Love for

MEANT TO BE

"If you're into swoony romances with a little bit of history thrown in, you'll love *Meant to Be*. I recommend it to anyone who loves Stephanie Perkins, Meg Cabot or the romantic bits of Sarah Dessen's books." —HelloGiggles.com

"Star-crossed characters, hilarious dialogue, and a perfect London setting. I loved *Meant to Be!*" —Robin Benway, author of *The Extraordinary Secrets of April, May & June*

"Entertaining and quick-witted." —*Publishers Weekly*

"Fate, humor, and first love collide—I couldn't stop reading." —Mandy Hubbard, author of *Ripple*

"Sweet, funny and romantic." —TheBusyBibliophile.com

"Sure to charm readers." —*VOYA*

"Readers of Jennifer E. Smith and Stephanie Perkins will revel in this debate about love ruled by the stars or as a matter of the heart." —Shelf-Awareness.com

"This book is so much fun!" —TheBookLife.com

"Oh how I loved this novel, let me count the ways . . . *Meant to Be* delivers on every level. The romance, the laughs, the great London adventure, and two memorable characters who are so different yet so *right* for each other." —*Ninja Girl Reads* (blog)

"A delightful, refreshing read." —*Pure Imagination* (blog)

"If you haven't found a fun, goofy, sweet and genuinely cutesy read since *Anna and the French Kiss* (I know I haven't), you have got to read *Meant to Be*." —*On Books!* (blog)

"I absolutely loved *Meant to Be!* I loved the writing, the characters, and the setting." —*The Reading Geek* (blog)

MEANT TO BE

Lauren Morrill

EMBER

Text copyright © 2012 by Paper Lantern Lit, LLC
Cover art copyright © 2012 by Trevillion Images (couple) and Timothy Passmore/
Shutterstock Images (sunset)

randomhouse.com/teens

Educators and librarians, for a variety of teaching tools, visit us at
RHTeachersLibrarians.com

The Library of Congress has cataloged the hardcover edition of this work
as follows:
Morrill, Lauren.
Meant to be / Lauren Morrill. — 1st ed.
p. cm.
Summary: During an educational trip to London, away from her
friends and the boy she thinks she is fated to love, Massachusetts high school
junior Julia Lichtenstein is paired with her nemesis, Jason, and begins seeing
many things differently.
ISBN 978-0-385-74177-4 (hardcover) — ISBN 978-0-375-99023-6 (glb) —
ISBN 978-0-375-98711-3 (ebook)
[1. Interpersonal relations—Fiction. 2. Dating (Social customs)—Fiction. 3. Travel—
Fiction. 4. London (England)—Fiction. 5. England—Fiction.] I. Title.
PZ7.M82718Me 2013
[Fic]—dc23
2011035519

ISBN 978-0-385-74178-1 (tr. pbk.)

Printed in the United States of America

10 9 8 7 6 5 4 3 2 1

First Ember Edition 2014

For Inger Sjostrom, my cheerleader always

MEANT TO BE

1

Down and Dirty at Thirty Thousand Feet

Have a gr8 trip—and feel FREE to
do anything I wouldn't do :) —P

There are certain things in life that just suck. Pouring a big bowl of Lucky Charms before realizing the milk is expired, the word "moist," falling face-first into the salad bar in front of the entire lacrosse team . . .

"Bird strike!"

Being on a plane with Jason Lippincott is another one of them.

Two rows ahead of me, Jason is holding his hands up in mock prayer as our plane bounces like it's on a bungee cord. Not that I would have any idea what bungee jumping feels like, since I would rather compete in a spelling bee in my underpants than leap off a crane with only a rope tied around me. At least I'd come away from the spelling bee with a medal.

As the plane drops several hundred (thousand?) feet, I white-knuckle the armrest. Jason's prayers may be a joke, but mine are very, very real. *God, please deposit me safely on the ground in London . . . and in the process, maybe you could find a way to get Jason to shut it?*

I hate to fly. Seriously. HATE. IT. It seems wrong to be hurtling through the clouds at warp speed in a metal tube. It makes about as much sense as being flung over the ocean on a slingshot.

I tuck my pocket Shakespeare into the seat back and carefully realign the magazines that have bounced out of formation on my tray table.

"We're going down!" That's Jason again, *of course*.

The plane bounces even worse than before. My knees crash into the tray table, sending my half-eaten package of peanuts and my entire stack of magazines raining into the aisle. I instinctively grab for the armrest once more, and the businessman next to me lets out a loud yelp.

Oops. Not the armrest. His thigh. (I thought it felt a little flabby.)

I mutter an apology and adjust my kung fu grip to the *real* armrest this time.

Breathe. Breathe. I close my eyes and try to picture Mark. Weirdly, the first image that comes into my head is his yearbook picture. He has the perfectly proportioned features of a model. A bright white smile with perfect teeth all lined up in a perfect row, except for that one tooth, three from the center, that is a teeny bit crooked, which I love, because it sort of shows off how straight the other ones are. And his thick, wavy brown hair is always in the right place, mussed just enough but not too much, without the aid of any greasy or crunchy hair product. Perfect. Just like him. I finally start to feel calm, like I'm coasting across the ocean on the back of a little songbird instead of strapped into a lumpy polyester seat.

Then Jason lets out a loud "Woooo!", shattering my Mark-inspired Zen.

I sit up straight in my seat. Jason's got his arms raised like he's on a roller coaster. A pretty flight attendant glides up the aisle toward him. Good. If God can't get Jason to shut it, maybe she can.

I crane my neck for a better view of the scolding I know is coming his way. Instead, I see the flight attendant pass him a folded-up napkin, which he immediately opens to reveal a stack of chocolate chip cookies. From the way he's handling them, all delicately, I can tell they're still warm.

The flight attendant flashes Jason a smile. He says something to her and she laughs. He acts like a jerk and *still* scores first-class snacks!

"Oh my God. He is too much. Isn't he hilarious?" It's Sarah Finder, Newton North's resident TMZ. She's elbowing her seatmate, Evie Ellston, in the ribs, nodding in Jason's direction.

"Seriously. Adorable. And the Scarlet thing is over, right?"

"*Way* over. They broke up weeks ago." Of course Sarah knows. Sarah *always* knows. So far, during the three hours and twenty-seven minutes we have been on this flight, Sarah and Evie have left no student undiscussed (except for me, possibly because the last time there was any gossip about me, it was in eighth grade, when Bryan Holloman taped a felt rose to my locker on Valentine's Day. The only reason anyone cared was that, it came out the next day, the rose was actually meant for Stephenie Kelley). From my vantage point in the seat directly behind her, I've already heard about Amber Riley's supposed nose job, Rob Diamos's recent suspension for smoking cigarettes in the janitor's closet, and the shame Laura Roberts was undergoing, having received her mother's '00 Honda instead of the brand-new Range Rover she'd been telling everyone she'd get.

"Think he's all wounded and needy? On the prowl for someone new?" Evie has one of those oversized mouths attached to an oversized face that makes all her vowels sound a mile long.

"Doubtful," Sarah answers. Then, lowering her voice: "He said he's trying to join the mile-high club."

"Seriously? Isn't that, like, when people . . . you know . . . on a *plane*?" From the way Evie's voice jumps to Mariah Carey octaves, it's hard to tell if she's horrified or interested in signing herself up as a willing partner.

"Shhh! And yes. Totally. You know how he is. Up for *anything*," Sarah says.

Gross. I say a silent prayer that God can add Sarah to the list of

People to Render Temporarily Mute while he's working on keeping our plane in the sky. I mean, I am totally not one of those prudes who believe having sex as a teenager is some kind of mortal sin or social death. I don't have a problem with sex. I just don't happen to be having it. And if I *were* having sex, I certainly wouldn't be getting it on in an airplane *bathroom*. Who wants to get down and dirty in a place so . . . cramped and dirty?

I close my eyes and try to get Mark back, but Sarah's voice keeps slicing into my visions like one of those infomercial knives. *Cuts cans, shoes, and daydreams.*

Without imaginary Mark to keep me company, there's only one way to simultaneously block out Newton North's biggest mouth and chase away visions of airmageddon. I pull my iPod out of my purple leather satchel, which is tucked safely under the seat in front of me. I unwind my headphones and click on some mellow tunes (Hayward Williams being my choice music of the moment. It's like someone put gravel and butter into a blender and out came his voice). But as I reach back to put in my earbuds, I encounter something wet and sticky nested in my curls. I pull the end of my ponytail around to my face to find a wad of what looks, smells, and feels like grape Bubble Yum.

A fit of giggles erupts behind me, and I turn to see a little boy, maybe seven, wearing a Buzz Lightyear tee. He's grinning maniacally, his mother snoozing peacefully beside him.

"Did you?" I whisper, furiously shaking my hair at him.

"Oops!" he exclaims before dissolving into another fit of hysterical laughter, his fat cheeks burning red under his mop of blond curls.

Add children to the list of things I hate. Flying and children.

After several minutes of careful picking, followed by some full-on tugging (all while I thank my parents for making me an only child), it becomes clear: I am going to have to leave my seat and go to the bathroom, in total defiance of the pilot-ordered Fasten Seat Belt sign.

I don't use airplane bathrooms. As a rule. And I *really* don't like breaking rules. (It's kind of one of my rules.) I mean, if I'm going to plummet to my death, it's *not* going to be with my pants around my ankles. Then again, a big wad of grape gum in my ponytail definitely constitutes an emergency, no matter how little I care about my over-chlorinated, wild chestnut waves. I carefully unfasten my seat belt, keeping my eye on the flight attendants' galley, and make a beeline for the lavatory.

As I pick at the purple gooey mess my head has become, I can hear faint giggling coming through the wall. What is it with everyone on this flight acting like it's a day at Six Flags? I'd rather be on the *Titanic* at this point. At least there I'd be traveling in comfort, with crystal glasses and warm towels.

I finally yank the last gob of gum out of my hair and step out of the lavatory, wrestling with the little sliding door, which has grabbed hold of the sleeve of my hoodie. I fumble around, bashing my elbow on the doorframe, before finally freeing myself and whipping around to leave. Right then the plane bounces hard, and I am shot out of the bathroom like a cannon ball. A pair of arms saves me from bashing my head into the narrow doorway. I look up to see Jason Lippincott steadying me on my feet.

"Book Licker!" he says, invoking my least favorite junior-high nickname. He grins, several freckles on his forehead scrunching together. "Enjoying your flight?"

I pull away from him. "It's Julia," I reply as calmly as possible, adjusting the hem of my pants, which have hooked themselves over the sole of my sneaker.

"Of course," he says, gesturing down the aisle. "After you."

"Um, thanks," I say. Maybe he can tell how badly I want to get back to my seat belt.

As I make my way down the aisle, I begin to notice my classmates' eyes on me. The looks quickly turn to snickers and then full-on laughter. Ryan Lynch, Newton North's lacrosse captain, is grinning stupidly at me. Sarah is whispering furiously to Evie, her eyes trained in my direction. I have absolutely no idea what is going on, and I immediately wonder if there is more bubble gum in my hair or it somehow landed on my face. I reach to pat my hair down when a wild gesture catches the corner of my eye. I turn to see Jason making a thrusting motion in my direction, winking at Ryan, who reaches out to give Jason a high five.

Oh my God. No way. They think it was *us,* in the bathroom, with the mile-high club and all that. They think it because he's *making* them think it! How could they think I would do *anything* with Jason Lippincott, much less anything in an airplane bathroom! My eyes dart back to Sarah, who is still in full-on gossip mode, her gaze locked on me. If Sarah knows, everyone knows, which means it's only a matter of time before the news gets back to Mark. And by then, who knows how crazy the rumor will get? Newton North is like one giant game of telephone sometimes.

One thing is certain: good, sweet, kind, thoughtful Mark is going to want nothing to do with me if he thinks I've been even semi-naked with Jason on a transatlantic flight.

Though Jason has stopped thrusting, he's still laughing and air-fiving his seatmates. Air-fiving. Yeah. First he calls me Book Licker; then he pretends I got down and dirty at thirty thousand feet!

All I can do is turn and hiss, "Stop it!" before dropping into my seat. I cram my headphones into my ears, crank the volume on my iPod, and try to drown out my humiliation with some tunes. At this point, I'm almost *hoping* for a crash.

2

Lattes and Long Legs

Is it too late to come w/u instead? —Jules

I spend the entire rest of the flight seething. I wish my best friend, Phoebe, were around; she would know *exactly* what to say to Jason and how to tell him to shove it. She is the queen of good comebacks.

When we land in London and I march straight up to him at the baggage claim, I'm ready.

"Listen, if you want to behave like some overcaffeinated child, that's your prerogative, but leave me out of it. I would *never* make out with you, and I certainly wouldn't . . . " At the last second, I can't even say it, not with Jason still grinning at me like an idiot. I take a deep breath. "Not on a plane or anywhere else. Never. So back off. Forever. Okay?"

"Prerogative, eh?" He chuckles, unwrapping a hunk of grape Bubble Yum and popping it into his mouth.

"It's an SAT word, so perhaps you've never heard it before." Okay, that was a little *I'm rubber and you're glue,* but I didn't make it past my opening line as I was writing my script.

"Oh, I know it. Seven twenty verbal," he says, and then leans in close. The smell of grape gum wafts into my face, and I wrinkle my nose to block the odor. "But don't tell anyone. Might ruin my 'over-caffeinated child' rep."

I start fumbling for some kind of comeback, but I'm saved by a tiny terror smashing me in the knees. I look down to see the kid from the plane, his Buzz Lightyear tee wrinkled, his blond curls in knots.

"Watch it!" I say, but he's too busy giving Jason a high five before racing off toward the luggage carousel (and his parents, I hope). "What was that about?"

Jason is tearing the gum wrapper into smaller and smaller pieces until it barely maintains the molecular structure of paper. It rains down onto his shoe. At that moment, the mischievous giggle rings in my ear and my hand flies up to my hair.

"You!" I cry as I watch Jason blow a perfectly round bubble that takes up half his face. I can still see the faint outlines of freckles through the bubble, and I desperately want to jam my finger into it and splatter gum into his bangs. See how he likes it. "You can't give little kids gum!"

"Why not? He seemed bored." Jason shrugs, turning toward the baggage claim. "Jeez, Mom, how 'bout we try to take the stress level down a notch or twenty, okay? This is *vacation*."

"It's *not* a vacation, it's educa—" I start, but Jason cuts me off with a shush maneuver I think I've seen on *Dog Whisperer*.

"You know what your problem is, Book Licker?" he says, rocking back on his heels. He gives me a quick wink. "You don't know the word 'fun.' Maybe because it wasn't on the SATs."

He brushes past me toward the baggage claim.

I am left reeling, hating him with the heat of a supernova. I'm so flustered I miss my bag as it rolls past on the carousel, and have to wait for it to come back around again. As I crane my neck, looking for my big green duffel, twin shadows overtake me.

I look up to see that I'm flanked by a pair of human storks. They're wearing matching skinny jeans and strappy tanks and have identical multicolored scarves wrapped around their swanlike necks. The only thing that distinguishes them is that one has a high, tight auburn ponytail, while the other has a high, tight blond ponytail and is clutching a giant iced coffee the size of her face.

"I swear to God, if our flat has bunk beds, I will walk my Manolos right onto the next flight back to the States," the blonde says. "Last time I came for fashion week, we had to bunk *four* to a room. I felt like I was at fashion camp. I am *so* not doing that again."

"I can handle the bunk beds, as long as Ursula isn't there," the brunette replies, hiking her tote higher on her bony shoulder. "She snores like a lumberjack."

Holy wow. Real models, in the flesh. Or bone. They certainly *look* overcaffeinated and starving. That's when I notice that there are a lot of women over six feet tall roaming the baggage area. The airport has been overtaken by Glamazons with hollow cheeks and black wheeled suitcases. They're all strutting across the linoleum in four-inch heels, looking like they stepped out of *Vogue Italia* and not off a six-and-a-half-hour flight.

"Do you know which shows you're doing yet?" the brunette on my left asks, scanning the carousel for her suitcase.

"I've got some go-sees tomorrow," the blonde replies. She gives her vat of iced coffee a lazy, uninterested shake. "My agent said Stella McCartney is totally a lock, though. And of course Marc Jacobs, like, loves me."

I catch the brunette rolling her eyes while she plucks her suitcase from the conveyor belt in one graceful, fluid movement. I've been so distracted by their conversation I haven't noticed that my duffel is about to pass me by again. I dive for it, my fingers barely closing around the nylon handle. I throw my weight backward to heave it off the carousel, but thanks to all those guidebooks I packed, the bag is heavier than I thought. I feel it throwing me off balance. I'm going down.

As I start to tip backward, though, a body breaks my fall. Unfortunately, it's the blond supermodel, whose waifish figure is not ready for my muscular frame and ten tons of luggage to come flying at her like a stealth bomber.

"What the—" she screams, falling backward off her platform wedges. We go down in a tangle of arms and legs, her coffee in a flood on the floor, now soaking itself into my sweatpants.

"Oh my God, I'm so sorry," I mumble, completely mortified. I struggle to scramble to my feet, and I'm nearly up when my foot catches in the handle of my duffel and I fall again, landing butt-first in the puddle. I can feel the cold, sticky liquid soaking into my underpants. Great—after the rumors about my joining the mile-high club, a suspicious stain on my sweatpants is the last thing I need. Did I mention that I *hate* flying?

I untangle my foot, grab my duffel, and make a run for the nearest sliding doors before I'm subjected to a supermodel-style tantrum. "Sorry!" I yell over my shoulder.

"You owe me a coffee!" the blonde screams at me, but I don't look back.

When I get to the curb, I scan the crowd for my group so I don't miss the bus. I spot Jason and start to head toward him, but I quickly realize that he's not with the group. He's busy chatting up a raven-haired supermodel who's poised to climb into a shiny black sedan. Of course.

Another black sedan screeches to a halt right in front of me. The tinted windows provide a perfect reflection of my appearance postflight. My hair is a wild mess, my eyes are bloodshot, and now I have coffee splattered from head to toe, including a large wet spot on my behind.

Great. I've arrived in London looking like a homeless—and incontinent—crazy person.

I hoist my duffel over my shoulder. I finally spot my classmates gathering in front of a giant blue tour bus. Mrs. Tennison is bustling around, counting heads and checking things off on her clipboard. Nearly everyone else has boarded the bus by the time I'm dragging my monogrammed duffel toward them.

Flying, children, models, and being late. And Jason Lippincott. The list of things I hate is getting longer by the minute.

I board the bus behind Deirdre Robinson and her ginormous fluff of curly blond hair and slide into an empty seat at the front, hoping it stays empty except for me. Yes, there are twenty students on this trip, and I'm close friends with exactly none of them. It's going to be a long ten days.

When everyone in junior-year lit class had the chance to go to London over spring break, I thought at least a handful of my swim teammates would come along on the trip. Yet despite my careful planning and organization, I managed to sign up and turn in my deposit before realizing that it conflicted with the MetroWest Invitational swim meet. It's the meet where I set the state freestyle record last year!

So I am here, and my teammates are not.

Missing the swim meet has me feeling sort of twitchy, and I start tapping my toe inside my sneaker. I promised Coach Haas I'd do extra laps while I'm here (our hotel has a pool, thank God), and hope he hasn't replaced me by the time I get back in ten days.

"Relax, Julia," Coach Haas told me when I told him I'd stick to my training. "Just try to have some fun while you're there, okay?"

Apparently no one understands that my version of fun includes laps, guidebooks, and following the rules.

Joel Emerson ambles lazily down the aisle, and I see him pause next to my seat, so I quickly drop my carry-on into it. Joel will spend the entire bus ride miming lacrosse plays, which I'm pretty sure will make me carsick.

Dammit, Phoebe, I'll kill you for ditching me.

Phoebe's parents refused to let her skip the Lis' family reunion, hosted every five years in Chicago. No amount of pleading from either of us budged them an inch. Phoebe even pulled out the "it'll look great on my college applications" card, but to no avail. Not that Phoebe needs to be worried about her college applications. She's an amazing artist, and she's totally getting into Rhode Island School of Design. And hopefully I am going to get into Brown, and then we'll share an apartment in a big Providence Victorian with bright walls and a turret.

"Hey, at least there's a beach," I told her last week. After months of begging, I'd finally convinced her to reorganize her closet. Phoebe says it's sick, but organizing other people's stuff is sort of a hobby for me. There is something incredibly satisfying about putting everything in its proper place.

"It's Lake Michigan—that hardly counts as beach," she said, then stuck out her tongue while checking a yellow T-shirt for holes of the unintentional variety. She tossed it into the "donate" pile.

"The Chicago Chamber of Commerce begs to differ," I replied, putting a pile of brightly patterned sundresses onto hangers one by one. I held up a purple houndstooth-printed minidress with an egg-sized rip in the hem. "Is this a keeper?"

"I can totally fix that," she said, adding it to the sewing pile next to her desk before gathering her long, shiny black hair into a messy ponytail. I'm so jealous of Phoebe's hair. It would take me two hours with a flatiron and the entire Kiehl's counter to get my hair that straight. And thanks to all the chlorine, it wouldn't be anywhere near that shiny. "Anyway, even if it was a real beach, it's only warm enough to swim in for, like, three weeks in August. It's March. That's practically the Arctic in Chicago!"

I sighed. "It'll be painful for me, too! There's going to be so much preppy on this trip I might come back with a full frontal lobotomy and a new wardrobe consisting of only skinny jeans and Tiffany bracelets." I tried to focus on folding her massive pile of screen-printed T-shirts and not on how lonely I would be. "Seriously, what am I going to do without you there?"

"You're going to enjoy London," Phoebe said, her eyes widening as she wound up for one of her famous, mile-a-minute diatribes, "a city filled with studly British scholars who read Jane Austen and the Brontë sisters. And every once in a while, you'll pause for a moment of silence for your best friend, who is busy scarfing down kimchi and casseroles made by great-aunts while you're enjoying tea and scones."

So my best friend isn't here to save me. But I am in London. For free. Without any parents. With an itinerary (highlighted and underlined, of course) full of visits to places I've only read about or imagined and a duffel bag full of guidebooks, notable passages flagged with an array of colorful Post-its.

It could be so much worse. I could be traveling with my aunt Matilda, who uses up most of every visit hinting that perhaps if I spent less time in the pool and more time in a dress, I'd have my very own boyfriend. I could be touring London with a convention of high school principals or infomercial hosts. All of those would be worse than this (I think). So it's decided. This trip is going to be awesome. I take a few deep breaths, pull out the itinerary, and begin psyching myself up for tomorrow's visit to the Tate. I have already printed out the online pamphlet describing the special exhibits. I plan to spend the evening (which is designated as "settling-in time" on the itinerary) rereading the Tate passages in each of my five guidebooks. Just the thought of the museum and my books, and my stress starts to ebb away.

Mrs. Tennison scurries onto the bus last and begins surveying the crowd. Her palazzo pants and floral tunic whip students in the face as she rushes down the aisle.

"Do we have everyone? Is anyone missing?" she asks, counting heads, then wringing her hands. "It appears we're one short!" Her mostly penciled-in dark brows furrow together.

"I'm here! Never fear!" Jason bounds onto the bus, laughing, and squeezes down the aisle past Mrs. Tennison. "Thanks for holding the bus for me, Mrs. T."

"Jason, please stay with the group. It is very important that we all stick together." Fifteen minutes in London, and already Mrs. Tennison is massaging her temples. Clearly, this is going to be a rough ten days for her, too.

"Sorry, Mrs. T. Never again, Scout's honor." He grins, shuffling down the aisle. He pauses by my seat, his nose crinkling. "Hazelnut, Book Licker? I would have taken you for a black-coffee kind of girl." I clench my fists.

Babbling brooks and cool breezes. Birds and hearts and rainbows and Mark's third tooth to the left of center . . .

"Thank you, Jason," Mrs. Tennison sighs, pulling out a thick file folder. The bus rumbles to a start, and Mrs. Tennison has to grasp the nearest seat so as not to fall into someone's lap. She nearly grabs Deirdre Robinson's fluffy head of crazy-curl hair, but Deirdre executes a quick duck-and-weave maneuver that I'm guessing she picked up on the fencing team (of which she is the sole member).

"Okay, everyone, listen up," Mrs. Tennison says, clearing her throat. "I've got some good news. There was a mix-up with the hotel, and everyone ended up in single rooms."

A cheer rises from the bus—a cheer even I join in on. A single room means I'll be spared from sharing with Sarah Finder and her explosion of designer jeans and faux Louis Vuitton bags. Thank GOD. This trip is getting better by the minute!

"Okay, okay," Mrs. Tennison says, waving her hands to shush us. "Moving on. Your curfew will be at ten p.m., and you *will* respect it. I will be holding on to your keys for the night so I can be sure you're in your rooms and not . . ." She trails off, and I know that she's imagining half the bus getting arrested and the other half getting pregnant.

All the other students begin grumbling and groaning. Evie even squeaks out, "But that's fascist!" I'm pretty sure she doesn't know what "fascist" means.

I don't mind the curfew. Early to bed, early to rise and swim my laps.

Mrs. Tennison goes on: "The way we're going to ensure that no one wanders off on their own is an old standby: the buddy system."

All around me, people are grabbing hands with their buddies, but having attended many summers at Camp Tanasi, I know exactly what's coming, and I feel a cold knot of dread building in my stomach.

"I've *assigned* partners for the duration of the trip. Not only will you be responsible for keeping track of your buddy, but they'll also be your partner for all activities and assignments. Remember, this is an *educational* tour of the UK."

"Ugh, don't remind me," Evie mutters from two rows back. Evie spent the end of the flight paging through *The Fashionista's Guide to London Shopping*. It's the first book I've ever seen her read.

"You will be responsible for your partner for the duration of this trip," Mrs. Tennison continues, winding up for a speech I suspect she practiced in her bathroom mirror before we left. "Their success is *your* success. You'll not only be together on our regularly scheduled tours, but you'll be keeping each other company during assigned cultural hours. You're probably thinking, What are cultural hours?"

"Um, no." Evie's eye roll is practically audible in her voice. Luckily, Mrs. Tennison doesn't hear her.

"Your cultural hours are daily two-hour blocks of time, in which you are permitted to explore London on your own. With your partner, of course!"

"Shopping time!" Evie squeals.

This Mrs. Tennison *does* hear. She shoots Evie an evil eye before charging on. "*Cultural* hours are to be spent exploring even more of the *culture* of London," she says, not so subtly emphasizing the words, "and this does *not* include shopping. I will be keeping track of your hours via your daily reflection papers, where you will write about all the wonderful British experiences you've had throughout the day."

My classmates continue their chorus of groans. I don't know what they expected. Contrary to popular belief, this isn't a vacation. It's for credit, and I plan to get an A.

Mrs. Tennison begins running through the list of partners, and I strain to hear my name. As she moves through the list, I start to notice a pattern. Brian Arnett is paired with Jamie Barnes. Evie Ellston with Sarah Finder. Tony Harrison and Logan Hunt. Lucy Karns and Adam Landry. Uh-oh. This can only mean . . .

"Julia Lichtenstein, you'll be with Jason Lippincott."

No. No no no. I *cannot* be with Jason. First of all, I just told him to leave me alone. Forever. I can't even *look* at Jason, much less tour castles with him. Second of all, what will we even talk about? Aside from our brief encounter today, Jason and I haven't so much as interacted since he stuffed tampons into my locker in ninth grade. He sits across the cafeteria with his lacrosse teammates and their giggly groupies at lunch and spends most of class time trying to embarrass our teachers with "that's what she said" jokes. I don't know how to play lacrosse, and I'm pretty sure he's never read . . . well, a book. Plus he's going to spend 90 percent of the trip figuring out ways to meet girls, which is going to be supremely annoying for the person who has to keep track of him. Which, apparently, is me.

But before I can ask if there is any room for negotiation, Mrs. Tennison pulls out a box filled with identical silver cell phones, each topped with a sticky note containing the phone's number in neat script. (Mrs. Tennison may be a psychotic mess, but she has beautiful penmanship.)

"These are your temporary cell phones—or 'mobiles,' as they say in

England," she says, tittering a little, as she moves up the aisle, distributing phones. My sticky note reads: **+442026415644**

I stare at the jumble of unfamiliar numbers, trying to commit them to memory. The standard country code is 44, so that's easy. Twenty . . . That was dad's jersey number in high school; he was captain of the football team. The numbers rearrange in my head, forming different patterns. Then I see it: 26 April, 1564. It's Shakespeare's birthday! That must be a sign.

There's only one remaining number to memorize, and that's easy enough: the last four is my GPA. Dad's jersey number, Shakespeare's birthday, my GPA. I mouth it silently to myself until it's committed to memory.

Mrs. Tennison is prattling on. "These phones are pay-as-you-go. They've been preloaded with twenty minutes' worth of credit, which is exactly the amount of time you should need to call the police, a taxi, or me. This means these phones are meant for *emergencies*." She says the word with as many syllables as she can stretch. She places the last phone in Susan Morgan's tanned palm and then whirls around to face the crowd. "Any credit you use beyond those twenty minutes you will need to purchase on your own. However, I am not giving you permission to spend this entire trip on the phone. Excuse me, Miss Ellston?"

I turn around to see Evie with her nose already buried in her phone, her manicured fingers tapping furiously at the keys. At the mention of her name, her head snaps up at the exact moment she snaps her phone shut.

"Yes, Mrs. Tennison?" she says brightly.

"What were you doing on that phone, Miss Ellston?" Mrs. Tennison crosses her arms over her chest and mimics Evie's peaches-and-cream tone.

"Oh, nothing," she says. Her voice gets even more syrupy, which happens whenever she's lying to an authority figure. I've been in at least a dozen classes with her, so I'm kind of an expert.

"Miss Ellston, thank you for reminding me to bring up one final point. As I have said, these phones are for emergencies. They are *not* for texting or Twittering or Facebooking or connect four-ing or socializing or anything else that will keep you from truly experiencing your time here in London. This trip is an opportunity for you to disconnect from technology and connect with a vibrant city full of art, culture, and history. If I discover that your phone use is proving too much of a distraction, I will confiscate it immediately. You will then have to rely on your partner's phone for the rest of the trip. Do I make myself clear?"

The bus breaks into a scattered chorus of yeses and some random grumbling. I flip my phone open, wishing I could use it to send an SOS to Phoebe. I even start typing a text. *Help! Partnered with Jason! Suicide likely, homicide imminent!* But because I'm a rule follower, I flip the phone shut without sending it.

3

⌒∾⌒

Less Bath, More Robe

Why does every1 think a girl who prefers bks to ppl
must be in want of a life? —J

The bus pulls away from the airport, and I practically press my nose against the windowpane. I refuse to miss a single second of England just because I'm stressing about Jason. We merge onto the M4 and begin speeding toward London. Everything looks *greener* here than at home. I gaze out over rolling hills dotted with patches of wildflowers and huge shade trees. It's a cool but sunny spring afternoon. I wish I could open my window and breathe in the air, because it looks like it smells earthy, heavy, and sweet.

The green hills give way to a vista of dense row houses and large supermarkets. For a minute I'm disappointed; we could be in Cleveland, Ohio. Then we veer off the busy motorway, and the street suddenly gets narrow, the buildings more opulent. This is the London I've always imagined. Everything looks like it is or was, at one time, a castle. Even the McDonald's, with its stone facade located beneath a stately brick apartment building, looks impressive.

Our bus disappears underground, rolling through a tunnel before emerging onto the street. We pass a lush green garden filled to the brim with beautiful flowers. I can't wait to take my old copy of *Pride and Prejudice* and read it in a real English garden. Although knowing me, I will probably get attacked by a wild goose or something. (I have goose-related issues. Don't judge me.)

Before I know it, we're in the thick of the city, passing locations I've heard my mom describe to me since I was a kid: Kensington High Street, Imperial College, Hyde Park, Piccadilly Circus. For a second my throat tightens up and I find myself holding my breath. London is where Mom and Dad went on their honeymoon, and they always talked about coming back here. Dad used to joke that Paris was the city of love for unimaginative folks. "Give me those guards in the big fuzzy hats any day," he'd say, laughing and planting a kiss on Mom's forehead. They'd even saved up for a tenth-anniversary trip, but when Dad got sick, the trip was quickly forgotten.

My parents met as teenagers attending rival high schools. Mom had watched Dad across the football field for two seasons, always wanting to talk to him. One day she twisted her ankle while out on a run, and Dad's was the first car to come by. He picked her up and drove her to the emergency room, and they were together all the way until he died. My mom has always said that it was fate, and I know she's right. It could have been any old Good Samaritan who picked her up, but fate brought her my dad.

Most people I know have parents who are separated or divorced or somewhere in between. But in all my memories of my parents together, they're always laughing or dancing around the kitchen or holding hands. They had more bliss in the decade they were married than most people get in a lifetime.

Fate worked for them, and it'll work for me.

That's why Mark Bixford is the guy. I know it. I've only been in love with him since we were *five,* when he was my next-door neighbor. We did all the usual kindergarten-neighbor stuff: running through the sprinkler, riding bikes, trying to swing so high we'd flip over the bar. We'd pretend we were spies, war heroes, teachers, royalty, the president. . . . We even had a pretend wedding once. Mark went home to put on his black T-shirt (the closest approximation a five-year-old has to a tuxedo), I threw a pillowcase over my head for a veil, and an old stuffed lion I named Growly presided over the blessed event under the willow tree in my backyard. The wedding ended with my very first kiss, and I've been smitten with Mark Bixford ever since. On my sixth birthday, he presented me with a gallon-sized Ziploc bag filled with only the lemon Starbursts, my absolute favorite flavor. (They sort of remind me of lemon Pledge, and my favorite chore as a kid was helping my mom dust all the antiques in our house.) Mark had saved up his allowance to buy a case of Starbursts, then picked out the yellow ones for me.

You see why I love him?

But the next year his dad got transferred to Pittsburgh, and I thought he was gone forever. I resolved to find a new crush, but over the years I kept thinking about Mark, wondering if maybe our "wedding" might have been a sign, or a premonition.

Now Mark's back. As of August 19, exactly 232 days ago today. And I haven't even looked at a single other guy since.

Unfortunately, Mark has hardly looked at me at all. Phoebe once said he's probably silenced by the force of his love for me, but I suspect he's long since lost the memories of our backyard vows, of how we each took a turn snipping off a small tuft of Growly's ratty old mane to symbolize our eternal bond. The slightly shorn lion still sits on the top shelf of my closet, looking a little lumpy and sad.

So for the past 232 days, I've loved him quietly and from afar, waiting for the serendipitous event that will bring us together. It's not that I'm too chicken to talk to him (okay, maybe a little bit). I simply think that if he's the one (and he totally is), it'll eventually happen naturally. I know it defies all logic and reasoning, but that's how fate works.

I've seen it.

Surrounded by London's tiny cars and cabs, our bus seems monstrous, like an elephant lumbering through a field of kittens. The only things even close to our size are the double-decker buses, which are *everywhere*. I keep having little moments of panic during which I think our bus driver has gotten drunk and is about to career into an oncoming car, only to remind myself that here in England they drive on the *other* side of the road.

We pass signs for the London Underground, which look like the T-shirts I've seen at Urban Outfitters. The buildings around us curve with the roads. It's exactly like I imagined, and yet still somehow better. And so far I've only seen it through the foggy window of a motor coach.

When we escape the snarled traffic of Piccadilly Circus, we turn onto a street so narrow I'm sure our bus is going to get wedged between a pair of buildings. It's a bit cloudy now, and with the height of the buildings around us, it's hard to make out the area from my window seat.

Finally, the bus rolls to a stop in front of our hotel. I stifle a gasp. The Soho Sennett Hotel is located in the trendy district populated by theaters, clubs, and record stores. The hotel itself looks like something out of a fairy tale. As I step off the bus onto a plush red carpet, I can tell I'm not going to have any problem with this. No problem whatsoever.

"Right this way, miss." A man in a heavily brocaded burgundy jacket gestures toward the double doors, which are already open and ready for us. A red-and-gold sign reading WELCOME, FRIENDS AND FAMILY sits on an antique brass stand.

The hotel is owned by Mrs. Tennison's husband's brother (or Mrs. Tennison's brother's husband—I forget which). His company bought it last year, when it was only a row of town houses, and they recently finished a full gut renovation. Thanks to Mrs. T's connection (and a rumored need to make up for some kind of family snub), my classmates and I are going to be some of the hotel's first guests. We're here to give the new staff a good trial run. Because really, if a hotel staff can survive twenty American teenagers, they can survive anything.

It's kind of unbelievable, really. Last year's class stayed in a hostel, and Jenny Davis's mattress had an infestation of bedbugs. She came home looking like she had chicken pox, and no one would go near her for a week.

As soon as we're in the door, Jason drops his bag on the floor and strolls over to the check-in desk, where a pretty redhead in a low-cut black wrap dress is tapping away at her computer. He folds his long torso over the marble counter and peers down at her screen. Before I can even wonder what he's up to, the clerk is giggling and grinning and tossing her hair. I look away. I mean, really, I'm going to be watching this very same scene over and over again all week. No point in spoiling the disgusting film with a gross preview.

Mrs. Tennison weaves through the group, pressing key cards into our palms and checking things off on her clipboard. Once I have mine, I drag my duffel to the grand staircase. On the third floor, I stop to roll my stiff shoulders, feeling completely sore and exhausted from the long flight. I make my way down the narrow hall, papered with a rich royal-purple-and-gold pattern. At the end of the hall, I arrive at a heavy mahogany door with a loopy number 315 stamped on a brass plate. After two tries with the electronic key card, the door swings open and my jaw hits the floor.

The room is unbelievably small, maybe the size of a large walk-in closet, but it's hard to care about that, given what's inside. A queen-size bed dominates the room, anchored to the wall by a floor-to-ceiling distressed brown leather headboard with oversized brass buttons, which create a quilting pattern. A mountain of fluffy bright white pillows breaks up the color scheme, and a thick bronze-and-burgundy comforter shines across the top of the bed. Mahogany end tables flank the bed, and a matching armoire is sandwiched in the corner; its door is slightly ajar, revealing a sleek flat-screen TV and entertainment system.

At the foot of the bed, on a raised bamboo platform nestled in the bay window, where one might normally find a window seat or a wing-back chair, stands a lacquered bright white claw-foot bathtub. A beautiful, glistening, perfectly me-sized bathtub.

I almost do a happy dance right there. (Okay, maybe I *do* actually do a small happy dance.)

Two sets of roman shades cover the window, a white set for privacy and light and a burgundy set for sleeping. A recessed light overhead shines a spotlight down on the whole tableau. Outside, I can hear my classmates shouting down the halls. I hear the words "down comforter" and "Wii," but all I can focus on is how desperately I want to climb into the tub and never leave.

Something tells me there won't be any bedbugs here.

But before I can submerge my aching feet in the bath, I need to get unpacked. I cannot live out of a suitcase for ten days (okay, technically nine, since today is Friday and we leave next Saturday). I can practically *feel* my clothes wrinkling. Plus I think some of that iced coffee may have seeped through my duffel. I heave my duffel onto the luggage rack and then open it to get things unpacked and organized.

I've started separating my socks and underwear into different drawers in the armoire when I come across a pair of heels buried underneath my favorite Harvard hoodie. Phoebe insisted I bring them. She came over to my house the day before I left for the trip to help me pack, toting a few "necessities" (according to her) in her bag.

"You *must* take these!" she said, holding up a pair of four-inch black leather gladiator heels with brass detailing.

I scrunched up my nose. "Um, Phoebs? Aren't those your prom shoes?"

"I decided to go with the silver dress, so these don't match." Phoebe has great style, the kind you can't find on the pages of *Teen Vogue* or *Seventeen*. Her wardrobe is a mess, an explosion of neon and distressed denim, pieces spanning numerous decades and as many styles. But get an outfit on her and step back? She always looks effortlessly cool. Of course, the designer mafia at school doesn't recognize her genius. Marc Jacobs? Yes. Vintage? In theory. But Phoebe's blend of Goodwill and DIY? They won't have it. Her outfit that day consisted of a Rolling Stones logo tee that had been refashioned into a pencil skirt, and a pencil skirt refashioned into a vest. A little bit insane, but on her, it worked.

"Don't you want to return them?"

"Hell no! They're cute, and I'll definitely wear them at some point," she replied, dangling them in front of my face and wriggling her sparkly teal fingernails at me. Her aluminum bangles smacked together like an army marching a two-step. "And until that point comes, I definitely think that you, oh best friend of mine, should break them in."

"Those aren't exactly ideal sightseeing footwear."

"It's London! Adventure happens." Phoebe doesn't quite believe in fate the way I do. She says you have to *chase* your destiny, and she always expects life to be like a romantic comedy: all you have to do is dress the part of the heroine, and pretty soon you'll be kissing some hottie while fountains spew and music swells in the background. Unfortunately, my life is more often like one of those cable-access channels with the grand-motherly woman who tells you how to make pies.

"Not on a class trip," I said, crossing my arms over my chest and firmly shaking my head. "And not to me. Besides, they won't fit in my suitcase."

"Maybe if you leave a couple of these behind," she said, rolling her eyes as she pulled out a stack of books. "Dude, seriously, you can borrow my Kindle."

I made a face. I have my own e-reader, but I hardly ever use it. I need to fold down pages and flag passages with sticky notes. I need to *experience* books, not just read them. I never go anywhere without a book in my bag, and to travel across the ocean, I'd packed more than my fair share. "No thanks," I said. I leaned over the bed toward her, but she danced to the other side of the room with my books. "I need book smell to drown out stale-airplane smell."

"You are such a grandma sometimes," Phoebe said. I leaped over the bed and ran to grab them, but she held the stack high over her head, and I had to jump a little to try to reach them.

"I need them!" I protested, reaching for the stack, which she quickly tugged away.

"You don't," Phoebe replied, putting them back on my bookshelf. "You're going to London, not Uganda. Even if you manage to finish your stash, they do have these things called *bookstores* there. I've heard tell that if you give them money, they let you leave with a book."

"Ha-ha."

"I'll take that as a yes." She tossed the shoes into my suitcase, in the spot where my books had been.

Now, with an ocean between us, I pull out the heels and line them up next to my flip-flops and my sensible sneakers in the closet. At least they'll remind me of Phoebe. I pull out the five guidebooks I brought, flagged with approximately 212 Post-it notes, wipe the travel dust off their glossy covers, and stack them neatly on the nightstand. I step back to admire my handiwork. My end table looks like a page out of a travel magazine.

Reaching back into my suitcase, I pull a small yellowed photograph from one of its interior pockets and smooth the edges, which are soft and curled from age. It's my favorite picture of my parents, from their wedding day. My mom is wearing a simple white linen dress with an Empire waist and lace sleeves. Dad in his marine dress blues is behind her, his chin resting on her head. They're both laughing hard at some off-camera joke, Mom starting to double over from whatever it was.

As I tuck the photo into the frame of the mirror hanging over the vanity, I start to feel a knot forming in the pit of my stomach, tears welling up in my eyes. I deal with this the only way I know how: by dropping to the floor for a few quick push-ups. I will not cry on my first day in London. When I've cranked out a solid twenty push-ups, the tears are gone and the knot has loosened. Now for that hot bath.

I jump up and set about lining up all my toiletries on the counter from tallest to shortest. I step out of my clothes, depositing them into the hotel-provided laundry bag, and slip into the white heavy-but-soft terry cloth robe bearing the monogram of the Soho Sennett Hotel. It's clearly been designed for the supermodel who will probably have this room when I'm gone, and I have to pick up the front like a ball gown to make my way around the room. The sash is so long that I tug it off and hang it back on the hook. I drape a towel over the edge of the tub and crank the silver faucet to hot. As the tub fills with steamy water, I grab my tube of spot cream, this amazing organic zit stuff my mom picked up in Boston. The herbs in it give off an incredibly relaxing scent, but they also turn the cream an unfortunate shade of green. I start dabbing, and when I'm done, it looks like I've decorated my face with split pea soup. I drop my robe and put one foot into the hot water when I hear a knock at the door.

"Who is it?" I call through the door, hoping it's housekeeping and I can tell them to save it for tomorrow.

"It's Jason."

It takes me a full minute to realize that it's Jason Lippincott standing outside my door and not some bellboy named Jason or the hockey mask–wearing psycho killer from the movies (who, honestly, is a more likely candidate to be standing outside my door than Jason Lippincott). I turn off the water and grab my robe. I can't imagine what he wants, which means I have to open the door to find out. I tug my robe closed around my naked body, suddenly missing the sash, as I frantically try to shake some soapsuds off my right foot and hop toward the door.

"What's up?" I ask as I swing the door open, trying to act casual despite my state of undress. But I instantly forget that I'm (for all intents and purposes) naked when I see that he's standing on the other side in perfectly distressed jeans and what looks to be a deep blue cashmere V-neck over a plain white tee. The sweater intensifies his blue eyes, and for the first time I understand why he won "Best Eyes" in last year's yearbook superlatives. The faint smell of cologne wafts through the doorway, and I notice he's added some kind of product to his hair to make it look like he walked out of a wind tunnel. This was not what he looked like during our bus ride through the city, when he had on a North Face fleece and a ratty Sox cap over his mop of rusty-red hair. The only thing that's the same is the big wad of purple gum he's smacking away at.

As I'm standing there, taking in his suspiciously groomed physique, he fishes a pen out of his pocket, uncaps it, and steps toward me with the tip aimed straight at my face.

"What are you doing?" I shriek, swatting his hand away.

"Connecting the dots," he says matter-of-factly. My hand flies to my face and comes away with a palm full of chartreuse speckles. "Good look, by the way. Very avant-garde," he calls out as I rush to the sink to scrub the green goop from my face.

Instead of responding, I march back to the door and give it a good hard swing, not really caring if it catches his pen, or one or two of his fingers. He's too quick, though, and throws a hand up to stop it.

"Wanna hit up a party?" he asks, stepping into my room as though I didn't attempt to slam my door on him.

"A what?" I adjust the robe. Clearly I haven't heard him right.

"A party," he repeats, a wide grin spreading across his freckled face. "A lively gathering, typically involving music and drinking . . ."

Too many questions are spinning around in my head to even land on one to ask. We've only been in the city about three hours, and most of that was spent on a tour bus with twenty of our classmates and one very frazzled English teacher. How did he get invited to a party? Where is this party taking place? And why on earth is Jason Lippincott standing at my door asking me to go with him? But I can't ask all of these at once, so I settle on the simplest question that comes to mind.

"What party?"

"Well, I was downstairs in the bar, talking to this guy—"

"You were in the *bar*?"

"Chill out, officer, I was having a Coke," he says, holding up his hands. "Anyway, there was a soccer game on TV—"

"Football," I say, correcting him. I have no idea why.

"Whatever. Anyway, he's got this girlfriend, and her parents are in Czechoslovakia—"

"I think you mean the Czech Republic," I say, correcting him again. I realize I sound like a shrew, but I'm kind of a stickler for history. And geography. And . . .

Oh my God, I suddenly understand why people call me Book Licker.

"What?" he asks, crinkling his nose in confusion. Of course, I can't just let it go.

"The Czech Republic. Czechoslovakia hasn't existed for almost twenty years. So unless her parents are visiting 1992, they're in the Czech Republic."

"Well, that certainly would make for a better story, now wouldn't it?" he replies, smiling as he leans into the doorframe.

My mind is drifting back to my bath and my book, so I'm ready to get this interaction over with. I pull my robe tighter around me in hopes he'll realize I'm prepped for something other than a party right now. He doesn't catch my drift. Body language much?

"The party?" I prod.

"Oh, right. So her parents are visiting *another country,* and she's having some people over. So he invited us."

"Us?"

"Well, he invited me, but you're my buddy, so by proxy, you get an invite, too. So how about it?"

I don't think I've ever been this confused by a conversation with anyone. Ever.

He's asking me because I'm his *buddy*? When have rules ever mattered to Jason? Case in point: he's planning on sneaking out to party. If you're going to break one, why not break them all?

Me? I'll go for breaking none, thankyouverymuch.

"I don't think so," I say. "And I really don't think you should be going, either."

"Why not?" He takes a step toward me. I take a quick step backward, unconsciously giving him room to enter. He lets the door swing shut behind him. Dammit.

"Because I don't think it's a good idea to go to a house party in a foreign country hosted by the girlfriend of a guy you met in a bar while watching soccer." As I tilt my head to meet his eyes, I'm reminded again of how freaking tall he is.

"Football," he says. He crosses his arms and cocks an eyebrow at me.

"Whatever!" I exclaim. I take a giant step backward so he's not towering over me. "You don't even know these people. They could be drug dealers or ax murderers. They could be cult leaders trying to get you to wear a choir robe and drink Kool-Aid. But all that aside, we're not supposed to be going out on our own."

"Ah, the rules," he says, sticking his hands in his pockets and chuckling to himself. "You do love those rules."

"I don't *love* rules," I say, starting to get pissed. "I just acknowledge their existence! And I don't want to get in trouble for *your* ridiculousness."

"C'mon, Julia. If it's the rules you're concerned about, then get dressed, because I'm pretty sure the number one rule is 'Don't lose your buddy.'"

"I'm not so sure a house party with British strangers is the cultural experience Mrs. Tennison had in mind," I reply.

"Mrs. Tennison could use a party! She needs to loosen up a bit, too. Think we should invite her?"

I don't like the way he says "too." I'm plenty loose. There's a difference between preferring books to parties and preferring sixteen cats to seeing the light of day.

"The answer is no," I say, hoping to end the conversation. I tap my toe frantically under the robe. If he doesn't leave soon, I'm going to have to jog to Glasgow to release this stress. "Besides, Mrs. Tennison will have my key. How do you suggest we get around that? Or were you thinking of sleeping in the lobby tonight?"

"That's why I have these," Jason says with a grin as he reaches into his pocket and fans out two key cards, one clearly marked 315. My room.

"How did you get—"

"I make friends, Book Licker. It's what I do best. Stick with me and maybe one day you, too, will learn how to do that." He tries to thrust the key card into my hand, but I push it back.

"I don't want that!" I cry, wondering what the punishment would be if I was found with a stolen key card I'd used to break curfew so I could go to a party hosted by strangers in a foreign country.

I think that slate of charges surpasses detention.

"Okay, fine," he says, dangling the key card in front of my face. "If you *really* want me to hang on to a key to your room . . ." He trails off, waggling his eyebrows at me suggestively.

I snatch the key.

"That's what I thought," he says with a smirk. Just then, he catches sight of my bathtub. "Holy crap, is that a *bathtub* at the foot of your bed? That's awesome! Can I join?"

"Hilarious." I can feel heat flooding my face.

"I'm not kidding. You, me, some bubbles . . ."

"You're insane," I say. My face is so hot I feel like I've already submerged in scalding water.

"It's all part of my charm." He tries to dodge me and grabs the bubble bath. I grab it back from him and turn around to place it in its rightful spot at the edge of the tub. But as I turn, something tugs on me. I look down and see the white rubber toe of Jason's sneaker planted firmly on the hem of the robe.

I'm moving, but the robe isn't. As the information makes its way from my eyeballs to my brain, I feel the robe slip off my shoulder.

"Hey!" I shout, and shove Jason backward. He pitches back onto the bed but grabs hold of the front of my robe. Before this can turn into a major wardrobe malfunction, I twist away from him, clenching the robe closed, but manage to get my feet tangled in the hem as it falls down toward the floor. Instinctively, I reach out to break my fall. Without my hands holding it shut, my robe flies open and billows out behind me. With my back to him, Jason can't have seen a thing, but my terrified scream pretty much serves as a high alert. He sits up in time to see me crash to the ground in a naked tangle of arms, legs, and terry cloth. As soon as I can discern my bare butt from my elbow, I pull myself into the fetal position and yank the robe over my head like a blanket.

It feels like an eternity before Jason stops laughing. He finally slows enough to choke out, "Are you going to stay huddled under that robe all night?"

"Go away!" I yell through the fabric.

"I'm sorry, I couldn't hear you," he says, still chuckling. "Why don't I turn around, and you can crawl out from under there? Then we can discuss this party situation further."

"How do I know you're going to turn around?"

"Well, you could trust me."

"Yeah right," I mumble.

"Or you could stay under there all night long," he replies. I think about that prospect for a moment, but the wood floor is not comfortable on my knees. Thinking quickly, I decide to feel my way around to the other side of the bed, where I'll be able to slightly shield myself from Jason's view. I army crawl across the floor, trying to keep the robe draped over me. Underneath yards of white terry cloth, I must look like some kind of turtle ghost.

When I make it around the bed, I peek my head out to see that Jason, true to his word, is facing the opposite direction. I let out a huge breath, adjust my robe, and scramble back to my feet.

"You good?" he calls over his shoulder.

"I wouldn't go straight to 'good,'" I say.

"Great." He spins on his heel, the soles of his sneakers squeaking on the polished floor. "Now hurry up and get ready. Let's party!" He grabs my purse off the dresser. I'd already packed it for tomorrow's excursion to the Tate. He tosses the bag to me. Faced with the prospect of releasing the robe to catch the purse, I decide to just let it whack me in the face, then bounce onto the bed. I've been naked enough for one day, thankyouverymuch.

"Now get dressed. We're going out."

"I said—" I say, stamping my foot like a little girl.

"I heard what you said. I choose not to believe you," he says. His mischievous grin quickly dissolves into something resembling seriousness. "Look, stay in with your books, or come out and get a life. It's your call. Personally, I think a little adventure would do you good. I'll be in the lobby. You've got ten minutes, then I'm out, at which point you will have officially lost your buddy."

The door slams, and I'm standing alone in the room, fuming. Get a life? A life! I have a life. A damn good one, too. I have friends, I play sports, I have fun, I have—oh crap, I only have ten minutes. With Phoebe's voice echoing in my ear—"It's London! Adventure happens."—I realize I need to do this. I need some adventure. Because my name is Julia. Not Book Licker. I'm Julia Lichtenstein, and even though I alphabetize my bookshelf and have, from time to time, quoted Dante at swim team dinners, I can have fun! I *am* fun. And if this is what it takes to prove it to Jason Lippincott—prove it to *myself*—then this is what I'll do.

And if I'm going to break the rules for perhaps the first time in my life, I'm going to look good doing it. I grab the only skirt I brought to London, an airy yellow number that hits just above the knee. It pairs nicely with my white polo and my black Converse high-tops, but as I look in the mirror, all I can see is Book Licker staring back at me. I'm dressed for a hayride, not a London house party. I look like a fifth grader on a field trip.

With mere minutes left before I lose my chance (or my nerve), I roll the skirt at the waist, transforming it into some approximation of a mini, and switch out my polo and Chucks for a strappy tank I brought to sleep in and Phoebe's heels. At least now I've got a little height, so I feel less like a gremlin. My hair is hopeless, so I leave it in the ponytail, hoping I can rock the bedhead look (with actual bedhead). I smear some eye shadow on my eyes and attempt to create some kind of smoky effect, but with such a limited time frame, it's looking more like I've been sleeping next to a coal furnace. Then I dash out the door (as fast as I can in four-inch leather gladiator heels), sliding my key under Mrs. Tennison's door on my way to the elevator. I'm half hoping I've missed him, half hoping I haven't, fully wondering why it's me he's even waiting for and not, say, Evie or someone like that.

The elevator is moving at a glacial pace, and I'm starting to have second thoughts. This is a bad idea. Very bad. I'm sneaking out to go to a party hosted by strangers in a foreign country. I'm putting my GPA and my permanent record (however mythical it may be) in jeopardy. To go to a party with Jason Lippincott. What am I doing?

If this doesn't constitute an emergency, I don't know what does. I pull out my assigned cell phone and dash off a quick note to Phoebe that ends up being the text-speak equivalent of "Going to a party with Jason Lippincott. Am I flap-my-arms-and-fly-away, speaking-in-tongues, barking mad?" How much can one little text cost, after all?

As the elevator doors slide open, I am once again face to face with Jason.

"Ready for this?" he asks, a wide grin spreading across his face.

In my hand, my phone vibrates.

Do it! And report back. Better be wearing the shoes! —P

"Ready," I say, dropping my phone back into my bag next to my pocket Shakespeare. "Let's go."

4

Boys and Drinks and Phone Numbers . . . Oh My!

Omg—Mark news! Must discuss.
Why aren't you picking up? —P

A half hour and a very expensive cab ride later, I'm standing in the living room of an opulently decorated town house, wearing a skirt that is turning out to be entirely too short. Everyone around me looks like they stepped off the pages of *Vanity Fair*. I feel like I need to find the kids' table.

An amateur MC is rockin' the mic (or attempting to, anyway) in the corner. Flanked on both sides by speakers, the deejay looks completely out of place surrounded by heavily ornamented and brocaded antiques. The furniture can best be described as "stately," an adjective that does not compute with the punky, flashy teenagers currently draped around it, glasses and bottles of various shapes and colors in their hands.

"So this is cool, right?" Jason asks.

"Oh, definitely. The coolest!" I reply, with entirely too much enthusiasm. I feel like such a dork, and the embarrassment coursing through my body causes me to teeter on my too-high shoes. Jason just rolls his eyes.

"Let's get some drinks," he says.

Oh yes! Let's! Because sneaking out isn't bad enough, so let's get drunk, too! Jason's already moving through the crowd, about to disappear behind a girl who looks like a praying mantis in leather pants. I hurry after him, because my desire not to be alone is overshadowing my desire to be on good behavior. I guess I've already screwed up the "good behavior" thing, anyway.

We make our way across the front room and into the kitchen. From a cabinet Jason procures two glasses, each of which looks like it cost more than my plane ticket. The marble-topped island in the kitchen is covered with various bottles and mixers. Jason splashes liquid from a few different bottles into the glasses, then hands one to me. As soon as the glass is in my hand, I tip it back and take a big gulp. I don't even ever *drink* alcohol, but it's as though my hand works automatically, bringing the glass to my mouth before my mind has time to be like, *What are you* doing? Coach Haas would kill me if he knew I was drinking during swim season.

Instantly, I feel like someone threw a match down my throat. As much as I want to be cool right now, my body takes over.

"Ugh," I grunt, my face contorting into a tight pinch from the shock.

"Uh, cheers," he says, laughing. "Too strong?"

"No, it's fine," I say, taking another (more careful) sip, wondering if the expression "when in Rome" applies to London, too. This sip burns less, but it still tastes like lighter fluid, despite Jason's having mixed in a good amount of lemonade. I'm sure he can tell from all the wincing that I'm in virgin territory here. What can I say? My mom is of the classic suburban-protective variety, and as I've made abundantly clear, I'm not much for rule breaking. But now that I'm at a party—a *London* party—full of strangers, it's like there's a whole new handbook of rules. I wonder if I can get a copy.

"First drink, Book Licker?"

"It's Julia," I reply, "and no." It's not a *total* lie. Gramma Lichtenstein always gives me a sip of her syrupy-sweet port at Christmas. That counts, right?

"Whatever you say," he says, shaking his head and taking a sip from his own glass. "Listen, I mixed that drink light, but you still need to go easy." I'd like to pretend he's genuinely trying to protect me from alcoholic embarrassment and/or danger, but I suspect he's making fun of me.

"Yeah, thanks," I say, but Jason's already walking away. I guess those were his parting words of wisdom, because five seconds later I spot him in the corner of the kitchen, already chatting up a gorgeous Brit girl who manages to make her punky neon-pink highlights look glamorous. Great. Now I'm at a party, surrounded by strangers, in a skirt that's too short, and I'm all by myself. I'm like a walking after-school special. I pull my glass closer to my chest to shield it from wandering roofies and date rapists.

"Well, hello there," says a high-pitched, distinctly American voice, and as I turn toward the figure that has sidled up next to me, I come face to chest with a very tall guy. A quick look up reveals perhaps the gawkiest of gawky boys, hair gelled within an inch of its life, wire-rimmed glasses perched atop an acne-covered nose. (I'm not mean! I'm descriptive!)

"Um, hi," I reply, already scanning the room to plot an escape.

"Lame party, huh?" he asks, resting an elbow on the counter and leaning into my personal space. "I've been to way better at the embassy."

"The embassy?" I ask, instantly regretting my curiosity, as I have now entered this conversation as a willing participant.

"A fellow American!" he says when he hears my accent. "Yeah, my dad's a diplomat. I've met basically everyone–everyone who matters, I mean. And I've lived all over the place."

Oh God, unattractive *and* pompous. A winning combination. My inner control panel is screaming *ABORT! ABORT!*

"That's really great," I say, continuing to formulate my escape route.

"It totally is," he says, oblivious to my desperation. He actually thinks I'm charmed by his ridiculous boasting. "I mean, I'm only sixteen and I've got three senators willing to write me recommendations to Harvard. Or Yale—I'm not sure which I'm going to choose yet. We'll see who offers me the sweetest package."

"Wow. That's . . . wow," I reply, choking back what I'm really thinking, which includes the phrases "shove it" and "butt munch." I toss back my glass and manage to mask my disgust for the drink and the company in one fell swoop.

"Can I get you another drink?" he asks.

"Oh absolutely," I reply, thrusting my glass into his hand. As he turns to fill it with who knows what, I dash through the nearest exit and down the hall. I duck into an open door, hoping it's a bathroom, but instead find myself in what appears to be a study. The walls are lined with leather-bound books and partygoers. A giant mahogany desk dominates the center of the room. If it weren't for the thudding bass and all the raging hormones in the air, I'd feel right at home. I plop down on an overstuffed, shiny leather couch and find myself sitting next to another male partygoer. He's wearing a rumpled oxford shirt and an even more wrinkled blazer. A gold crest on the lapel gives him away as a prep school boy. He's nursing a cut glass tumbler of some kind of brown liquor, which gives him away as a *drunken* prep school boy. His drink smells so strong I fear it will singe my nose hairs, and the smell gets stronger as he drapes his heavy, drunken arm over my shoulder and turns his face to mine.

"Whatcha thinkin' about?" he slurs.

What I am thinking about is the weight of the tiny book in my purse, and how I should be immersed in a hot bath right now, thumbing through its well-worn, highlighted pages. Not even one day as Jason's buddy, and already my worst fears have come true. Instead of a bath, I find myself in some kind of live-action video game nightmare, where the object is to shoot down as many drunk, irritating teen boys as possible. Is this what all parties are like? Because if so, I obviously haven't been missing out on much. The book is just pulsing there in my bag, taunting me for my stupid decision to come here.

"As You Like It," I blurt out, instantly regretting the words.

"What?"

I can feel the splotches of anxiety creeping onto my face. "Um, yeah, it's a play. And there's this girl, Rosalind," I start, going with it, as if this guy is in any mood for a literature lecture.

And clearly he's not, because he pulls me closer and says, "Listen, Rosalind, wanna go upstairs?"

"Um, no. *I'm* not Rosalind," I say, wrenching away from his embrace. "Rosalind is from *As You Like It.*"

"I *do* like it," he replies, shooting me a lecherous smile. "Let's go." He grabs my hand and starts to pull me from the couch, but my nerves have made my hands clammy with sweat. As he leans his body backward to haul me off the couch, his hand slips right out of mine. He stumbles back a few steps, pauses, wobbles, and then stumbles back a few more. One more step, and the back of his knee makes contact with the wide glass coffee table behind him. He is entirely too drunk to catch himself, or even protest. In fact, he seems only awake enough to enjoy the fall. That is, until his butt makes contact with the sheet of glass beneath him.

The crash is deafening. It can be heard well over DJ Rock the Mic and the din of fifty-plus chatting, laughing partiers. The entire party goes silent as every eye whips toward the pile of glass and the drunken boy in the middle of the room.

I'm the first to get my wits about me (probably because I'm the soberest one in the crowd), and I quickly jump up to help get him off the ground. He looks miraculously unscathed but is unlikely to stay that way if he starts stumbling around in a pile of glass shards.

"What in the bloody hell?" screeches a tall blonde, teetering into the study on giant stilettos that make my strappy sandals look like baby booties. From the look of horror on her face, I gather she must be the hostess of this fiesta.

Shockingly, the first person to speak is Drunky McDrunk, who mumbles from the floor something about Rosalind coming upstairs with him. He points a droopy finger my way.

"My name's not—" I say, but I'm quickly cut off.

"Ugh, whatever," she says, grabbing him by the hand and pulling him straight up. I'm surprised by her strength in heels, but maybe the adrenaline from an actual party crash is fueling her. Unfortunately, she turns that superhuman strength toward me. "Listen, Rosalind, Gabe's an arse and I don't blame you for launching him into inanimate objects. Just remember that there's a lot of priceless crap around here, so watch where you chuck him, right?"

She then turns on her heel, her blond hair whipping with such force I nearly duck, and drags Gabe toward the door. I'm left standing amid the glass shards while the party continues around me. Apparently, the show is over, and no one much cares that there's a shattered table left behind.

A tall, dark figure who looks like he stepped out of an Armani ad breezes past me. "Hot name," he says, leaving a trail of some strong-smelling cologne in his wake.

"I'm not . . . ," I start again, quieter this time, but there's no point. Armani is gone.

That's when it hits me: I *could* be Rosalind. I could be *anyone*. Nobody seems to know the difference between Julia the rule-following, Shakespeare-reading, freestyle record–holding übernerd from Newton, Massachusetts, and Julia the girl who attracts all males of the species, who coolly disposes of boys by shoving them into glass-topped tables. I could be someone cooler, more confident, just for tonight, just for this party. I can be the über-Julia. The Julia who says witty things and drinks and has boys, sober or otherwise, hanging on her every word.

I'm imagining myself in a circle of guys, a veritable buffet table of sexy hair and accents, when someone stumbles into me.

"Oh jeez. So sorry. I swear, I'm quite the klutz, falling into lovely girls in the hallway," says a very handsome sandy-haired Brit. "Though not as klutzy as poor Gabe, apparently. I saw what happened in there. Nice deflection. I'm Avery. Rosalind, was it?"

"Actually, it's Julia," I say. Between Jason, always calling me Book Licker, and Gabe the town drunk, I've had enough of people mistaking my name, thankyouverymuch.

"Ah, Julia, then," he says, taking a sip of beer. His blond hair is starting to fall over his eyes. He reminds me a little bit of Mark, which sets my mind drifting to Phoebe's text message, wondering what the "Mark news" could be.

Avery does one of those casual hair flips that boys do, saying, "That was a pretty crazy scene in there. You didn't cut yourself, did you?"

"Oh, I'm fine," I reply. "No big deal. He just came on a bit too strong is all."

"Gabe's an arse," he says. "But at least you can defend yourself."

"Oh, I'm ready for battle at a moment's notice." I flex my bicep, which I realize is shockingly defined from my regimen of laps and push-ups. I let my arm drop awkwardly before he mistakes me for some kind of she-hulk and runs away.

"So you're single, then?" he asks, his dark brown eyes looking at me expectantly.

"What?" I shift in my heels, trying to dislodge one of the leather straps from my pinkie toe while I attempt to untangle the rather abrupt change of conversational direction.

"I mean, if you don't need defending," he says, a little bit of red creeping into his cheeks, but on him it only gives that ruddy, athletic look of a rugby player. "I mean, er, well, I meant you don't have someone to defend you. I guess. Well, that made very little sense. I was trying to be sly and find out if you had a boyfriend, but that was the opposite of sly, eh?"

My mind is experiencing a thousand mini explosions. I have an Abercrombie ad standing in front of me, and he's nervous. *Talking to me.* I try to be calm, but my hands flutter from my hair to my skirt to my purse. I take a deep breath, rest my hand on my hip, and get control of myself.

"No worries," I reply coolly. *(Coolly?)* "I do have a boyfriend, actually, but he's back in the States. Hence the self-defense." The lie comes effortlessly. I'll have to thank Phoebe for dragging me to that week of drama camp at the community rec center.

Shockingly, he looks *disappointed.* But he continues with questions. "So you're from America, then?"

"You couldn't tell from the accent?"

"First impressions often lie," he says. (Oh, if only he knew . . .) "Where in the States?"

"Boston," I reply, which sounds much more cosmopolitan than Newton, a suburb of Boston that is basically the most boring place you can live and still see the skyline. But somehow even Boston doesn't seem to fit, so I go on. "But I'm living in Manhattan right now."

"Wow," he says, taking another sip of his beer. "I've always wanted to go to New York. What do you do there?"

For a second my mind goes blank; I'm not sure which is more distracting: his gorgeous accent or his chiseled jawline. Then I remember the giraffe-like girls at the baggage claim, their coffee and their rolling bags and their shiny sedans. I remember the beauty Jason was chatting up at the curb. "Modeling," I blurt out, rising up on my four-inch heels in hopes that he won't notice that I'm more suited to join the Lollipop Guild than the cast of *America's Next Top Model.* He appears to be buzzed enough to buy it, so I go on. "I've got a place downtown. I live with some of the other girls."

"That's awesome," he says, his eyes growing wide. I see him clutch his glass tighter. "Is that why you're in London?"

"Oh yeah," I say, studying my nails. "I'm here for fashion week and doing a little print work." Print work? Where the hell did I come up with that one? The lies have rolled off my tongue effortlessly, and I can already picture Mark in the role of my handsome American boyfriend who is oh so supportive of my modeling career but still misses me desperately when I travel. Avery hands me a heavy beer bottle, which makes my storytelling even more vivid. I'm talking about a *Vogue* spread when he pulls out his phone and asks me for my number. Old Julia screams in my head, *This isn't an emergency!* But über-Julia knows better. What could it hurt, really? He hardly seems like a sex offender, what with the stumbling and mumbling. Plus he's deliciously cute, and I'm not actually planning to *answer* his calls—if he calls at all. So I tell dorky Book Licker to shut it while über-Julia takes his iPhone out of his hand and taps my school-issued cell number into the shiny screen. Dad's jersey number. Shakespeare's birthday. My GPA. Done and done. I hand the phone back to him, letting my fingers linger on his palm for just a second.

"I look forward to hearing from you," I say before flashing him a smile, turning on my heel, and heading out of the room. I'm not quite sure where I'm going, but leaving seems like the cool thing to do. And I don't even teeter on my borrowed heels as I go.

5

꩜

Shentensh Shtructure

Wait, wa? Mark has publiclyyy. // announced his luv 4 me??
Haaaa a girl cn dreem. Too trd will skype toMorrr. —J

I'm definitely teetering on my heels a couple of hours later, when Jason finally appears at my side in the living room. I was chatting with a handsome bloke wearing Bob Marley's face on his ratty T-shirt, but he left to get me another drink. I was standing near the fireplace, using the mantel to support my weight. It seemed as good a time as any to respond to Phoebe's text.

As I lean away from the mantel to drop my phone back into my bag, I realize I'm wobbling. I'm not sure what all went from the various glasses and bottles into my body, but it seems to have done a number on my equilibrium. That's a good word. Equilibrium. Equillllibriummmm . . .

"What are you mumbling about?"

"What?" I snap toward Jason's voice.

His freckled face and bemused grin sway into focus. "You keep saying 'equilibrium.'"

Oops, was that out loud? "Nothing, never mind."

"Having fun?" he asks, raising his reddish-brown eyebrows at me.

I notice they look like little sunburned caterpillars, which causes me to break into a fit of giggles and hiccups so epic all I can do is nod in response. Jason pretends not to notice that I've come completely undone.

"Great, let's get out of here then, shall we?" He puts his hand on my lower back to steer me.

"What's the rush?" I ask, though it sounds more like "watsha russssssss." I'm following him toward the door, using his shoulder to steady me and desperately trying to resist the urge to pet his soft cashmere sweater.

"What do you mean?" Jason says, not even stopping in his pursuit of the exit. "I practically had to drag you kicking and screaming to this party, and now you want to stay?"

"No, I'm fine to go," I say—er, maybe slur. "But I do not need to be dragged around by you. Wait, that was bad shentensh shtructure."

"Great, a grammar lesson from a drunken Book Licker," he mumbles, nudging someone out of his way as we barrel toward the door.

"I'm not a Book Licker! I'm not a prude! I'm a PARTY GIRL!" I shout, and then let out one of those party girl "Woooooo!"s that I find so annoying when I'm sober. But they're really fun to do. Really fun. I totally get what's going on with the woo. Fun! "Wooooooo!"

"All right, party girl," he says, grasping me firmly by the hand. "But it's time for the party to end."

"Why are your pantsh suddenly so on *fire* to get out of here?"

"No reason," he replies as we burst out onto the stoop, but not before a deep voice booms from within the house.

"Hey, you little American shit. You assaulted my girlfriend."

Jason and I wheel around and come face to face with a very large, very drunk, and very mean-looking Brit with skunk-like neon streaks in his spiky bleached-blond hair. Even in my own drunken state I know immediately who his girlfriend must be: the girl Jason was talking to in the kitchen, the one with the emo-streak hair.

"I absolutely did not," Jason replies with way more courage than he should have when talking to this human mountain.

"Jason, this is not the time to stand up for your"—hiccup—"character," I whisper, finding a little clarity in my intoxication.

"My mate said you were talking to her," the guy says, challenging him. His eyes are angry and shot with red.

"Well, sure, we had a chat," Jason says with a shrug. "Mostly we talked about her wretchedly possessive and terribly unattractive boy-friend, which I take it is you." I grab Jason's arm, hoping to get him to stop talking. He rolls his eyes. "But I never touched her."

"Like hell you didn't," the human wall growls. "I'll make you sorry."

"You don't want to do that, friend," Jason says, snarkily placing a hand on his shoulder.

"And just why is that?"

"Because my dad is a lawyer, and he'll ruin your life if you lay a sin-gle fat finger on me." It occurs to me right then that Jason is a little drunk, too, which can be the only reason he's baiting this giant hunk of man.

"Piss off," the guy says, clenching his fists.

"You know, I'm not particularly familiar with that British expression. Does that mean 'Have a lovely night'?"

"Jason!" I hiss, willing him to cool it so we can leave. I'm becoming more and more aware of my own intoxication, and the realization that I snuck out to go to a party on a class trip to get this way is really starting to freak me out. The thought *I don't want to be drunk anymore, I don't want to be drunk anymore* runs on a continuous loop through my head as I grasp on to the railing on the stoop, trying to stay upright.

The British guy sneers at Jason. "It means I'm going to beat you into a bloody pulp and they'll have to mail you back to your mum in a lunch box," he says, rearing back a meaty fist. This makes me giggle a little, because it's funny to hear a British meathead use the phrase "lunch box."

Luckily, Jason ducks in time for drunken prep school Gabe to walk by and receive the full force of the punch. Poor kid can't catch a break, but I suspect he's so drunk he's not feeling much of anything at this point. Blazer and tie flapping out like wings, his body goes flying down the stoop and into the street, where a group of Arsenal fans are heading en masse to the closest tube station from a pub. They've clearly had a few postgame drinks themselves and are none too happy to be taken off their feet by a couple of teenagers.

"Bloody hell! What do you think you're doing?" shouts one of the men, grabbing drunken Gabe by the collar and shoving him back up the stoop and into the angry boyfriend, no easy feat. I've been completely rooted to the ground in shock, but as Gabe sails past me, I step back to avoid being taken out. I nearly topple off the stoop and into an ornately pruned rosebush in the process.

"Piss off!" the boyfriend shouts, clearly lacking a deep repertoire of comebacks. A crowd is starting to form as teenagers push their way out of the house to get a peek at the action. Angry Boyfriend grabs a beer bottle from one of the spectators and launches it at the middle-aged men now crowded on the sidewalk.

"You little pink-haired bastard!" shouts one as they rush up the steps to grab Angry Boyfriend.

"Get the little punk!"

"Piss off!"

"You'll wish ya had!"

"Arsenal sucks!"

"You suck!"

"Kick his ass!"

Before I can even blink, a full-on street brawl erupts on the sidewalk, middle-aged football fans tangling with drunken teenagers. Fists fly, insults are shouted, and I feel a pain in my shoulder as someone grabs my faux-leather hobo and the handle snaps clean off. The contents of my bag scatter across the stoop and underfoot of the madness.

"Dammit!" I yell, dropping to my knees on the rough stone stoop in an attempt to gather what I can. I spot my phone perched on the edge of the top step, but as I reach out to grab it, I'm shoved violently from behind. I tumble down two steps and land in a pile of arms and legs at the bottom.

"Nice panties," I hear, and look up to see Jason offering me his hand. "Let's get the hell out of here."

"My phone!" I shout, pulling myself to my feet. "It was right there." I point to the top step, but the phone is gone.

"I've got it," Jason replies, holding up a shiny silver cell phone. "Let's go. Now."

He grasps my hand, and we take off down the sidewalk at a full sprint. House after house whizzes by, and at the end of the block he hangs a sharp left. I have absolutely no idea where we are or where we're going, and I have no idea if Jason does, either, but I manage to fall into a good stride, keeping pace right with him in four-inch heels. The shouts of the fight fade far into the distance as we run block after block away from the party. I try not to think of the many ways these shoes are ripping my feet to shreds right now or the rest of my belongings, scattered clear across a street that is now surely half a mile away. The purse is cheap, easily replaceable with twenty dollars and a trip to H&M, and I have plenty of extra pencils and tubes of lip gloss. I even have a spare calculator in my suitcase. But my heart sinks into my insensible shoes as I think of my dog-eared, note-filled pocket Shakespeare, probably resting in a puddle underneath that stupid rosebush.

6

❧

The Morning After the Night Before

U ok? No public pronouncements of love but Mark has
def been acting weird. Talk soon! —P

BEEP BEEP . . . BEEP BEEP . . . BEEP BEEP . . .

My eyes flutter open to the rhythm of a foreign sound emanating from somewhere in my room. It takes me a moment to remember that I'm not in my bedroom in Newton. I'm not even in the United States. I'm thousands of miles across the ocean in London. With my classmates. And the new fuzzy friend that seems to have grown on my tongue overnight.

"Ugh," I groan, peeling my eyes open from the deep sleep that's encrusting them. I don't *feel* disgusting. I *am* disgusting. The pure embodiment of grossness.

BEEP BEEP . . . BEEP BEEP . . .

My head starts to thud in time with the beeping, and I fling my arm over the mahogany nightstand, giving my travel alarm clock a hard thwack. The sliver of light peeking out from the sliver of space where the roman shades don't quite meet the floor is cutting straight into my eyeballs like a laser beam.

BEEP BEEP . . . BEEP BEEP . . .

Well, it's not my travel alarm clock, since that's now in a pile of plastic parts on the floor. What is happening to me? My head pounds even harder, bringing back the memory of the thudding bass from last night. My memories start flowing as if rapped by DJ Rock the Mic himself. The house party. The short skirt. Jason. The beer. The embassy geek. Gabe. Rosalind. The broken glass. The bass. Oh God, the bass. Avery.

BEEP BEEP . . . BEEP BEEP . . .

My night is flooding back to me, with that incessant beeping providing the beat. What in the hell *is* that?

BEEP BEEP . . . BEEP BEEP . . .

And then the last piece of the puzzle falls into place. My phone! I manage to extricate myself from the tangle of my sheets, and I realize I'm still wearing the rolled-short skirt from last night. It has migrated practically to my chin. The left strap of my tank top somehow found its way over my head, so both straps are hooked over my right shoulder. One glance in the mirror tells me I look like I tried to get dressed while riding a roller coaster.

Ugh. I am NEVER. DRINKING. AGAIN.

BEEP BEEP . . . BEEP BEEP . . .

I need to make the beeping stop, which will hopefully also stop the room from leaning sharply to the left. My bare foot, now covered in angry red blisters, lands on something small and cold. I lift it to find the shiny silver cell phone, still beeping and flashing a nasty red light at me. The old Julia must have remembered to set an alarm.

I flip it open and press every button I can find on the unfamiliar phone to silence the blasted thing. Thank God I manage to hit something right, because the beeping stops and a text message appears on the screen, glowing a warm blue.

It was amazing 2 meet u last night. I was dying
2 kiss u. U free to chat? —Chris

WHAT?

My brain goes into mini-meltdown mode. My phone bears a message from a guy who wants to—no, is *dying* to—kiss me.

WHO?

Chris? Which one was Chris? I concentrate, trying to remember the sequence of events that led to this text message. Everything is clear up until the broken table. Unfortunately, the rest of the night is mostly a blur. I know another beer was put into my hand, then another. I started talking more and more, getting bolder and bolder. The beer helped, but so did the idea of being the über-Julia, this whole new person who bears no resemblance to Book Licker. And it turned out that über-Julia was *quite* popular with the boys.

There was the Irish lad who sang "Danny Boy" (only slightly off-key). I gave him my number, mostly so he wouldn't launch into his likely very deep repertoire of Flogging Molly covers. Then there was the prep school kid with the posh accent who kept talking about his family's jet. He was another who'd received the number simply so I could get rid of him.

But then there were the tall guy with the shaggy hair who played guitar in a Shins cover band, the blond university student studying twentieth-century Eastern European literature, and the young Scottish artist with deep blue eyes who told me about his latest installation using tinfoil and Beatles lyrics. I dazzled them all with my wit, charm, and beer-induced confidence, matching the literature buff book by book, dissecting "Revolution 9" with the artist, and humming along as the musician strummed his guitar.

It never occurred to me that any of them would try to contact me. The only calls I normally get from guys fall into two categories: questions about homework and requests for tutoring. As I attend school with exactly none of the guys from the party, I didn't expect to hear from any of them. Ever.

Which one was Chris?

I read the text message once more, hoping something will jog my memory. Dying to kiss me? They were all cute, so I'm pretty sure I'm dying to kiss him, too.

I mean, none of the boys I met was *the one*. Not like Mark. But Mark's not here. And kissing a boy might still be good practice. And practice makes perfect, which is exactly what I want to be when Mark and I finally get together. It's not like I get these chances very often. Whatever I was doing last night—I guess it's called flirting—obviously worked. Let's hope I can re-create that sober.

Because I repeat: I am NEVER. DRINKING. AGAIN.

Now the real question: what the *hell* am I supposed to write back?

A loud banging starts up on my door.

"Julia? The entire class is waiting for you! Would you please get your ass downstairs, like, ten minutes ago!" Sarah Finder's voice does a remarkable job of piercing the thick wood door and driving straight into my ears like a spike. I glance at the time on the phone and see that I am, for the first time in my entire life, late. So I type the first thing that comes to my alcohol-addled brain.

> Great to meet you too! Can't talk!
> Rushing off to all-day photo shoot. TTYL —J

It just seems easier to continue with the lie I started yesterday than to think of a whole new one. I hit send before I can realize what I've done. I make a mental note to check my available phone credit later, then fly out of bed and gargle some mouthwash. I quickly replace my rumpled skirt with a pair of jeans, toss my tank in favor of my favorite blue thermal, and throw on some sensible sneakers in hopes of placating my very angry feet. Drinking, flirting, lying, and now late? Can the old Julia please come back now?

7

໒ঐ৩

Toe Curling, Tongue Kissing, and Tate Wrestling

Wow. All clear. Now I know I should have kissed u. —C

"In this room, you will find a veritable feast for the eyes, with colors exploding like fat, ripe berries of passion all over the canvas. Taste with your eyes the juicy flavors of impressionism, paint swirling into itself like a delicious gravy of art." The tour guide's speech is interrupted by snickering. My head hurts too much for me to turn and find out who's laughing at the "berries of passion"—or to point out the tour guide's use of mixed metaphor.

All I want right now is to crawl back into bed. The only reason I haven't barfed yet is that I have too much respect for the Tate museum to leave my breakfast on the floor. But if our tour guide keeps going on about feasts and gravy, I may not be able to stop myself.

He finishes his spiel on impressionism before leaving us to explore the contents of the room. Students start milling about, taking in various works of art.

"Miss Ellston!" Mrs. Tennison stomps across the gallery to Evie, who is holding her shiny silver international cell phone in her French-manicured hand. "I fail to see how you can be paying attention to the art around you with your nose in that phone."

As Mrs. Tennison reaches for Evie's phone, her jangly adobe bracelet catches on the fringe of Evie's leather hobo bag, pulling it off Evie's shoulder and sending its contents spilling onto the floor. Among the assortment of nail polish bottles, tubes of lip gloss, and three different hairbrushes, I see about twenty plastic cards emblazoned with the words "Talk 'n' Text!!"

Mrs. Tennison looks from Evie to the phone cards on the floor, then back at Evie again. Evie's eyes have gone wide and all the color drains out of her face until only her artful application of blush remains. Evie's family may be loaded, but even I've heard the stories about how strict her father is. If Mrs. Tennison calls him, someone is getting her Audi taken away.

"Miss Ellston, what did I say?" Mrs. Tennison barks.

"Um, about what?" Evie replies, her voice barely above a whisper.

"About *phone* use, Miss Ellston!" Mrs. Tennison takes a deep breath and then raises her voice so that all the students in the gallery can hear. "Class? Everyone gather around."

We shuffle together. Someone in the group smells like the onions in their morning omelet, and I have to take a few steps away from the circle, feeling dizzy with nausea. Mrs. Tennison's tone cuts right through the cool air of the gallery. She holds Evie's phone above her head.

"Miss Ellston seems to think my instructions regarding the intended purpose of these phones—and what they are not intended for—were mere suggestions. Let me be clear. You are to remain present on this trip, in mind *and* body. Therefore, you will not talk, text, or tweet on these phones unless you are having an emergency. Remember, your behavior on this trip will impact not only your grade, but your disciplinary record back at home. You *will* face classroom repercussions should you disobey my rules."

"I'm sorry," Evie mutters. I can hear my mom's voice in my head: *She's not sorry; she's just sorry she got caught.* I hate when Mom says it to me, but I'm not going to lie: I get a little thrill from watching Evie's face as her cell phone disappears into Mrs. Tennison's ugly old carpetbag full of guidebooks.

"Yes, I'm sure you are," Mrs. Tennison says. "But I'm afraid the damage has been done. I will be holding on to your phone for the time being, and if there's an emergency, you can borrow your partner's phone."

Students scatter back to various corners of the gallery, and the thrill of seeing Evie get in trouble quickly disappears. All of a sudden I feel like my stomach is going to fall out of my butt. *Classroom repercussions?* I flip open my phone and scroll through the text messages. Will Mrs. Tennison find out? I try to figure out a way to connect the texts on my phone to a cultural aspect of the trip, but thoughts of the party last night only reignite my pounding headache. I need to reload my phone with credit to erase whatever damage the texts may have done.

I put my phone back into my bag and set about doing what I've been doing all morning: pretending to examine a piece of art while actually just standing still, trying to keep it together and not throw up. This is how I've managed to hide my hangover from my classmates and Mrs. Tennison. Let me tell you, it has been no easy feat. Even though I've been looking forward to this excursion for months, I can't enjoy a minute of it. I feel like my eyeballs are going to fall out of my head and my brain will ooze out my ears. And that's just what's happening above the neck. My stomach is doing a cha-cha. I managed to choke down a piece of toast on my way out of the hotel, but it definitely wants out.

I see a bench in the middle of the gallery, conveniently located in front of a very large sculpture. I lurch for it, sighing with relief as I collapse onto its cool marble. I stare intently at the statue as if I'm taking in the wonder. Really I'm clamping my mouth shut and willing my stomach to calm down. I think of the text message I sent this morning, and though I didn't know it was possible, I feel even worse.

I hear a jangling coming in from the right. Mrs. Tennison and her oversized jewelry swoop in next to me. She sighs. Playing strict teacher 24/7 is obviously taking its toll on her.

"It's just lovely, isn't it?"

"Gorgeous," I reply, barely glancing at the huge sculpture in front of me. I recognize it from my art history book as Rodin's *The Kiss*. It's huge and shockingly white. With my pesky hangover, I practically need shades to look at it. It depicts two lovers, naked, arms encircling each other for an epic make-out session. I'm hoping Mrs. Tennison will want to take in the beauty in silence, but no dice.

"Rodin really knew the body," she says, sighing again. "He high-lighted every physical manifestation of attraction. Look at how the man's spine is tense as he pulls her close. Even her toes are curled into the rock with lust. Every inch of this piece is meant to inspire passion."

"Impressive," I say, trying to sound engaged without opening my mouth too wide.

"You know, I've often imagined myself in this piece," she says, and my stomach really starts to have a go. "Locked in a tight embrace, never feeling close enough. His lips on hers, skin on skin, the lust of—"

"Gross!" I exclaim, my hands flying to my mouth.

"Excuse me?" Her head whips around, and she narrows her eyes at me so that I can see her liberal application of turquoise eye shadow.

"Oh! Uh, well"—I panic—"it's just, uh, um, a gross oversight that, uh, the rest of the class isn't as taken with the piece as you are, Mrs. Tennison."

"Oh yes, it certainly is," she says, letting out a long breath. "I just hope one or two of your classmates manages to trip and fall into some cultural experiences." She smiles at me before wandering off to humili-ate another student with her presence. The adrenaline rushes out of my body, and I'm left exhausted. I lean over and put my head in my lap, hoping I can get one moment of peace before we have to move on to the pop art collection. But again, no such luck.

"Hey, buddy, you doing okay?" Jason plops down next to me on the bench. He must have been hovering nearby, waiting for Mrs. Tennison to leave.

"No," I say into my jeans, too tired and sick to lie.

"Hangover? That sucks, dude," he says, doing a little seated tap routine with his green high-top Chucks. I swear the kid can't be still for a second.

"How are *you* feeling okay?" I manage to ask before clamping my mouth shut again. I look like roadkill, and this guy is sitting here with sparkling blue (non-bloodshot) eyes. I sniff, expecting to catch a whiff of at least beer, if not stale cologne, but there's nothing. If I can make out anything, it's the scent of the hotel-provided bar of soap.

"Practice," he replies with a laugh. He digs in his pocket until he produces a purple-and-white scrap of paper. A gum wrapper. "Are you gonna make it?"

"That's unclear. I'm trying to recover from the trauma of last night," I say, sitting up. "I can't *believe* I let you convince me to go to that party. And then I got drunk? God, I totally embarrassed myself last night."

"Embarrassed? No way. It looked to me like you were a hit." He folds the gum wrapper over and over on itself, until it's nearly a speck.

"What?" I ask. The faint smell of grape is wafting off the paper, and I have to turn away so I don't gag.

"Yeah, about an hour in, I came to find you to take you back, but then I saw you with that guitar guy." He flicks the wrapper toward a nearby wastebin, but it banks off the edge and lands on the floor. "You looked like you were having fun."

I sit straight up and turn to him. "Guitar guy? What guitar guy? Did you catch his name?"

"Um, Bono? No, I didn't. Why?"

"No reason," I say, trying to sound nonchalant. I'm pretty sure the squeak in my voice gives me away, though, because Jason frowns at me.

"What's up, Julia? You're acting even more wacko than usual this morning." Jason has made no move to pick up the wrapper, which is still lying several feet away from the trash can. Of course Jason would litter in one of the most famous museums in the world.

"I told you. I'm hungover," I say. I stand up deliberately and make my way to the abandoned wrapper, which I pick up and pointedly deposit into the bin. I definitely don't need *Jason Lippincott*—who until this trip had spoken a total of three words to me in my life—telling me I'm a wacko.

"Yeah, it's not that." Jason stands and shuffles after me. His sneakers are squeaking across the floor of the museum like an annoying, yappy puppy.

"Really?" I stop in my tracks and whirl around to face him, mostly so he'll stop too and the squeaking will stop with him. "Because it's all I can think about right now."

"We're in a museum, Book Licker," he says, pointing at a late Picasso painting. "It's like your mother ship, and you're not paying attention to anything. Seriously. Did something happen last night?"

There is a touch of concern in his voice, and it softens me for a moment. But then I imagine what would happen if Jason knew all about my texting. He teased me enough when he barely had any ammunition.

"I do *not* want to talk about it," I reply. I turn my back to him. In front of me, the surface of a Mondrian painting explodes with oranges and blues.

I hear the telltale squeaking of his sneakers as he loops around me so we're standing side by side. "You don't want to talk about it, or you don't want to talk about it with *me*?"

I can't seem to shake the guy. "Both. Equally."

"C'mon, Julia," he says, nudging my shoulder with his. "I know you feel like hell this morning, but last night it seemed like you were having something resembling a good time."

"I was," I concede, still avoiding looking at him.

"So I helped you have a memorable first night in London?" Pride creeps into his voice.

"Oh God, more than you know," I say. As if on cue, my phone buzzes in my bag. I pull it out and flip it open to find another text from Chris. *Hopefully soon,* it reads.

"Excuse me, isn't that your school-provided cell, Miss Emergency Only?" Jason asks, and when I finally do look at him, sure enough, a sly grin is spreading across his face. There is no doubt he is enjoying my new rule-breaking spree.

"Can you leave me alone now, please?" I sigh, and snap my phone shut quickly. Since when is Jason so interested in harassing me? Since when is he so interested in even acknowledging my existence?

"Oh, come on, I'm your buddy. You can tell me anything." He throws an arm around my shoulders. I'm startled by the gesture, which is apparently exactly what he wants. He quickly uses his free hand to snatch the phone out of mine before taking off at a sprint into the next gallery.

All hangover symptoms melt away in an instant. I take off after him. I have to wander through two different rooms before I find him in the corner of a gallery dedicated to Warhol. He's clicking through my phone underneath one of Warhol's camouflage prints. I snatch the phone from his hands, but I can tell from his mischievous grin that the damage is done. He's read all the texts. Blood rushes to my face.

"What is the matter with you? Were you dropped on your head or something?" I snap. I'm so embarrassed I feel like someone has shoved my whole head into a pizza oven.

"A photo shoot?" Jason laughs.

"It was the first thing that came to my head. Thanks to *you,* I wasn't exactly thinking clearly." I stuff the phone back into my bag, spin around on my heel, and march away, trying to muster up whatever dignity I can.

"Hey, no one forced drinks down your throat," he says, following me once again. "Well, aren't you going to text back? That *is* the proper etiquette."

I turn around and hold up both hands.

"Shut up! Just shut up. For the rest of the day, I need you to shut up," I burst out. I glance over his shoulder to see a Warhol print of a handgun. *If only* . . .

"Will do," he says, miming a zipper across his lips. But that only lasts a split second before he unzips and says, "But first I need to hear the story."

"What story?" I ask impatiently.

"The one about this Chris character. Who is he?" Jason's face looks like he's doing his best not to start laughing hysterically, which makes me more furious than ever.

"I don't know!" My headache is starting to return, so I once again head to the nearest bench and plop onto it.

"You don't *know*?" Jason, of course, sits right next to me, since apparently he has decided that today we're besties.

Maybe because I want him to stop bothering me, maybe because I hope he has a clue to Chris's identity, or maybe (in fact, definitely) because I'm too exhausted to resist anymore, I tell him the whole story: about Gabe and the shattered table, about Avery and giving out my number, and about all the rest of them, one of whom is named Chris and sent me the text message Jason is now grinning about.

"Let the teasing commence," I say, dropping my throbbing head into my hands.

"What? Tease you? Me? Surely you jest," he says, reaching for my cell inside my bag. "I only want to help."

"Yeah, help me right into a suspension," I reply, jerking it away.

"Julia, you are my 'buddy,'" he says, using the requisite air quotes. "I would never put you in harm's way."

"Oh, right. You'd only take me to a party full of strangers in a foreign country and abandon me. Then get me caught in a street brawl, where I lose all my stuff including my pocket Shakespeare."

"Your pocket what?" He raises an eyebrow. He probably thinks I'm talking about a mini-Shakespeare action figure. (Actually, I *do* have one of those. But I left it back in Newton, *thankyouverymuch*.)

"Never mind. The point is, why would I accept help from you?"

"Look, I can get anyone to fall in love with me," Jason says.

I snort. "That seems *highly* improbable."

Jason doesn't take offense. "Okay, okay. I can get anyone to fall in serious *like* with me. Anyone. Guaranteed. And I would like to extend that talent to you. Want this dude to fall for you? I can make it happen." He holds out his hand to shake on the deal.

"Oh, and you're going to help me out of the goodness of your heart?" I ask, eyeing him.

"Hell no," he says brightly. "You're going to help me out, too."

I stare at him suspiciously. "What do you want?" I ask.

"You're going to write my reflection papers for me," he says like it's the most obvious thing in the world.

"Are you kidding?" I cry out. "You want me to help you cheat?"

"No such thing as a free lunch, Book Licker." He crosses his arms and leans against the wall. "Take it or leave it."

"No way," I say. I walk away from him before I can change my mind. I expect him to come after me, pecking at me like some rampant chicken, but he doesn't move.

"Then good luck in your texting adventures," he calls out. "May the force be with you."

I stop right in the middle of the gallery. My phone feels heavy in my bag. When I pull it out and flip it open, I see the text from Chris still floating on the screen as though it's taunting me.

"Oh, come on, Book Licker," Jason says. I yelp and spin around. I didn't notice him oozing his way off the bench and slinking up right behind me. "So you write a few extra essays. It won't kill you. Besides, I'm sure you're already worried about how badly *my* writing is going to hurt *your* average. What better way to protect your GPA than to do it yourself?"

My mind flashes to my cell phone number. Four. My perfect GPA. The number I've worked so hard to achieve.

"Is that a threat?" I ask. I try to keep my tone steely, but I can hear the slight quiver in my voice.

"Not at all!" he says, but he grins at me in a way that's no longer just mischievous. It's devious. "I'm just saying I'm not the best with the spelling. Or the grammar. Or the finishing things on time."

"You *are* threatening me!" I say.

"I'm giving you all the facts," he retorts. "What you do with them is your concern."

"You sound like a lawyer," I say, loosening my grip on the phone.

"Like father, like son," he replies. "C'mon, Julia. It's a couple extra essays. You'll probably even like it. Now would you give me that thing?"

He takes the phone from my hand and flips it open, then types furiously on the keypad. "You need to sound confident, even cocky. Guys like confidence." He hits a couple more keys. "That should do the trick."

" 'Actually, I think I should have been the one kissing you,' " he reads aloud, and I instantly flush.

"You *must* be hungover if you think that's even in the same universe as something I would say," I reply. "There is no *way* I'm sending that to him."

"You just did," he says, snapping the phone shut and pressing it into my hand.

"What!" I flip it back open and scour the message log, hoping he's lying just to scare me. But alas, there's the message in the "sent" folder.

"Well, you were yapping about how you'd never do it, so I did it for you," he says. He's clearly proud of his good work.

I am about to have a total meltdown when the phone vibrates in my hand. I'm so shocked I nearly send it right to the wood floor.

"What's it say?" Jason asks, leaning over the display, eager to find out the result of his little experiment.

At this point I'm so sick and shocked and at a total loss for words that I simply pass the phone to him.

" 'There's always tonight . . . ,' " he reads aloud. "See? I told you I could do it," he says to me, grinning hugely.

"But what now? He wants to meet tonight!" My mind is racing.

"Which you cannot do," he says firmly, flipping the phone shut.

"What? Why not?"

"First of all, you don't even know who this guy is. He's a total stranger; you can't meet up with him after two text messages. Too dangerous. But more importantly, you don't want to seem too eager. Play hard to get a little. It's old school, but it works."

"Seriously?"

"Of course," he says. "And let's be honest: you're going to need a *lot* of help before you can handle Chris on your own. Without my guidance and tutelage, you *will* royally screw this up."

Sadly, I realize Jason is right. I was reckless last night, and I was lucky to escape with only a fun, mysterious, sexy text message. And what will Chris think when he discovers I'm not some gorgeous supermodel, but a Book Licker from Newton, Massachusetts? He'll probably run screaming in the opposite direction. I need time to think.

"Besides, you told this guy you're at a photo shoot," Jason points out, as if reading my mind. "You can't see him until that's over, Kate Moss." He chuckles to himself.

"Shut up." I fake-punch his arm but can't help cracking a smile.

"Hey, I'm not the one who claimed supermodel roots!" he says, holding his hands up.

"I never called myself a supermodel!"

"Oh, you didn't tell him about your runway work in Milan, super-model?" he says, pointing an accusatory finger at my nose. I swat at him. He jerks away from me, tripping over the toe of his sneaker, and then springs to his feet.

"What, are you gonna throw that phone at me, Naomi Campbell?" He laughs, shielding his face with his hands in mock fright.

"Maybe!" I say, playfully tossing it at him. He catches it with ease, flipping it open to dash off another text, then tosses it back to me. He looks like a little kid who stole an entire birthday cake. *What did he do?* When I see what he's written, I flush so deep I'm afraid I look purple.

You couldn't handle me tonight.

Ack!

"You jerk!" I swat at him again.

"Such language and violence, my lady." He ducks from the blow, and I only get a whiff of his jacket. I lunge to get him again when the phone rings. I look down and see Chris's number blinking at me. Not a text message—an actual phone call. In my frozen shock, Jason has time to grab the phone back from me and flip it open.

"Hello there, sexy," he answers, making his voice phone-sex-opera-tor deep.

That does it. I totally break every museum rule known to man or beast and launch myself at him, taking us both down to the hardwood floor. He rolls away, but I reach out and grab a handful of his shirttail, pulling him back. Just as soon as his hand is within reach, he holds his lanky (and surprisingly muscular) arm over his head. I have no choice but to climb on top of him if I'm going to have any chance of getting the phone back.

"Having fun?" he asks before executing some kind of ninja flip that finds him over me, pressing my shoulders into the floor. "Because I am."

With the call ended, Jason rolls off me and sprawls out on the floor next to me. He's laughing and sighing, happy with his victory. Great. What will Chris think after Jason answered the phone? I *never* should have trusted him.

"Mr. Lippincott! Miss Lichtenstein!" Mrs. Tennison comes flying up to us, her Birkenstocks slapping angrily on the floor. "What in God's name are you doing on the floor of the Tate?"

Instantly I scramble to my feet, mortified. I haven't been chastised by a teacher since the fourth grade, when I got caught hiding in the locker room during a game of dodgeball.

"Uh, falling into some culture?" Jason, still on the floor, says with his trademark smirk, which has probably gotten him out of legions of situations just like this with teachers just like Mrs. Tennison.

I step consciously away from him, as though I can physically shake off his bad influence. "Mrs. Tennison, I'm so sorry. What happened was—"

Mrs. Tennison doesn't let me finish. "Honestly, Julia, I am shocked by this behavior from you. You're acting like children, and in one of the greatest museums in the world!" Her hideous necklace, which looks like it's made out of adobe Christmas ornaments, rattles as she gesticulates angrily.

There's no point in trying to explain. Instead, I croak, "It'll never happen again."

"Well, lucky for you, you're going to get another shot at appreciating fine art," she says in a tone reserved for teachers who have devised the perfect educational punishment. "Since you've wasted your time here at the Tate, you and Mr. Lippincott will be visiting another museum of your choice during your cultural hours. I want a thousand words from you on the cultural importance of art."

"A *thousand words*?" Jason asks, barely able to choke out the number.

"Not another comment from you, or I'll make it two thousand," she snaps. "Now rejoin the class. It's time to move on." She straightens her flower-print blouse and marches off, her shoes smacking against the floor as she goes.

"You are a *jerk*," I say to him in a low voice as soon as Mrs. T is out of hearing range.

"You started it," he replies, shrugging as he attempts to de-wrinkle his gray polo.

"What are you, five?"

"I'm rubber and you're glue." He sticks out his tongue at me.

"Great. I hope you can bring those creative writing skills to this essay."

"Uh, no. That's all you. Remember our deal?" Jason spots Evie and Sarah in a corner, huddled around Sarah's phone, and heads in their direction. He gets about four steps away, then turns back to me. "Cheer up, Book Licker. It's extra homework. Your favorite thing, right?"

"It's Julia!" I fume, but he's already jogged off to join the rest of the class.

8

Oh, Darling . . . Should I Believe You?

What is going on w/you and JL? Back off already —SF

Embarrassment, anger, misery: SF. Sarah Finder. Has to be. It's hardly a secret that she looks at Jason as though he's the best thing to happen to the world since fat-free cookies. I feel like my head is going to spin off my shoulders. Thank God she didn't bother to confront me in person, because I'm certain that would have pushed me over the edge. I would have barfed for sure.

I read the text again. Back off? I can't believe she thinks I'm *on*. She must have thought our wrestling match was *flirting* (gag). Apparently, she missed the part where I actually wanted to grind Jason into a bloody pulp. I chuck my phone into my bag in disgust.

"Would you please hurry up?" I call back to Jason. The afternoon has gone from bad to worse. First we went the wrong way when we left the Tate; then Jason made fun of me when I pulled out my guidebook, complete with Post-it notes and a flagged foldout map; then I tripped over a crack in the sidewalk and nearly tumbled into a group of tourists.

"What is your freakin' rush?" Jason snaps, trotting up to walk beside me. "Look around. It's gorgeous. Can't you calm down for one hot second?"

He's right, of course, but I won't admit it. We're finally heading the right way, east along the river through Millbank. The buildings all around us are carved stone and rusty brick and copper that's turned green over hundreds of years of rain. I know from my reading back in Boston that we're breezing past enough history to fill more than ten volumes. I nearly stop to point out the Chelsea College of Art and Design, which used to be the Royal Army Medical College, where they developed the vaccine for typhoid. But I know any mention of nineteenth-century history and disease will only be met with some epic eye rolling from Jason, so instead, I charge on along our path, shaded by trees and curving with the river.

"I want to get this over with so I can get back to the hotel and swim some laps before dinner," I reply, gazing over the low stone wall and on to the dark waters of the Thames. The fresh air rushing down is helping my headache, but I still want to dive into the pool and work out some of this tension. The invitational is today, and I can't help wishing I were there, especially after what happened this morning.

"Laps?" Jason arches one eyebrow.

"You have your hangover cures; I have mine."

"You any good?" he asks, quickening his pace to walk next to me.

"Excuse me?"

"Swimming. You any good?"

"I'm okay," I reply, wondering what kind of answer he's looking for.

"Just okay?" he says incredulously. "Didn't you win state in the women's hundred-meter butterfly the last two years in a row?"

"And the hundred-meter freestyle," I add. Then I stop. "How did you know that?" I whip around on the street so I'm face to face with him. He immediately takes a step back.

"I mean, I think I saw something about it in the paper or whatever.

Don't get all obsessed with yourself over it," he says, pushing his hands deep into his jeans pockets, walking past me with his bobbing strut. "Where are we going, anyway?"

"I figured we could hit the National Gallery," I say, now matching his pace. "It's easy to get to, and it'll be easy to find good material for the essay. They have van Gogh's *Sunflowers* on display, and I would totally love to see that. Van Gogh always makes an interesting essay. Or we could write about a series of Renaissance paintings and their historical context."

"And by 'we,' you mean you," Jason says, still marching forward, dodging tourists taking photos of the view along and across the Thames.

"No way." I have to double my pace to keep time with his long, lanky legs, and I have the sudden realization that *I'm* now following *him*. "Our deal was for the reflection papers, which are only three hundred words. Thanks to you, we owe Tennison an extra *thousand* words, so I think you'll be helping."

"Actually, *you* jumped *me*. So I think that knocks my liability down to somewhere in the range of two hundred fifty words." Jason nearly walks into a woman teetering around on platform wedges. He jumps to her right to avoid a full-on takedown. "It takes two to tango . . . or wrestle on the floor of the Tate, as the case may be."

"You forced me into it!" I say. "Five hundred words, minimum." As the words come out of my mouth, I can hardly believe I'm negotiating with him.

"Three hundred twenty-five, and that's my final offer," he says over his shoulder.

"Whatever." I am not interested in starting another fight, and I clearly can't trust him to do the work, anyway. I'm starting to wish he would go back to ignoring me, as he has always done in the past. "If you could just cooperate with me for the next hour, we could get this essay done *and* actually learn something. I really want to see the Caravaggio!"

"Snooze!" Jason drops onto a bench along the path, tilts his head back, pulls his ball cap over his eyes, and starts loudly snoring. A giant red tour bus is emptying out right in front of us, its passengers already armed with cameras, ready to snap shots of the boats cruising along the Thames. An elderly man actually turns his camera on Jason, snapping a photo as if he's some kind of performance artist.

"And you have a better suggestion?" I say, trying to suppress my bubbling rage. He springs back to his feet and starts marching down the sidewalk, continuing east along the curved river.

"I do, actually. Follow me."

Jason gives me a wave and then mimes a dive right into a knot of camera-toting tourists. Americans, if the American-flag T-shirts are to be believed. I'm imagining what might happen if I ditch him and head to the National Gallery on my own when I catch a flash of Jason's Sox cap bobbing through the crowd. Before I can question the decision, I take off after it.

As we walk, the sun disappears behind a patch of clouds. The day instantly becomes one of those classic cloudy London-fog days. A cool breeze blows off the Thames. The river is dotted with rowers, clad in rugby shirts and Windbreakers, slicing through the water in shiny red boats. The low stone wall gives way to a wrought iron fence spiking up out of the grass. I can see the towers of Westminster Abbey peeking through the trees and buildings ahead. It's just like a movie. And even though I'm hungover, following Jason to god knows where, I am overcome with love for London. It has yet to let me down. Dad was right. Screw Paris; London is the city for me.

I'm taken out of my reverie, though, as Jason leads us off the paved path and down an embankment, where we crunch along a narrow gravel path closer to the river's edge. The path is dotted with broken glass and bits of trash, and it's clear that this is not meant to be traveled by tourists.

"Where are we going?" I ask.

"We're almost there," he says, charging ahead as if he isn't leading us somewhere creepy or potentially dangerous.

"That is *not* the answer to the question I asked," I reply. He slows a little so that I can fall into step next to him.

"Are you always this intense?"

"Yes," I reply, because I know that saying no would only be the start of another argument.

"Well, at least you're honest. Intense and honest," he says, trudging toward the base of a bridge ahead.

"Again, where are we—" I start, but Jason interrupts me.

"We're here." He points to the scenery before us.

"Here" is a kind of concrete cave bounded overhead by a bridge rumbling with car traffic. Underneath the bridge, the concrete curves alongside the hill leading up to the street, forming not only a perfect canvas for street artists, but an ideal half-pipe for the band of dirty skate punks risking their lives (without helmets!) zipping up and down it. Skaters are flipping and twisting off a few scattered ramps. We'd be in almost total darkness were it not for the swirling intensity of the spray paint covering every available surface, the bright colors giving the illusion of light. From any vantage point on the path or the bridge, the entire park would be completely hidden.

"What is this place?" I ask.

"Underground skate park!" he replies over his shoulder. He starts jogging around the space, vaulting off various ramps. "Cool, huh?"

"But what are we *doing* here?" I'm still feeling disoriented: the swirl of motion and colors is dizzying, and the space echoes with the sounds of kids shouting to each other. "In case you've forgotten, we're supposed to be writing an essay about art and culture."

"Are you kidding? There's plenty of art and culture here," Jason says, heading back toward a concrete barrier covered in colorful graffiti on the far side of the park. "Maybe even more than at the crusty old National Gallery."

I decide to let the comment about the National Gallery being "crusty" and "old" slide (especially since 187 years is practically a baby when you're talking about a city that was settled by Romans in AD 43) and instead follow him to the wall. Jason runs his hand over the concrete, chipped and cracked, but covered with some pretty impressive graffiti tags. There's no discernible shape or pattern, just swirls and explosions of paint. The color is so vibrant it looks like it's about to burst off the wall. It kind of reminds me of the Mondrian we saw earlier at the Tate.

"It's cool, right?" Jason asks, running his fingers over the wall. With his bright red hair, he looks almost like he could step right into the painting.

"Yeah," I admit, moving away from the wall toward a huge boulder closer to the river's edge. It's painted to look like a psychedelic Easter egg.

"Thank you," Jason says, taking a slight bow. "Better than the National Gallery?"

"I still want to see the *Sunflowers*," I reply, unable and unwilling to let him win so easily, "but this is pretty great."

"I'll take that," he says with a smile like that of a little boy who got an A on his very first test. He ambles off in the opposite direction, toward another concrete wall with a series of spray-painted stencils. They're not Banksy tags like the ones I've seen online, but they're good approximations. A series of spray-painted black rats depicts the evolution of man. There are also a number of poorly painted anarchist symbols, but most of the images are impressively detailed. In the middle of the wall, there's what appears to be a giant hole in the concrete, through which you can see a busy street scene. I actually have to step closer to realize it's all a spray-painted illusion.

In the corner of the park, a grungy-looking skater boy in skinny jeans and an even skinnier (and, I assume, ironic) Justin Bieber T-shirt picks up an acoustic guitar covered with an array of battered, peeling stickers. As he positions the leather strap over his shoulder, I half expect to hear a crushing rendition of the latest emo punk single. But instead, he begins gently plucking the opening notes to one of my all-time favorite Beatles songs, "Here, There, and Everywhere." I'm shocked by how talented he is: his version is beautiful and slow, with some small riffs on the melody. I close my eyes to listen, and for a minute, my hangover disappears. The Beatles played live on the banks of the Thames: a perfect London moment.

"You okay?" Jason asks, putting his hand on my shoulder.

"Yeah, I just completely love this song," I reply, leaning my head back to take in the sky and sucking in a deep breath. Mom walked down the aisle to this song, and my parents had a tradition of dancing to it every year on their anniversary, even if their dance was only a two-minute twirl around the living room.

"Yeah. The Beatles. Pretty good," he replies.

I snap my head around so fast I risk nerve damage, turning to stare directly at him.

"Pretty good?" I say incredulously. "Let me be clear: the Beatles are the best band ever to walk the face of the earth, and if you can't recognize their genius, I hardly understand how you have enough sense to dress yourself in the morning!" It's the exact speech my dad gave to my grandfather when he had the gall to question the Beatles' greatness. Of course, that was before I was born, but Mom still repeats the story from time to time, laughing about how Dad was so puffed up that Grandpa couldn't even formulate a response.

"Down, girl!" Jason says, holding up his hands. "I'm a fan."

He wanders away, I assume in an attempt to escape my insanity, and I turn back to some of the paintings around me. There's a spot where many layers of spray paint in a rainbow of colors have started to peel away. An industrious artist has taken some tool or another to carve out the lyrics to Queen's "Fat Bottomed Girls." It's somehow beautiful.

"Hey, Jason," I say, waving over my shoulder to show it to him, but when I turn, he's gone. I scan the park and see that he's wandered over to the street musician, who is adjusting the tuning on his guitar. Jason takes out his wallet and passes the guy some cash, which the guy takes, and in exchange he hands over his guitar.

Oh God. What is he doing?

Jason waves me over. At first I hesitate, but he's gesturing so frantically he looks like he's about to have a seizure. Finally, I trudge over to him.

"What are you–" I start, but he cuts me off.

"Sit," he says, and points to a bench, like I'm a dog.

I know he'll bug me until I agree, so I sigh and sit down where he indicates. I'm on the bench directly in front of him, so I have to look up a little to see his face.

"Happy now?" I ask.

Instead of responding, he launches into a perfect acoustic rendition of "Oh! Darling," but unlike skater boy, Jason sings. Sings!

Now, I normally do not like it when people sing near me, much less *to* me. I don't care if they're good, bad, or mediocre. It's all the same. Unless you're signed to a major label with music I can find on iTunes, I don't want to hear your live performance. It's why I can't watch *American Idol*. I keep worrying the contestants will mess up and be embarrassed, and then *I'll* be embarrassed *for* them.

But Jason is fantastic, and I'm mesmerized. His voice cuts right through the London fog, and I'm glued to the bench, unable to take my eyes off him. He stares right back at me, eyes sparkling. He hits every note, even Paul McCartney's trademark ooohs at various pitches.

"Believe me when I tell you (oooh!)," he sings, winding down, "I'll never do you no ha-arm." By the time he finishes the song, my jaw must be hanging down to the ground. And while I'm busy trying to figure out what I should say—in this moment when I should be totally embarrassed but instead I'm totally enchanted—he casually whips the guitar over his head, hands it back to the skater boy (who is applauding), and heads toward the far border of the park. I scramble off the bench and head after him.

"Where did that come from?" I burst out. He is pretending (I think) to examine more graffiti.

"I told you, I'm a fan," he says with a shrug, not looking at me.

"Sure, a fan, but I didn't realize that meant you were a mini Paul McCartney."

"Nah," he says, brushing the compliment off. "I just mess around. My mom used to play me Beatles records and all that."

I open my mouth to tell him about my parents, too, but something stops me. I don't like talking about my dad. I hardly ever do, even with Phoebe.

"Well, that was really good," I say, then pause before adding, "*You* were really good."

He shrugs and glances at his watch. "Hey, we can still make it to the National Gallery if we hurry. What did you want to write the essay about, again?"

"This," I say, willing him to look at me. "The graffiti. The 'gallery' of the park. It's amazing. There's art and culture here, you said so yourself."

"You think?" He finally turns to me.

"Yeah, of course," I say, walking toward the evolution-of-man illustration. "I've got my camera. We can take some pictures."

"Awesome," he says, his eyes lighting up. "Let's do it."

I reach into my tote and dig out my digital camera, checking the battery life. "How did you even find this place?"

"Oh, um, some guy—" he starts, but I'm already laughing.

"Of course," I interrupt. "You always know 'some guy.' "

"Yup, that's right," he says quickly. "I'm down with the shady characters." He points at a tag he wants me to photograph. "Are you sure about this? I mean, you aren't worried about your grade? I don't think this is what Mrs. Tennison had in mind."

"It'll be fine," I say, shockingly sure of myself despite the grade that hangs in the balance.

"Excellent progress," he says. He blows on his fingers, then brushes them off on his shoulders. "Good work on my part. You're making a lovely transition from Book Licker to Sexpot."

We spend the next few hours picking out the most interesting pieces from the walls and boulders all around the open-air park. By the time we leave, we've taken nearly forty pictures and have pages of notes in Jason's messy scrawl and my flat, loopy cursive; as we make our way back to the hotel, neither of us can believe it's nearly dark. I'm shocked that I've spent practically twenty-four hours with Jason Lippincott, and I actually enjoyed myself. I think this means we might actually be friends. Turns out Jason is full of surprises.

As we climb the hill and start toward the main road, I realize I haven't eaten in hours. Jason is busy on his phone, tapping out text messages with a furrowed brow. Either he's having a *lot* of emergencies or he's using his phone for decidedly un-school-related business.

I pull out my cell, wondering if there's another message from Chris that I missed, or maybe even a missed call from one of the other guys I met at the party. When I flip it open, though, the screen shows no alerts. I sigh loudly, but Jason keeps tap-tap-tapping away at his own phone. The sound is unnerving.

"I'm starving," I say. Either he doesn't hear me or he pretends not to. I kick a crumpled can on the sidewalk in front of me and it clatters loudly off the curb and into the street. "Want to grab some food on the way home?"

"Um, yeah, sure," he says, keeping his nose practically pressed to his phone.

"Great," I say. I can't believe I just asked Jason Lippincott to spend more time with me. I can't believe he actually *agreed*. I turn toward a pub on the corner, about half a block from the hotel. I have a total weak spot for fried foods, and I'm on an unofficial hunt for the best fish-and-chips in London. I reach for the door to head inside when I realize that Jason has stopped on the curb.

"Actually, no," he says, flipping his phone shut and putting it back into his bag. I wonder for a moment if he was texting the gorgeous-yet-punky pink-streaked girl from the party. I sneak another glance at my own phone. Still nothing. And now Jason is about to ditch me, too.

"No?" I ask, shoving the phone deep into my bag.

"I mean, not right now. I'm not hungry, and I think I really need some, you know, alone time. To decompress. I'm, like, really exhausted," he mumbles, stifling a possibly staged yawn.

"Okay, well—" I start, but I'm interrupted when Sarah Finder and Evie trip out of the pub. They look fabulous in their sightseeing attire, which includes skinny jeans and fashionably oversized button-ups. Matching plaid scarves are wound around their necks, and twin hammered-silver earrings dangle from underneath their shiny, perfectly wavy tresses. How have they achieved beach hair in London in March? I glance down at my favorite jeans, holes worn in the knees by me, not by Abercrombie or Fitch. Why am I the only one on this trip who seems to have packed for a field trip instead of a fashion show?

"Jason!" Sarah exclaims with a hiccup, rushing toward us to give him a bear hug. "Oh my God, where have you been? I haven't seen you since the Tate!"

The pair of them tower over me on their platform wedges, and I instinctively rise up on my toes so I don't feel quite so miniature.

"Seen anything cool today?" Evie purrs, draping an arm around his shoulders.

"Nah, nothing special," Jason replies, and I'm surprised by the little needles I feel poking at my spine when he says it. He's not looking at me, either. It's like suddenly I don't exist.

"Ugh, us neither," Sarah groans. "I don't know *how* I'm gonna write that stupid reflection paper."

"We're in London. *Everything's* special," I mutter. Then I clamp my mouth shut. I definitely did *not* mean to say that out loud.

"Oh, Julia, I didn't see you there," Evie says, giggling. "Having fun in London?" She doesn't even wait for my reply. Instead, she turns back to Jason.

"So where have you *been*?" She links an arm through his.

I wait for him to tell them about our afternoon at the skate park (and the mini concert), but several members of our class pour out of the pub and surround Jason. I find myself pushed nearly into the street by the throng. As they move back toward the pub door, Jason is swept along with them. I'm not quite sure what's going on, but I'm pretty sure their plan does *not* include fish-and-chips.

So much for alone time. I'm guessing it was Sarah he was texting on our walk. She probably invited him to the pub party. He was no doubt planning to ditch me before we arrived.

No wonder I got that weird, nasty text from her earlier. Luckily for Sarah, I was too hungover to respond, but even post hangover, I'm not sure what I would have texted. I don't need to be a part of Newton North drama, especially concerning Jason. Sarah is delusional, and she clearly has her sights set on him. And good for them, seriously.

She deserves Jason. And he deserves her.

I focus on the anger so I can't focus on the gross feeling churning in my stomach again, killing my hunger. One second he serenades me, the next he pretends I don't exist. Plus he ditches me after making such a big deal about the "buddy system," dragging me out to a party, and getting me in trouble with Mrs. Tennison.

So much for the new Jason. I can't believe I thought we might actually become *friends* on this trip. He's the same as he always was: a complete and total jerk.

Later that night, back in the hotel, I'm working on our essay. At first I set out to only do my half—five hundred words, no more, no less—but the more I typed, the less I wanted to deal with Jason at all. I'm nearly done with the whole thing now, and I'm not even annoyed. Jason clearly sees me as some kind of bummer or social ball and chain, and I'd prefer to limit our time together to our school-sponsored outings. No more house parties or detours to underground parks.

I take one more bite of my curry-chicken sandwich—which I picked up from a little grocer around the corner and have been working my way through as I've typed—and stretch my fingers. I'm about to get started on the conclusion when an email from my mom pops up with a bing.

> **Hi, hon! Just wanted to check in on your great London adventure. Have you fallen in love yet? Keep in touch. I'd love to hear all about your trip! I miss you lots and lots. Don't worry, I'm TiVoing all our favorite shows so we can watch them when you get back. Let me know that you landed safely! Lots of love my darling dear. — Mom**

Fallen in love? I know she means with the city, but I can't help thinking about the romantic jumble of boys I've met in the last twenty-four hours. I hit reply to start typing, but then hesitate, my fingers hovering over the keys. I can't really ask for Mom's advice without bringing up the drinking. And the sneaking out. And the ten thousand other rules

I've broken in the day and a half I've been on the other side of the ocean. I wish I could ask her for some words of wisdom, but I don't think there's a mom-safe version of this story. Instead, I dash off a quick response, telling her about our trip to the Tate and filling her in on tomorrow's adventure to the Tower of London. I end by telling her I miss her lots, which is true. My laptop makes its trademark "whoosh" sound as the email zips through cyberspace to my mom.

I click on the document to churn out the last two hundred or so words of my (or "our") essay, but the cursor blinks at me. I can't remember what I was planning to say. My brain feels like a cereal bowl with too much milk in it. I need a break. I grab my camera and start flipping through the pictures from the afternoon when I come across one taken by the skater-boy guitarist. Jason and I are posing in front of a tag of a red British-style phone booth. The Queen of England is painted inside, and the text coming out of the phone reads *London calling*. My arm is thrown over Jason's shoulder. We look like a set in our matching black North Face fleeces, his pink polo peeking out of his unzipped collar. Jason's Sox hat has somehow been knocked askew, his rusty hair sticking out from underneath it in all directions. I was feeling high off the hidden park, the mini concert, and the fun of discussing the graffiti with Jason. I'm wearing a giant goofy grin, and he's laughing hard in the picture.

It's only now, as I look at the image on the back of my digital camera, that I see why he was laughing.

He's holding bunny ears over my head.

Seriously? Is he *five*?

I throw my camera at my bed, where it bounces twice before dropping off the edge of the mattress onto the floor. Instantly, I regret it; I realize the warranty probably doesn't cover accidents provoked by Jason-inspired rage. I rush over to the side of the bed to pick it up. When I reach down, I see it has landed next to my phone, which is flashing with a new message.

Radio silence much? JL is SO NOT INTERESTED —SF

SF? I assume the text is from Sarah Finder again, like the nasty one I deleted earlier in my hangover-induced indifference. I guess she didn't take Mrs. Tennison's warnings about unapproved texting seriously—or else she thinks this constitutes a 911 situation.

It's almost laughable. She thinks I like Jason Lippincott.

But quickly, the humor starts to fade. If *she* thinks I do, is it possible that *he* thinks I do? Is that why he was so eager to ditch me? Why he was being so awkward and mumbly? Does he think I'm some sad crush girl? I could seriously melt into a *puddle* of embarrassment. It's one thing to *be* sad crush girl, but it's even worse for someone to think you're sad crush girl when you're not.

And if *Sarah* thinks I'm sad crush girl, then soon so will everyone else.

And that could get back to Mark.

I debate texting back—something like *I'd sooner drill out my own eyes with an unsharpened pencil than date Jason* should do it—but I'm worried that giving her any ammunition will only make things worse. Instead, I decide there will be no more semi-playful wrestling on the floors of any museums. Clearly it's giving people the wrong idea. Jason and I aren't even *friends*. He's the last person on earth I'd ever have a crush on. And I'm going to make sure that fact is obvious to Sarah and to everybody.

This whole day has turned into a fractured web of ridiculousness, and all I want to do is go to sleep. As I crawl into bed, my cell blinks again. I contemplate ignoring it, not wanting to know what snarky comment Sarah crafted this time, but I know I won't be able to sleep unless I read it. I flip open the cell and my heart skips a beat.

Chris.

9

Meta-Tweets and Tuna Fish

Absence makes the <3 grow fonder . . .
Can I see u? —C

W ell, that's it. I definitely can't sleep now.

There's only one thing I can do to calm myself down: I pull on my Kelly green Newton North–issued team Speedo and head to the roof to hit the indoor lap pool. I saw in the hotel welcome binder (which I've already read cover to cover . . . twice) that it's open until midnight every night, and it's only nine o'clock now. That gives me a full hour to get back to my room before Mrs. Tennison does her final check to ensure all the keys have been turned in. I still have the spare key tucked in my wallet, but I am *done* with Jason-style shenanigans.

No matter what side of the ocean you're on, the chemical smell of a pool remains the same, and I find comfort in the chlorine and the burn of my muscles as I pull myself through the water. When I'm underwater, the world is literally muted, and I'm left only to my own head.

I start out with a simple freestyle. Years of early-morning swim practices and weekend meets have built definition in my shoulders, arms, and thighs. My body is built like a little compressed spring, compact and strong. It looks like at any moment I could release my coils and take off into the air. On dry land this means my jeans are always too long, never big enough in the thigh. Tank tops can make me look slightly mannish. But in the pool, my body is perfect. It does exactly what I tell it to do, releasing its coils at exactly the right moment to power me through for win after win, record after record.

Unfortunately, tonight my head is muddled with boys. Chris, my mysterious text messenger. Mark, my one and only (if only he knew it). And now Jason, whose goal in life seems to be to throw me off balance and humiliate me in as many ways as possible. If harassing me doesn't work, he'll simply flirt with me. That must have been what that song was all about.

Because he was flirting with me. I know it. I felt it.

Didn't I?

Chris. Mark. Jason.

Chris. Mark. Jason.

They're beating a rhythm through my brain with every stroke. Freestyle isn't working. I need something harder, so I jump out of the pool, turn, and dive straight back in, attempting a fresh start with the butterfly, the hardest stroke, but also my favorite. This time, as I slice into the water with a perfect shallow dive, my mind goes straight to Dad. The summer I was five, he'd spent weeks teaching me the perfect technique for diving. Dad was always a great teacher. Tough, but patient. While most kids were getting a round of applause for a clumsy belly flop, Dad was standing next to me on the deck, demonstrating how I should bend my knees, how to tuck my head between my arms. He taught me to swim, too, when I was even younger than that. Sure, he let me flail for a second, but I never doubted that his firm hand would reach down and pluck me out of the water by my swimsuit as I gasped and spit. Dad would never let anything bad happen to me.

Instead, something bad happened to *him*.

My muscles burn as I pull myself through the lap lane, thinking about how fast he got sick. In my memory he was strong and healthy until the moment he wasn't. I remember visiting him in the hospital exactly one time. And even unshaven and pale, he still looked like a force. Like he could reach in and pull me out of whatever trouble I might find myself in. I don't remember much of the funeral—I was only seven—just the American flag draped over the casket, men in their dress uniforms everywhere, and the twenty-one-gun salute.

I count out twenty-one strokes down the lane, then pull myself straight onto the deck of the pool. Drops of water shake off my face, so no one would be able to tell that I'm crying. If I don't calm down now, it'll be only moments before I'm gasping for breath, my muscled shoulders shaking with tears. Most of the time the pool is my oasis, but sometimes when the memories creep in, it crushes me.

I clearly need help, and I only know one person with all the information to counsel me.

I take a few deep breaths while toweling off, then head back to my room, where I flip open my laptop and dial up Phoebe on Skype. She clicks in immediately. Her smiling face fills most of the screen, and I see she's wearing her favorite shirt, a commemorative tee from the release of the long-forgotten '90s flop *Dick Tracy*. The pumpkin-colored walls of her bedroom, dotted with various artwork purchased from Etsy, appear behind her. The sight of the whole tableau makes me feel the tug of homesickness. I have to concentrate for a moment to keep those tears at bay.

"Cheerio!" she says in a bright Mary Poppins accent, her cheerful mood chirping through my laptop speaker. "I was wondering when I'd hear from you again! Your last text was a little garbled."

"Oh yeah," I say, thinking back to my last drunken message to Phoebe. "Texts will be a little few and far between. In a single day Evie apparently racked up a bajillion dollars sending out tweets or whatever, and Mrs. Tennison went ballistic. She actually screamed at her in the Tate."

"Oh, I heard. Sarah already put an update on Twitter to say that there wouldn't be more updates. How meta is that?" We giggle at the ridiculousness of our classmates. "So you'd be totally proud of me. Guess what I'm doing right now, a full twelve hours before my trip?"

"Packing!" I say with a smile. Only Phoebe would get how much organization makes me happy. "Are you using the list?"

"Of course!" Phoebe replies, shaking a crumpled piece of paper containing my patented packing list. "Without this bad boy I'd probably arrive in Chicago with one pair of jeans, six hoodies, and exactly no underwear. How're things in jolly old England?"

"Ugh" is all I can say, covering my face with my hands.

"That good, huh?" Phoebe leans back in her paint-spattered desk chair, throwing her feet up onto her desk.

"Worse," I mumble through my fingers.

"Well, I've got something to take your mind off whatever the trouble is," she says. "A little bit of Mark gossip."

My heart jumps, and I lean in so close to my laptop I practically smack my head against the screen. "Oh my God, I totally forgot!" I say, thinking back to last night's text. "What is it?"

"Okay, so talk about fate," she says. "I was at the Polar Pop grabbing dinner for the fam, and *who* should be having dinner there but Mark."

"And?" I can hardly conceal my impatience. If I could, I would jump through the monitor right now.

"*And* he was with Ian Green, who was all, like, geeking out because apparently Serena Garner asked Mark out last night."

My stomach plummets. Serena Garner is tall, gorgeous, and graceful. Even worse: she's a *senior*. I glance at my muscled swimmer's shoulders in the mirror. I look like a linebacker standing next to Serena. There's no way I can compete.

Phoebe can see my face fall, so she quickly jumps in. "But he said no! He told Ian that Serena isn't his type, and he's not going to waste time on a girl who couldn't give him what he wants," she finishes triumphantly.

Not his type? I quickly catalog Serena's defining characteristics. She's beautiful. She looks like she's constantly on her way to shoot a shampoo commercial. She's been elected homecoming queen, prom queen, and student council president, and if there were a category in the senior superlatives for Best of Everything Forever the End, she'd probably win.

She's also dumb as a box of rocks.

Wait. Does that mean he likes smart girls? Smart girls like *me*?

"Oh my God, I love it!" I exclaim, grabbing the sides of my laptop as if I'm going to hug Phoebe through the screen.

"Yeah—pretty good, huh?" Then she wrinkles her nose. "Although I think it's a little creepy that he said she can't give him what he wants. What does that even mean?"

"It's not creepy! He's talking about MTB," I say, invoking Phoebe's and my trademark code for true love. "Meant to be." I'm thinking back to our backyard wedding, wondering if it's a sign that he remembers. Maybe he knew Phoebe was listening in on his conversation. Maybe he knew she'd tell me! Who needs texting when the love of your life is sending messages through your best friend? "I mean, you know Serena isn't the brightest crayon in the box. Remember that time we bought cupcakes from her at the dance team fund-raiser, and she couldn't remember how much a nickel was worth? He probably just means he couldn't carry on a conversation with her."

"Maybe." Phoebe shrugs, although she doesn't look convinced.

"Wait a minute, weren't you the one who last week tried to convince me to buy a yellow mini, telling me I could wear it on my first date with Mark?" I ask, eyeing her through our pixilated connection. "Now you're having doubts?"

"Julia, wake up! I don't care if you go out with Mark or the starting lineup of the football team or even Joey Benson—"

"Not even!" I cry. Joey wore a cape, a floor-length black velvet cape, to school in the eighth grade with no sense of irony. He's been undatable ever since.

"I don't even care if you go out with Jason Lippincott—"

"You shut your mouth!" I shout, leaning straight into the mic, but Phoebe charges on, looking stern.

"All I want, oh dear friend of mine, is for you to go out with *someone*. Do something, even if it's not the magical, wonderful thing you had in mind. Don't sit around for one more second pining away for some fantasy that might never come along, because it might not even exist."

"It will come along," I insist, "and it does exist. I saw it."

"Maybe it will," she sighs, chin in hand, knowing not to challenge me when it comes to Mom and Dad. "Maybe it won't. But while you're sitting around pining and waiting and wondering and hoping that this perfect love happens, lots of guys and lots of dates and lots of kisses are passing you by."

"But that's it," I say. "Kisses. Or *The Kiss*. I was staring at it today, live and in person at the Tate." So, okay, I'm kind of recycling Mrs. Tennison's weirdo speech from earlier, but maybe she had a point. I mean, teachers have to know *something*, right? "That's what I want. I want toe-curlingly awesome kisses. One-of-a-kind kisses, from a one-of-a-kind boy."

"I hate to break it to you, Julia, but Rodin made many casts of *The Kiss*," Phoebe says, rolling her eyes. "There are dozens of versions of *The Kiss*, in museums all across the world. Oh, and by the way? Those figures in the statue are supposed to be the adulterers from Dante's *Inferno*. The world's most romantic cheaters."

"But Mark—" I start to protest.

"Maybe he's MTB," she says, cutting me off, "but maybe not. And until you figure that out, I'm just saying there are other fish in the sea, Julia. Big fish. Tasty fish. Tuna fish!"

"Maybe I already caught one," I say, resigning to end the argument and move on to some juicier conversation. I begin telling Phoebe all about the party and Chris and the text messages. "And the last one said, 'Absence makes the heart grow fonder.' And then he asked to see me!"

Phoebe is gaping at me through the monitor. The way she's leaning in toward the camera makes each of her eyes look approximately the size of a fishbowl. "Jules, that is awesome! Are you going to meet him?"

I pick at my fingernails. I never paint my nails, because the chlorine inevitably causes the polish to chip off. Chipped nails pretty much drive me to distraction; they're like my own personal kryptonite. "I don't know. I've got Jason shackled to me, making things difficult. I mean, he answered the phone today when Chris called."

"Which probably just made him jealous and more interested," Phoebe says. "I mean, he sent you the text about seeing you *after* that, right?"

"Yeah," I admit.

"See? He's interested. And you should be, too. Text him back!"

"But what about Jason? And Sarah? She's watching my every move and practically glued to her phone," I protest. "I don't think she's nearly as afraid of her parents as Evie is. And I don't want to come back from this trip with a reputation and a permanent Twitter record of my every move."

Phoebe flaps a hand dismissively. "Just forget them. Everyone knows ninety percent of Sarah's gossip is bogus, and the other ten percent is only partially true," she says, affecting the soothing tone she's honed over years of friendship with me. "So you have to spend these outings with Jason. It's all business, right? He's just screwing with you, and Sarah is loco. Don't let them get to you, okay?"

It only takes another ten minutes of prodding before she has me convinced. Not that Mark is wrong for me, but that I should be having some fun with some other fish–er, guys. Phoebe also thinks it's a bad idea to get together with a sort-of stranger in a foreign country before I know a little more about him, so when I sit down to text him back, I enter the message we've agreed on.

Been thinking of you too. But need to know u better b4 we meet again. More texting? —J

I flip the phone shut and set about my nighttime routine. With my face washed, my teeth brushed and flossed, every part of me moisturized, and my clothes set out for the next morning, I'm finally ready to end the day. By the time I crawl into bed for the night (dangerously close to the time I need to wake up in the morning), I'm feeling much better. I am, after all, a very lucky lady. I'm curled up in the most comfortable bed ever (seriously, it feels like sleeping in a hug), in a gorgeous hotel room in London. I have eight more days of exciting and interesting travel and a mysterious stranger who wants to kiss me. Bet Phoebe didn't have that in mind when she instructed me to find adventure in London.

What I need is a plan. I love plans, especially when they're written down with my favorite pencil using pretty little bullet points, but I'm too tired to get out of bed now. Instead, head sinking into the feather pillow, I lie back, staring at the stylishly tarnished brass chandelier over me, and start to think.

First of all, I *have* to get off this rule-breaking kick. Sneaking out? Drinking? I'm lucky I didn't get caught. I also have to find out who Chris is. Besides, I'd like to have some more time to charm him with my wit–or at least my proper use of grammar–so he doesn't bolt in the opposite direction when he realizes I'm not *exactly* the model I've been claiming to be.

Of course, this whole situation is made a thousand times more complicated by my getting dragged through London by the king rule breaker himself, Jason Lippincott.

Suddenly, I realize that being tethered to Jason for the next eight days may not be such a bad thing. Sure, he's supremely annoying and has more than once nearly ruined my life, but that kid probably has plenty of devious spy tactics to help me find my mystery man. Let *him* break the rules, and I'll trail behind, reaping the reward, hopefully in the form of awesome European smooching—or snogging, as the Brits would say—with my mystery guy. And if I have to write a few extra essays and tolerate a few extra hours with Jason to do it, well, then that's a deal I'm willing to make.

Who knows? Maybe by the end of this trip I'll have fallen in love with more than just the city.

10

Various Forms of Torture

Mark who? :P —J

When my alarm buzzes, my head is so clear, and my outlook so sunny, there might as well be chirping birds flitting around the room and cheerful little mice waiting to dress me for a ball. I stretch my legs, still a little tight from last night's lap session, then throw back the plush hotel comforter and bound out of bed.

I step into my favorite jeans, topped with a tank and a vintage flannel button-up Phoebe gave me last year. It's so old and worn it's like wearing a basket of kittens (but not in a weird way). I double-check my bag to be sure I have everything for the day's visits (guidebook, map, agenda, fully charged phone, a book in case I get caught somewhere with nothing to do, ibuprofen, gum, a pencil case with four fully sharpened number-two pencils . . . you know, the basics). Satisfied, I head down to the hotel dining room.

Last night's laps cleared my head, but they've also awakened my swimmer's appetite, and I realize I'm absolutely *starving*.

The hotel kitchen staff is ready for me, though, and when I arrive downstairs in the dining room, I'm greeted by the most incredible buffet table I've ever seen. Rows of gleaming silver chafing dishes are overflowing with golden French toast, pancakes dotted with fat red berries, crispy bacon, fluffy scrambled eggs, and home fries (is that what they call them here?). Past those I spy a separate table nearly sagging under the weight of various pastries, baked goods, and bowls of whipped butter and clotted cream. I heap portions of everything onto my gold-rimmed plate. If there's a heaven, it's this buffet—inside a library with no one around but me. And maybe Phoebe. And my mom.

And Mark.

"Carbs much?" Evie says sarcastically as she flounces past me.

I nearly lose my grip on the heavy plate, and the Belgian waffle perched precariously on top of my two scones nearly tumbles to the ground, a dollop of maple syrup oozing onto my sleeve. She rolls her eyes, placing one half of a grapefruit on her otherwise empty plate, and flounces off to join Sarah at a table in the middle of the room. I make a face at her receding back, wipe the syrup from my flannel, and find my way to an empty table in the corner.

I dive into the food along with my copy of *Pride and Prejudice*. I'm lost in the scene where Mr. Darcy proposes to Elizabeth when I feel someone hovering over me. It's Jason, in his standard uniform of jeans that look like they haven't been washed since before ninth-grade gym; a ratty, pilled old North Face fleece; and his Sox cap, perpetually askew. I'd bet all the money in my pocket that underneath his fleece is a Bruins tee.

"Where'd you disappear to last night, Book Licker?" he asks, as though *I* were the one to ditch *him*. He balances a plate even more overflowing than mine.

"Back to the hotel," I reply coldly. I make a conscious—and, I think, very mature—decision to ignore the nickname. I feel good, and I'm going to hold on to that mood. I plop a spoonful of clotted cream onto a bite of waffle, wondering if my blood sugar is too high for me to get angry right now. I might be experiencing some kind of food euphoria.

"By yourself?" His eyes grow wide.

"Yup," I reply. I shovel a forkful of waffle into my mouth and try to sound confident. "I wanted to get some swimming in."

"I see," he says. He brushes his bangs from his eyes. They fall right back over his face, and after two more attempts, he finally gives up and shoves them under his baseball cap. "You really shouldn't wander around by yourself, you know. There are some crazies out there."

"Right," I say. "Because being with you is totally normal."

"Ha-ha." He slides into the seat across from mine, unzipping his fleece. I see that I'm right about the Bruins tee. "Seriously, Julia. I would have walked you back to the hotel. Just let me know next time."

He seems genuine, but his tone makes me feel even lamer, like some pathetic lonely girl who can't even get someone to walk home with her. That's twice in the past ten minutes someone has tried to make me feel like a loser, and I'm kind of over it. It's time to take control of this day, so I decide to set my newly hatched plan into motion.

"Well, I wanted to text with Chris," I say. I peek over my fork to catch his reaction. Jason just rolls his eyes.

"Continuing your little *textplorations* solo, eh? That's a dangerous game," he says. He grabs a bread item slathered with something I don't recognize and takes a giant bite. Immediately, his nose crinkles and his mouth screws up into a deep grimace. He swallows hard, then grabs my napkin off my lap and starts furiously wiping his tongue.

"What are you eating?" I ask.

"Marmite," he spits. He steals my glass of cranberry juice and slugs it down. "Ugh, it tastes like a salty dirt pile."

"Why did you cover your toast in it if you didn't know what it was?"

"When in Rome," he says. He flips his toast over so the offending

Marmite is no longer facing him. "Isn't that why you're on this random text adventure?"

I open my mouth to reply but am interrupted by Sarah, who practically skips up to our table, her loose blond waves bobbing on her shoulders.

"Oh my God, are you so psyched about the Stratford-upon-Avon trip?" she asks, her eyes trained on Jason. In her world, I'm not even here.

"The what?" he asks, raising an eyebrow at her.

"Stratford-upon-Avon," Sarah repeats slowly.

"Shakespeare's birthplace," I say, jumping in. I run my finger through a river of maple syrup and lick it off. Sarah wrinkles her nose at me, but I don't care. This maple syrup is liquid love. While she's watching, I pick up a cheese blintz and take an enormous bite. Sarah looks like she's tallying calories in her head.

"Evie saw online that there are going to be a bunch of other American schools there from all over the place," Sarah explains, turning away from me and back to Jason. "It's going to be a *major* party scene."

"Screw literature; let's drink," I mumble to myself through crumbs of cheese pastry.

"Excuse me?" Sarah glares at me.

"Nothing," I reply, tossing my napkin onto my plate. "Sounds awesome."

"I'm psyched we're actually getting out of London for a day," Sarah sighs exaggeratedly. "I'm already bored. So you're going?"

"We're all going," I say. "It's required."

"You heard the lady," Jason says, pointing a thumb in my direction. "I guess we're going."

"We?" I ask with heavy skepticism, though it's purely for show. I'm, to quote Sarah, "so psyched" for the Stratford-upon-Avon trip. Not only is it Shakespeare's birthplace, it's where my parents got their wedding rings, and I definitely plan on stopping by the little antique shop where they found them.

"Yes, buddy," he says, tapping the table with his fist for emphasis. "You and I are buddies, and as buddies, we will show our buddy-ness by attending the Stratford-upon-Avon trip. Together."

"*Or* because you *have* to be with your buddy," Sarah says in that obnoxious tone of voice she's so fond of. She adjusts her brown leather hobo on her shoulder, spins around, and skips back toward Evie.

"Look," I say as soon as Jason turns his attention back to me. "Let's get one thing straight. I am really excited about this trip, and not for the major party scene or whatever you call it. As soon as we get there, we'll be parting ways. My liver and I are not interested in a repeat of the other night. You can party, and I can take in the culture."

Jason smirks at me. "You and I have very different definitions of 'culture,' Book Licker."

"You and I have very different definitions of everything," I say.

"Speaking of culture . . ." Jason leans over and snatches a plump strawberry off my plate. I was saving it to dip in the powdered sugar left behind by my waffles, and it's all I can do not to reach over and take it right back. "You haven't forgotten our little agreement, have you?"

"I'll write your stupid essays," I snap. I catch myself and say in a more normal tone of voice, "So long as you keep up your end of the bargain."

"You have yourself a deal," he says. He holds out his hand. I roll my eyes and shake.

"A deal with the devil," I mutter. I hope I haven't traded away *too* much of my soul.

"Okay, everyone!" Mrs. Tennison calls from the other side of the room. "Bus is here! Finish up your breakfasts!"

I stand up and head toward the bus without waiting for Jason. I can only hope that today's adventures will be a little less adventurous than my last adventures.

✳ ✳ ✳

"It's huge!"

"That's what she said!"

Cue riotous laughter as our bus rumbles past Big Ben.

I want to roll my eyes, but I'm afraid pretty soon they're going to get stuck in the back of my head, and penis puns are really not worth my permanent facial damage.

By the time our bus pulls up to the Tower of London, my expectations for the day are somewhere in the basement. Call me a cynic, but since Jason spent the *entire* time we toured Big Ben talking about how satisfied Mrs. Ben must be, my guess is that a landmark famous for its *crown jewels* is not going to bring out his most charming comments, either.

But from the moment we walk in the door, he is quiet. He's not cracking jokes or laughing or snorting or high-fiving anyone. He's simply following the rest of the tour, listening to the guides and (can it be?) actually reading the historical markers along the way.

We leave the Waterloo Barracks, home to the crown jewels, and Mrs. Tennison tells us to find our partners and discuss what we've seen so far.

"Remember, this is *perfect* subject material for a reflection paper," she says, her eyes aglow with the excitement of homework. "Don't simply *discuss. Dissect!* The work will be easier later!"

I find Jason in a corner, looking at a glossy brochure the tour guides gave us when we arrived. I don't expect much in the way of dissection. I will, after all, be writing his reflection paper.

"Crazy, huh?" he says, flapping the brochure at me. "You know they used to torture people here, right? Weird that everyone knows it mostly for the bling."

I stare at him. He goes on to talk about the juxtaposition of the famous jewels and the political prisoners who have been held within the tower walls. He actually uses the word "juxtaposition." I couldn't be more shocked if he donned a hat made of fruit and danced the cancan in the middle of Westminster Abbey.

"And a lot of the prisoners weren't even real threats, you know? I mean, sure Guy Fawkes tried to blow up Parliament or whatever, but they were more afraid of what he was *saying*," he says. I remember Guy Fawkes from our unit on European history. "Hey, did you take that political protest class Coach Hudson taught?"

"Not yet," I say. "I was hoping to get it next semester." "Coach" Hudson actually coaches the debate team, but he's just as respected as our soccer coach. Maybe more so. I've been dying to take his class.

"Dude, you *have* to take it," he says, his face animated. "You'll be totally into it."

I blink at him. Jason Lippincott's recommending a class to me is like my offering makeup tips to Evie. Fortunately, before I have to think of a response, the tour guide signals for us to move on.

As we continue the tour, I try to see the place from Jason's eyes, but every time we pass a darkened corridor, the hair on the back of my neck stands up. I imagine invisible hands snatching me off to some prison cell, where I'm left to bed down on a pile of rotting hay, rats scurrying all around me. The tour guide keeps mentioning that the whole place is haunted with the ghosts of people who have been beheaded there. I can only imagine what their corpses would look like wandering around; somehow I don't think they're going to be as friendly as the ones in Harry Potter. I try not to linger too close to the dank stone walls, in case there's lingering tuberculosis or bubonic plague. I instinctively feel around in my bag for my travel bottle of hand sanitizer.

"Can you believe people were imprisoned here? Some of them for *nothing*," Jason says. He leans against one of the tubercular walls and I suppress a shiver.

"Well, odds are at least some of them were guilty of something," I reply. I'm not totally sure if I believe it, but I'm not going to get through an entire field trip without contributing *something* to a discussion with Jason. I clear my throat and channel Coach Hudson's debate skills. "It's naive and unfair to judge history by our standards. It's what they had. It's what they knew. And people *should* be punished for breaking the rules, so long as the rules are fair."

"And who decides if the rules are fair?" he asks.

"Society," I reply, keeping my tone even.

Jason raises his eyebrows at me and opens his mouth to reply, but then he shuts it. I feel a flicker of triumph. Does that mean I won?

We wander into the next room, an interactive prisoner exhibit. It's a little bit cheesy, with videos of reenactors with hammy British accents playing the roles of various historical prisoners. All around us are instruments of torture with historical placards explaining their uses.

Jason practically skips across the room. When he gets to the far wall, he whips off his belt with a flourish and strings it through a set of iron rings built into the stone wall high above his head.

"Jason," I say. "What—"

"Oh, flog me. I've been a bad boy!" His voice echoes around the room. "All the partying, all the girls, all the fun. It goes against society's rules. It goes against morality! Punish me, Julia!"

All my blood rushes directly to my face. Strangers are staring, mouths open, while my classmates giggle and whisper.

Without meaning to move, I sprint across the room. "What is your problem?" I ask, leaning in. "Are you mental or something?"

Jason just starts moaning, loud and long, writhing against the stone wall. I'm sure it looks *awesome* what with me standing so close to him. I leap back so fast I nearly fall ass over teakettle into a giant iron maiden.

A group of British schoolgirls in matching plaid uniforms explode into laughter.

"I love American boys," one girl says.

"*So* funny," the other agrees, and then she actually gives him one of those finger-wiggling waves. I have to keep myself from visibly gagging. How can they be charmed by him? This is *London,* where people have class. Can't they see he's essentially an overgrown seven-year-old?

I scan the room for Mrs. Tennison. Surely *she'll* put a stop to this ridiculousness, but she's nowhere to be found. Seriously? She's been hovering over us like a thick cloud of mosquitoes since we got here, and she chooses *now* to walk away? You'd think someone as anxious as Mrs. T would learn to hold it until the wild group of teenagers leaves the building containing priceless artifacts. I wait for a guard to throw us out, but even security seems uninterested. In fact, I catch one woman trying to suppress a smile.

Jason finally unhooks his belt from the metal rings. His grin is fading into a smirk.

"What's the matter, Julia?" he asks. "Let me guess—you're not into domination? Maybe you want to *be* dominated. They say it's the most controlling people who look for someone to tell them what to do. Look, if that's your thing, I'm sure we can make it work. . . ."

I'm so embarrassed—and angry—I could reach out and smack him. Instead, I ball up my fists and feel my nails digging into the flesh of my palms.

"Why do you have to be such an ass?" I ask in the calmest, coldest tone I can muster. "Why do you feel the need to get attention every moment of every day? Were you ignored as a kid or something? Did Mommy forget to love you? Do us both a favor and get over yourself, okay?"

Jason's face has turned stony. "Dude, you need to chill out," he says.

He tries to put on his belt but drops it; it clatters to the ground. "I'm having fun, Julia. F-U-N. You don't have to be such a bitch all the time, you know that?"

I open my mouth to reply, but he's already stalking away from me. My cheeks are burning, and to my horror I feel tears welling up in my eyes. I will them away.

I can't believe he called me a bitch. I feel like I've been plunged head-first into a bucket of ice water.

The class is gathering at the entrance of the exhibit to move to another gallery, and Jason goes to stand in the back of the crowd, a little bit separate from everyone else, shoving his hands deep into his pockets and staring resolutely in front of him.

So much for not letting Jason get to me. So much for using him to help me get Chris.

My phone buzzes against my thigh, making me jump. I pull the phone out of my messenger bag with shaking hands and flip it open.

> Was @ Globe last night and thinking of u,
> thinking of me? —C

My heart leaps into my throat, and I swallow furiously, trying to put it back where it belongs. I wish I could run to Chris right now—which I realize is more than a little weird, considering that I can't even remember what he looks like. I press reply and stand staring at the blank screen and the blinking cursor. I have no idea what I can say that won't ruin it.

"Let me guess—Chris." Jason is staring at me from across the now-empty gallery. The rest of our class must have moved on. His eyes are expressionless. "You haven't scared him off yet?"

"*What* is your problem?" I burst out.

"I thought you already knew." He raises an eyebrow. "Abandonment issues and immaturity. Got any more to add to the list?"

I feel guilt squirming in my stomach. But he deserved it. He did.

I look away from him. "You don't have to embarrass me all the time." My voice comes out all squeaky. "I embarrass myself enough as it is, okay?"

There's a moment of silence. Then squeak, squeak, squeak as Jason crosses toward me. He holds out his hand.

"Give me your phone," he says. He's not smiling, but his voice is softer.

"No way."

"Say the wrong thing and you might never hear from him again," Jason says. I can tell that he has forgiven me for what I said. I guess I can forgive him for calling me a bitch. I may occasionally be a little . . . outspoken. "You know you need Dr. Love-in-Cott to help out."

"Ew," I say, making a face.

He leans into me and nudges me with a shoulder. "Seems like your tactic thus far has been to lie and dodge. Is that working for you?"

I feel like my stomach is going to do a dance right out of my belly button. I'm not going to ruin it. Am I? I stare down at my phone in my hand.

"Suit yourself," he says. Jason begins skipping backward, still watching me. Now the smile is back in his eyes. "Best of luck to you."

I feel like I'm in some kind of horror movie, standing at the front door, trying to decide if I should let the vampire in to defend me from the snarling werewolf. One will tear me limb from limb; the other will suck the life out of me. I can't decide which is worse.

He's nearly to the exit when I call out to him. "Wait!" I say, and he skips back over to me.

" 'Was at the Globe last night and thinking of you,' " he reads aloud as I show him the phone. "First of all, good sign. Thinking of you? That means he's—"

"Thinking of me?"

"Exactly," he says, ignoring my sarcasm. He plows on. "And the

Globe. That's got to be a clue. Well, it looks like we have a little mystery on our hands, Julia Lichtenstein! And possibly some adventure." He rubs his hands together like a super villain. "The Globe is like the old-school version of a movie theater, right?"

I stare at him. "If by 'movie theater,'" I reply, "you mean the world-famous theater in which the majority of Shakespeare's plays were first performed."

Jason laughs. "Chill out. I'm with you. I'm not a *total* moron." His face lights up. Even his freckles seem to get brighter. "Maybe Chris is a theater geek. A nerd, like you!"

I stifle a nasty retort. Our class is heading out of the exhibit and down the stairs, another tour finished. Soon we'll be on the street and splitting up to "enjoy" our cultural hours. Our classmates' voices bounce off the stone walls, and I can hear them excitedly planning their next steps (most of which involve shopping or going to a pub to watch football). Jason and I hurry after them.

"So what do you think I should do?" I ask when we find ourselves back on the sidewalk.

"Well, I think this is a clue, and we should follow it," he says, looking around for some kind of direction. "And figure out who he is. And then you can live happily ever after reading books and going to museums, or whatever it is you nerds do."

"Ha-ha," I say, snapping the phone shut. "I'm not just a nerd, you know. I mean, I'm not a nerd at all. I just happen to find history interesting. And literature. And political structures. And—"

Jason cuts me off. "Please," he says, looking pained. "Never go into law. You put up a terrible defense." Then he perks up again. "So . . . feel like checking out some British theater? We should swing by the Globe. Ask around. Maybe he works there or something."

"And when do you suggest we go?" I ask. I'm torn between my desire to do some major sleuthing on Chris and my vow not to break any more rules. I've got our itinerary in my bag, and there's not much free time on the schedule.

"No time like the present," he says, without missing a beat. "We'll use our cultural hours."

"We're supposed to use that time for independent tours so we can write our reflection papers," I say, trying to mask my exasperation.

"I think the sentence structure you're looking for is 'so *I* can write our reflection papers,'" Jason says. He bends down to tie his left sneaker, the lace of which is fraying and dirty. "Besides, half the class is using that time to hit pubs and go shopping. We're actually going somewhere that Mrs. T would call culturally relevant."

It's honestly not a bad idea, and I've wanted to see the Globe Theater ever since I first read *Romeo and Juliet* in the sixth grade. Even if Chris isn't there, at least I'll be fulfilling a lifelong dream.

Still, I'm conscious of the fact that I'm about to follow Jason through the streets of London while he supposedly helps me hook up with a guy. I think if someone had written that sentence down a week ago and showed it to me, my brain would have exploded and oozed out of my eye sockets.

"Come on, Julia, your destiny awaits, or whatever," Jason says, already a few steps down the road.

I know better than anyone that it's impossible to argue with destiny. I heave my bag up higher on my shoulder and start down the street to catch up.

11

Various Uses for Toilet Paper

wow, I guess you've got a new mtb . . . —P

"Dude, this place is seriously vintage. Can you believe Shakespeare might actually have stood right here?"

Jason and I are standing on the sidewalk, looking up at the Globe Theater in front of us. The sky is gray and looks on the verge of dumping on us, but it just makes the theater even more imposing. Jason once again seems to be intrigued and impressed by history, and I'm once again a little thrown off by it.

A cold, damp wind blows through and whips my curls directly into my face. I sigh heavily, tossing my head around, trying to wrangle my hair. I've been wrestling with my mane since we left the Tower of London, and the half-hour stroll along and finally across the Thames to arrive at the Globe has turned it into a Bride of Frankenstein–esque tangle.

"It's a reproduction," I reply, rummaging around in my bag for a hair elastic. I normally carry at least two.

"Seriously?"

I look over at his face, which registers the same kind of shock you expect to see when you've told your five-year-old cousin that fairies aren't real.

"Yup. This is actually the third one," I explain, winding my wild hair into a messy ponytail. "The first burned down during a show in the early 1600s, the second was demolished about thirty years later, and this one wasn't built until the late 1990s."

"See? Who needs Tennison when I have you as my tour guide?"

Great. I've gone from Book Licker to pathetic high school English teacher. I suppose both are improvements over sad crush girl, so I can't really be choosy.

Jason pops a piece of grape gum into his mouth. "Let's go find your lover boy," he says, taking off up the steps. "Race ya!"

When I get to the top of the stairs, I find Jason studying the theater's schedule in a glass display case.

"There was a show here last night," Jason says, tapping his finger on the glass next to a production of *A Midsummer Night's Dream*. "Maybe your mystery man was here."

"Well, what are we going to do?" I ask impatiently. "Review security tapes?"

"Not a bad idea, *CSI: London,* but no," he says, gesturing toward the box office. "We'll go a little lower tech and ask that guy."

All the ticket windows are closed except for one at the end, where an old man with bushy eyebrows and a gin-blossomed nose is reading a thick leather-bound book. The nameplate in the window reads FELIX.

Jason sidles up to the window, but the man is too engrossed in his book to notice. We stand there for a moment, clearing our throats and trying to make ourselves known, but Jason finally just taps on the glass.

"What's that about?" Felix grumbles. His big, watery eyes peer at us over his wire-rimmed glasses.

"Yes sir, so sorry to bother you," Jason says, "but we were hoping you might be able to help us out with something."

"Whatssat?" he mumbles, clearly *not* particularly interested in helping us out.

Jason takes off his hat and twirls it around his finger. "Well, you see, my friend here is looking for *her* friend Chris . . ."

"'Scuse me?" he says. Now he's not even trying to conceal his irritation.

"We're hoping you might tell us whether my friend was here last night," I say, putting on the sweet, polite voice I use to get grown-ups to do what I want.

"Young lady, do you have any bloody idea how many people were here last night? It was a full house." Felix directs his attention back to his book.

I turn away from the ticket booth and let out a long sigh. It doesn't look like we're going to get anywhere.

"A full house?" Jason asks, undeterred by the lack of information. "Now, Felix, how many people is that?"

Felix jabs a finger to the wrinkled, weathered sign that reads MAXIMUM CAPACITY: 1500 in the corner of his tiny ticket booth. "Last night we was chock-full of schoolkids, so there's no way I could tell yer if your lad was here."

"Schoolkids?" Jason presses his nose against the window, straining to see the papers on Felix's desk.

Felix slams his book down onto the counter and whips off his glasses. I can tell he was hoping this conversation would be over by now.

Felix leans in close to the glass. It almost looks like he and Jason might bump noses. "Yes, young man. A whole gaggle 'a kids from St. Bonaventure's Academy. Some kind of class assignment or some rubbish."

My ears perk up at the mention of a class trip. There were *definitely* some prep school boys at the party. I can picture the little gold crests on their blazers. Chris could have been one of them!

"Excuse me, um, sir?" I say, putting my grown-up voice back on and bumping Jason out of the way with my hip. "Could you possibly point me toward St. Bonaventure's?"

"Get the phone number," Jason whispers behind me. "Get the phone number!"

"Okay!" I snap, giving him a jab with my elbow. "And, um, maybe you have the phone number? That would be great, too. I promise, after that, we'll leave you to your book."

Felix looks at me with eyes narrowed, like he doesn't quite believe we'll *ever* leave him alone. His gaze settles on Jason, and he smartly realizes that Jason is a professional when it comes to being annoying. Seconds later, he's pulled up the phone number.

"Gimme a pen," Jason says, fishing unsuccessfully in his pockets for one. What comes out instead is a handful of change, some pieces of lint, and half a pack of gum.

I reach into my bag, pull out my pencil case, and offer Jason one of my fully sharpened number twos.

"Who carries pencils?" he asks, looking at it like I've offered him a quill and scroll.

"I do," I reply, my mouth set in a straight line. I want the phone number, and I don't want any guff with it. I haven't carried pens around since ninth grade, when, while cutting through the gym en route to the library, I found myself in the middle of a full-contact game of dodgeball. The next thing I knew, I was on my butt, the pen in my back pocket spilling dark red ink all over the back of my white linen pants. Evie went around telling everyone I got my period, and convinced a few boys—including Jason—to deliver tampons to my locker. I've been Team Pencil ever since.

"Do you want it or not?" I ask. I hold it out to Jason point-side first, visions of jamming it right into his eyeball bouncing through my head.

"Yes please, Miss Lichtenstein, ma'am," he says, doing some kind of ridiculous bow to me (his left eye coming perilously close to the sharpened point, I might add). He snatches the pencil from my hand, along with the mini spiral notebook I also keep tucked in my purse. He leans over, the pad perched on his knee, and starts to jot down the phone number. He barely gets the first number down before I hear the telltale snap. He picks up the pencil and stares wide-eyed at the now-empty tip.

"It broke!" he says.

"You pressed too hard," I inform him.

"This is why people use pens, Book Licker. Why don't you have a freaking pen?"

"Pens leak."

"Pencils break."

"Yeah, but you can always sharpen them. What do you do with a broken pen?"

"Sharpen them? Who carries around a pencil sharpener? What is this, 1943?"

I reach into my pencil case and produce a small red pencil sharpener. Then I take the pencil from his hand and, looking him straight in the eye, jam it into the sharpener and give it three hard twists.

"You're whacked," he says, snatching the pencil back from me.

When we've got the number down, we thank Felix (who grunts back at us) and step away from the window. Jason pulls out his phone, sets it to speaker, and dials the number. I lean in close, not wanting to miss a minute.

"Hullo?" A cheerful female voice chirps out of the speaker.

There's a moment of silence, as we forgot to discuss which one of us was going to do the talking. I'm overtaken by sudden panic and can only let out a gurgle, so Jason jumps in.

"Y-yes ma'am, hello," he stammers, clearing his throat. "Um, I'm looking for a student of yours. I thought possibly you could help me."

"It's possible," she says, a smile still in her voice. "What's the student's name?"

"Chris," Jason says before giving me a panicked look. I wonder what he's worried about when the woman on the other end of the line continues.

"Last name?" she chirps. Oh. Right.

"Um, that's the thing," he says, giving a little laugh to smooth things over. "We're not totally sure. You see, my friend met him—"

"Him?" the voice cuts in.

"Yes ma'am," Jason replies, "and, well—"

"Oh dear," she says. "I'm afraid you must have rung the wrong number. St. Bonaventure's is a girls' academy. No boys here, I'm afraid."

The air goes right out of my lungs. Our only clue, and now it leads to nothing. Jason mumbles a polite thank-you into the phone and snaps it shut, then shoves it back into his pocket.

"This is a bust," I say, staring back up at the Globe. "We're no closer to finding Chris than we were when we got here."

It's starting to drizzle, and despite my obsessive packing and checking this morning, I still managed to forget my mini umbrella back at the hotel. I really need to get my head on straight; this is *so* unlike me.

"Well, I don't know about you, but I'm starving," Jason says as he hops under a nearby doorway to avoid the rain. "What do you say we find someplace to eat and wait out this weather?"

"Sure," I reply. My stomach *does* feel kind of hollow, and I still haven't made any progress on my search for the best fish-and-chips. I reach for my guidebook in my messenger bag, but Jason reaches out a lanky arm and swats my hand away.

"Dude, it's raining," he says. "This is no time for guidebooks. We must be spontaneous. We might have to pick a place we haven't read a *single review about.*" He puts on a shocked expression, his hands pressed to his cheeks. "Gasp! Can you take it?"

We circle around the theater and find a Starbucks. I definitely did *not* come all the way across the ocean to have the same overpriced beverages

and baked goods I can have every other day of my life, but unfortunately, as we're standing in front of the ubiquitous green sign, the sky
opens up and the rain really starts to come down.

The tinkle of a tiny bell announces our arrival to the nearly empty
'bucks. There're the same display of white-and-green mugs, the same
towers of ground coffee, the same glass case of pastries as in the nine
billion other Starbucks stores I've visited in my life. The one notable
difference, though, is the array of artwork hanging on the walls. Near the
counter, above the containers of straws and drink sleeves, a spidery
metal sculpture that looks like it was made out of wire hangers takes
up almost an entire wall. There's a portrait of the queen done entirely
in M&M's and a matching Margaret Thatcher done in Starburst
wrappers. There's something in the corner that looks like the artist un-
spooled an entire roll of toilet paper and stapled it to the wall. Underneath each piece is a tiny white card noting the artist and how much the
work is selling for. And there are a *lot* of zeroes after each pound sign. I
wonder what Phoebe would think of this display. It would certainly silence her parents' fears that a career as an artist is a "one-way ticket to
living in a cardboard box," as her dad is fond of saying.

"Do you think people actually buy this stuff?" I whisper to Jason.

"The real question is how they're going to get that toilet paper off the
wall in one piece," he replies, and I can't help giggling.

We make our way through the maze of tiny round tables until we're
at a glass case filled with baked goodies on brightly colored ceramic
plates. Hanging overhead is a series of vintage chalkboards, drinks and
prices scrawled across in a carefully careless-looking script.

"So what are you going to get?" I ask, surveying the offerings.

"I don't know yet. You? Cuppa tea?" he asks, affecting an English
accent.

"Ugh, no," I reply, wrinkling my nose. "Tea is gross."

"Seriously," he says, checking out the baked goods. "Tastes like yard."

The girl behind the counter, who has pierced eyebrows and electric-blue bangs, rolls her eyes.

"I want one of those," Jason says, jamming a finger against the glass case toward a large fluffy-looking scone dotted with chunks of chocolate.

"Make that two," I say, my mouth already beginning to water.

"Make that four," he says, pulling out his wallet. "My treat."

Jason grabs our plate, piled high with baked goods, and I grab two glasses of water. We park at a small café table in the corner by the window. As we take our seats, I notice that Jason has deposited his wad of purple gum on the edge of the white porcelain plate. I grimace and reach over to scoot my scones to the other side. Jason already has crammed half a scone into his mouth, and as much as I want to give him a dirty look, it's hard to glare with my own mouth stuffed full of pastry. As we chew quietly, our eyes glued to our snacks, I again think of how strange it is to be sitting elbow to elbow across the table from Jason. We're usually sitting at opposite ends of the cafeteria.

But I feel surprisingly relaxed. The silence between us is strangely comfortable. We've reached some kind of truce, and it's not bad. From one window I can see collections of tourists gathering outside the Globe, some with dignified umbrellas, but most draped in those horrible trash bag–like ponchos you can buy in tourist-trap shops. They're trying to wedge themselves under various ledges overhanging the buildings around the theater, but there are too many of them. They're starting to seek shelter in the Starbucks, and as they pour through the door, I imagine they're an army of angry, overstuffed trash bags staging an invasion.

"So, can I interest you in a diorama containing plastic dinosaurs and old tubes of ChapStick?" Jason asks through bites. He gestures at the piece of what can generously be termed "art" hanging on the wall over my head.

"You know, I really think that would tie my bedroom together." I laugh, rolling my eyes.

Then, out of nowhere, Jason asks, "What's MTB?"

Cue a thousand mini explosions in my brain.

"Excuse me?" I choke, and bits of scone fly out the corner of my mouth. I desperately hope he didn't see.

"MTB," he repeats casually, swiping the debris off the edge of the table. Great.

"Where did you hear that?" I flip through my mental file of memories, wondering if he might have overheard me talking to Phoebe, or if maybe I—or should I say *über-Julia*—drunkenly blurted out something between my model stories? Oh God . . .

"Oh, one of those girls in the tower said it. I had no idea what it meant," he says, taking a very large bite of his scone. "I figured it was some British thing. And what with all your book learnin', I thought you might know."

"Hardee har har," I retort. I pause to break off another chunk of scone. Really I'm stalling, hoping that he'll get distracted by something else and let it go.

"Come on," Jason presses. "Tell me."

"I dunno," I say cautiously. "I mean, when Phoebs and I use it, we mean 'meant to be.'"

Now it's Jason's turn to choke.

"What?" I say, instantly defensive.

"So when you say 'MTB,' do you mean, like, guys?"

I clear my throat a couple of times and try to sound casual. "Yeah," I reply. "I mean, we might say, 'So-and-so are totally MTB,' as in, that couple is totally meant to be. Or 'That guy is totally my MTB,' meaning that we're totally meant to be together."

Jason snorts. I can tell he doesn't buy it. "So do you have an MTB?" he asks.

The question startles me. I mean, I've been saying Mark is my MTB for as long as I can remember, but there's no way I can tell Jason that.

Fortunately, I don't have to come up with a response, because Jason charges on.

"Meant to be . . . ," he says with a little chuckle. He takes a stack of brown raw-sugar packets from the container on our table and starts slapping them against his palm to loosen the sugar. "What a load of crap."

"What do you mean?"

"You can't *actually* believe that. I mean, you're smart. You know stuff. So you've gotta know that it's all a big fairy tale. A marketing tool. Chick flicks and Hallmark cards and Valentine's Day and diamond rings. Bullshit." He rips the tops off the three sugar packets, tips his head back, and pours them into his mouth. Great. With all that sugar, now he's going to go supersonic.

"You don't think you'll ever fall in love?" I ask, leaning back in my chair, the metal curlicues digging into my back.

"Sure, I think I'll fall in love," he says. He crumples the empty packets in his fist, then drops them. They bounce and scatter across the table. He ignores them, scraping together a little mountain of crumbs on the plate, licking his finger, and pressing it into the pile. "Many, many times. And when I do, I don't think it's going to be about fate or destiny or 'meant to be.'"

"Then what will it be about?" I fire back. I reach for the wrappers, gathering them up and placing them on our plate. Why am I always picking up his trash?

"I don't know, I've never been in love," he says, pulling apart chunks of his remaining scone, "but I imagine it'll be about her thinking it's funny when I make a fool of myself and laughing at my dumb jokes and liking the same music."

"So you're looking for someone just like you?"

"Sure." He shrugs. Then he grins widely. "But with boobs."

I instinctively cross my arms over my own (sort of flat) chest.

"Nice," I say, narrowing my eyes at him.

"Whatever. Point is, maybe some people wouldn't want to be around me all day, but there are people out there who would. And they're smart and funny. And they like some of the things I like and hate some of the things I hate, but they also introduce me to all kinds of new things. That's as close to 'meant to be' as I can imagine."

"So there's no 'the one'?"

"Nope," he says. "Ones. Plural. Many ones. Which makes me a lucky guy." Another grin spreads across his face and he winks at me.

"You're gross," I reply. I toss my napkin at him. He catches it in midair.

"I'm right," he says. He chucks the napkin back at me.

"You're not." I duck, and the napkin sails over my shoulder and bounces off the window.

"We'll see," he replies.

I want to say something clever and cutting, but all I can do is mutter back, "I guess we will."

"Flirtation is no different from mounting a good argument or coming out ahead in a deal," he says. He starts batting the last chunk of his scone back and forth across the table with his fingers. "It's manipulation, Julia. Good convincing. Hell, it's practically theater."

Suddenly, I feel almost *sorry* for him. Manipulation? Theater? This is what he thinks when he thinks of love? It's sad, really. Everyone knows that Jason's dad and stepmom split in an epic disaster of a divorce. Jason's dad is a pretty big-deal lawyer in Boston, so the details were splashed all over the Internet. There were quite a lot of name-calling (his) and some rumored cheating (hers), as well as a very public tossing of a plate of risotto at a charity function (also hers). I don't know anything about his biological mother—no one does—but I know that now he never sees his stepmom, who had been around since Jason was little. Can you imagine? She was practically his mother, and now she's gone. According to Sarah Finder, his dad is always running around with one leggy blonde or another, each younger than the one before. No wonder Jason has a warped view of love.

I guess that's Reason Number 725 that Jason and I are completely and totally different.

Probably only a few more minutes and we can head out. I reach into my bag, now slung over the back of my chair, to pull out *Pride and Prejudice*.

"GOOOOOOOAL!"

A chunk of scone bounces off my chest and onto the floor, leaving a spray of clotted cream from my shirt down. I look up and Jason has his arms raised above his head. Before I can protest (or protect my clothes), he flicks another chunk toward me; this one misses me and instead splatters on the dinosaur diorama directly behind my left shoulder.

The barista with the blue hair and the metal in her face is *unamused*, to say the least. She wads up the rag in her hand and chucks it at the floor with quite a lot of force, looking like she's about to head around the counter and toward us. To kick us out, probably. But I'm not in the mood to be chastised today (or any day, really), so I grab Jason by the hand and jerk him toward the door.

"What are you–" he asks, but I shush him and nod toward the angry barista.

"Julia, I was trying to win the World Cup," Jason whines, trying to stall. "I just need one more shot!"

"Come on." I pull Jason hard by the hand, and together we stumble into the rainy street.

12

The Spy Mission, or Mick Jagger Strikes Again

hey P, what is your fave line from Shakespeare?
(I forget) —J

"Ouch!" I yank my finger back from the brass knob on my dresser. I stick it in my mouth, trying to soothe the pain of a truly shocking electric shock. I've got all my shirts in a pile on the floor, and I'm refolding them and placing them back in the drawer one by one, long sleeves on the left, short sleeves on the right. As I hold each one up to fold, I give it a quick once-over for stray lint, picking off tiny bits of fuzz whenever I spot it. With all the quick dressing I've done in the last couple of days, my bureau is looking really disorganized, and it's time to clean it up.

It's five p.m., the hour on our itinerary marked "rest period." Clearly, Mrs. Tennison intended this to be *her* rest period. Did she think the rest of us would need a juice box and a nap? Not even halfway through our trip, and already the woman needs to escape. I don't know how she's going to get through the next seven days.

I really should be working on my reflection paper (or papers, plural, I guess), but my brain can pretty much only tolerate searching for lint right now. I wonder what my classmates will be writing about, since, as Jason already pointed out, most of them have spent the time trolling pubs and shopping. I might as well have gone with them, because even though I've taken in some *actual* culture, I'm having a really hard time focusing.

The rain outside my hotel window is tapping lightly on the sill, lulling me into a little bit of a post-dinner coma, and the blinking cursor on my laptop seems to be taunting me for my inability to crank out a simple one-page paper. At least reorganizing my dresser seemed like a good way to take control of *something* in my world. "Reorganize the room, reorganize the mind," my mom always says. But all I can think about is my conversation with Jason a couple of hours ago at the café. His words keep playing on endless loop: *You've gotta know that it's all a big fairy tale.*

I guess it's hard to believe in love when the people who are supposed to be your role models call each other playboys and gold diggers in public.

I reach for the picture of Mom and Dad. I know, it's very *Brady Bunch* to idolize your parents, but mine really did have a perfect marriage. I think that's why Mom's been single since Dad died. Can you imagine trying to find perfection a second time?

I try to conjure up an image of Mark, but it keeps coming up all blurry. I try focusing on his perfectly imperfect smile when my thoughts are interrupted by a persistent buzz. I reach for my phone to find another text message.

@ cue-2-cue, know it? —C

Chris! And I was *just* thinking about my MTB. I mean, sure, I was thinking about *Mark,* but maybe this is supposed to be a sign. Like maybe Chris could be my MTB. And he's given me an actual location where he might be *right now.*

A quick trip to Google pulls up only one hit for a Cue-2-Cue location in London (because I'm guessing Mystery Chris is *not* chilling in

Turkmenistan), and it turns out to be an indie music shop right here in Soho, only a few blocks from the hotel. Probably only about five minutes away. I could go there right now and . . . and what?

Definitely not meet him. Jason was right about one thing: Chris will be disappointed that über-Julia has morphed back into . . . well, Julia-Julia. But I could go and scope him out from afar. Maybe I'll *finally* recognize him from the party.

I click reply and start typing a message about being busy, but I realize that if I tell him I'm not coming, he might leave. No. I want him to stay right there. Instead, I ignore his text. I'll pretend I never got it, then scoot over to the record shop and do a little detective work.

Forgetting all about my vow not to break any more rules, I quickly jot down the directions from Google, tuck them into the pocket of my coat, and get ready to head out. I'm about to grab my mini umbrella when there's a knock at the door. I peer through the peephole to see a fish-eyed Jason leaning against the entryway. Dammit.

The door swings open and Jason hops inside before I can slam it in his face.

"What do you want?"

"Now that's no way to greet your buddy. Hello to you, too, sunshine."

"Sorry. I was working on my paper and you interrupted me." Homework: that's sure to scare Jason off.

"Oh, great. That's what I'm here about," Jason says, his grin practically taking over his lightly freckled face.

"What?"

"Just checking to see if you got my paper done," he says. He dodges me neatly and steps all the way into my room. "I may have to do a little editing, you know, so it's in my own words."

"Not done yet," I reply. I need to keep things short and sweet if I hope to be rid of him. I'm not a very good liar. "Soon."

"What, you're having a little trouble reflecting? Your inner mirror a little foggy?"

"No," I say. "It turns out that twice the work takes twice as long." I shoot a glance at my phone. It's still open on my bed, the text message visible. "I'll text you when I'm done, okay?"

"You'll text me? Gee, you're getting awfully liberal with those texts," he says, raising an eyebrow.

"The longer you stand here bothering me, the longer it takes me to write," I say. I fling the door open and gesture him through it. "Now go."

"Fine, then. Back to work! Chop-chop!" he says. Then his face turns suspicious. His eyes flick to my packed messenger bag, which is sitting on the bed. "Wait a second. Were you going somewhere, Book Licker?"

"No," I say, a little too quickly.

"Then why are you wearing your coat?" he asks, leaning in to pick some lint off my shoulder. "Feeling a draft? Catching a chill? Trying to put out your pants, which seem to be catching on fire, you liar liar?"

"Fine!" I explode, just to get him to shut up. "Yes, okay. I was maybe thinking of possibly going somewhere. Are you satisfied?"

He crosses his arms and raises his eyebrows. "Without me? My, my, you really are turning into a regular rule breaker. Let me guess. You got another text from Loverboy."

I ignore the "Loverboy" part and extend my phone to him. He rubs his chin as he reads the text. I notice he has a tiny bit of stubble coming in along his jawline. It makes him look more grown-up, which only makes the mischievous look in his eyes more noticeable.

"Cue-2-Cue is a music shop," I mumble through my embarrassment. "I was thinking of heading over there."

He squints his bright blue eyes at me. "Well, then it's a good thing I showed up," he says as he turns toward the door. "I'll get my coat. Be back in a flash."

I think about making a run for it but instead pull my door shut, tug on it twice to make sure it locked, and wait in the hallway. In seconds he's trotting down the hall, his rusty, messy hair bouncing across his face.

"I thought you didn't believe in love," I say as he leads the way to the elevator.

"I don't," he replies over his shoulder.

"Then why are you coming along?"

"Because I think this guy could be a fun adventure for you, Book Licker. You need to loosen up, and having a little foreign fling might just be the ticket. Maybe it'll cure you of your ridiculous fairy tale."

I sigh, but let it slide. I *like* my fairy tale, thankyouverymuch.

Cue-2-Cue looks like it came right out of the last century. Every inch of wall space is taken up with dust-laden CDs. Long tables dip under the weight of milk crates stuffed full of records. These tables make up the narrow aisles of the shop, and there's a row of wooden windowed listening booths, like a row of old phone booths, along the far wall. It smells like dust and must and that special cocktail of vintage-BO.

There are a few customers in the shop. Three of them are girls. One of the two guys in the shop is the middle-aged clerk, bearded and clad in an old moth-eaten blazer. The other is a boy of about thirteen, who's glued to a display of Rush's entire catalog.

"I don't think he's here," I whisper to Jason.

"Why are you whispering?" he whispers back. "This isn't a library."

"Whatever," I say a little louder, clearing my throat. "I don't think he's here."

"Are you sure? *He* looks like a likely candidate," Jason says, and he gestures to the kid flipping through Rush albums. "And he looks like your speed, too! Beginner level."

"Hey, I have been on plenty dates before, you know," I retort. Okay, three dates—but Jason doesn't need to know that. I'm not a *total* loser.

"Oh really? And who are these lucky bachelors? Members of the robotics club? Mathletes?" Jason crosses his arms and leans against a rack of concert T-shirts, like he's daring me to prove him wrong.

"Kevin Heineman. And some other people you probably wouldn't know." *Because they don't exist,* I mentally add.

Jason feigns nearly falling over. "Kevin Heineman? Are you kidding? I totally saw that guy eat his own boogers."

"Oh, when was that, first grade?"

"Last year," he replies, laughing. "C'mon, Lady Marmalade, let's go check the listening booths in the back."

I follow him down the aisle and off to the left, toward the row of four narrow wooden booths, which are plastered with torn and fading posters. A handwritten sign stuck to the front of each booth reads *Only one guest per booth!* The first two are empty. The third contains a girl clutching a Tori Amos album and scowling.

"Nasty breakup," Jason says, winking at me, before moving on to the last booth. His eyes grow wide. "Well, I think we might have something here."

My heart leaps into my throat, and I move slowly into the view of the window. Chris? I don't see anyone at first, but when I glance at Jason, he's pointing toward the floor. I look down to see a pair of teenagers in school uniforms sharing a pair of headphones and furiously making out. The girl catches me staring and gives me a dirty look before giving me the finger and returning to her business.

"Nice, Jason," I say. I try to arrange my face into the same dirty look Miss Makeout gave me.

"What?" he asks, giving me that innocent look he seems to have perfected.

"Let's get out of here," I say, turning to head toward the door, feeling deflated. Yet another blown opportunity to see Chris.

"What, we walk *all* the way over here, and now you want to ditch out after a few minutes just because your mystery lover isn't here?" Jason pulls open the door to the first booth in the row, gesturing for me to go in.

"I am *not* going in there with you," I say. The booth is barely big enough for two people, and I can't help flashing back to what Sarah Finder said about Jason's desire to join the mile-high club.

Jason rolls his eyes. "I promise to play nice. Come on. We're here. We might as well enjoy it." He spins around toward the nearest bin of records. Dramatically wiggling his fingers, he closes his eyes, drops his hand into the records, flips for a moment, then pulls out a colorful album cover at random. He glances at the cover, then hugs it tightly to his chest, his arms crossed over the back so I can't see.

"This is perfect," he says, his eyes sparkling. "It's time for a love lesson, Book Licker. There's no time like the present."

He opens the door to the booth and practically shoves me into it. Jason steps in behind me and pulls the door shut before I can protest—or make an escape. A table in the corner holds a teetering stack of lumpy stereo equipment. There're a tape deck, a CD player, two big speakers, and resting on top of the stack, a turntable. Jason nudges me with his shoulder a few times to get me out of the way, then executes a little hula maneuver that turns out to be a hip check. We do a little circular shuffle, practically nose to nose, until he's the one by the stereo and I'm pressed up against the door. He keeps bumping into me as he works to keep the album cover hidden from view.

"Uh, Julia, you saw the sign," he says, tilting his head toward the window of the booth. "Only one person per booth. Soooooo you better duck, okay?"

"Are you kidding?" I glare at him.

"Do you want to get in trouble for breaking the rules?" he asks, arching an eyebrow. Darn it. He knows me too well.

I lower myself to the floor and pull my knees into my chest. Jason turns his back to me and places the record on the turntable. He presses a couple of buttons on the stereo, then lifts the needle.

"Okay." He holds the needle dramatically over the spinning record. "This song is the essence—the quintessence!—of music about love."

"Quintessence?"

He ignores me. "It's pretty much guaranteed to get you kissed, and I have it on good authority that Ryan made it to third base with Evie while listening to this song."

I stifle a gasp. Ew. So ew. I didn't know Evie and Ryan hooked up. It's amazing that either one of them could be pried away from a mirror long enough to fool around.

Jason drops the needle, then joins me on the floor. He leans against the back wall, his knees against my knees, facing me.

A full band starts up, led by what sounds like six electric guitars and a synthesizer. It's loud, but it's also slow and dramatic. I look at Jason, who's staring back at me so hard that I have to drop my gaze to my knees. The song is soft, the tension building. I hear some crowd noise, so I can tell it's a live version. I glance back up and Jason's eyes are still trained on me. My heart starts thudding in time to the rhythm. I hug my knees closer, my hands starting to sweat. This *is* a good song. . . .

Then the singer comes in; it's a man's voice. "Love on the rocks, ain't no surprise. Just pour me a drink, and I'll tell you some lies. . . ."

What?

I look at Jason for explanation, but he's starting to crack up. "Your face!" he says between chuckles. "You were so into it!"

"What *is* this?"

"C'mon. Don't tell me you don't recognize the Diamond!" He pulls the album cover out from under his butt. He shows me a picture of Neil Diamond, decked out in the tightest pair of jeans I've ever seen on a man and an American flag–printed silk shirt, unbuttoned low enough to show *way* too much Diamond for my taste.

I don't even know what to say. I stare at him openmouthed. "You're sick," I finally manage to say. "*This* is your epic love song?"

Jason laughs. "Jeez, Julia, didn't we already have this conversation? Love is a fantasy. And *not* in a good way!"

I feel of flash of anger, but just as quickly it passes, and I'm sad for him again. Maybe Jason can tell that I feel sorry for him. He jumps up so fast the record skips. There's a little scratching, and then there's applause as a horn section kicks up. Jason's face immediately lights up, his grin so wide that all his freckles look like they're running together.

Neil's voice comes in, in that sing-talking, soaring way it does when he's performing live.

" 'Sweet Caroline'!" Jason says between lyrics. "C'mon. It's just like home! Sing with me!"

"You are not serious," I reply, still crouched on the ground. He reaches down, grabs my elbow, and in one swift move hauls me right to my feet.

"Hey, lady, you're from Boston," he says as we're practically nose to nose again. "You can't dis Neil, or half of Fenway is gonna jump you." He picks up the needle, moves it over a bit, and drops it in just the right spot for the opening notes of "Sweet Caroline." He spins the Sox cap around, pulling it down low over his eyes so I can see the logo, and air-guitars along with the chorus. He looks ridiculous, and I can't help laughing.

"You know the words!" he says. "Sing!"

After another moment's hesitation, I do. I burst out the lyrics just like my dad taught me, adding the "So good! So good! So good!" as if I were at Fenway Park. When the chorus ends, there's a light tap at the window, and I turn to see the shop clerk motioning us frantically out of the booth. My hand flies to my mouth.

"Oh my God, he can hear us! *And* we're not supposed to be in here together." I point to the little sign.

Jason raises an eyebrow. "Of course he can hear us. Why do you think they have the headphones? The booths aren't soundproof."

"So embarrassing!" I cry, leaning back against the side of the booth. "Come on, we're going to get in trouble."

"Don't stress it. You were showing some hometown love." He bumps the door of the booth open with his hip, then gestures for me to shimmy out first. When I get back into the aisle, I lean against a crate of soul records and Jason squeezes next to me. "Besides, now I know we can be friends," he adds.

I look away so Jason won't see how much the idea pleases me. It feels nice to think I might have a friend on this trip after all, and it beats pretending to be friends with Sarah or Evie. "Why's that?"

"Because you're clearly a Sox fan." He swivels his Sox hat to the side and grins.

"Hate to disappoint, but I haven't been to a game in years." I shrug.

"What?" Jason explodes, staring at me like I've confessed to having a tail.

"I used to go with my dad," I reply. The words fly out of my mouth before I can think about what I'm saying. "He was a *huge* fan. But after he died, I didn't want to make my mom take me. I thought it would make her too sad."

Instantly, I wish I could take the words back. I never talk about my dad. There's a moment of awkward silence, the kind that makes you realize you've unintentionally sucked the wind out of a conversation. I stare at the ground, pretending to be fascinated by an old hair elastic that has found its way into the corner. I try to think of something to say to lighten the mood again, but my brain feels like it's covered in chalk.

Instead, Jason speaks up. "But things work out, you know. Even if it doesn't feel okay for a long time, or even if it feels like things will never be okay again, everything works out in the end." I look up, surprised by the softness of his voice. Now he looks like he feels sorry for *me*. My neck gets warm, and I'm glad I'm wearing my hair down so he can't see the splotches that I know are forming. I take a breath, and my body sways toward him a little. In the small space, it brings me awfully close, and I worry he can feel the pounding of my heart. I want to say something, but I don't know what, so we end up staring at each other for way too long.

Then he pulls the wad of grape gum out of his mouth and sticks it to the side of a record crate.

"Oh, gross!" I cry out. Just like that, the intensity of the moment is over.

Jason laughs and turns to a cardboard display of the Rolling Stones. Mick Jagger's mouth is wide open, mid-lyric. In one quick move, Jason grabs Mick and gives him a deep dip, his arms wrapped around his cardboard waist.

"What are you doing?"

"Getting me some satisfaction," he replies.

"I don't think that's the lyric," I say.

"Yeah, I'm getting that," he says. "Mick won't kiss back, rotten prude." Jason throws the cutout at the floor and accidentally takes Keith Richards and Brian Jones down with it. Before I can even blink, the entire cardboard band goes flying, knocking over a stack of CDs near the register. Everyone's eyes snap toward us at the sound of the clatter, including those of the shop clerk, who is putting price tags on a stack of vintage albums at the register.

"Oh my God, I'm so sorry," I say to no one in particular, and reach down to pick up some of the CDs. But before I can make any progress, Jason grabs my hand and pulls me toward the door. Once again, an outing with Jason culminates in disaster and the pair of us sprinting down the street away from trouble.

And once again, my head is full of more questions than answers.

13

༄

Just Call a Tassel a Tassel

is Jason still being a total ass? —P

"And this window treatment was selected by Queen Victoria herself, the first monarch to live in the palace, just before the first attempt on her life," our tour guide says, his voice rising in excitement as he gestures toward some truly hideous drapes. Then he chuckles softly to himself. "One hopes the two things were unrelated!"

I clutch my notebook, scribbling furiously. *Q. Victoria. Drapes. Assassination attempt?**

Underneath this, I add my own commentary: **Why are we learning this?*

Our tour guide at Buckingham Palace today has been about as interesting as a Latin translation of the Boston phone book. He's got a monotone voice and only shows hints of excitement when discussing the historical significance of the different draperies throughout the palace. He can't stop talking about fabrics and color swatches. I'm a fan of symbolism and all, but sometimes a tassel is just a tassel, okay, guy? I'm willing to go out on a limb and say the gold thread in the drapes in the throne room has very little to do with the signing of the Treaty of Versailles.

I turn to say this to Jason, but he's planted himself in the very back of the crowd. He's been cranky all morning. He started the tour at my side, following our guide closely while I scribbled notes in my book. He kept looking at his phone, then snapping it shut in disgust. He barely paid attention to anything our tour guide said, and as we moved through the palace, he quickly drifted away from me.

Our tour guide leads us down a hallway and into a library. My heart quickens as I gaze over the shelves of leather-bound books. I stop to run my fingers along a shelf full of gorgeous editions of Shakespeare, but the tour guide is at it again. This time it's the fabric on a gold-striped wing-back chair in the corner. Something about how Churchill once sat here on a visit. If he can connect that chair to Churchill's leadership during the Blitz, even *I'll* be impressed. I flip to a clean page in my notebook and scurry back toward the front of the group. I get almost right to the front, but Deirdre is blocking my view of whatever our tour guide is gesturing to now. Her giant, unruly blond mane could seriously block the sun. I stand up on my tiptoes and dance around a little, trying to get a good view, but there's no seeing around or over her hair. I'm going to have to get physical.

I clear my throat a little, then sort of step widely around her, giving her a gentle hip bump along the way.

"Hey!" she whispers.

"Oh, sorry," I reply, giving her a sympathetic look. "I'm such a klutz!"

I turn to see what we're looking at now, and I instinctively give a half-whispered yelp of fear and take a quick step back.

Perched atop a table is a perfectly taxidermied goose, wings spread as if in mid-flight.

"Are you okay?" Deirdre asks, surprisingly forgiving, considering I just hip-checked her to get a better view.

"Yeah," I reply, trying to tear my eyes away from the animal in front of me. "It's just . . . geese. I hate them."

"Oh yeah, totally," she whispers back with a little laugh. "There was this one time when a goose *crapped* on my new messenger bag, which thank God was waterproof, and . . ."

Deirdre charges on, but I'm not listening. I'm already thinking about my own horror story. I was five years old, and my family was at a neighborhood picnic held at a local park. I was playing with some of the other kids near a pond when a flock of geese landed nearby. I toddled my little kindergarten legs over to one and tried to pet it.

From my fuzzy little-kid memory, that bird let out the loudest, longest, scariest screech I'd ever heard from any animal of any kind, and snapped toward my hand. I screamed like a banshee and ran like hell, and that bird chased right after me. I thought I was going to die (or at least that's what I screamed like, said my dad). Dad ran over and scooped me up, and all of a sudden I was bigger than that dumb bird. With me held high in his arms, we chased that stupid goose together.

Still, I've always been afraid of them. Whenever I see one, it's a reminder that I've got to chase the geese on my own now. At least this goose is stuffed and shellacked and mounted on a wooden platform. Phoebe-the-vegetarian would kill me for saying so, but it kind of gives me a sick sort of satisfaction.

Luckily, our tour doesn't linger long. When we finally make our way back to the grand hall, the class disperses to wander around the room, looking at the portraits set into the walls and examining the marble staircase. I tuck my notes into my bag for safekeeping and hurry over to where Jason is gazing out an oversized window. He's tossing his phone back and forth between his hands, and I'm guessing he's *not* contemplating the political ramifications of the purple brocade covering the window.

"Everything okay?" I ask him. "You get up on the wrong side of the bed or something?"

"What?" Jason starts, as though he didn't even notice I'd appeared at his side.

I wave a hand in front of his face. "You haven't made a sex joke in, like, two hours. Are you feeling okay? Do you have a fever?"

Out of nowhere, he blurts out, "Is Mark Bixford seriously your type?"

My brain powers down completely. "Excuse me?" I say. It's all I can do not to choke on the words.

"I mean, he seems kind of shallow," Jason says. My face must not be betraying the fact that I'm having a mini meltdown that is happening in my brain.

"Where did you hear that?" I say, struggling to keep calm, struggling to keep the panic from my voice.

"Where else? Sarah Finder, Queen of Gossip."

Of course. Suddenly, I feel sick. The gilded room is spinning around me. Who else has Sarah told? Does Mark know? And how the hell did *she* find out?

Oh my God. Did she tweet about this?

Jason charges on. "But then again, he's probably really *charming,* and not a complete *ass* like me." His voice hangs on "charming" in a way I don't like. I hoped we could forget about my flipping on him yesterday. He certainly didn't seem mad last night when we went to Cue-2-Cue, but he's clearly still a little pissed about it now.

"I don't know what you're talking about," I finally squeak. I hope he doesn't notice the beads of sweat forming on my forehead.

"You can chill out," Jason says. "Like I even give a crap who you swoon over. I'm not going to tell anyone."

"I'm not swooning over Mark. And even if I *was,* why do you care?" I try to sound confident and dismissive, but all I can think about is that my knees are wobbling like they've been replaced with mint jelly. I try to casually drape my arm across the back of a wingback chair for support, but instead, it looks like I'm clinging to a piece of furniture as the *Titanic* is sinking. I hope the chair isn't a priceless piece of history in case I pass out in it. Or barf on it.

"I don't," Jason replies. He plops down in the chair, and I imagine we must look like we're posing for some bizarro portrait. Only I probably look like I'm participating at gunpoint.

"Then why did you bring it up?" I demand. My face is burning.

"You totally don't get it," Jason says, rolling his eyes.

I plant myself directly in front of him. "Listen, don't hate on Mark just because he's everything you're not," I say right to his face.

"Excuse me?" Jason looks up at me, his eyes narrowed to angry slits.

"You heard me. Mark *is* charming, and respectful, and he's not always vying for attention." Jason opens his mouth, but I charge on before he can say anything. "He's a really great guy who's never said a bad word about anyone, and for you to trash him for no reason is pathetic."

"You know what, Julia? You—"

Before something really nasty can come out of Jason's mouth, my phone starts buzzing in my back pocket. I hold up a finger at him, the international symbol for "'Scuse me, I have something more important to pay attention to, so you're gonna have to hold on." I glance around for signs of Mrs. Tennison, but unwilling to take any chances, I crouch behind one of Queen Victoria's fancy-pants drapes and flip open my phone to find a new text from Chris.

Sitting in a café with a burnt caramel mocha
watching the rain dreaming of u . . .

My face burns even hotter. No one has ever sent me a text this sweet before. I read it again. And again. Then I feel a finger poking at me through the drapes.

"You in there?"

I push on the drapes, trying to find my way out, but Jason is in the way and I can't find the opening. I feel his hand poking me, but I can't follow it out from behind the drapes. I have a brief, panicked fear that I'll never get out of here, and my mummified body will become part of the palace tour.

I finally have to drop to my knees and wiggle out the bottom. When I emerge, Jason is rolling his eyes and giving me a total "you're the chief resident of crazytown" face.

"What is your problem?" I ask, trying to pretend I didn't stage an epic battle with a set of velvet drapes.

"If you're soooo obsessed with Mark, if he's your MTB"—here he makes air quotes—"or whatever, then why are you chasing after this dude Chris? For someone who probably irons her underpants, you're pretty all over the place, aren't you? Just like all the girls you look down on."

"I don't look down on people!" I protest.

"Don't you? Haven't you spent most of this trip thinking that all your classmates are shallow horndogs who couldn't appreciate the history and literature of London if it kicked them in the teeth?"

"Well, Sarah and Evie *are* shallow," I retort. "*Especially* Sarah. Why can't she mind her own business? She acts like other people's lives are her personal *Us Weekly*."

"You don't even know her," he replies. "If you spent a second reading a Sarah Finder guidebook, you'd know she's in everyone's business because she wants to protect her friends. You're too busy in Julia Land to notice anyone else."

"Whatever," I mutter. My throat is having spasms. Jason makes me sound like an awful, uptight, self-involved monster. I'm not like that! He thinks he knows me! He doesn't know me at all. I inhale deeply and lower my voice. "Mark is none of your business, okay? Just because you've dated a bunch of girls doesn't make you an expert on love. I mean, yeah you've had girlfriends, but have any hung around for more than like a week?" I bite my lip, regretting the words as soon as I've said them.

"If I'm such an idiot, then why did you ask for my help?" He tosses something small and silver at me. I catch it before it smacks me in the cheek. My phone! "Here. Good luck with your texting."

"What? How did you– When did you–" I sputter.

"Slimeballs like me have sticky fingers," he deadpans.

Oh my God. The drapes. When he was trying to "help" me out, he must have snatched my phone. My breaths are coming fast and deep, like I've just climbed out of the pool after a hard sprint. Everything is upside down. If there is such a thing as spontaneous human combustion, I fear I'm about to experience it.

"Leave me alone" is all I can whisper.

"Gladly." Jason brushes past me, bumping me hard with his shoulder. I take a stumbling step backward . . . and run smack into a suit of armor.

The whole thing starts to teeter on its tiny base. I reach out to grab it, but it's too late. It seems like slow motion as the armor, surprisingly heavy for a mini replica, crashes to the ground. The sound bounces across the marble floor and swirls around the room like a tornado. I stand frozen in horror. Everyone is looking at me, including Jason, his face registering a mixture of annoyance and amusement.

Our tour guide gives a tight, choking laugh and says to the staring faces, "Just a reproduction, just a reproduction. Do be more careful, though, won't you, miss?"

"Julia Lichtenstein, what has gotten into you?" Mrs. Tennison stage-whispers through clenched teeth. It's clear she doesn't want to make even more of a scene in front of our tour guide, but she is capital-*P* Pissed. She plods heavily across the floor in a pair of beat-up Uggs, which Mrs. Tennison probably thinks make her look trendy, though actually she looks like she has clubfeet. She takes me by the arm and leads me quickly over to a side hallway.

"Miss Lichtenstein," she begins, winding up for a serious talking-to, "your behavior on this trip has been *completely* unacceptable. I was hoping you would be a role model for your classmates, but instead you have been impulsive, thoughtless, and disrespectful. I did *not* expect this from you, of all people."

Her words pack a punch right to my gut. I feel like all the wind has been knocked out of me, and my eyes burn with tears. I've *never* been talked to like this by a teacher. *Ever.*

"I'm so sorry," I whisper. Suddenly, my throat is squeezing shut and I realize I'm about to cry.

"Really. What *has* gotten into you?" she asks, staring me hard in the face, eyes narrowed. She turns on her heel toward the rest of the group, waving me along after her. Apparently she wasn't looking for an answer, which is good, because I don't have one. What *is* wrong with me? Did a teacher just seriously refer to me as *impulsive?* And *disrespectful?* Jason's calling me shallow; Mrs. Tennison is calling me thoughtless. . . . What's next?

I trudge after Mrs. Tennison, rejoining my classmates. As I wipe the tears from my cheeks, I catch a glimpse of Sarah Finder, standing near the back of the room. I expect to see a smirk, but all I can see is . . . pity. She actually looks like she feels *sorry* for me. Which doesn't make me feel better. In fact, it makes me feel worse. Maybe I *am* shallow. Whatever. I just know that I'm sick of being ignored, pitied, judged . . . by everyone.

14

❧

Love May Be Blind, but I'm Not

lovers quarrel? do tell! —SF

I quickly type back *as if* in response to Sarah's text, then wander through the rest of the tour like a zombie, trying to remain expressionless and emotionless. *I will not cry. I will not cry. I will not cry.*

When the tour ends, we make our way to a pub curiously named the Only Running Footman. It's listed in my guidebook as one of the best places for "true British grub," though unfortunately, my book doesn't tell me where it got its wacky name. It's located in what my book tells me is the Mayfair district. I want to flip and cross-check just what that is, but my head hurts too badly to focus on the index. Once inside, my classmates spread out among the tables and the black vinyl booths. They place orders for shepherd's pie and fish-and-chips, giddy over the delicious-smelling pub fare. Ryan attempts to order a pint, but he has to laugh it off like it's all a big joke when Mrs. Tennison whips around and shoots him the evil eye. This would be the ideal place to continue my quest for the perfect fish-and-chips. They even offer what the menu calls "proper mushy peas" as a side, but I'm not hungry. I keep thinking back to Mrs. Tennison's angry voice, her finger wagging in my face.

Instead of ordering, I take a small table in the corner and flip open my notebook, hoping I can focus on going over my notes and drafting some of today's reflection paper, but what I see on the pages are not my standard, neatly lined-up notes with indents and symbols. My system is nonexistent and my notes are a hot mess. I can't get anything right today. *I will not cry. I will not cry. I will not cry.*

A shadow swallows my notebook. I look up to see Jason. He's holding two porcelain white plates of fish-and-chips, perfectly rounded scoops of tartar sauce and mushy peas on the sides. He has two bottled waters tucked under his arms.

"You can't leave England without eating some fish-and-chips," he says. When I don't respond, he says, more softly, "Come on, Julia. I know you can eat like a running back."

He drops one of the plates in front of me, and it clangs loudly on the table. One of the fries escapes its pile and plops down on top of the mountain of tartar sauce. I instinctively reach for it, dabbing the sauce on the side of the plate before returning it to its pile.

"Thanks," I mumble, but I have to push the plate back across the table. The smell of the beer batter reminds me of our night of drinking at the house party, the start of all the rule breaking that led me here. I drop my head onto my folded arms, my messy curls spread out across the table.

"Mind if I sit?" He doesn't wait for a response, of course; he deposits the other plate in front of the empty chair next to mine and plops down beside me. A few minutes pass in silence, other than the sounds of his noisy chewing. I keep my head down, but the smell of the French fries is starting to work its telltale magic. I finally raise my head, and Jason immediately slides my lunch in front of me.

"Listen, I really appreciate that you didn't bring my name into that," he says, passing the malt vinegar my way.

"What are you talking about?"

"Back at the palace. You were mad at me; it was my fault you ran into that suit of armor." He has to swallow back a laugh as he says it, which only reminds me of how awful and embarrassing the whole situation was. He quickly continues, "Anyway, I appreciate that you didn't say anything to Tennison. If Mrs. T gives me a terrible grade for this trip, my grade for the semester is screwed, and frankly so is my GPA."

"What happened to that seven twenty verbal score?" I reply, an edge in my voice. "Shouldn't you be cruising through classes with those smarts?"

"I'm very smart," Jason says matter-of-factly. "But as you yourself have pointed out, I'm also not the most . . . serious student in the world. If my GPA takes another hit, I won't get into a good college. And if I don't get into a good college, I won't get into a good law school. Doth sayeth my father, anyway. And if I don't get into a good law school, trust me—I won't even be welcome at family holidays anymore." His laugh comes out forced.

I want to continue being mad, but I feel a stab of sympathy for him. My dad wouldn't have cared what I did with my life, as long as I was happy. I can't imagine having pressure like that from my parents. So I swallow back my snotty retort and instead stare at my plate.

"Look, you're pissed. I get that. I'm sorry for what I said before, okay? I want to make it up to you." For once, he seems sincere.

"How do you plan on doing that?" I sigh.

"Well, that text from Chris . . . ," he says, reaching into his pocket. He pulls out a crumpled piece of paper; it looks like a receipt, with his trademark chicken scratch on the back. "He mentioned having a burnt caramel mocha. Turns out there're only two places in London that have them on the menu. I Googled," he explains as he holds the paper out to me. I see that he's written the addresses on it.

"Where in the hell did you Google?"

"The girl sitting at the security desk. She was cute. She thought I was cute. . . ." He trails off, and I get it.

"So she was blind?" I say.

"Hardee har har. I guess I deserved that." He nudges me with an elbow. "After lunch is cultural time. So what do you say? I say burnt caramel mochas are *very* culturally relevant."

I fiddle with my napkin. I know Jason is trying, but I'm not totally ready to forgive him yet. Still, maybe the café is somewhere Chris hangs out regularly. He might even be there right now, even though he sent the text a while ago; Phoebe and I used to practically *live* at the Beanstalk.

"Okay," I say. "Fine. But you write your own paper this time."

"We'll leave that discussion for later," he says. He pumps his fist in the air. "Oh, and you should write back to that text. Say . . . say 'wish I could be there to warm you up.' "

I stare at him like his red hair is actually on fire, but when he doesn't flinch, I give up. I pull out my phone and type it in, word for embarrassing word. What have I got to lose, anyway?

When we finish lunch, we walk the eight blocks to the first café he's noted, but from the moment I walk in, I'm sure this cannot be the place. The wall is plastered with heavy wallpaper covered in roses the size of my head. There're so many of them, red and pink and fuchsia, in a repeating pattern that I start to worry that they're closing in on me. Each round table is topped with a handmade doily, and cross-stitched Bible verses in wooden frames adorn the walls. The only patrons in the café are of the blue-haired set, and they appear to be holding a book club focused on the latest Nicholas Sparks sob fest.

"Can we please get out of here?" Jason whispers to me as the elderly woman at the counter waves a porcelain floral teapot threateningly in our direction.

"God yes," I whisper back, a fake smile plastered on my face for the patrons. We rush out before they start showing us pictures of their grandchildren.

We have to take the tube to the second café, and I notice that Jason is nice enough to stand between me and the creepy guy who smells like oatmeal and sweat. Turns out even Europe has subway weirdos. Or *tube* weirdos, I guess they say in London.

When the train glides to a stop, Jason leaps out. Then he bolts toward the exit. I make it out of the train right before the doors slide shut again, and take off after him. He's weaving through crowds of commuters, dodging around people like he's on a slalom course. When he gets to the base of the escalator, he barely gives me enough time to catch up.

"What was that about?" I ask, but the words are barely out of my mouth before he takes off again, running up the escalator, taking the steps two and even three at a time on his long legs. I run after him, and when we finally burst out onto the street, we're both panting and laughing.

"Where's the fire?" I ask through gasps.

"Daily cardio, Book Licker," he says. He's bent over slightly, his hands on his knees, catching his breath. He stands up and raises a hand high. I have to hop a little to return his high five. "Nice work," he says.

"Thanks," I reply. I ball my fists and hold them up like the track champion I'm definitely not. Even though I'm winded, I feel incredibly energized. "So what's with the mad dash?"

"Don't you want to meet this mysterious Chris? Isn't he worth running for?" Jason gives me a strange look. I open my mouth but realize I don't have anything to say.

An uncomfortable feeling worms its way into my stomach. The truth is I'm not sure how I feel about seeing Chris. All I know is it feels nice to be wanted, to be pursued, to be *flirting* for once.

And a tiny little minuscule piece of me might be enjoying Jason's company, too.

Jason guides me across a square and toward a narrow coffee shop squished between a used-book shop and an Internet café. When we get inside, I hustle straight to the register to take a peek at the menu. Sure enough, burnt caramel mochas are listed right at the top, a house specialty.

"Think we should order one?" Jason asks, coming up behind me in line. "We did scour all of London to find them."

"Nah," I say, gazing around the shop. "I'm not much of a coffee drinker." I'm not much for caffeine of any kind. It makes me so jittery that I feel like I could read the entire Harvard library in one night, or flap my arms and take flight off the roof of the Hancock Building. The last time I drank a latte, I decided the best way to study for the SATs would be to memorize the entire dictionary. My mom found me the next morning surrounded by multicolored flash cards that looked like they had been written by a serial killer. I was drooling in the middle of the *K*s. It was a month before I could look at a *K* word without getting the shakes.

There are a few people in the shop, and most of them look older, like graduate students. One is pounding away angrily on his laptop, and I'm pretty sure he can't be Chris. I would have remembered the jagged scar across his cheek (I hope). Another is engrossed in a paperback novel, but I don't think he's Chris, either, as I'm certain a chest-length red beard would have been fairly memorable.

There's only one other candidate, and he's reading what looks like . . . No. It can't be.

It is. A pocket Shakespeare sits on the table next to his mug (a burnt caramel mocha, perhaps?).

It's him. It has to be.

My stomach flips. He's got horn-rimmed glasses and short, messy black hair. He's that kind of rugged, nerdy handsome. Part emo, part mountain man. In a word, the boy is hot. If he has a British accent, I might actually suffer a romance-induced stroke and keel over dead right here in this coffee shop.

My hands instantly go clammy and the blood drains from my face.

"Think that's him?" Jason nudges me.

"Dunno," I say, limited to one-word answers by my fear.

"Are you going to go over there?"

"Nope." I hope I don't look as panicked as I feel. I shove my hands into the pockets of my pants so no one can tell they're getting so sweaty it's like I dipped them in a vat of movie theater popcorn butter. My heart is beating as if someone is playing speed metal inside my rib cage.

Jason studies me for a second. I catch myself bouncing up and down on my toes. Okay. So I almost *definitely* look as panicked as I feel.

"Fine," he says, brushing past me. "Then I will."

"No!" I shout, drawing the attention of the few patrons. I reach out and grab the hem of his shirt, pulling hard.

He jerks backward, then whirls around to face me. "What is going on? We've been running all over London to find this guy. Now there he is, and you can't go over there? You've got to take the training wheels off sometime, Julia."

"I . . . I just . . ." My mouth bobs open and shut like I'm some poor fish that's been plucked out of the ocean. I don't know what to say. The truth is now that I've seen him, I *can't* go up to him. He's HOT. And I'm . . . well, I'm me. Not to mention I've been telling him I'm a supermodel. He probably only believed it because he was as drunk at the party as I was. One look at me in the sober light of day, and the whole thing crumbles to the ground about my short little legs.

"I can't do it," I finally manage to croak.

"Isn't that your book?" Jason prods. "Your pocket Shakespeare, or whatever?"

I'm shocked he remembers. Last time I mentioned my pocket Shakespeare, he looked at me like I'd been carrying a live fish in my purse.

"I'm not ready," I say quietly, almost in a whisper. I turn away and head toward the door. Jason trots after me.

"You're serious?" he asks.

I can only nod.

I feel a thousand emotions, everything from fear to anxiety to sadness. . . . I wish I had the confidence to stroll right up to Chris and smile at him. Evie and Sarah would. Phoebe definitely would. But I don't. I can't. I'd say something to screw it up, or I'd trip over myself or knock coffee into his lap, and I wouldn't be able to stand the disappointed look on his face.

When we get out to the street, I have to lean over and take a few deep breaths. My legs buzz with energy, and I want to take off running. Instead, I inhale three more breaths, then turn and face Jason. "I think I need some more time."

Jason looks at me for a moment, and I brace for the teasing. But shockingly, it doesn't come.

Jason scans the street and suddenly brightens. "I've got an idea," he says. He grabs my arms and starts pulling me down the sidewalk. "This'll cheer you up." He ducks into the used-book shop next door, which appears to specialize in antiques and rare editions. The place smells like a library attic, and from the moment I step through the door, the little bell tinkling behind me, signaling my arrival to the shopkeeper, I'm in heaven. This is definitely more fun than standing in that café, morphing into a quivering pile of nerves.

Shelves jammed with books of all sizes take up nearly every square inch of the store, leaving only narrow aisles down which you can browse.

A fat gray cat snoozes in the corner on a lumpy red pillow, a basket of yellowed Penguin Classics next to him. Soft strains of music are wafting through the shop, a familiar tune I can't quite place, but I hum along anyway. I walk over to the glass display case where highly polished leather volumes with gilded pages and borders practically sparkle. As I stare at a copy of *The Collected Works of Shakespeare,* I realize I've been holding my breath since I walked in. I let it out in one long, satisfied sigh.

Jason has wandered off down one of the tall, narrow aisles, no doubt in search of the DVD section (which he won't find in a place like this). I hope he doesn't knock anything over. I wander down the closest aisle, looking for him.

The back of the store opens up into a small café area with a stage at the back. There are several people gathered at the tables, drinking coffee and tea out of chipped mugs. A young-looking girl with loose braids is carrying an acoustic guitar offstage, and three raggedy-looking guys push past her onto the tiny stage, where their instruments are waiting. The guitar player turns a few knobs on his Gibson while the drummer closes himself into the corner behind his drum kit. Within minutes, they've fired up the amps and the bass player is belting into a mic. Their music is loud and seems kind of out of place in the small, old-looking space, but it's also joyful. The rhythm starts beating its way through the floor, up through my body.

I recognize the song from the very first notes, from the ten thousand times I've heard it on my parents' old record player to the time just the other day when Jason played it at the skate park. I lean into a bookshelf in the back of the room, close my eyes, and listen as they begin to sing, "Oh darling . . ."

Jason taps me on the shoulder.

"C'mon," he says. Before I can protest, he pulls me toward the stage. We weave through the maze of tiny tables and patrons, and at first I'm afraid he's going to jump onstage and sing (again). He stops short of the stage, though. He bumps an empty table with his hip, scooting it over to make some space for us. Then he holds out his hand.

"What are you doing?" I whisper. I can feel the audience's eyes on us. We're standing in front of the entire room, only a few feet away from the band.

"What does it look like I'm doing?" he responds neutrally. "We're going to dance." He grabs my hand, pulling me into him, and the next thing I know, he's got me in a classic ballroom pose. I feel strange in his arms, like I should be on my guard. I anticipate a tickle attack of some kind or kamikaze pantsing at any moment. Or maybe he'll dissolve into some goofy fox-trot or tango. Instead, he loosens up and starts a slow sway. I giggle into his shoulder.

"What's so funny?"

This is fun, I almost say. But instead, I shake my head and say, "Nothing." I breathe in the smell of his shirt, which is equal parts detergent and cedar.

He begins humming along with the bassist. "This should be our song."

"Yeah, one where a guy begs for forgiveness," I say, rolling my eyes.

"He's not begging for forgiveness," he says, pulling back a little so he can give me a look. "He's asking for her trust."

"Probably because he *broke* that trust at some point in the recent past," I retort. I pull back a little, too.

"Why so cynical all of a sudden?"

I feel my cheeks heating up. Jason's eyes are locked on mine. I can see bits of gold swimming among the blue. "You're the one that's suddenly sentimental!"

"Sorry," he says breezily. "I thought you were the one that believes in love and all that." He pulls me back in, eliminating all the space between us. He's warm. I can feel the heat from his body pulsing through me, from the top of my head down to the tips of my toes.

"Yeah, I am," I reply, "but if this is, in fact, our song, then I'm going with the alternative interpretation."

"Okay then, Professor Lichtenstein," he says, chuckling.

"You don't see it that way?" I say, my cheek now dangerously close to pressing into his chest. He leans down to my ear.

"Love looks not with the eyes, but with the heart," he says. His breath tickles my neck and a chill shoots up my spine. I'm so shocked I end up stamping hard on his foot. Where did that come from?

"Ow!" he says, hopping a little. "Watch where you stomp those things, okay? They're small but deadly."

"Um, it's 'Love looks not with the eyes, but with the *mind*,'" I say, correcting him, trying to shake off the surprise of hearing him quote Shakespeare, however incorrectly. "'And therefore is winged Cupid painted *blind*.'"

I feel funny saying the lines to him. It's different from the thousand other times I've corrected him on something. This time I feel a little warm, and I can't look him in the eye. It's my and Phoebe's favorite Shakespeare quote, and I've always imagined Mark whispering it into my ear right before planting a soft kiss on my lips. Instead, I'm being squeezed a little too tightly by Jason Lippincott, who's not even saying it *right*.

I look up. He's looking right at me, one eyebrow raised and a slight glimmer in his eyes. I worry he's going to start teasing me about love again, but instead, he starts spinning me around. The band is really winding up now, the amps buzzing with the wailing of the lead singer. Jason spins me faster and faster. I lose my balance and break away from him, stumbling backward into a waiting café chair.

"I think that's enough dancing for me," I say. My fingers clutch the bottom of the chair as the room tilts in front of me. I feel dizzy from the spinning, and maybe a little from the conversation, too.

Jason's still staring at me. There's no glimmer in his eyes now. His expression is totally unreadable. "Whatever you say," he replies. He puts his hands deep into his pockets, then turns on his squeaky heel and heads for the front of the shop. In a blink, he disappears between the shelves. I take a deep breath. I can still smell him—grape gum and fabric softener and something else, something I can't identify. My stomach does a little flip, and I tell myself it's only nausea from the spinning. In the distance, I hear the tinkle of the bell on the front door.

"Hey, wait up!" I call. I scramble after him, overcome for a moment by that head-rushing blackout sensation. More people turn to stare at me, but I ignore them. I can see Jason through the glass door, his back to me, his red hair curling underneath his ball cap. The butt of his jeans is worn, the ancient outline of a wallet visible in his back left pocket. One of his belt loops is ripped and dangling, causing his brown belt to droop a little near his hip.

I pause for a second to make sure that all the dizziness is gone. Then I push the door open. When the bell tinkles, he doesn't turn.

"I didn't know you could dance," I say to his back.

He pauses for a split second and shoots me a glance over his shoulder. "There's a lot you don't know about me," he says, and then he's gone.

15

His Keeper or Whatever

i want 2 get 2 know u better. —C

"**C**an I sit here?"

I'm surprised to find Susan standing over me. Her perfectly flatironed hair is held back by a red headband with a dainty little bow. It matches the red in her cardigan and the red patent leather flats on her feet.

"Uh, sure," I reply, scooting my notebook closer to give her room at my standard corner table. I'm frankly happy to have her join me. I figured Jason might sit with me at dinner, but he's been ignoring me since the impromptu dance performance at the bookstore.

As if on cue, I hear riotous laughter coming from across the dining room. Jason is sitting with a group of guys and they're launching dinner rolls off their forks. Typical. I notice Ryan is sitting with them. Their table is full, which explains why Susan is sitting with me and not over there, hanging on every "dude" Ryan is uttering.

Awesome. I'm the reject table.

"So what have you been—" I say, but Susan has already pulled out a thick copy of *British Vogue* and is engrossed in its pages. Susan probably joined me at my table because she figured it was the place to page through her magazine without being bothered.

A dinner roll sails over our table and bounces off the wall behind me. I look up to see Ryan and Jason raising their forks in triumph.

"Ugh, isn't he the worst?" Instantly, magazine forgotten, Susan whips around to stare at the boys' table. "Such a child."

"Seriously," I say. Thank God Susan Morgan and I have *something* to talk about: our mutual dislike for Jason. "It's like he's incapable of acting like a normal human. And that gum! What high school boy do you know that chews that much grape gum? So gross."

Susan looks slightly puzzled. "What?" she says; then she shakes her head. "Oh, I meant *Ryan*. He's, like, so ridiculous."

"Oh," I reply. I guess Susan and I don't have anything in common.

"Jason's actually not that bad," she continues. "He totally bailed me out last spring when my computer ate my final paper for Freeman's AP English class. He lent me his computer right away—and his notes were *soooo* much better than mine! I would have, like, totally failed if it weren't for him."

"Oh," I say again. Even though I'm sitting down, I feel curiously disoriented. Jason lent Susan his computer just to be nice? Even stranger, Jason takes *notes* in class?

"Yeah. Jason's kind of the best, actually," Susan chirps. Then she returns to her magazine, and just like that, I'm alone again.

I turn to my own notes, trying to make sense of all the madness I've been writing. I'm going to have to crank out a reflection paper later, and there's no way I can be thorough with the mess I've got in front of me. My brain feels like it's doing freestyle laps through a pool of lime Jell-O. Well, maybe I can't blame my notes *entirely*. It was a long walk from the café to our hotel, but we somehow made it all the way back without ever mentioning a *word* of what had just happened.

I'm not even sure what *did* happen—whether we had some kind of a moment, like we did in the record store, or whether I imagined the whole thing.

And then there's the text I got from Chris, which of course binged onto my phone as soon as we got back to the hotel. I was tempted to show it to Jason, but after the dancing, I felt funny about it. And what did he mean, 'There's a lot you don't know about me'? What is he hiding? Why can't he just be *normal*? One second we're friends, the next second he acts like I have leprosy. It's enough to give a girl whiplash. It's like he gets off on confusing me, like it's some little game.

Well, I don't want to play anymore.

But I *do* want to get to know Chris better. Or more accurately, now that I've seen him, I want *him* to get to know *me* better so that when I finally work up the courage to meet him, he may not be too dismayed or shocked to find out that I'm a five-foot-tall swimmer and not a six-foot-tall supermodel. Even if he weren't the single hottest guy I've ever seen (after Mark, of course), he seems totally perfect. I mean, he was reading Shakespeare. In a café. The *same* book I was reading.

I glance up at Susan, who's completely engrossed in an article about the return of the feather boa. She probably wouldn't care in the least if I walked away, but I still feel bad abandoning her.

"Do you mind?" I ask, nodding toward the elevator. "I need to get a jump on this paper, and that tour guide was completely useless today."

"Whatever, totally fine," she says. She glances back at Ryan's table, where a seat has opened up. She grabs her stuff and bolts for it. So much for thinking he's a child.

While I ride the glacially slow elevator to my floor, I pull out my phone and stare at the text from Chris. As the elevator dings past each floor, I take a deep breath and type out a reply.

Definitely. Same. —J

I figure my best bet is to keep it short and simple. That way, I can't screw anything up . . . hopefully. I've just arrived at my floor when my phone buzzes with a reply.

Ready to meet up? —C

I gasp and flip my phone shut. I can't reply to this in the hallway. I need to do some thinking. I get back to my room and I flop down on my big fluffy bed, my laptop open and ready for another reflection paper. Only I still can't reflect. I can't think *at all*. I keep seeing those glasses and that shaggy hair. He's *so hot*. This is worse than when I had no idea who he was. Now I can perfectly visualize his face . . . and his inevitable look of disappointment when I approach him.

What on earth will I say to him? *Oh—hey, Chris! Here's the thing. When I said "supermodel," what I really meant was "high school student." And when I mentioned "photo shoots," I was actually referring to a field trip. So essentially, I'm a dirty liar. I'm from Massachusetts, not Manhattan, but please still fall madly in love with me, okay?*

I slam my laptop with enough force that my cell phone bounces onto the floor. I pick it up and look back at the text from Chris. He wants to get to know me better. So I'm guessing now is not the time to let him know I've been basically stalking him all over the city. I want to be flirty or witty, but I'm too scared, so instead I go with Plan B: honesty.

not yet. things are complicated.

"Complicated" is the understatement of the year, but if I were to try to describe how things are on the T9 keyboard of my crappy little loaner cell phone, it would take me days. And even then I probably wouldn't have it right. Because I have *no idea*.

I pull my laptop back into my lap and stare at the blank screen. I take another stab at my notes, this time attacking them with my favorite green highlighter. I flip through the pages of my script, trying to pull out themes, or even a starting point. As my flipping gets more manic, I cram the highlighter into my mouth, running my fingers along the lines to find something, *anything* I can write about. The further I get from a finished paper, the closer I get to a full-on breakdown. This is *useless*.

My broken travel alarm clock glares at me with angry red cracked lights, taunting me for how long I've been grinding away at this assignment. I jump up from the bed, charge over to the wall and lean against it, then drop into a low squat. Wall sits. A good burn in my thighs ought to take the burn out of my brain. I start counting the seconds. Thirty. Sixty. Ninety. They tick by, but nothing is happening. I get to nearly two minutes, and my thighs start to quiver, but I'm still feeling crazy. Somewhere around the three-minute mark, my legs give out, and I plop to the floor right on my butt. I massage my thigh, breathing heavily and trying to figure out what to do.

It's like I'm groping around in my brain with two hands and a flashlight, yet I can't find a single word to name what I'm feeling. All I know is there's no way I can write two of these stupid reflection papers, especially since Jason has been little or no help to me lately. In fact, he has been the exact *opposite* of helpful (help-empty?).

If he doesn't hold up his end of the deal, I won't hold up mine.

And I'm going to tell him so. Now.

I run my hands over my stomach, smoothing my wrinkled shirt, take a deep breath, and then slip into the hall, wedging a shoe in the door so it doesn't lock closed behind me, since Mrs. Tennison has already collected key cards for the night.

I stop in front of Jason's door, and before I can think or talk myself out of it, I give it a hard knock.

Nothing.

I press my ear against the door, but I don't hear music or the television or any rustling around. Maybe he's asleep? I glance at my watch. It's ten-thirty already. Jason must have snuck out.

I knock again. I lean close as if I'm going to see in through the peephole, and my forehead smacks on the door.

"Ow," I mutter, rubbing my forehead.

"Dude, he's not in there." The voice startles me, and I whirl around to see Quentin Phillips, lacrosse player and stoner extraordinaire, poking his head out of the room directly across the hall.

"Excuse me?"

"Dude, you have . . . stuff . . . on your . . ." He can barely get the words out between laughs.

"What? What is it?" I snap.

"Your lips are green," he says, and raises a finger to point directly at my face. Suddenly, the memory of the green highlighter, stuck between my teeth while I was trying to write my reflection paper, comes flooding back. Excellent. I lick my fingers and rub furiously, but without a mirror I have no idea if I really got it off.

"Where did he go?" I ask, and Quentin doesn't laugh, so I assume the green is mostly gone.

"He's out," Quentin says in his bizarre surfer accent. (I know for a *fact* the kid was born and raised in Boston.)

"Do you know where he went?"

"Not sure, dude," Quentin says slowly, watching me through eyes narrowed to slits. "Some kind of anti-liquor protest, I think."

"I'm sorry, what?" I don't speak faux surfer, so I *must* have misunderstood.

"I dunno, dude," Quentin says, a lazy grin spreading across his face. "He was talking about prohibition, and I was kinda tired at the time, but I'm pretty sure that's where they, like, think booze is the devil, right?"

"Are you sure about that?" I ask. Prohibition? For real? What in the world is this kid smoking? I mean, even if there *were* some kind of throw-back anti-liquor rally going on in London, I think Jason would sooner set his hair on fire than participate. He seemed to be pretty pro-alcohol the other night.

"Look, man, I was getting back from a run and I saw him in the hall and I was all like, 'Hey, dude, where ya going?' and he was all like, 'I'm going to prohibition,'" Quentin says, getting a little testy. "I'm not his keeper or whatever. Isn't that *your* job?"

A lightbulb goes on in my brain. It's not a protest; it's that expat bar we passed on our first day here. It's *called* Prohibition. Of course Jason went out drinking. He snuck out *again,* and this time he didn't even bother to tell me.

I stomp back to my room and give the door the hardest slam I can muster. The gilded mirror rattles on the wall. I grab one of the heavy silk-covered pillows off my bed, bury my face in it, and let out the loud-est, longest scream I think I've ever heard.

I throw the pillow back down on my bed and look at myself in the mirror. I look *pissed*. Actually, I look crazy. I've been running my hands through my hair so much that it's starting to frizz and stick up in funny places. My eyes are slightly bloodshot, and my cheeks seem to have ad-opted some kind of permanent blush. My hotel room is starting to feel tiny and stifling. The air is thick and stale and sticky all at once, and I have trouble drawing good, deep breaths.

I need to get a hold of myself. Now.

I whip open my bureau and pull out my running shorts. I dress, tie my running shoes, and pile the frizz ball that is my hair into a messy bun. Then I fish around in my suitcase for my broken purse. In the inside zipper pocket, my hand closes around the plastic key card, the one Jason stole for me. I haven't used it since the night of the party, when I told myself I wouldn't be breaking any more rules. Boy, was I wrong.

I open my door and poke my head out, glancing up and down the hall. No one. Then I step out into the hall, take a deep breath, and let the door shut behind me with a mechanical click. I test the key to be sure it still works, and I'm happy to see the little green light flicker next to the knob, indicating that all is good to go. I tuck the key into the pocket of my running shorts, then take off for the stairs.

I run for blocks. For miles. For what feels like hours. I run until I'm no longer tired, until my legs don't ache anymore, until I'm on autopilot. I run to the rhythm of my pounding heart. It's late and dark, but there are plenty of people out, so I'm not worried about ending up in some abandoned back alley. No one seems to pay any mind to the short little American girl sprinting through the streets in neon-pink gym shorts.

As I'm finally starting to relax, to ease into the rhythm of my run, my sneakers catch something. I stumble and then tumble to the ground. I get my hands down in time to avoid bashing my knee on the sidewalk, but my palms sting and I manage to scrape the skin off my left thumb.

"Great," I mutter as I pick myself up carefully. My left shoe is completely untied. I must have stepped on the lace. I was in such a rush to get out of the hotel, I forgot to double knot my laces.

I bend down to retie my shoes.

"Sweeeeet Caroline!"

Even though his voice is slurry, I recognize it right away: Jason. I turn around and see him stumbling out of a pub.

I ran right to Prohibition. Of course I did.

I consider tucking my head and bolting. But then I see that he's in bad shape. He stumbles over a trash bin in the street and laughs a little.

Uh-oh. He is definitely drunk.

He doesn't seem to see me. He just rights himself and starts down the block. He's stumbling a lot. I dart after him. I'd better make sure he doesn't get into any *more* trouble. After all, I am, as Quentin so artfully put it, "his keeper or whatever." I barely get five steps down the block before he whirls around on his heel and plows right into me.

"Oh!" I yelp in surprise, trying to figure out what I'm going to say about why I'm following him from a bar and down the street in the middle of the night.

"Wow, lucky me," he slurs, "bumping into a hot girl like you."

It would mean more if his eyes weren't clamped tightly shut. In actuality, I'm red and splotchy from my run. My old Newton North High T-shirt is soaked with sweat, and stray bits of my hair have escaped from my bun and are glued to the sides of my face and my forehead.

Jason rubs his eyes as though he got maced.

"It's me, Julia," I snap, trying to pull his hands away from his eyes, but he resists. When I let go, his left fist snaps back kind of hard and he ends up punching himself in the eye.

"Ow!" he shouts, still rubbing his face. "Wazzat for?"

"It's for sneaking out of the hotel *again* without telling me," I snap. I use the hem of my T-shirt to wipe some of the excess sweat from my face as I sigh into the damp fabric. "And for getting so wasted—*alone*—that you apparently can't even open your eyes."

"Not alone! With friends! Lots of new friends . . . ," he says, trailing off, but I see no sign of these supposed friends around.

"Where are these awesome new friends?" I ask.

"Just left." He shrugs. "And I'm leaving, too." He takes a step down the sidewalk and promptly trips over his untied laces. I grab him before he can hit the pavement.

"You're not going to make it anywhere on your own in this condition," I say. I lean him against the wall of a small sporting goods store, then drop down to tie his laces. Quentin was right. I really *am* Jason's keeper.

"What are you, my mom?" he slurs, leaning into a nearby lamppost.

It comes out like "Whadda yous, my maaaam?" Apparently Jason has quite the Boston accent when he's drunk.

"Maybe you could use one," I retort, and he drops his hands from his eyes, which are watery and red. "What *happened* to you, anyway?"

"This guy bought me this shot and it was called a stuntman and when you do it you squirt a lime in your eye and it sounded like a weird idea but like the shot was free ya know and what kind of ugly American would I be if I turned down a free shot," he explains in one long, continuous sentence, only stopping to take a big gulp of air.

"Reaaally smart, kid ace," I reply, throwing his arm over my shoulder and guiding him back onto the sidewalk in the direction of the hotel. I wish I had thought to bring cash, because then I could shove him into a cab and be done with it. Instead, sweating from head to toe, with legs full of lead, I have to practically drag Jason through the streets. Jason is skinny, but he's still a head taller than me, which adds a lot of weight. Deadweight, which is now draped around my neck. As we're inching our way forward, he stumbles again and again. I glance down at the ground to see if maybe his shoes have come untied, but they're still in perfect double knots.

"Lissen," he says after falling with his entire body pressed into mine. "I was jus doin' some recon, ya know? Like a spy." He hiccups with his whole body, and I have to hold him tighter around the waist so he doesn't face-plant on the pavement.

"What are you talking about?" I grunt, making sure we're clear of traffic as I gingerly lead him across the street. TEEN TOURISTS FLATTENED BY DOUBLE-DECKER BUS. That would be a lovely headline for the hometown paper.

"I'm tawkin' about the Globe, Julia," he says like I know exactly what he's talking about. "Iss not justa name of some stupid, fake old musty theater that's not even the real one"—hiccup—"iss also this underground club. Ya know, like this cool place no one knows about! Maybe your dude, Chris, was there."

The more excited he gets about his inside info, the less steady he gets on his feet. He's gesturing wildly, and his hand brushes up against my boob. My face burns and an electric shock goes from my belly button to my spine, but Jason didn't notice, so I keep quiet and keep guiding him back toward the hotel.

"Isnit great, Julia?" I look up and he's beaming at me, happier than I've seen him in days. "We should check it out! Less go!"

"You are not checking out anything besides your bed," I say firmly. I take the next left onto Regent Street, a busy road populated by boutiques and restaurants. We're only three blocks away. Almost home.

He seems to be walking a little more steadily, so I loosen my grip. Jason takes that moment to lunge away from me and press his nose against the glass of a snooty-looking restaurant. A French name is painted in gold scroll across the window.

"Look, Julia! Meat! I love meat!" He starts tapping on the window like it's a fish tank, pointing toward a middle-aged couple in front of us who are feasting on what looks like a leg of lamb. They look pretty pissed, no doubt because they did not order a side of drunken teenage boy.

I grab his arm and try to tug him up the street, but he resists me. I get closer, putting my arm around his waist again, and start to pull. I mouth an apology to the couple in the window. Then my gaze lands on something sequined sparkling just behind the woman. My stomach drops into my toes. It's a silver sequined bolero jacket, and it's draped across the shoulders of a frizzy-haired woman who is sitting across from a tall, thin, balding man in a three-piece suit.

Mrs. Tennison.

I feel a dual urge to laugh and scream. Apparently it's not all tea and crumpets for our chaperone. I don't know what shocks me more: that

Mrs. Tennison snuck out, too, or that she's apparently getting more action than me.

She's waving her empty wineglass in the air and trying to get the attention of a waiter who is bustling his way toward the window, probably to command Jason and me to clear off.

As soon as her head starts to pivot toward the window, I grab Jason by the back of his shirt and yank him to the pavement. Fortunately, he's not in any condition to do anything other than crumple.

"Hey," Jason says. He tries to stand again and I pull him to the ground. "Watcha doin'?"

"Resting," I say.

"Yeah, I need a rest, too," he says. He leans his head on my shoulder and sighs. "This is nice."

"Yup," I reply. I place my hand on his head to keep him from popping up into Mrs. Tennison's sight line. "It's nice, until our chaperone comes out and finds you drunker than a cast member of an MTV reality show."

"MTV sucks," Jason mumbles.

Even though I agree, I ignore him. "Now here's the plan. You and I are going to scooch down the sidewalk until we're away from the window. Then we're going to walk back to the hotel, where you can go to sleep laying on your stomach like you're supposed to, okay?"

Jason nods rapidly. "You have great plans, Julia."

"It's about time you noticed," I mutter. I grab him by the hand and drag him with me while I crab-shuffle along the wall of the building. He shakes me off, then rolls over and crawls sloppily behind me. When we've moved away from the restaurant, I haul him back onto his feet, throw my arm around his waist, and propel us both down the last three blocks to our hotel. As we make our way through the revolving door, Jason pancakes himself to me, his chin resting on my head, his arms wrapped tight around me. He smells like grape gum, stale beer, and some kind of spicy cologne that makes me lean in for another whiff. I try to breathe through my mouth so I can stay focused on the task at hand. When we get all the way around, Jason lunges toward the lobby without letting go of me and we both tumble onto the plush red carpet. I say a little prayer that none of our classmates are around, and a quick glance tells me that for once my prayers have been answered.

"Julia, help me," Jason whines from the floor, his arm stretched up to mine as I scramble to my feet. I grab his hand, haul him up, then guide him straight to the elevator. I punch the button to summon the elevator so hard one of my fingernails bends backward, and I jam my finger into my mouth to dull the pain.

"Are we home yet?" Jason mumbles.

"Just about," I reply. "Are you seriously this drunk?"

"Eh," he says, waving me off. "Iss not so bad. 'Specially now that you're here. You're the best buddy ever. The best!"

"Well, I try," I say. "Almost home." I hope we can get upstairs before anyone sees us.

The elevator arrives after what feels like an eternity. When the brass doors slide open, I say a silent prayer of gratitude that it's empty. I shove Jason onto the elevator and leap on right behind him. Instead of plopping down on the plush red bench inside, Jason opts to drape himself back over me for the brief ride upstairs. I sigh, putting my arms around his waist so he doesn't fall down.

"Thanksh, Jules," he mumbles into my hair.

As the elevator doors slide shut, I shoot one final glance into the lobby . . . and see Sarah Finder. She's by the reception desk, but she's turned straight toward us. Her arms are crossed, her hip cocked to one side, and she's giving me the evilest of evil eyes.

"Excellent," I mutter as the doors finally close and we're gliding upstairs. As if my problems weren't huge enough, now I've got Sarah to contend with. Again. I should wake up to some friendly texts from her tomorrow, I'm sure, and probably some crazy stares from the rest of my classmates. Wonderful. Life was much easier when my name was on some kind of gossip blacklist. Who knows what people are saying about me now? I need to ask Phoebe for a report from the home front. Thank God Mrs. T forbade Twitter updates on this trip.

The tiny elevator is full of the smell of his cologne, whatever it is. Thankfully it conceals the smell of my sweat.

As soon as the elevator reaches our floor, Jason bolts out and down the hall. Great, *now* he can walk on his own.

I run after him, catching him right in front of his door. He's pulling his stolen spare room key out of his pocket and trying to jam it into the little mechanical slot. He keeps missing, though, and trying to push it straight through the wooden door itself, the key card falling to the carpet at his feet.

"Here, let me," I sigh, but I bend down at exactly the same time he does and we bash heads.

"Ouch!" Jason starts to laugh. "Your head is haaard."

My patience has almost completely run out, so I pluck the card off the ground, jam it into the lock, and push the door open. Jason stumbles in first. I hesitate for a second, then decide I should probably follow. I'm trying to remember what we learned in health class about "overconsumption." I *think* I'm supposed to make sure he doesn't sleep on his back.

Inside, Jason falls onto his bed, freshly made, thanks to a visit from housekeeping. I head straight into his bathroom and grab a glass, which I fill with cool water. On my way out, I snag the small trash can from under the counter and place it next to his bed. Just in case.

"So comfy," he mumbles.

"I know," I reply, arranging the glass of water on his nightstand. "I can't wait to get in mine."

"Is yours comfy like mine? I bet it's not."

"I'm sure all the beds came from the same distributor and are thus identical in their . . ."

"C'mon. Try it out." He looks up at me through narrow eyes and pats the vacant spot next to him.

"I don't think so," I say, my cheeks flaming. I point to the water. "That's for you. Drink up."

Jason rolls over onto his stomach. "Don't need it. Feel great." His voice is slightly muffled by the piles of pillows all around him. "You're the best. Have I said that yet? Because you are. The best."

"Yup, thanks," I reply, brushing my hands off on my shorts. "Okay, well, good night. Don't sleep on your back, okay?"

I don't get a reply. Within seconds, he's snoring.

I leave his key on the bedside table where he's sure to find it in the morning, then reach into my pocket to fish out my own.

Only there's no key in my pocket.

In fact, there's hardly a *pocket* in my pocket: my fingers slide through a big tear in the lining and straight out the leg of my shorts. Oh God. My hands and feet are starting to feel a little tingly as the reality of the situation is beginning to set in.

I don't have my key.

I close my eyes and can instantly picture the tiny white card lost somewhere in the streets of London along my twisting, turning running route.

"Oh, frig," I mutter to myself, and Jason snorts from his bed.

"Just say the bad word, Julia," he mumbles. Apparently he's *not* quite asleep.

I take a deep breath and think through my options. I could try to convince the front desk to give me another key, but there's a fine for a lost key, and Mrs. Tennison will know that I was out of my room at (I glance at my watch) twelve o'clock at night. Great. I look back at Jason, sprawled almost spread eagle across the comforter. A little puddle of drool is starting to form on the pillow. There's no way I'm getting in there with him.

I grab one of the pillows from the pile on the floor and the decorative throw that's draped over a chair in the corner. Since Jason's bathtub, unlike mine, is located in his bathroom, the foot of the bed is taken up by an oversized rug. I create a little makeshift bed and curl up for the night.

But after only fifteen minutes, I know there's absolutely no way I'm falling asleep. The rug has these little decorative knots in it that keep digging into my back. Plus I can't get out of my mind the fact that I'm sleeping on the *floor*, which is where people walk with their dirty feet. I practically have feet all over me. So I just lie there, blinking at the dark ceiling overhead, knots digging into my back and feet crawling all over me.

I can't do this. But my only other option is . . . and I can't . . . I won't . . .

I pop my head up at the foot of the bed to see that Jason has curled up on his side, taking up exactly half of the queen-size bed. There's enough space that I could climb in next to him without actually *touching* him.

I take a deep breath and ease onto the bed. He barely stirs as I lie down. I'm so tense that I worry I won't be able to fall asleep, but within seconds exhaustion grips me and pulls me under into dream.

16

Eye for an Eye, Text for a Text

Ah well. "the course of tru luv never did run smooth."
;) —C

A sliver of light is shining directly into my eyelids. It burns, and I try to pull the covers up over my head, but I can't, because I'm sleeping on top of them. No covers? How am I not cold? I always get cold without covers. . . .

My eyes creep open and I see a pile of dirty laundry on the floor in the corner. Why didn't I fold my clothes last night? I squint harder at the pile. My jeans don't have holes placed in them by Abercrombie & Fitch. . . .

Then I remember where I am. I'm in Jason Lippincott's room. And I know why I'm not cold. I'm lying on my side, my cheek nestled in a heavy feather pillow. My knees are bent and tucked up toward my chest. I feel warm and cozy, like I'm sleeping in a giant hug.

Then it hits me: I *am* in a giant hug. The weight over my waist is an arm. And that's not a pillow tucked up in my knees. It's another set of knees. Ohmygod. I think I'm spooning. With Jason. I'm spooning with

Jason, and his face is buried in my hair and I can feel his breath on my ear and OHMYGOD I'M SPOONING WITH JASON.

If there were a red light and a siren in my brain, you'd be able to hear the screeching and see the flashing all the way back in Boston. I have exactly eleven minutes before our class is supposed to meet in the lobby for some cultural hours touring. I still don't have a key to my room, and there's no way I, rumpled and half-asleep, can sneak down to the lobby to get a key, change, and make it back downstairs in time.

As much as I want to bolt straight out of bed, I don't want to risk waking Jason and confronting the fact that I slept (oh my God) in his arms last night. So I carefully reach over and slowly shimmy my way across the mattress, careful not to disturb him. I'm nearly home free, about to swing my feet onto the floor and make a run for it, and I hear a snort and a cough coming from the other side of the bed. Jason's arm flings across the mattress, hooking me around the waist and pulling me clear back across to him. All that work, and I'm spooning with him again.

I start my escape again, slower this time, but I barely get an inch away before I hear him mumbling. It's muffled, but I definitely hear the words "another kiss" coming from his pillow.

OH. MY. GOD. I'm spooning with Jason Lippincott and he's dreaming about kissing? I give up on the slow and steady and instead launch myself off the bed. I land on the floor, my butt cushioned by a stray pillow that was apparently flung aside at some point in the night.

I spring up and catch a glimpse in the mirror and curse myself for ever leaving my room last night. I'm still wearing my neon running shorts and the "Reading Is Sexy" T-shirt that I wore all day yesterday. I'm not sure if I'm popular enough for people to notice my attire, but I do *not* care to find out today. Besides, Sarah saw Jason and me stumbling upstairs together last night. If she sees me in the same clothes today, there will be no end to the rumors, much less the barrage of text messages. Thankfully, my phone was in the *other* pocket.

The floor is littered with various articles of clothing. I start plucking things up off the carpet, holding them between my thumb and forefinger while I sniff for freshness. I recoil in horror when I realize that some of these shirts are definitely *not* fresh. I drop to my hands and knees, crawling around in search of something–anything–that is clean, or even semi-clean. I finally strike gold when my hand lands in a pile that's been kicked halfway under the bed. I sprint for the bathroom and throw on the green 2008 Celtics Championship tee, which falls well below my knees. If I had a belt, I could pass it off as some kind of minidress (and probably look trendier than I have all week), but beltless I'll just have to hope that homeless chic is still a thing. I run my fingers through my tangled hair, pulling the elastic off my wrist and winding it into a messy bun. I splash some cold water on my face and make a valiant attempt at brushing my teeth with a squeeze of Jason's toothpaste and my index finger. When I step back and survey my appearance in the mirror, I still look like roadkill. The shirt is a wrinkled mess and about six sizes too big. My cheeks are splotchy, with the impression of the pillow, and chunks of my hair poke out of the bun at severe angles. My shorts feel grimy from an entire day (and night) of wear, but there's nothing I can do. I have to go.

I emerge from the bathroom to see Jason still dead asleep on the bed. If I don't wake him up, he'll miss the trip. If I do . . . well, then I have to face him and possibly explain how I ended up in his bed all night long.

"Sorry, Jason," I whisper, grabbing his fleece off the back of a chair and creeping out the door.

Mrs. Tennison doesn't hand back our keys until we are all gathered in the lobby, ready to head out to Notting Hill. For someone who was up late last night having her own illicit adventures, she looks surprisingly chipper.

"Where's your buddy?" she asks me as she finally presses my key into my hand. It's clear that I am out of the doghouse with Mrs. T.

"He's not feeling so well," I blurt out. This is the understatement of the century. "He thinks he might have a stomach flu or something."

As Mrs. Tennison narrows her eyes at me, I do my best "I'm Innocent!" expression. Hey, it worked in third grade after I accidentally dented Mrs. Hardwell's Toyota hood during a game of stickball. I somehow managed to convince her that a squirrel must have pegged it with a massive acorn.

"That's a shame," Mrs. Tennison says finally. "I hope he hasn't given it to you."

This is how I end up third-wheeling it with Ryan Lynch and Susan Morgan. Sarah gives me a scathing look and whispers something to Evie. My cheeks begin to burn. I remember how she saw Jason draped around me in the elevator last night. Oh God . . . if she somehow figures out we slept in the same bed . . .

I take a deep breath. Nobody knows. Nobody will know. Nothing happened.

Mrs. Tennison shoos us out the door and points us in the direction of the nearest tube station.

"Where are we going?" Evie's voice quavers. Today's excursion was noted on the agenda as "shopping." Clearly, the idea of a luxurious day spent in the finest boutiques in London is getting her all worked up.

"We're headed to Notting Hill," Mrs. Tennison replies, constantly counting and recounting our group as we make our way up the street.

"Like in the movie?" Sarah squeals.

"What movie?" Mrs. Tennison asks, and Sarah just stares at her, mouth gaping. Mrs. Tennison shakes her head and returns to her unceasing head count. "We'll be exploring the street markets, home to some of the most exciting and interesting antiques in the world!"

"Antiques?" Evie cries. I can practically see visions of cashmere and

Jimmy Choos melting away before her eyes. I know from my reading that it also features a pretty impressive secondhand clothing market, but I don't want to give her the pleasure of knowing. Besides, Evie hardly ever wears the same outfit twice; she definitely wouldn't be down with vintage.

I smile thinking about all the used-book shops in Notting Hill. I'll have to settle for browsing, since all my money is in my broken purse in my locked-up room. It's going to be a long day.

✴ ✴ ✴

Unfortunately, with Ryan and Susan, used-book shops do not appear to be on the agenda. I try to lead them into a crowded, narrow shop with a shockingly blue facade, but Susan rolls her eyes, grabs Ryan's arm, and drags him off down the street. It's soon clear I won't be observing any impressive antiques today. It appears I'll have to write my reflection paper on the awkward flirting techniques of one Susan Morgan, with footnotes detailing the equally awkward behaviors of Ryan Lynch, the object of her apparent affection, and his inability to pick up on a single clue. Part of this intricate mating dance appears to be a strict adherence to the belief that I'm not here at all.

At least I don't have to worry that they'll notice I'm clad in Jason's clothes. They wouldn't notice me even if I ripped off this shirt and ran around the market in my bra, arms over my head, laughing maniacally. I've never slept in the same bed as a guy before. Which makes Jason, literally, the first guy I've ever slept with. *That* thought makes me want to scream or wet my pants or transfer schools.

I spot Sarah at a stall full of jewelry made out of broken clock pieces and quickly duck around a different vendor's stall to avoid her. I'm bracing myself for another mean text from her. In fact, I'm somewhat surprised it hasn't already binged in my in-box. The only text I've gotten today is from Chris. I haven't written back. How can I? I have no idea what to say to him.

While Susan stops to buy an ice cream from a street vendor, I finally get the opportunity to look around a little more closely, and I spot a table filled with rows of teacups and matching saucers. Each one is made of delicate porcelain and hand painted with brightly colored floral arrangements. It looks like if you breathe on them too hard, they'll shatter into a million pieces. They look so fragile and vulnerable out here in the open. I close my eyes and instantly have an image of Jason executing some kind of ninja kick for fun, accidentally flipping the table and sending shards of porcelain raining down on the road. I open my eyes to see the cups all still intact and feel weirdly disappointed.

Oh my God.

Am I actually *missing* Jason? Okay, maybe not *missing* him, exactly. But I realize that without him, these tours are definitely less exciting. Maybe it's Susan's ridiculous mooning over Ryan, or maybe it's that I've never gotten giggly over shopping, but I'm bored out of my mind.

"Um, are you *coming*?"

Susan is dragging Ryan up the road by his sleeve again, a melting ice cream cone in her free hand. I sigh and trudge along after them. I *have* to get out of here. All this flirting makes me want to barf.

I scan the crowd for Mrs. Tennison, who is luckily only two booths away, looking at porcelain figurines of farm animals. I walk over to where she's standing, holding up a sheep about the size of a fist with a creepy smile painted on its little sheep face.

"Have you ever seen such an adorable thing?" she asks. Oh, no. I should have known. Mrs. Tennison is one of those women who never quite outgrew their doll collections. I bet she collects embroidered pillows, too.

"Um, Mrs. Tennison? I'm not actually feeling so well," I say. I place my hand on my stomach, hoping this will help my cause. "I–I think I maybe did catch something from Jason." I try to think of something that will make the color drain from my face, but all I can think about is waking up next to Jason, which has the exact opposite effect. I can feel myself blushing like a madwoman.

"Hmmm." She frowns, setting down the sheep. "You do look slightly feverish."

Yes!

"I feel really hot," I say, going with it. I dab at my forehead like I'm about to break into sweats.

"Well, I'll put you in a cab, you should probably go back to the hotel and lay down," she says, taking my elbow and leading me down the street. "I certainly hope there isn't some bug going around, or you will all have a very uncomfortable flight home. Have you two been sharing food or swapping drinks?"

The thought of swapping spit with Jason is enough to make me choke a little, which only helps my cause. Mrs. Tennison rubs my back, muttering, "Oh dear," to herself and sighing.

* * *

"Welcome back, miss," the doorman says, holding open the heavy door to the hotel with a white-gloved hand.

I give him a weak smile. I don't feel like a "miss" this morning. First I woke up in a boy's bed; then I wore an outfit that was half-stolen, half-grimy; and *then* I lied to Mrs. Tennison about feeling sick. I just couldn't take watching Susan giggle at Ryan anymore while he lazily scoped out British hotties passing by.

When I get back to my floor, I stroll right past my own door and head straight for Jason's. I pound hard on the door; then–thinking back to my own hangover–I switch to a gentle knock.

"Jason?" I call softly, but loud enough that he can hear. "Jason, are you in there?"

The door flings open. Jason's wearing the same clothes he was wearing when I left him this morning, the same clothes he was wearing last night. His eyes are bloodshot, probably partly from the hangover and partly from that asinine shot he did. His red hair is sticking up in crazy clumps, a giant cowlick protruding from the top of his head. So much for never getting hungover.

"What?" he mumbles. He presses his hands to his temples in what may be an attempt to hold his brain still.

"You need food," I say, marching into the room past him. "You need to clean up, and you need some fresh air."

"Ugh," he grunts, throwing himself back onto the bed. I walk to the dresser and fling open the top drawer, but it's empty. Same with every drawer underneath it.

"Where are your clean clothes?" I ask with the efficiency of a drill sergeant. I am not taking my chances with the piles on the floor again.

He mumbles into his pillow and his hand falls out to his left, pointing toward the corner. I follow the point to see his suitcase, overflowing with wrinkled T-shirts and holey jeans. Of *course* he didn't unpack. I rifle through his suitcase and pick out a pair of jeans and a T-shirt, trying to ignore the fact that I've added a pair of navy blue boxers with battleships on them to the top of the pile. I toss the clothes onto the bed next to him.

"Get up," I say. "This will be good for you."

He makes another unintelligible noise into the bed that sounds like a cross between a grunt and a groan.

"Get up," I repeat, marching to the bathroom and turning on his shower. "This is your last chance before I start singing show tunes as loud as I can. And I'm a *terrible* singer."

He lies there for another moment, so I take a deep breath and launch into the opening lines of "Tomorrow" from *Annie*.

"Ahhhhh!" he yells, springing up off the bed. "Fine! Geez, they should send you to Guantánamo."

"Excellent," I reply, heading toward the door. I do *not* want to stick around for Jason's dropping his pants. "I'll be back in ten minutes. Please be showered and ready to go, or it's *Bye Bye Birdie* for you!"

I skip back down the hall to my room, suddenly in an excellent mood. I feel like I've stepped off the podium at a meet, a gold medal around my neck. Back in my room, I quickly swap Jason's oversized clothes and my dirty shorts for my favorite pair of cords and the Scottish wool sweater my mom got when she and Dad were here all those years ago. The sweater is older than I am; I found it in my mom's closet a couple of years ago and have been wearing it every winter since.

When I return, I see that there will be no need for more Broadway numbers. Jason is clean and dressed, though he still looks a light shade of green under his freckles, and his eyelids hang heavy as ever. I return his clothes, folded in a neat stack, to his dresser (the only items of clothing actually *in* his dresser, since everything else is tossed around the room).

Jason doesn't say much as we wander out of the hotel and down the street. In fact, he doesn't say anything at all except to grunt and point to a restaurant.

" 'Wagamama'?" I read off the sign. "I've never heard of it."

"Hangover food," Jason says.

"I thought you didn't get hungover," I reply.

"I said it takes a lot," he replies, pushing open the door to head inside. "And that's what I had. A lot."

Wagamama turns out to be this great noodle shop, and we both order heaping bowls of ramen with chicken and veggies. As Jason tucks in his meal, his color starts to return to normal. His eyes clear up a bit and that lopsided, lazy smile returns.

"So how did you get out of today's tour?" he asks me.

"I took a page out of the Jason Lippincott playbook and claimed to be sick," I reply. "And by the way, you have me to thank for getting you off the hook, too."

"Well played," he says into his soup. "I owe you one."

"Did you get some sleep?" As soon as I ask the question, I realize I'm inviting conversation about our super-awkward sleeping arrangement. Though I'm not even sure if he remembers it. He was pretty drunk when he fell asleep, and I left before he woke up.

"Yes, thank God," he says, abandoning his chopsticks for a nearby spoon. "I slept like a baby. Probably the best sleep I've had in a while. You?"

"Uh, yeah, good." I blush, wondering if he knows that I stayed in his room. In his bed. The little spoon to his big spoon.

"You laugh in your sleep."

My head snaps up from my lunch. So he does know. "I what?"

"Yeah, don't get excited," he says, smiling to himself. "It's not cute. It's kind of creepy. More like a cackle. You *are* whacked, Book Licker."

"Oh, shut it," I say, tossing my chopsticks wrapper at him. It lands right in his bowl, which is almost all broth now. He picks it up and tosses it back, but his hangover has affected his aim. It sails right over my shoulder.

I tell him about my shopping trip with Ryan and Susan, and he jokes that they need to buy themselves new personalities. I tell him he was lucky to sleep through it and I wish I could have claimed the same.

"You can sleep in tomorrow," he offers. "I'll cover for you. Tell Mrs. Tennison you got lost in a gigantic encyclopedia or something."

"No way! I cannot *wait* for tomorrow's tour," I say, ignoring the jab. "It is seriously going to be the highlight of the entire trip."

"What's tomorrow?"

"It's the Stratford-upon-Avon trip," I say, shocked that he doesn't remember.

"Oh yeah. Right. What's so great about visiting Shakespeare's old crib, huh?" Jason asks. He slurps broth from his spoon with such force that bits of it spray back onto the table.

"Shakespeare is probably *the* greatest writer of all time," I say. "It'll be inspiring to see where he came from. Maybe he wrote some of his sonnets there. 'Shall I compare thee to a summer's day—'" I break off, embarrassed.

"I guess so," Jason mumbles before tilting his bowl into his mouth to finish off the broth. I make a face at him.

"I know *you* don't believe in love, but I do," I reply, lining my chopsticks up neatly next to my empty bowl. "And Shakespeare knew exactly how to write about it. Chris would understand. I bet *he* appreciates Shakespeare."

"Why, because he's British? I think that's racist." I look up to see the edges of his mouth turned up. He's teasing me. That's a good sign. He looks up from his noodle bowl. "Hey, I never said I don't believe in love. I just don't think it comes in perfect, predictable packages."

I roll my eyes at him for the ten zillionth time, and he ignores it for the ten zillionth time. It's an exchange that's starting to feel routine, and almost comfortable. Even with the soup slurping and the teasing, I'm much happier now than I was this morning, though I'm sure that's mostly to do with my bespectacled text friend and tomorrow's Stratford trip.

"So what's next, Book Licker?" Jason asks as we make our way out onto the street.

"Well, first of all, you could can it with the 'Book Licker' stuff," I reply. "I lied to a teacher to come take you out to lunch. The least you can do is call me by my real name."

"Okay, okay. I didn't realize you were such a rebel," he says, laughing. "So what's next, *Julia*?"

I hadn't thought that far ahead. "I dunno, whatever you want to do, I guess. I really need to pick up another phone card. I don't know how much these texts are costing, but they can't be—"

"London Eye," he says, cutting me off midsentence.

"What?"

"The London Eye. I want to go on a ride," he says. I hesitate and he cocks an eyebrow. "You *said* whatever I wanted to do, and that's what I want to do."

It takes me a minute, but I finally cave. It's not like I'm *afraid* of heights, but . . . Okay, so I'm a little afraid of heights. The London Eye is mentioned in each of my five guidebooks (and in the three I left at home). It's the largest Ferris wheel in Europe, and each book mentions that the views are breathtaking. I was kind of hoping to take in its majesty from the ground, but it looks like that's not in the cards.

My dad always lamented that the Eye hadn't been built yet when he and Mom were here. He always said that on their next trip, they would take one ride for each year of their marriage, and Mom would smile and say, "We better get there before we're old and gray, then." I guess this means I should take ten rides in their honor, but one will have to suffice.

When we get to the London Eye, I realize it's not exactly a Ferris wheel—more like a Ferris wheel on steroids. Each windowed pod can fit at least twenty people, and the entire contraption creeps along so slowly it takes half an hour for it to complete a full revolution.

Jason pays for my ticket—"My idea, my treat," he says firmly—and we step on board. The pods are made up almost completely of windows, which the inhabitants can crowd around to view the Thames below and all of London laid out before them. A wooden bench takes up the middle of the space, but only one woman sits on it and I think that's because she genuinely *is* afraid of heights. She keeps taking deep breaths and periodically putting her head between her knees. I hope she doesn't barf, because I'm not sure I could take being trapped in a glorified hamster ball filled with stranger puke.

As we rise, I take in the view. It is truly spectacular. I've seen videos, bird's-eye views from past riders, but nothing can begin to compare. It reminds me of the scene in *Willy Wonka* when Charlie escapes the factory and flies high over the city in a glass elevator. The sky is clear blue. Fluffy animal-shaped clouds drift across the clear blue sky. I feel like we're going to end up straight in the belly of a fluffy cloud kitten. The tour boats cruising down the Thames look like toys as we get higher and higher. Even Big Ben starts to look tiny as we approach the peak. I almost expect Jason to make a joke about it.

"I used to love this thing when I was a kid," Jason says instead, and I look over to see him gazing out over the people on the ground, who are now little more than specks. "I think I was one of the first people to ride it. I haven't been back in ages."

"I didn't realize you'd ever visited London before," I reply, keeping my gaze, like his, on the city below us.

"Well, technically I haven't *visited*," he says, shrugging. "I'm a British citizen. My mom is English. So I guess it's not like I'm a tourist."

"I'm sorry, what?" I ask, taking my eyes off the view to stare at him in shock.

"It's a formality, really," he says, not meeting my eyes. "I mean, I have dual citizenship. I'm still an American."

I don't really know what to say. I never knew anything about Jason's real mother, but I figured she was your typical upper-middle-class Boston suburban mom. I never would have guessed she was British, and I certainly had no *idea* Jason was, too. I think about what he said the other day: *There's a lot you don't know about me.* He wasn't kidding.

I watch him closely, trying to judge how much I should pry, but he's completely distracted. He's staring over the Thames toward a small cluster of buildings to the left of the expansive green Buckingham Palace Gardens.

"See that little spire over there?" he asks abruptly. "The blue one that looks like it could almost be a little crooked? On top of that church?" I follow his finger to the spot in the distance, and sure enough, there's a little blue spire that has such an odd design it looks almost bent. I spot it as he drops his finger. He reaches into his back pocket and pulls out a leather wallet that's so old it's now mostly made of duct tape. He flips it open and extracts a small crinkled picture from inside. It has been cut and cropped to fit snugly next to his Newton North ID card.

It's a picture of London, taken from the roof of a building some-where. The whole frame is jammed with roofs and chimneys. He holds the picture up to the glass, and the scenery in the picture begins to line up with the view. The picture was taken from a much shorter distance than our spot up in the sky, so everything is larger, and I can easily make out the small crooked spire. He points to a little green roof about three over from the crooked spire.

"That's where I lived until I was five," he says. "Before my mom left and my dad moved back to the States."

There is a moment of stunned silence as I take in what he just said. So not only is Jason's mother British, but he actually *lived* in London? I always thought Newton was small enough that everyone knew every-thing about everyone else, but no one's ever mentioned Jason's living in the United Kingdom.

"What was it like living here?" I try to guess which of the little chim-neys belonged to him.

"I don't remember everything," he says, a slight smile creeping into the corner of his mouth, "or anything, really. Our house was pretty small, but I remember one Christmas how we still managed to wedge a giant Christmas tree into the corner. I made my mom string popcorn like I'd seen in the movies, and she kept poking herself in the finger. And while she was stringing popcorn, I was eating it off the other end. We never did get any popcorn on that tree." He's laughing to himself now.

"That sounds like a great memory," I say, thinking of my own Christ-mas memories from when my dad was alive. He always told me that kids who don't believe in Santa don't get any presents. On Christmas Eve, he always arranged for a neighbor to come ring our doorbell, and when I'd answer it, I'd find a pillowcase with a few wrapped gifts inside. Dad always made a big show about how Santa would come visit the especially good little girls and boys early. I believed in Santa, really believed, all the way up until Dad died.

"Yeah, those were the days," he says, though his chuckle now sounds a little harsh. He wedges the picture back into his wallet, then shoves the wallet into the back of his jeans. "Funny, now the only holiday memories of my mother are the Christmas cards she sends each year. I don't even know if she's the one signing them."

There's a moment of thick silence between us before he gestures again toward the little crooked spire. "Forty-two Ebury Street," he says. "Just thataway."

I glance at my watch, realizing we'll have plenty of free time once our ride is over before Tennison and the others make it back to the hotel. "Do you want to go over there and see it?" I ask. "We totally have time if you want to go check out the old neighborhood."

"Definitely not," he says, his tone suddenly sharp. I don't push any further. I want to say something to break the tension, but I can't come up with anything that isn't just plain silly. Instead, I fidget with my watch.

Suddenly, the London Eye jerks to a stop, our pod dangling midway over the river, and our little capsule shudders for a moment. A few people stumble, losing their footing slightly at the sudden stop in movement. Jason, hands buried in his pockets, stumbles into me. I try to jump back, but the couple behind me is in the way, and I bounce like a pinball back into his chest. I put my hands out and grab for his shoulders, but he's too tall and my hands end up on his waist.

I don't let go right away. I tell myself it's because I don't want to fall again, but the couple behind me has moved toward the middle of the capsule. There's plenty of space.

Jason's head is tilted straight down, and now, at last, he is looking at me. He holds my gaze for what feels like a full minute. There's heat coming from somewhere between us, and I shift awkwardly, feeling like I might start sweating. I finally let go of him and quickly look down at my shoes.

I open my mouth to say something, maybe apologize, but before I can find the right words, the pod shudders again and resumes its descent. I'm just as unprepared for this jolt as the first, but I push my weight back instead of forward. I'd rather fall on my butt than accidentally hug Jason again.

As I fall, though, Jason jerks his hands out of his pockets and reaches out. His arms circle *my* waist this time, and he pulls me upright with enough force to bring me back to his chest. The shock pushes some of the air out of my lungs. I have to breathe deep to fill them again. Our pod is gliding gracefully toward the ground, but still Jason doesn't let go. The feeling of his arms around me is becoming way too familiar, from the dancing at the bookstore to the spooning this morning in bed.

I'm losing my balance again; I start to tip backward, but Jason tightens his grip, pulling me upright and even closer. If I look at him, we'll be face to face, nose to nose. Instead, I focus on my sneakers, on my double-knotted laces, afraid of what might happen if I look up. After a few moments, his hands drop away, and I sense them shifting back into his pockets.

As our pod makes its way back toward the ground, I finally find the courage to glance up. He has turned away so that he's standing next to me again, looking out over the river below.

As we inch closer and closer to the ground, Jason turns back to me. "Do you think you might actually meet up with this Chris guy?"

I'm not really sure how to respond, partly because I don't know the answer myself and partly because I'm still stunned by what just passed between us. Because something did pass between us—I'm sure of it. I finally settle on an answer that seems honest and true.

"If it's meant to be, we'll find each other," I say before hopping off the still-moving capsule at the bottom. I trot up the path through the little park leading to Belvedere Road, and Jason is close behind me.

"Julia, I need to tell you something. I think—" he starts, but his phone buzzes in his hand. He glances down at the screen.

"What?" I ask. "What do you have to tell me?"

He studies his phone for another beat, absentmindedly pushing his bangs under his ball cap. "Never mind," he says. He tucks the phone back into his pocket. "It's nothing."

"You sure?" I study him, trying to see if I can decode his expression. He's already arranged his face into that crooked smile.

"Yup," he replies, taking off his hat and swiping a hand through his hair: casual, easy. "So that Stratford trip. That's tomorrow, huh?"

"Yeah," I say.

"So, little Miss Guidebook," he says, patting the bag that's on my hip. "Tell me some fun facts and trivia about Mr. Bill Shakespeare's birthplace."

"For real?" I say. Jason shrugs.

"We've got nothing else to do," he says.

I dig out my guidebook and flip to one of the many multicolored Post-it notes hanging out the side. We settle on a bench in the shadow of the London Eye, a line of trees overhead, and I start reading passages to him. As I read, Jason tilts his head back, his face pointed directly at the sky while he takes long, labored breaths. I worry he's using this opportunity to take a nap, but he blinks a few times, so I know he's awake.

I want to ask him about the stumble on the Eye, the tilt, the look, but I don't know if I want to know the answers. Instead, I plow ahead, reading about Henley Street and Shakespeare's birthplace. If he's going to ignore it, I will, too.

17

The Wild-Goose Chase

OMG—I think u might be right about ur MTB! It's F8.
We need 2 talk ASAP. Skype? —P

The bus speeds down the M40, passing towns with names that sound like they've come straight out of a Harry Potter novel, like Boltmore End and Tiddington. Mile after mile of vivid green rolls by. I can barely sit still in my seat. I even have to put my book back in my bag. For the first time in my life, I can't concentrate on *Pride and Prejudice*. Every time Mr. Darcy goes and says something smarmy, my memory flashes to Jason, then to the moment high over the Thames when Jason and I shared . . . what? A long gaze? An almost kiss?

Jason hasn't acknowledged me, other than to hip-check me out of the buffet line this morning to get a second slice of French toast. Despite Mrs. Tennison's directions to sit with our buddies on the bus, Jason skipped my seat and instead sat down in the row behind me, next to Sarah. Which means I'm stuck with Evie instead. Jason and Sarah have been tossing notes back and forth, giggling to each other and otherwise being obnoxious.

"No freakin' way!" Sarah exclaims with another explosive giggle.

"I wish they would just get back together already," Evie mutters into her copy of British *Cosmo*. "I mean, holy sexual tension!"

"Wait, what?" I can't tell what's more confusing: that Evie is talking to me (or *at* me), or what she just said. "What do you mean, 'get back together'?"

"Hello? Catch up, jeez. They used to date. Freshman year, remember?" Evie says, rolling her eyes with a "you don't know anything" scowl. She throws her feet up on the back of the seat in front of her and lazily flips a page. "And from the looks of things, a reunion is in the cards."

No wonder Sarah has been sending snarky texts all week! She wants Jason back and thinks I'm in the way. I'm *so not,* though. I am in no one's way when it comes to Jason.

Sure, sometimes Jason is nice, like when he sings Beatles songs in the park or dances in the aisles of a bookstore. But that's only about 10 percent of the time. The other 90 percent, he's making fun of me or—even worse—pretending I don't exist.

Still, the idea of Sarah and Jason together makes my stomach churn.

And that 10 percent . . . I mean, Jason was singing *to me* and dancing *with me*. Right?

I spend the rest of the bus ride with my thoughts careering over the past few days of our trip. Even though Jason and I have been searching for Chris and I know that Mark is my MTB, I can't stop thinking about Jason and Sarah together.

I close my eyes and command myself to think about Mark and his golden smile or even Chris, sitting in the café and casually pushing up his glasses as he pages through his pocket Shakespeare, but I've lost total control of my brain. I feel like I'm watching a movie of the last few days with Jason while someone holds the fast-forward button. The flashing images are starting to make me feel ill.

Thank God the bus soon shudders to a stop. One deep breath of fresh country air and a look around me, and it's hard to stay stressed.

The town is absolutely beautiful in that quaint, British-countryside kind of way, and I'm not going to let Jason (or anyone else, for that matter) stop me from enjoying it.

The bus has let us off near the Royal Shakespeare Theater, which is surrounded by cute little shops and gorgeous views of the River Avon. Unlike during most of our time in London, which has been stereotypically gray, the sun is shining brightly today, and the feeling of excitement I had when we left London this morning returns.

We make our way to Henley Street, where we find ourselves in front of an old half-timbered dwelling, surrounded by bright bursts of pretty wildflowers and lush gardens.

Shakespeare's home. It's what I've been waiting to see since the trip was announced, and now I'm so excited I seriously might wet my pants.

Unfortunately (and unsurprisingly), Shakespeare's birthplace appears to be a pretty popular tourist destination. Throngs of people crowd every path through the gardens and spill out onto the street. A family of five are having their picture taken near the door to the house, and a large on-deck area is packed with people holding cameras, waiting to do the same.

Mrs. Tennison waves us in the direction of the entrance, where yet another tour guide is waiting for us. I race to the front of the group. I've visited plenty of old historic sites in my life, and I know they tend to be pretty small and cramped. I'm not going to be the schmuck stuck in the back of the room straining to see and hear. I whip my notepad and a newly sharpened pencil out of my bag.

Our guide is a tall, thin man who looks to be in his midfifties. When he speaks, an odd tremor creeps into his voice, as though he is overtaken by nerves.

"Hullo," he says, clearing his throat. "My name is Bertrand. Welcome to the birthplace of William Shakespeare. I'm delighted to be giving you this tour today, as it's my first ever." He's trying his best to seem dignified, but he keeps giggling nervously.

My classmates start to snicker, but I resolutely ignore them. I've been obsessed with Shakespeare since I found my mother's heavy, dusty gilded copy of his collected works in sixth grade. I flipped straight to *Romeo and Juliet.* I'd heard of Shakespeare before, of course, but never read a single line of his plays.

I knew even then that writing like his was somehow important. I remember stumbling through the lines, having to read and reread them to make sense out of the language. Still, it took my breath away. I wanted to devour the play over and over again, followed by everything else he'd ever written.

Bertrand gestures for us to follow him inside, where he launches into a brief history of Shakespeare's life. Our guide might have appeared nervous at first, but as soon as he begins his speech, he becomes a different man. It's almost like Shakespeare himself, clad in an argyle sweater-vest, is leading us through his own home. Bertrand spouts stories about Shakespeare's lost year, gossips about his marriage to Anne Hathaway (maybe a shotgun wedding?), and peppers his presentation with quotes from some of Shakespeare's greatest works.

I'm in absolute heaven. I scribble so hard and so fast my pencil breaks and I have to quickly fish for another before I miss a single word. Let's be honest: Bertrand had me at "hullo," so my intricate system of check marks, asterisks, boxes, and bullets flows out onto the page. I find it easy to ignore everything else, Jason included. Especially Jason.

Okay, maybe that's a slight overstatement. Maybe, when I turn for a second to make sure that he hasn't gotten lost or, I don't know, arrested, and I see him chatting with Sarah and not even pretending to pay attention, maybe I feel a teensy nudge of disappointment.

Maybe I even feel a teensy bit jealous.

But I quickly squash it. *Stupid. You don't even like Jason. And of course he's with Sarah, because he's not your MTB, and he doesn't even care about Shakespeare. Mark. Marrrrk.* He *would get this. I know he would.*

"Now, students, if you'll follow me, we're going to take the short walk to Holy Trinity Church, where we'll be visiting Shakespeare's grave," Bertrand says, and with a slight flick of his hand directs us back out onto the street. "I don't have to tell you that the proper respect is required."

As if on cue, Jason and Ryan race to be the first through the door and end up wedged in the frame, shoulder to shoulder. Neither can budge until Susan comes up behind them and gives Ryan a shove, sending them both tumbling through the doorway. They end up sprawled on the walk, hysterically laughing. Mrs. Tennison rushes toward them, and as I pass, I hear her threatening them with extra essays.

That is one essay I will *not* be writing. I leave them to their scolding and hurry after our tour guide.

Bertrand leads the way down Henley Street. Mrs. Tennison and I march right on his heels; the rest of our class trudges behind us. The road is lined with old half-timbered cottages that look like if you blew on them too hard, they'd tip over and collapse. We reach the end of the road, wind around a little roundabout, and are dumped out at the top of High Street. The narrow road is crowded with shops, colorful awnings, and cafés with tables spilling out onto the sidewalk. Everything is called Something-or-Other Cottage or Ye Olde Whatever. It's touristy as all get out, but I don't care. I love it.

As we walk, I peer down side streets, hoping I might catch a glimpse of the tiny antique shop my mom has been describing to me forever. I must have heard the story a million times. Mom and Dad didn't get rings when they first got married, since Dad had just joined the marines and they were dirt-poor. They were wandering around the tiny town, no maps, playing "which way does this road go?" on the twisty streets. They came upon a tiny secondhand shop, where they found matching gold bands. Mom said it was a sign that they were on the right path. Neither ring needed to be sized a bit; they fit perfectly. They look like the gold was hand-molded, with little bumps and imperfections all around.

Dad always liked to show me how Mom's ring fit right down into his. Now both rings live in my mom's jewelry box, nestled in the blue velvet, her ring tucked inside his.

After a few blocks, the shops give way to little town houses and brick offices. The sidewalk narrows and we have to march down the road in a straight line, one after the other. We walk along quietly for a few minutes; then the lane widens and the trees grow dense. A church spire pokes up in the distance. We're standing at a wrought iron gate. A low stone wall surrounds a tree-lined property.

Bertrand signals for us to gather around, and once again I press myself practically under his nose, notebook poised and pencil prepped. We're about to visit Shakespeare's grave. If I knew how to genuflect, I would.

"Welcome to Holy Trinity Church, often referred to simply as Shakespeare's Church," Bertrand says after taking a deep breath and clearing his throat. "William Shakespeare was baptized here in 1564, and fifty-two years later he was interred here at a depth of twenty feet to prevent theft of his body."

"Oh, that's just gross," Evie says, and there are several soft snickers.

Quentin says, in his perpetual stoner's voice, "*Romeo-and-Juliet-meets-zombie-killer. All right!*"

"Braaaaiiiiinnnnnssss!" Ryan raises his arms toward Evie's head and lurches at her, his tongue lolling out to one side. She giggles and skips away, ducking behind Jason. Susan stands off to the side, pouting.

So much for respect. I inch away from my classmates and offer my most sympathetic look to Bertrand. I want him to know I'm on his side.

Once inside the church, everyone scatters. Susan drags Ryan up the center aisle toward the altar, looking like she's about to burst from happiness. He, on the other hand, looks like he'd rather be taking the SATs in Latin than standing at the altar with her. I don't blame him.

I make a beeline for Shakespeare's grave. A bust of him stands over the altar, a blue silk cord that marks his grave lining the stone floor. A plaque above it reads:

GOOD FREND FOR JESUS SAKE FORBEARE TO
DIGG THE DUST ENCLOASED HEARE.
BLEST BE YE MAN YT SPARES THES STONES AND
CURST BE HE YT MOVES MY BONES

I read the words again and again to myself. I imagine my parents standing here, barely twenty-two years old, newly married, Dad's arm draped over Mom's shoulder, Mom leaning into his chest. And once again, I'm struck by how much I want that. This time, when I close my eyes, I have no problem imagining Mark here with me, standing beside me, his arms around my waist. I lean back into the imaginary embrace—maybe a little too hard, because I actually start to fall backward.

"Whoa, Book Licker!" Jason's hand lands right on my back and shoves me upright. "Been sipping off the Communion wine?"

"Very funny," I say. I hate that when I open my eyes, *he's* the one standing behind me. I want to see Mark and his perfect crooked smile and his dark wavy hair, not Jason's smirk and his messy, shaggy red hair.

"Students, gather around!" Mrs. Tennison's nasally voice bounces off every surface of the church, driving daggers into our ears. I'm grateful to have a reason to escape Jason in this moment. Her itinerary is in her hand, and she is simultaneously studying it and using it to fan herself. She waves us out of the church and into the churchyard, which is shockingly green. The grass looks so full and fluffy I want to lie down in it, and looking around, I notice a few of my classmates already are. Sarah and Evie have taken residence under a willow tree and are whispering about something. (Please, oh please, don't let it be me.)

"Well, class, it appears I've miscalculated our itinerary today," Mrs. Tennison says, creases of worry forming around her eyes. Her hands are quivering, but that may be more attributable to the tea she's been mainlining since we stepped foot on British soil. This trip has definitely taken at least a decade off her life. I know from looking at the itinerary, oh, twelve or thirteen thousand times that we've got at least an hour before we can check into our hostel for the night. She is clearly not prepared to entertain twenty seventeen-year-olds for an hour. Mrs. Tennison eventually folds her stack of papers, crams it back into her carpetbag, and takes a deep, cleansing breath. "Looks like we'll be having an unexpected cultural hour."

People begin giving each other fist pumps and high fives. Ryan Lynch shouts, "Shakespeare rules!"

"*With* your partners!" Mrs. Tennison calls as we begin breaking up. "I mean it . . . *cultural* hour! I expect to see mention of what you've done in your reflection paper!"

Everyone starts pairing off and heading in different directions. I know I should go over to Jason, who is standing with Evie and Sarah, but I hate feeling like a little tagalong. I hear Sarah say something to them about shopping. Jason shakes his head, and Evie and Sarah scurry up the road back toward High Street.

Pretty soon Jason and I are the only ones left other than Mrs. Tennison, who sags onto a bench under a willow tree across the yard. Clearly, she needs a Zen moment.

We stand across the grass from each other for a few moments, Jason kicking at something invisible on the ground. After a torturous minute of silence, I can't take it anymore.

"Well, I guess we could go make rubbings of some of the gravestones, then write about the people buried there," I say.

"Graves? Dead people? Wow, you're a real ray of sunshine, J," Jason says. He unwraps a piece of gum, biting off half of it and then wrapping up the other piece. He shoves the remaining half back in his pocket, for later, I guess. Ick.

"Do you have any bright ideas?" All I want to do is ignore Jason. He has, after all, been ignoring me all day. Then I'll have time to look for my parents' antique shop, or daydream about Chris. I mean, Mark. I mean . . . well, both.

"Want to wander?" he asks.

"Wander?" I ask. I feel something in my messenger bag digging into my back. I heave it over my head and flip it open to see what's out of place.

"Yes! No guidebooks, no historical facts, just taking off in a random direction, without any specific reasons."

I find the source of the jab. It's my pencil case, which should go in *front* of my notebook, not behind it. I quickly rearrange things, then reposition my bag. Much better.

"I know what 'wander' means, *thankyouverymuch*." I don't mention that the only place I wander around in is the library. Hey, Google Maps was invented for a reason!

Jason fake-bows and gestures down the road in the opposite direction of Henley Street and the rest of our class. We fall into step in silence. He stuffs his hands deep into his pockets. His legs are long and his bobbing stride wide, and I have to work double time to keep up.

"So. Anything in particular you want to see?" he asks.

"I thought we were wandering," I say.

Jason holds up both hands. "Listen, you were the one getting all hot and bothered about coming here. I just want to make sure your literary fantasies come true."

"Well, I was hoping to find this little antique shop—" I start, but Jason doesn't let me finish.

"Oh, hell no," he says, stopping in his tracks. "If I wanted to go shopping, I would have followed Evie and Sarah."

I consider letting him know that this is *nothing* like shopping, but that would mean telling him about my parents. "Where do *you* want to go?"

"Nowhere in particular," he says. "I'm a fly-by-the-seat-of-my-pants kinda guy. You know. Carpe diem and all that. Never know what's going to happen next." I roll my eyes at him, but he has picked up his pace and doesn't see me. I sigh and follow him.

We take off down the road, away from our classmates, past a series of gardens. We stroll past the Royal Shakespeare Company but don't stop, because it's choked with tourists and children and cameras and backpacks. We "wander" along the river, where ducks paddle lazily and people in rented boats glide along the water. Jason and I have lapsed into silence, but it doesn't feel awkward. The scenery is so breathtaking that there really is no need for words, although I definitely see how Shakespeare produced such beautiful sonnets here. The grass smells freshly cut and sparkles under a layer of dew. There is a heavily sweet smell of flowers suspended over everything. Birds are chirping and frogs croak throatily underneath them, and I start to feel like if I sat down with my notebook and pencil, I might produce something great and beautiful, too. Everything is like a dream—until the sun gets eaten up by increasingly ominous-looking clouds, and it looks like any moment it may start to pour.

Jason leads us across a bridge to the other side, where the houses and shops give way to fields and paddocks, the roads getting narrow and the grass getting high. I don't want to ask, but as we get further and further away from town and deeper and deeper into who knows where, I can't help myself.

"Where are we going?" I ask.

"I said, 'wandering,'" he repeats, as if that's a proper destination.

We stumble across the Stratford Butterfly Garden and an old graveyard. It is getting darker by the second. I've never seen clouds move so fast before. I don't know why I ever think following Jason is a good idea. Even if he *did* know where he was going—which he obviously doesn't—he would still lead us straight toward trouble. I will never learn.

Jason starts trotting down the road as the sky opens up and sheets of rain begin driving down, hard.

"Do you know where you're going?" I call over the sound of thunder. We hardly need to hurry now; within thirty seconds, we're already soaked to the bone. Jagged lightning tears across the sky. Thunder booms and I jump.

"I think we can make it back to High Street quicker if we cut through Bancroft Gardens," Jason says, surveying the scenery.

"I don't know about that," I reply, mentally trying to conjure up the maps I'd pored over before the trip. What I wouldn't give to have my iPhone . . . "Besides, aren't you supposed to *avoid* open fields during lightning storms? I don't want to get electrocuted."

"Well, either you stand here in this rainstorm, or you take a chance with me," he says, and as if on cue, a clap of thunder echoes through the trees.

We hop the wet fence and set off through the tall grass. It's not a difficult walk for Jason, whose long legs stride effortlessly through the terrain, but my wee little legs are not as quick. It probably doesn't help that every time I hear thunder, I crouch down into the lightning-safe position we learned in fourth grade. What? I'm not taking any chances with my life! I have to incorporate little hops into my gait as I try to keep up with Jason. My sweater clings heavily to my skin, and my jeans are making suction-y sounds with every step. As we cross the field, the rain slows down to something more like a heavy mist. I've got my eyes on the ground, making sure I don't step into any puddles or holes, when I hear a noise that makes me stop short.

Jason charges ahead a few steps but quickly realizes I've fallen behind. "What's going on?"

"Did you hear that?" I ask. Sure enough, it happens again: like a horn honking, if the horn was thirty years old and covered in sawdust.

"What, the geese?"

"What?" I shriek, my eyes darting around. "Where?"

"Chill out," he says, chuckling. "They're not going to attack you."

"Are you sure?" I cross my arms. "I am not taking a single step unless you can swear to me–"

"There are no geese, you wuss," he interrupts, patting me on the top of my head like I'm a five-year-old. "No need to have a meltdown. What's your problem with geese, anyway?"

"I don't want to talk about it," I mutter, and take off ahead of him. I get about six or seven strides ahead when the ground levels out and I find myself face to beak with a flock of about nine geese, their beady eyes trained on me, mouths–or bills–curled up into demonic smiles.

I let out a loud, long bloodcurdling scream. I whirl around and take off at a sprint, no longer paying attention to how much work my short legs have to do to get me through the mud and the grass or how I could get struck by lightning at any second. I hear the heavy stomp of Jason's footsteps behind me.

"Slow down!" he manages to choke out. "Julia, wait!" He runs a little farther before doubling over and starting to laugh hysterically. I pull back, running straight toward him.

"You jerk!" I give him a hard punch in the arm, which I doubt he feels, what with all the hiccupping and chortling. "You said there were no geese!"

"I didn't see them!" he says through wild gasps. "That was an incredible scream. I thought you'd seen a dead body! Holy wow!"

"Can we please get out of here before–" I start, but I'm too late. Thunder booms again while lightning zigzags across the sky. The mist turns all at once to liquid, and it begins to pour again. Jason seems not to have noticed, as he's still laughing hysterically. No doubt we could both be electrocuted and he would still be laughing. I don't know why I've trusted this stupid "wandering" plan for this long. I dig for my phone, then find Mrs. Tennison's number in the address book. I've been in the United Kingdom a week, and I've yet to use my phone for any legitimate reason.

But when I hit the green button to call for directions, my phone beeps and a message appears on the screen.

0 Minutes Remaining

"What!" I shout, literally stomping my foot in the puddle that has formed around me.

"What's your problem?" Jason asks, finally pulling himself together.

"Well, besides standing in a field, lost, in the pouring rain, about to get attacked by disease-carrying birds or possibly electrocuted by lightning," I snap, "my phone is out of minutes."

"Wow," Jason says, looking at the blank screen. "I would have thought someone like you would have planned ahead enough to reload it before we left the hotel."

"I probably would have," I snap, tightening my grip on the phone so I don't throw it at his stupid head, "but I think your immaturity is rubbing off on me."

"I know you are but what am I?" he retorts, crossing his eyes and poking me in the ribs.

"Please shut up and give me your phone," I say, holding my hand out. Damp strands of hair keep getting glued to my lips.

Jason abruptly stops laughing. He gives me a strange look. "My what?"

"Your. Phone," I say, enunciating each word slowly. "We're lost, and I want to get us out of here as fast as possible. I can call Mrs. Tennison for directions. Or you can call."

"I don't think that's a good idea," he says, turning away from me.

"Why not? She's not going to be mad," I say, following after him. "I mean, not if you give her one of those silly Boy Scout salutes that seems to get you out of so much trouble."

"Look, if we call her, she's going to know we weren't experiencing the culture of Stratford-upon-Wherever-We-Are. Besides, we don't *need* directions. If we keep walking, we'll get there eventually," he says, picking up the pace through the field. I have to accelerate to a jog to keep up.

"I don't want to stomp through the mud and rain any longer than I have to," I say. "Either you make the call, or I'll make it for you."

"Unlikely," Jason says, marching forward.

"Jason, this is dumb," I call, my voice rising with my anger. "Just give me your damn phone!"

"No!" he yells over his shoulder.

"No?"

"No!" And then he's breaking into a full-on run.

"Jason!" I shout, stamping my foot in the mud. "This is *so not the time* for a game of keep-away!" But he's not stopping, so I take off after him, and he underestimates my swimmer's legs at a full sprint. I'm close enough that I could reach out and grab a handful of his fleece. Without thinking, I take a flying leap onto his back. At first he keeps running, me clutching him in a sort of bizarro piggyback ride, but then he stumbles. We both crash to the ground. I dig my hand straight into his pocket and pull out his phone.

"Hey!" he shouts, and just like back in the Tate, he flips himself over in two moves, and suddenly, I'm on my back, in the mud, wetness seeping through my sweater. The air goes out of my lungs, and while I'm gasping for a breath, he snatches the phone and flashes that obnoxious, lopsided grin. He holds the phone high over his head and grins down at me, his blue eyes locked on mine in what looks like pure triumph.

"Let me up!" I scream, trying to wriggle out from underneath him.

But he doesn't. And then something changes and I realize Jason's lying on top of me, staring at me, and his lips are inches from my lips, and there is rain dripping off his hair, curling it around his ears, running down onto my neck.

My heart pounds and I feel the tingle starting in my toes again.

Jason drops his phone in the grass and uses the free hand to brush a fat, wet curl out of my eyes. His fingers brush my cheek and I feel that pull in my belly button that goes straight through to my spine. As he tucks the hair behind my ear, his hand cups my chin. It's surprisingly soft, and I nuzzle lightly against it. He leans down slightly, then pulls back a bit.

So many thoughts are whirling around in my head at once, I can't hold on to any of them. Is he—? Does he want to—? Do I want to—?

Are we going to—?

And then he's kissing me. His lips press against mine, hard at first, hungry, and for once I'm not worried about what is happening or whether this is the right thing to be doing. I relax into it, enjoy it, float away. His tongue gently traces my upper lip. I part my lips, but instead of jamming his tongue down my throat like Billy Russell did when we were at the multiplex in eighth grade, Jason lets it venture slowly into my open mouth. I sigh into the kiss, my arms around his waist, my fingers digging into the wet fabric of his T-shirt. He kisses me for what seems like hours, until I can barely catch my breath. I can hear thunder in the background, but suddenly, it no longer matters. I feel like the ground is opening up and pulling us down inside. The weight of everything rests on top of me, but I don't feel crushed. I want more. I pull him closer, harder, heavier.

Jason finally pulls away, and I blink at him. I want to ask him why he kissed me, and whether he meant it, and what it means. But I decide it's probably best to keep my mouth shut so an unending stream of gibberish doesn't pour out. Jason rolls over to the side of me, propping himself up on his elbow, as though we're lying on a sun-drenched field instead of a mud pile with what has become a very light drizzle falling down on us.

"Can I ask you something?" he asks. My stomach drops, and I wait for the inevitable "who the hell taught you to kiss like *that*?" inquiry.

"Yeah," I reply, bracing myself, but Jason comes out of left field.

"Seriously, what's with the geese?"

I look up to see his eyes flashing, his mouth set in a tight line to suppress his riotous laughter.

"Oh, it's a dumb childhood thing," I say. I roll over onto my stomach, then lay my cheek down in the wet grass. My mind is still swirling, my heart still racing.

"Come on, you know I'm still basically a dumb child," he says, giving me a poke in the ribs. "Spill."

So I tell him the story, a mixture of my fuzzy little-kid memories and the endless rehashings from my parents. As I talk, I remember how my dad used to act out chasing the damn bird away, me tucked safely in his arms, both of us screaming back at a little goose. By the time I finish the story, Jason and I are both flat on our backs in the grass, clutching our stomachs in laughter.

"Your dad sounds like an awesome guy," Jason says when his laughter has finally slowed.

"He was," I reply, sighing deeply.

"Was?" Jason props himself up on an elbow. I can feel him staring at me.

"He died when I was seven," I say, my eyes trained on the sky above me.

"Oh, right. I'm sorry," he whispers, reaching his arms out and pulling me close. He buries his face in my hair, planting a soft kiss on my temple. I reach up and grab on to his arm, which is circled around my chest. I give it a squeeze, simultaneously blinking back tears. I breathe deeply, taking in full breaths of thick, damp, grassy air. I can't believe it, but lying in the grass, enveloped by Jason, is better than being in any hotel bed or swimming pool could ever be. I don't care that I'm shivering from my damp clothes and the cool wind. I don't care that I'm covered in so much mud I could build my own hut. I don't care that my hair has probably wound itself into such a tight knot I may have to shave my head. I close my eyes and settle in, ready to lie here forever.

I take a deep breath, breathing in the air, heavy with the smell of rain. Jason hasn't said anything for a few minutes. My heart is pounding out of my chest, but I have to ask.

"Jason, does this mean—" but the question catches in my throat. I feel fat raindrops roll down my face, sticking to my eyelashes.

"We should—" Jason says, and the rest of his sentence is cut off by a clap of thunder. We both scramble to our feet. Jason grabs my hand and takes off running. I don't know if he knows where he's going (I certainly don't), but I'm happy to be pulled along. My feet sink deeper into the mud with each sprint, splashes flying up my legs. My jeans are fully soaked, and mud is caking deeper and deeper in my sneakers, but I don't care. I shake my curls, heavy with rain and covered with grass and mud, and they slap across my face, sticking in my wide smile. We run clear across the expansive field. I fall into a perfect pace with him, grasping his hand tightly, thinking back to that first night in London when we ran from the house party, thinking of how much has changed.

We slow to a stop underneath a huge shade tree, a bright blue bike leaning against its trunk. It's one of those rickety old cruiser styles, and it looks like there's more rust than bike there. Jason quickly tests the wheels, giving it a few rolls, before climbing on.

"Hop on," he says, his wet hair plastered across his forehead.

"Where?"

"Right here," he says, patting the slippery handlebars as I raise my eyes at him. "What, you want to stay out here?"

I look up. All I can see is a sheet of gray clouds.

"Are you hoping the sky is going to drop a helmet?" Jason says, teasing me.

"Or a Volkswagen," I mutter, giving the sky one last look. "Fine, fine. I guess it's safer than hitchhiking." I scramble up onto the handlebars, and as I try to settle in, Jason grabs my shoulders and gives me an effortless lift. Next thing I know, we're speeding down the narrow lane back toward town.

18

Meant to Be or Not Meant to Be, That Is the Question

I've made a HUGE mistake —J

We're staying in Stratford for the night, in a little hostel that has the personality of a mental hospital. The walls are white; the beds are white; the sheets and towels are white. I'm sharing a room with half the girls on the trip, packed into bunk beds like we're booked on a steamer ship. My bed is old and metal, and every time I turn over, it squeaks. And I'm turning over *a lot*. Everyone in this room probably hates my guts. I say a little prayer that they all sleep like the dead before turning over for the billionth time. I can't help it. My brain won't quiet enough for me to fall asleep.

I want my mom. She's a champion at calming me down, a skill she's honed over years of dealing with my minor freak-outs. I want nothing more than to be home, curled up on the couch, watching TiVo and eating animal crackers, under the big afghan that Gramma Lichtenstein made for me when I was born.

But I don't have the afghan. Instead, I have this awful, scratchy hostel blanket that smells like asparagus and bleach.

Every time I close my eyes, I picture the kiss. It comes with such intensity that I can practically feel it. It was the perfect kiss in every way except for one: it was with Jason Lippincott. Was that supposed to happen? Was that meant to be? Is *he* meant to be? This whole time I've been chasing after Chris, but I haven't gotten any closer to him. I *have* gotten closer to Jason, apparently. Close enough to lock lips. And then I'm off again, reliving the rain and the grass and the kiss.

But just as soon as I'm feeling blissful, I hear Jason's voice in my ear calling me Book Licker. I hear him telling me that finding the one is "bullshit." I hear his dirty jokes about Big Ben and see him stringing himself up to a wall and embarrassing the living hell out of me. I even picture him depositing tampons in my locker in ninth grade and scrawling on Phoebe's painting.

This was clearly not meant to be. I mean, sure I've learned to tolerate Jason on this trip, but I still fundamentally don't want to be around him. I'm pretty sure that as soon as we get back to the States, we'll go right back to ignoring each other. We are not friends. We are less than not friends. We don't have anything in common.

My MTB won't be an annoying, immature, uncultured, dirty-joke-making boy like Jason. He won't be an attention whore who is spending every waking minute trying to be the loudest person in a room. He won't be a guy who hasn't even read a single book, much less a Jane Austen novel!

It was an accident. We were wrestling, and we fell, and we got caught up in the moment. He bewitched my hormones with his crooked, mischievous smile, his ridiculous freckles, his mess of a mop of hair, his low voice, making fun of me like it's all some kind of inside joke, like he's known me forever . . . and before I know it, I'm back to the kiss, reliving it again. . . .

The rain . . .

The soft pressure of his lips . . .

The feeling of his hands in my hair . . .

✻ ✻ ✻

The sounds of my classmates rifling through their overnight bags wakes me. I guess I finally did fall asleep after all. I sit up too quickly and smack my head on the ceiling.

"Ouch," I yelp, rubbing the quickly growing goose egg on my forehead.

"Well, look who's awake," Sarah Finder grumbles. "Glad *someone* could get some sleep. The rest of us were kept up by some major squeaking."

"Seriously," Evie whines, tossing her toothbrush back into her Louis Vuitton tote. "It was like you were doing the nasty with someone up there."

"Sorry," I mutter, turning bright red. I don't even want to *think* about what Sarah would do if she found out about Jason's kissing me. She would probably convince the whole school that I had a third nipple or an STD. I miss Phoebe. As soon as I get back to the hotel, I'm writing her an email and begging her to get on Skype.

"Can I have my charger back, please?" Evie sticks her palm out and taps her toe theatrically on the floor. I didn't know "please" could sound like an insult, but she has managed to pull it off.

The perk of us all having the same phone? We all have the same charger. I "borrowed" hers last night after she went to sleep.

Down in the lobby of the hostel, a rumpled employee is handing out sack breakfasts. Inside, I find a semi-stale croissant, a foil-wrapped pat of butter, and a small container of cranberry juice. It doesn't matter. My stomach is all jumbled up. I couldn't eat if I wanted to.

As I climb the steps and shuffle onto the bus, I look for Jason, but he hasn't made it on yet. I take a window seat toward the middle, wondering if he'll eventually plop down beside me and steal my breakfast. A few minutes later, that rusty head of baseball cap–covered hair pops up in the front of the bus. My stomach turns a somersault.

Jason starts down the aisle, nodding to people as he passes. When he finally notices me and the empty seat beside me, I'm not totally shocked that he doesn't take it. I *am* shocked that all I get is a half nod before he plops down into a seat two rows ahead of mine. Not even a snotty good morning when he calls me Book Licker? Not a *word*?

I crane my neck over the seat in front of me, thinking maybe he'll turn around and say something, but the bus shudders to a start and we set off down the road. Jason doesn't even glance back in my direction.

When I lean my head against the bus window, I can make out Jason's arm resting against the glass two rows up. I can see him passing something to the seat in front of him, but I can't make out what it is. I wait and watch closely, but I can't tell. The next time I see him make a move, I stand up and fake stretch, and that's when I see what he's doing. He's passing a note to Sarah Finder.

I fall back into my seat so hard I feel the metal springs poke me in the rear. I don't care. Frankly, it feels good to have a reason for the tears welling up in my eyes, even if it is a literal pain in my butt. I shut my eyes tight before a single tear can fall, and conjure up all those things about Jason I listed last night—how he's annoying and calls me names, embarrasses me, hates the books I love, has to be the center of attention—and before I know it, I hate him again. But now I have an even bigger reason.

Because he gave me the best kiss of my life—my first real *kiss* kiss—and is now pretending it never happened. Even worse, he's flirting with Sarah in front of me.

The rest of the ride is miserable. I try to listen to my iPod, but every song seems like some sappy love song. Jason was right. What a bunch of crap.

When we're just outside the city, my phone buzzes against my thigh. I dig it out of my pocket and flip it open to see a text.

Just wanted to say hope ur having a good day —C

I've never been so happy to have a charged phone in my life. A sweet text from Chris is exactly what I need. And it's finally a text I don't have to analyze or decode. One that doesn't need some kind of witty response. I can actually respond to this one all by myself with (gasp!) honesty.

I've had better . . .

Seconds later, a response comes.

"If ur going through hell, keep going." —Churchill

I laugh. My dad used to say that all the time, and my mom would swat at him for saying "hell" in front of me.

I like that 1
How bout the Frost quote?
3 things about life: It. Goes. On.

I press send and imagine Chris in some café somewhere, a burnt caramel mocha and a book on the table, his phone in his hand. Maybe he pushes his glasses up the bridge of his nose before he sends each reply; maybe he's got to push up the sleeves on his worn flannel shirt. I imagine his hair falling over his eyes as he types, and my heart gives a little flutter.

UR awesome. Meet up soon?

The bus shudders to a halt, and I'm thrown forward into the back of the seat in front of me. My phone clatters on the ground, and I have to contort like a pretzel to reach it from underneath my seat. As I get up, I see Jason ahead, his head bobbing down the aisle. I fling my bag over my shoulder and make my way up the aisle, but something in a seat two rows up catches my eye. It's a small white piece of paper, probably a receipt, folded tightly. Writing is scrawled on the back. The note.

I want it. I feel the same itching intensity I normally feel while standing on the starting blocks at a swim meet. Just give me the signal; I'm ready to bolt.

I reach out and snatch it up, and when I turn around to see Deirdre peering out under her frizzy hair to give me a strange look, I smile at her. "I can't believe people would leave their trash on the bus for someone else to pick up," I say, rolling my eyes. I stuff the note into my bag.

Back in my hotel room, I latch the chain, as if someone is going to bust in and accuse me of stealing. I unfold the note and read the two sets of handwriting: Sarah's loopy cursive spelling out *What happened to you guys last night?* and Jason's trademark chicken scratch replying, *I screwed up. In more ways than one.*

I read it over again. And again. And then a fourth time. After the fifth, I wad it up in my hand hard and fling it with all my might across the room. It's only a small scrap of paper, though, so it flutters and then drops limply near my feet. I don't know what else to do, so I stomp on it hard. And then again. And then I jump up and down on it.

When I finally stop, I'm out of breath, but a sense of calm comes over me.

So it was a mistake. We *do* hate each other. We *are* complete opposites. It *was* just hormones. It didn't mean a thing.

I won't think about it again, ever, not even for a second.

It feels like my brain has been cooked into scrambled eggs. All I know is I need to get the anger *out,* so I drop to the floor, flat on my back, and do a hundred crunches. When I'm done, my abs are tight and burning, my lungs begging for more oxygen.

I sit down on the big fluffy bed and pull the comforter around me like a cape. Then I drop back on the bed and fall asleep, gaining back all those lost hours from last night.

When I wake from my nap, I realize I've missed lunch. Oh well. I still have negative appetite. I spot my towel from the hotel pool hanging over the rack. As soon as I slip into my suit, I feel my muscles start to burn, begging for a good workout.

Up on the rooftop pool, I execute a perfect dive into the water, barely making a splash. I start freestyle, pulling myself hard through the water, but it's not long before I switch to the butterfly. It's not my best stroke, but it works my body so hard I can't think of anything else.

Except the kiss. The kiss that was a mistake. The water isn't doing its job today. Nothing is muted. In fact, it all seems louder. The kiss was a mistake? But then why did it feel so right at the time? I've had enough kisses in my life (okay, *four*) to know that what happened yesterday was different. Special. Downright awesome. My mind wanders back to the moment in the grass, right before the rain, when I could feel his breath in my hair. I'm about to get lost in the memory when reality clicks in and brings me back. Apparently, the "different" feeling was that I'd never been kissed by *accident*. I'd never been kissed by someone who didn't want to kiss me back. (Even Johnny Cafferty, who *had* to kiss me during spin the bottle at summer camp, *wanted* to kiss me. He told Phoebe and she jostled the bottle at the last second so it landed on him.)

When will I *ever* understand *anything* about love?

Between Mark, Chris, and Jason, I keep getting it wrong. Mark is a dream, Chris is a mystery, and Jason is a mistake. Or maybe they're all mistakes? I don't even know anymore.

Then it hits me: all this time, Chris has been asking to see me, to meet up. And I keep turning him down. Why? Because I'm afraid, and that's a stupid reason to run away from someone who actually likes me—who is actually happy he met me—even though he doesn't know the *exact* truth about who I am.

If my parents' relationship has taught me *anything*, it's that things don't last forever–they can't–so I shouldn't waste a single minute. Connection is a matter of destiny: if Chris turns out to be my MTB, then he won't care that I'm not really a supermodel. He'll love me anyway. Besides, he has already met me. Dad always said great reward comes with great risk; it's time for me to risk something.

I swim over to the edge of the pool where I've left my towel and my phone. I flip it open and dash off a new message to Chris.

How bout tonight? —J

I click send, then snap my phone shut and dive in for another punishing lap. I'm halfway through when I realize there's someone standing on the edge of the pool, right at the end of my lane. I come up for air, swiping the water from my eyes.

"Julia!"

Impossible. I blink, several times, realizing I *must* have a lot of chlorine in my eyes. There's *no way*. I'm dreaming.

"Fancy meeting you here! I totally forgot the juniors were staying at this hotel."

Mark Bixford, Man of My Dreams, MTB original, is standing on the pool deck, smiling down at me.

19

❧

Three's a Crowd . . . Even in an Actual Crowd

UR on. Meet me @Camden market 2nite for some
mulled wine & meandering? —C

My phone beeps with a new text, but I'm too stunned to look at it. Or maybe it's just my brain beeping—some inner alarm going off. MTB! MTB!

"What—what are you doing here!" I exclaim. The combination of the hard workout and the shock makes me sound sputtery and shrill. I grip the side of the pool, resting my chin on the ledge, trying to conceal as much of my body as possible. My Day-Glo swim team one-piece doesn't exactly have major sex appeal.

"Uh, well, I heard there was a pool on the roof, so I figured I'd come up here and check it out," he says, shrugging.

"I meant in London," I say. I'm still blinking chlorine out of my eyes, but I don't blink too fast, in case he's some kind of mirage and I could accidentally blink him away.

"My dad got called in last minute to cover fashion week," he explains, and I remember that his father is kind of a big-deal photographer. Not only does he regularly have spreads in *Vogue* and *Harper's,* but he volunteers photographing cancer patients at the children's hospital. He donates a photo shoot to the Newton North PTA's charity auction every year. Obviously, Bixford Senior has transferred his awesomeness to his son. "Since I had no spring break plans, he brought me along. I figured a London adventure would be fun."

"But I thought the hotel wasn't even open yet. To regular guests, I mean." *As if that even matters right now, Julia. You are a conversational wizard.*

But Mark doesn't roll his eyes or sigh or crack a joke. He just nods and explains that his dad knows Mrs. Tennison's husband's brother (or whatever), too, and in exchange for some photos to hang in the hotel's dining room, the Bixfords are staying in the hotel for the rest of the week.

A shiver passes through my body, and I have the sudden realization that Mark Bixford, my MTB, is standing here, and I'm in a pool. I put my hands up on the ledge of the pool and start to haul myself straight up onto the deck. I make it about halfway out of the water when it strikes me that I'm about to be standing in front of Mark Bixford, my MTB, *wearing a wet bathing suit.* The horror sends me plummeting backward into the pool, water splashing onto Mark's perfectly white sneakers.

I have a moment when I think about staying on the bottom of the pool until I die . . . or Mark leaves, whichever comes first. But that only lasts a minute before I burst back to the surface, gasping for breath.

"Do you need help?" Mark bends down and offers me one of his hands. *I need a pair of jeans and a sweatshirt. And possibly a lobotomy, because my brain is, like, frozen from shock.*

I grasp his hand and he pulls me straight up onto the deck in one fluid motion. I can feel his eyes on me in places I only imagined Mark Bixford's eyes would go. I'm simultaneously horrified to be wearing my swim team suit and thankful I'm not in a teeny bikini. I cross my arms in front of my chest, then drop them to my sides, then cross my hands at my waist. I must look like I'm doing some kind of half-naked Macarena, so I dive past Mark for the towel I left before I got into the pool. I wrap it around me like a cape.

"I, uh, well . . . ," I mumble, praying that my brain will emerge from its watery fog and start to actually function. "I'm going to head downstairs. I need to get dressed."

"I'll ride with you," he says. He follows me toward the elevator and jumps in front of me to punch the button.

The elevator dings down each floor. The noise is loud and crisp and somehow chipper, a signal of something exciting about to start. I can't believe Mark is actually here and talking to me, not just because he thinks he should. I have to keep sneaking glances at him to be sure it's not a dream. I hope he doesn't notice.

I focus on not staring at him, and try not to think about the silence stretching between us, either. I won't speak, because if I speak, I'll blow it. There's water in my left ear—I can feel it—but I refuse to try to shake it out. I am not going to start hopping up and down like a lopsided jackrabbit in front of Mark.

Mark is here.

I keep repeating it over and over in my head, but it still doesn't totally feel real. I want to pinch myself. Or him. Or both. Or have *him* pinch *me.*

I must have gotten water in my *brain.*

I stare into the brass elevator doors, which reflect the image of Mark standing next to me. He's leaning against the back wall of the elevator, his arms crossed over his chest. His sleeves are rolled up, and I can't stop staring at his tan skin. There are a few freckles dotted along his arm. I want to run my fingers from one to the next, tracing them like some kind of constellation.

Mark is *here.* And talking to me. *Me!*

"I heard you had some, um, excitement on the flight over," he says, arching an eyebrow.

"Oh yeah, the flight was crazy bumpy," I reply. "How did you—"

Before I can finish my question, the elevator dings twice to indicate that we've arrived at my floor, and as the doors slide open, Mark's reflection disappears . . . and is replaced by the real-life Jason, who is waiting to get into the elevator.

His dark green thermal has a hole near the hem and the sleeves are all stretched out over his fingers. His messy hair appears to be staging an escape from underneath his crooked baseball cap.

Jason's eyes flick back and forth from Mark to me, me to Mark.

"Hi!" I shout, entirely too brightly. I push past him before he can do something to embarrass me, and Mark follows me into the hall.

"Hey there," Jason says, swiveling around to face me, although he keeps his eyes on Mark. Now that I can see them standing across from each other, I can't believe I was ever hung up on Jason for even .2 seconds. Mark is *perfect*. Jason was right: the kiss was a mistake.

Jason's expression is hard to decipher. He looks very calm. Unfortunately, it seems like the kind of calm that comes before a tornado whips through your town and deposits three cows and a Pizza Hut on top of your house. I feel my body tense as I wait for the inevitable funnel cloud.

Mark, to his credit, is oblivious.

"Hey, man, good to see you," Mark says, and offers his hand. Jason eyes it for a moment before leaning in for one of those half-high-five, half-hug back-slap maneuvers guys seem to be so good at. Jason thuds Mark so hard on the back that I think I hear a low "ugh" escape.

"You too, *man*," Jason replies, a faint note of sarcasm in his voice. Jason turns to me. "So, buddy, I was just looking for you. We've got that outdoor-space assignment, so I was thinking we could hit up Covent Garden. You know, sniff some flowers and stuff."

"It's not actually a garden," I reply.

"What?" Jason looks puzzled.

"It's a shopping district," I say. I glance over at Mark nervously. I don't want him to think I'm some kind of boring know-it-all. Luckily, he doesn't seem to be paying attention. "There are markets and the Royal Opera House and stuff."

"Whatever," Jason says. He positions himself between Mark and me. "Do you wanna go?"

"It doesn't really fit the assignment," I reply, uncomfortably adjusting my towel-cape.

Mark glances at his watch. He moves easily around Jason, and I practically melt into a puddle when he smiles at me. "I'm headed over to Hyde Park in a few. My dad's doing a shoot, and he wanted me to meet him. You could come with me if you want."

I have a teeny, tiny sliver of a moment when it seems like Mark Bixford might be asking *me* out on a date, but Jason quickly stomps his foot down on that hope and dream.

"That sounds great," he says, a heavy, affected enthusiasm dripping from his words. "Don't you think that sounds great, Julia? Almost, I don't know, *meant to be?*"

I shoot a warning eye at him, and he seems to get the message: *Don't. Just. Don't.* I want to slap that snotty grin right off his freckled face, but instead I take a deep breath and smile at Mark.

"Yeah, that'd be fun," I say, hoping my voice sounds appropriately enthusiastic without too much of a tinge of OMGYESPLEASERIGHT-NOW! "I'll go throw on some clothes," I say.

"Are you sure?" Mark smiles at me and raises his perfect eyebrows. "I'm sure the people of London would love to see you touring in your swimsuit. I certainly wouldn't mind."

Jason shoots him an irritated look, but I don't really care, because at this moment, a thousand tiny Julia Lichtensteins are doing cartwheels in my brain. *He's not just talking to me; he's flirting with me!*

"Just hurry up, okay?" Jason says. "I don't want to wait all day for you to find the perfect outfit."

"Yeah, 'cause *that* sounds like me," I mutter. I really don't want to start a fight with Jason right now. I don't know what's spurred this sudden interest from the guy who has occupied 94.32 percent of my brain ever since he moved back to Newton. All I know is whatever this new reality I've entered into is, I worry it's being held together by Popsicle sticks and old rubber bands. I'm not about to fight with Jason and disturb this delicate, miraculous occurrence.

"Well, hurry up, okay? I want to get going," Jason says. He slams a button to summon the elevator again. A ding signals its arrival. The doors slide open, and Jason steps in. "I'll meet you in the lobby."

"I'll go with you," Mark says, throwing his arms into the closing elevator doors. They pop back open and Mark strolls in. "I'll grab some road snacks. Anything for you, Jules? I don't know if they make Starburst in the UK."

The elevator doors slide closed before I can respond, which is probably good. I wouldn't have been able to speak anyway. I'm too busy hopping up and down, doing a happy dance, my hands over my head, my wet hair whipping back and forth.

The first thing I do when I get back to my room is give myself a once-over in the mirror. My hair is hanging in heavy wet waves, sticking to my shoulders in chestnut clumps. My suit hasn't ridden up anyplace embarrassing, but still, a Speedo isn't the attire I'd pick for my first conversation with Mark Bixford in five years. I resist the urge to Skype Phoebe right *now* and shout through the Internet that Mark is talking to *me,* Mark is going on a date with *me* (well . . . sort of). I have to be downstairs in like, five minutes ago, so our gossip session will have to wait until later.

I change in record time, opting to let my hair air-dry and hoping that it won't turn into a crazy ball of frizz. While I brush my teeth, I close my eyes and see his smile when he said my name. I see that one tooth that lies on top of the other tooth, making him look just a little bit more—I don't know—mortal. I mean, it sounds like he remembered our wedding. And *smiled*. What else could *possibly* matter right now?

When I get to the lobby, I spot Jason and Mark sitting opposite each other in plush wingback chairs. I arrive in time to hear the end of their conversation. Jason is looking toward the bar, where a group of stray models seem to have stopped in for a midafternoon drink.

"Seems like a lot of easy prey around here for you," Mark says. *Gross.* I don't want to know anything about Jason's "prey." I can't believe I actually let him kiss me.

As soon as the thought comes to me, though, the sensation of our kiss in the grass surges through me like an electric shock. I suddenly feel too warm, with the kind of heat that brings little pinpricks of sweat right to your temples. I gasp and have to give my head a little shake to get the image to go away. The noise alerts the boys to my presence, and they look up at me.

"Ready?" I ask, a little too brightly.

"Uh-huh," Jason grunts, and starts for the door without even a glance in Mark's direction. Not the greatest start.

It takes us about twenty minutes to walk to the entrance to Hyde Park, and every minute is agonizingly awkward. Mark tries to make conversation about London; Jason snorts or rolls his eyes in response; and to compensate, I end up acting like every single word out of Mark's mouth is a jewel crapped out by a fairy princess. I'm bordering dangerously on reenacting Susan's ridiculous flirting techniques.

If nothing else, at least the weather seems to be cooperating. Mrs. Tennison seemed so proud of her little "outdoor spaces" assignment, designed to get us off to one of London's famed parks and out of the pubs and boutiques my classmates are so fond of. After the last two days of rain, I was starting to think our outdoor-spaces assignment was going to be an epic disaster.

I breathe a huge sigh of relief when we finally arrive in Hyde Park, because I hope it means we'll have something concrete to talk about. Maybe we can even ditch Jason. Except, of course, I can't. I mean, I shouldn't. Because that's against the rules. And I don't break rules. Except *with* Jason.

I can feel Jason's hands in my hair again, his lips on mine, and I'm gasping for breath.

"You okay, Jules?" Mark asks, stopping to see if I need a slap on the back or mouth to mouth (um, maybe?).

"Fine," I reply. "I just, uh, swallowed a bug, I think." *Oh. My. God. Did I seriously just say that? Mark is going to think I'm gross.*

Fortunately, he just laughs. "Swallowing can be a hazard," he says, like we're sharing some kind of inside joke. I relax again, grateful to him for making me feel at ease.

Jason, on the other hand, is definitely not making me feel at ease. He's stalking four feet ahead of us—just far enough to seem deliberately rude, but not far enough that we can converse freely without his involvement. I only know one way to distract them from the awkwardness, so I pull out my guidebook and start flipping the pages until I find the listing for Hyde Park, which I marked with a blue Post-it the first time I read this book back in Boston.

"According to my guidebook, Speaker's Corner is really close by," I say, my eyes glued to the page.

"What's that?" Mark asks, peeking over my shoulder at my book.

"It's an open-air space for debating," I say, trying to hide the fact that his closeness is practically giving me heart palpitations. "Anyone can get up and speak about . . . well, anything."

"I think you should speak, Julia," Jason says, turning around to shoot me another indecipherable look. "I think you should dazzle us with your theories on MTB!"

I nearly drop my book.

"What's MTB?" Mark asks, looking closer over my shoulder as if he's going to find the answer in my Frommer's guide to London.

"Oh! It's . . . uh . . . just this thing. From social studies," I say quickly, my mind racing to come up with three little words. "It's the, um, Massachusetts . . . Terminal . . . um, Budget. Yeah, Mass Terminal Budget. Or as it's more commonly known, the MTB."

Jason bursts out laughing. I could kill him right now. Since I'm pretty sure homicide is just as illegal on this side of the ocean, I turn on my heel and start walking in the opposite direction, cutting across the grass and toward Speaker's Corner. I'm happy to see that Mark follows.

Speaker's Corner reminds me a little bit of back home on Boston Common, minus the tour guides wearing Revolutionary War garb. Various people are milling about in the space. Some speakers are standing on literal soap boxes, others on chairs. Some have constructed elaborate displays; some are waving posters; others are gesticulating wildly.

In one spot on the path, leaning against a fence, is a man speaking out against overpopulation. Directly across from him is a scruffy-looking university student standing on a step stool, trying to convince passing tourists of the virtues of a vegan diet. Runners zip through the crowd, headphones fixed firmly on their ears, and mothers with children hurry by as quickly as they can. But many people have stopped to listen. Occasionally, people shout back at the speakers. One guy keeps yelling, "I'd go vegan if bacon grew on trees, mate!"

We wedge ourselves through the crowd. Most of what I hear just seems stubborn, reactionary, or downright crazy. I start to feel that tense skin-crawl of discomfort. I don't like crowds, and I don't like yelling . . . which means I definitely don't like yelling crowds. I start to feel a little dizzy: the swell of voices makes my head spin.

I look over my shoulder to make sure Mark and Jason are still close, and as my back is turned, I bump into someone.

I whip around to see a balding man in a shabby suit standing silently in the middle of the path. He's holding a sign, stark white with bold black block letters. It reads DON'T BELIEVE ANYONE, INCLUDING ME.

"I'm sorry," I mutter, but he doesn't say anything. He just gives me a creepy little smile. "Julia, you okay?" Mark appears behind me, a hand on the small of my back. The heat of his touch seems to anchor me to reality again and draws me back to the present.

Mark is reading the man's sign, too. "What's it mean?" he asks.

Again, the man just smiles in response.

Jason appears on my other side. "What's up?"

"Nothing, I—I want to get out of here," I say. I push past the man and his sign, and I start quickly for the end of the path where Speaker's Corner ends and the rest of Hyde Park begins. Mark walks after me, and Jason follows him.

"What was that about?" Jason asks.

"I wasn't into it," I say, which is the understatement of the century. "Too crowded."

"And loud," Mark says.

Jason shrugs. "I kind of dug it. Especially that last dude." Jason is keeping his eyes locked on the ground, kicking at pebbles every few feet. "Smart slogan."

"I don't really get it," I say. I have to sidestep awkwardly not to run right into him. Mark, who is walking next to me, moves his hand onto my elbow to steady me.

"What's to get?"

"I mean, what *is* he?" I ask. I feel frustrated. I'm confused by the cryptic message. I feel like there's a joke somewhere and I'm not in on it. " 'Don't believe anyone, not even me'? I mean, is it a political statement? Is it a party slogan?"

"He was probably just crazy," Mark says, shrugging.

"He seemed like the sanest one of the bunch to me," Jason retorts, then picks up his pace, putting distance between us.

"I still don't get it," I say. Trying to loosen my neck, I give my hair a shake. It's still a bit damp from the pool and it feels like it's weighing me down, like someone put a wet blanket on top of my head and is forcing me to walk around with good posture.

"Figures," Jason calls over his shoulder. Then, out of nowhere, he performs a cartwheel, right there, in the middle of the path.

I almost burst out, *What's that supposed to mean?* but I swallow back the words. I feel the buzzing building in my legs, like I want to swim until I reach the moon and back. Dealing with Jason and Mark is proving too stressful. I mumble something about needing water and head off toward one of the little food carts parked around the area. I give the vendor an assortment of heavy coins, and he hands me a cool bottle of water, dripping on the outside from being pulled straight out of the tub of ice. I twist the top and chug until half the bottle is gone.

"Easy there, buddy, save some for me." Jason is standing next to me, and I instinctively look around for Mark.

"He went to the bathroom," he says, rolling his eyes.

"Oh," I reply, bummed he walked away and annoyed that Jason noticed I was looking for him.

"For real, are you okay?"

"I'm fine," I say. I thrust the half-empty bottle into his hands. "Like you care."

"Oh, don't even start," Jason says, pushing it back into my hands. "You finish it. You look like you need it."

"Why are you doing this?" I burst out. Suddenly, I feel like I'm on the brink of tears.

Jason's eyes flicker. For a moment, he looks uncertain. "Doing what?"

"Making my life a living hell one minute, then acting like you care the next."

"I'm not acting," he says. He takes the bottle from my hand, chugs the rest, and tosses it into the recycle bin at the foot of the cart. He steps back into my little circle of personal space, closer this time, so that to meet his eyes, I have to actually tilt my head up. As I raise my gaze, his hand comes up to cup my chin. He leans in slightly, and the magnetism of the moment and his intense blue eyes nearly pull me in. His head turns slightly to the left. I start to tilt right to meet him, but the memory of his note to Sarah comes slamming back.

I take a quick step back. I stumble backward, nearly knocking down a businesswoman in a crisp black suit who is rolling a wheeled briefcase behind her. I mutter an apology. Jason snags my elbow and leads me away from Miz Business, who is about to have a full-on meltdown over a scuff I've added to her smart black pumps. He leads me off the path and into the grass. I keep my eyes on the ground, focusing on lining the toes of my sneakers up perfectly with the edge of the paved path.

"That's not a good idea," I say after what seems like an eternity of silence. Jason leans against a scrawny tree, and I worry he's about to send it keeling right over.

"It isn't. . . ." His eyes are dark. I can't tell from his tone if it's a question or if he's agreeing with me.

"No," I reply, still staring at my sneakers. "We both know that was a mistake. Let's not repeat it, okay?"

Jason is silent for a second. Then he says, "Yeah, sure." His bangs have fallen sloppily over his eyes. His gaze flicks over my shoulder, though, and when I turn, I see Mark strolling up the path toward us.

"What's next?" he asks, flashing that perfectly imperfect grin.

"More wandering," I reply. I turn to Jason, but he's already shooting ahead, executing a series of cartwheels down the path. Normally, his behavior would annoy me, but today I'm glad he's at least putting distance between us. I don't know what kind of game he's playing, but I'm not interested in participating.

Mark and I walk along the path side by side. Silence stretches uncomfortably between us. I'm so nervous and self-conscious about making a good impression that I don't even know what to say to him. I pretend to survey the land around me, letting my gaze skirt over his face several times, just for a second, so it won't feel like I'm staring. I notice a tiny scar under his right ear. It's perfectly round, like a pinprick. I have one just like it on the back of my neck. A chicken pox scar from when I was four. I wonder if that's how he got his, too.

"I'm glad I met up with you," he says, and now that he's spoken to me, I'm able to look straight at him without seeming like a creeper. "I'd be hella bored if I had to be by myself for this whole trip."

"I'm sure you'd find something to do," I reply. I have to work to keep my voice even. I don't want to betray the excitement that's bubbling in my stomach. *He's glad he met up with me!* My feet are tingly. I feel like at any moment they might break into some kind of Broadway-esque tap number, high kicks and all.

"Sure," he replies. As we walk, our arms swing slightly, and his hand bumps mine and he grabs it. "But this is way more fun."

I grin like an idiot, and to hide it, I stare at my shoes, then glance out over the park. We wander along the path, holding hands, and my heart feels like it is exploding with happiness.

Holdinghandsholdinghandsholdinghandsohmygodwe'reHOLDING HANDS.

Ahead of us, Jason continues to make a complete and utter idiot of himself. He jumps over benches, cartwheels through the grass, and jumps to swat at low-hanging tree branches. He's careering down the path like a battleship. Every once in a while a pedestrian has to leap out of his way to avoid being flattened by the S.S. *Inconsideration*. It feels like Mark and I are in charge of a hyperactive eight-year-old.

The path opens up, revealing a large pond on our right (thank God, goose-free). The scenery again draws memories of home, of walking along the Charles River on the Esplanade with my parents, petting passing dogs and feeding ducks. (Ducks are little and cute. Geese are huge and evil. Major difference.) Ahead of us, Jason stops and surveys the scene.

"Like home, huh?" he calls back. He does a double take when he sees Mark and me holding hands; he is in such shock that his freckles seem ready to leap off his face. For some reason, I feel incredibly guilty.

My immediate reaction is to wrench my hand away from Mark's and grab my guidebook, anxiously flipping through the pages until I find our location. "It's called the Serpentine," I say as I read the tiny black text. A small black-and-white picture accompanies the blurb, and I study it closely, hoping that neither boy can tell how uncomfortable I feel.

"That's a pretty incredible name," Mark says, stepping to the water's edge. "Does your book say where it comes from? Is it full of snakes?"

"Damn right!" Jason exclaims. He climbs on top of a bench, balancing perilously on the back, then flings out his arms, beats his chest, and shouts, "Behold the Serpentine!" His voice booms and echoes across the water. I take a few steps away from him. An older couple is passing us, and I shoot them an apologetic smile, which I hope communicates something along the lines of *How terrible to see madness in someone so young; I'm sure his keeper will bring him back to the asylum soon.*

"Um, my book doesn't say where the name came from, though it does mention that while people tend to call the entire body of water the Serpentine, it actually only refers to the eastern portion of the lake."

"Fascinating, Book Licker," Jason says. He leaps from the bench, landing hard right in front of me. "Just fascinating. But I have an idea. Why don't you take your nose out of your book and actually *look* at the damn thing."

Mark laughs, and I slam the book shut. I don't want Mark to think I'm a *total* nerd, and I *don't* like Jason making him laugh at me. I wrestle with my messenger bag to get the book back in its proper spot among my pencil case, wallet, phone, and copy of *Pride and Prejudice,* but the bag is putting up a fight. I walk over to a nearby bench and sling it down on the seat, where I'm finally able to make it all fit in its proper alignment again.

"That's more like it," Jason says, his wide grin more of a taunt than an encouragement. He takes off, leaping over benches and cartwheeling along the grass.

"Jason, would you knock it off?" I say through gritted teeth. "I really don't want to drag you to the hospital when you break your arm."

"Oh, come on, *Jules*," he says, his voice heavy with sarcasm. "Lighten up. Have some fun!" He turns to Mark conspiratorially and stage-whispers behind his hand, "Our girl is quite the planner. Seriously. You should ask her about her plans. Her long-term plans. She's *definitely* got some."

"Yeah?" Mark looks slightly puzzled. I start to fear Mark will connect Jason's lunacy with me, so I roll my eyes expressively to show that I have *no* idea what Jason is talking about.

"Definitely." Jason raises his arms over his head to execute another cartwheel. He gives me a wink, then flings his body headfirst at the ground. When he wheels over and pops back up on his feet, I can see right away that he has way too much momentum. He starts to fall backward but gets his feet moving into this crazy backward run to avoid falling on his butt, his arms swinging like an out-of-control windmill. I try to step out of the way, but before I know it, we end up in an insane bear hug and he's carrying me off my feet . . . straight into the pond.

I try to scream, but quickly shut my mouth as we go tumbling under the surface. Cold scummy water floods my nostrils and soaks into every bit of my clothing. I pop back up to my feet. Jason is laughing hard already and sputtering pond water, struggling to stand in the muddy depths.

"WHAT IS WRONG WITH YOU?" I scream, shoving Jason hard back into the pond.

"I thought you liked to swim," he says. He fakes a backstroke as he lies in the water.

"You. Are. Unbelievable," I choke out.

"C'mon, Jules." There's a leaf draped over his forehead, and he's struggling not to laugh. "It was an accident."

I'm so miserable and wet and pissed that I can't even speak. I can't believe this is the *second* time today that Mark has seen me completely drenched. I don't even want to think about the crazy things my hair is doing. I want nothing more than to drown Jason right here in the pond. Or at least give him a good kick in the teeth. I try stomping angrily out of the pond, but my jeans and sneakers are so heavy with water that I can barely lift my legs. The sleeves of my soaked sweater are now hanging well below my hands, and its hem is sagging close to my knees.

I make it about four steps before stepping on the elongated hem of my soaking-wet jeans and pitching forward face-first back into the water. As I struggle to stand up, I can hear Jason laughing behind me.

I can't believe I was ever confused about his place in my life. The only feeling I will EVER have for Jason Lippincott is complete and utter hatred.

Mark is standing at the edge of the pond, holding my bag. Unlike Jason, he's not laughing. He looks concerned.

"Jesus. What's your problem?" he calls out to Jason. Then, to me: "You must be freezing, Julia."

I trudge (carefully) through the water a few paces before Mark reaches out and offers his hand. I take it, and when I'm back onshore, I reach up and wring out my hair.

"Here, put this on," he says, pulling off his forest-green fleece and holding it out to me. I pull off my own sweater and throw the fleece on over my still-wet T-shirt. It's not a cold day, but there's a cool breeze, and walking back to the hotel in sopping-wet clothes would probably lead to the flu.

I think suddenly of my mom on the side of the road, her ankle swelling, when my dad pulled his car up to her. This is it. Mark is saving me. The thought warms me up as much as Mark's jacket.

Behind me, Jason fakes a swan dive into the pond and calls out, "Come on, Julia! Don't you want to stay in?"

The softness of Mark's fleece, still warm from his body, and the woodsy smell that permeates it serve to block out the anger. I pull my hands into the sleeves, tug the collar up around my cheeks, and take deep, soothing breaths.

"Better?" he asks. I nod. "Look, why don't we head back to the hotel so you can get warm and dry? I'll call my dad and tell him to meet me a little later."

"Okay," I reply. "If you're sure you don't mind . . ."

"I definitely don't mind." Mark puts his arm around me, pulling me close to him and rubbing my back for warmth.

"Hey, where are you going?" Jason calls out. He's still sloshing his way out of the water.

Mark swivels around. "It's none of your business." I lean into Mark. At this point, I don't care if I get in trouble for ditching my buddy. I don't care if I get booted off the trip, as long as I don't have to spend a single added second with Jason right now.

It's not until we're back on the block of the hotel that I remember I was supposed to set up a meeting with Chris. I stop short, a pinch of panic in my chest.

"Everything okay?" Mark asks, and once again his concern serves to release any tension I feel.

"Yeah, just fine," I reply. "I just forgot to do something, but it's, uh, no big deal."

Back in the hotel, I start for the elevator but am stopped short by a snooty little throat-clearing. I look up to see Sarah, giving me the up-and-down with her eyes. I can't even imagine what she must think, me soaking wet and fully clothed, dripping all over the plush crimson rug. She practically does a spit-take, though, when her eyes land on Mark.

She nudges Evie, next to her, and doesn't even try to hide that she's pointing at me, even though I'm looking right at her.

"Hey, so is it cool if I leave you here? I want to grab a bite to eat," Mark says, tilting his head toward the bar, where Evie and Sarah are still staring.

"No, that's fine," I reply. "I could come with you, if you want."

"No, you should go change," Mark says, taking a few steps backward. "I'll be fine."

"Okay," I say, trying not to betray that my excitement about the afternoon is melting into my sneakers. "Well, at least let me give you your fleece back."

"Don't worry about it," Mark says. "I'll get it from you later."

And just like that, I feel like someone is playing a bass drum in my chest. *Later? He wants to see me later!*

"Yeah! Later!" I call, but Mark is already heading into the bar, where Evie is giving him one of those cheerleader grins and Sarah is waving him over. Gag. I hop onto the elevator and pull the neck of the fleece up around my face, breathing in the woodsy smell of him. He spent his day with *me*. He saved *me*.

Back in my room, I dig out my phone, once again giving the universe a giant thank-you for my bag's not going into the pond with me. I flip it open and dash off a quick text to Chris, apologizing for standing him up. Only when I get to the excuse part, I realize I can't tell him I was touring London with my nemesis and my MTB. But as my thoughts linger on Mark and his arrival in London for fashion week, I come up with the perfect excuse.

Can't tonight!
Photo shoot running long.
Another time? —J

20

enn

Juggling Acts

Sounds like your life is spicy indeed. Luckily I like things
hot . . . If things settle, let's try again —C

I scrunch my toes into the end of my sneaker and give my foot a
shake. There's a teeny, tiny rock in my shoe that's been wedged
underneath my toes all morning. Every fourth or fifth step, I think it's
finally shaken free, and then it's back again, poking into the bottom of
my foot. As I shake my foot, I feel the pebble start to move a little, so
I shake harder. The morning is cool and breezy, and I pull my purple
Windbreaker tighter around me.

We've been walking all morning, first touring the London Pavilion
and the Criterion Theatre. I'm still not speaking to Jason, and every time
he comes within a ten-foot radius of me, I maneuver myself around my
classmates to avoid him. Mrs. Tennison finally released us to explore the
rest of Piccadilly Circus (which for my classmates means shopping). All
I can think about is how much I can't stand Jason.

Well, that and Mark. I haven't stopping thinking of Mark since he
left me in the lobby last night. I dreamt about him all night, thought of
him the moment I woke up, imagined him as I brushed my teeth and

washed my face, and even took him into account as I picked out my outfit. That's why I'm wearing my purple North Face Windbreaker. Mark has one just like it, only in forest green. He wears it almost every day, except for on rainy days, when he wears his Patagonia rain jacket. When it's cold, he wears his green fleece underneath, but not today, since it's folded neatly on my pillow back at the hotel.

Uh-oh. I'm definitely *worse* than Susan. I sound like a psycho stalker.

I look around for a place to sit, but there are people *everywhere*. I start elbowing my way through the thick crowd. Everyone is facing the same direction. I start to wonder what they're all looking at. I'm way too short to see over the crowd. I hear some muffled shouting, and every few seconds the whole group explodes in a thunderclap of laughter.

"'Scuse me," I say, wedging my shoulder between two little old ladies, their ball caps adorned with giant silk peonies. I squeeze past them but accidentally elbow the one in blue polyester pants. She begins cursing at me in what sounds like German.

Looking at the ground, I can see some free pavement through the legs of the line of men in front of me. That might be my spot. I squat low and push through, but my messenger bag catches on a pleather fanny pack, and I stumble forward into the open pavement. My bag, snapped free of the fanny pack, shoots forward and beans me, knocking my sunglasses down over my face.

"Excellent! A volunteer!"

I shove my sunglasses back to their perch on top of my head and shake my hair out of my face. I'm sitting right on my butt in the middle of a circle of tourists. The only other person in the middle of the crowd is a tiny old man with scraggly gray hair. His face is long and looks even longer with his aged skin sagging low around his chin. He's wearing the kind of black spandex leggings you see on male ballet dancers or circus performers, and a grubby white V-neck T-shirt hangs loosely on his bony body.

It's only when he points a long, bony finger in my direction that I realize he's talking about me. *I'm* the volunteer.

"Oh, uh, no," I say, scrambling to my feet and dusting the street grit off my butt. "I'm not, uh . . . What I mean is, I don't really want to–"

"Don't be shy, m'dear!" he says, giving me a wink. "Let's have a round of applause for our lovely volunteer!"

The crowd breaks into a booming applause. I scan the audience, panicked. The crowd is thick and heavy. There must be at least a hundred of them, and all their eyes are trained right on me. I feel a lump the size of a tennis ball forming in my throat.

"Please . . . you don't understand. . . . I don't really like–" Crowds. People. Volunteering. Being in public. All the words collide in my head at once, and I can't get a single one of them out.

"Just stand there and look pretty," the man replies. He's now holding my arm up, making me wave at the crowd. "Easy peasy."

Great. Now I have to embarrass myself in public in a foreign country, and I'm expected to look good while I do it. I liked it better when my biggest problem was a rock in my shoe.

The man introduces himself as "The Fire Man." This can't be good. Before I can repeat my protests, he whisks me off to the dead center of a circle and points at a wooden box painted bright banana-yellow. It's pretty tall, about half my size, and narrow. It looks like a stiff breeze might send it tumbling over.

"Stand," he orders. I stare at him.

"I'm sorry, what?" My brain feels as though it is a pile of oatmeal. The crowd thinks I'm making a joke, and everyone roars with laughter.

In response, this tiny old man who looks like he's made of toothpicks suddenly develops Hulk strength and picks me up by my armpits. In one quick motion, I'm standing on top of the yellow box. My knees start shaking immediately, which causes the box to wobble, making a little tap-tap-tap noise on the sidewalk.

"Hold still, now," he says loudly in a stage voice to the crowd. "As an American, you'll want to have very, *very* good insurance for this next bit."

"What?" I cry, but the Fire Man is already prancing away from me, shaking hands with the people in the front row, really working the crowd. Everyone is laughing and cheering, and I start to worry that they actually *want* to see me seriously injured. *I thought I was in London, not the Roman Colosseum!*

Standing—or, more accurately, wobbling—on top of the box, I can see over the crowd a bit, all the way back to the Shaftesbury Memorial Fountain, where people are lounging on the steps in the morning sunshine. I spot Jason in the audience, directly in front of me and about three rows back. He's standing with Ryan and the ever-present Susan, and they're smirking at me. (Well, actually, Susan's too busy making moony eyes at Ryan to smirk at me, but he's making up for it by smirking extra smirkily.) I freeze.

"Ah yes, that's much better," the Fire Man quips. "You'll want to hold absolutely still."

A young boy, maybe about ten or eleven years old, appears out of the crowd. He looks like a younger, miniature Fire Man. His hair is blond, stringy, and shoulder-length. He's wearing the same black tights and white V-neck, though his T-shirt looks a bit newer than Fire Man Senior's (or at least like it's been washed sometime in the last year). The boy takes his position to my left, never meeting my eyes, and the Fire Man stands to my right. I look back at the boy, hoping he'll take some pity on me and let me get down, but he just stares straight past me. I see a spark in his eye, which I realize quite quickly is a reflection of an *actual* spark.

Behind me, the Fire Man is holding what look like four bowling pins, and he's lit the fat end of each on fire.

ON. FIRE.

I yelp and make a move to hop down, but the Fire Man shouts, "HOLD STILL!" I freeze just in time for the first flaming bowling pin to go whizzing past my face. Within seconds, all four of them are in motion, back and forth between the old man and the little boy. They alternate in front of me and behind. I want to reach back and grab my ponytail to protect it from the flame, but I'm too petrified to move. I watch the flames fly back and forth, faster and faster. I can't take my eyes off them. As they move, I start to slip into a slight haze. The crowd seems to melt away and all I can see are the flames darting past my eyes. They're falling into a steady rhythm, and my thoughts go with them.

Mark. Mark. Mark. Mark.

Mark. Mark. Mark. Chris.

Mark. Chris. Mark. Chris.

Mark. Chris. Mark. Jason.

As Jason's image flies into my brain, my vision clears and I spot him in the crowd. He's staring at me with an expression I can't quite read, though it's definitely not his standard sarcastic smirk. I can still see the flaming bowling pins flying around, but I'm suddenly not afraid. I'm just tired. Talk about juggling. How did I get here? A little over a week ago I hated Jason, and Mark didn't speak to me. The biggest adventure I'd ever experienced was a Boston Duck Tour with Phoebe. (She pretended we were Swedish exchange students, which meant I mostly sat mute.) Now I've kissed Jason (but I'm back to hating him) and Mark is not only talking to me, but he wants to spend time with me. Throw in the fact that I've got the single hottest guy I've ever seen (after Mark, of course) reading Shakespeare and texting to meet me, and I feel like I've *Freaky Friday*-ed myself into the life of someone far cooler than I am.

What in the WHAT is going on with my life?

The crowd breaks out into thunderous applause, and just like that, I'm out of my trance. The pins aren't burning anymore, and the Fire

Man and the little boy are taking a bow. They gesture to me, and I give an awkward little curtsy from my perch on top of the box.

"Very nice, very nice," the Fire Man says, offering me a hand as I hop back down to the pavement. "Always good when our volunteers don't wear a whole lot of hairspray!"

The audience laughs, and I take the opportunity to dart back into the crowd. I push my way through to where I saw a few of my classmates standing, but they've disappeared. I push through farther until I've finally hit the outer circle of people. I reach the foot of the Eros Fountain and decide to finally take the annoying pebble out of my shoe. Out of nowhere, Jason plops down next to me. At this point, I'm too exasperated to think about moving, and I ignore him as I pick at my double-knotted sneaker until the lace finally comes loose. I pull my sneaker off and turn it upside down, giving it three good, hard shakes. Nothing falls out.

"Are you going to ignore me for the rest of your life?" he asks, nudging me with his shoulder.

The answer is yes, so instead of replying, I jam my sneaker back onto my foot and quickly retie the double knot. When I'm done, I hop up and step onto my newly adjusted foot, happy that I don't feel any kind of rock in there.

"Don't you want to enjoy the fountain? It's a famous landmark," he says. He reaches down and brushes a smudge off the white toe of my sneaker, and I can feel myself softening. "If you study the details, you could probably get an entire reflection paper out of it."

Even though the dirt on my sneaker is now gone, I reach down and rub at it anyway.

"C'mon, Julia," Jason says. He reaches down and pulls my guidebook out of my bag. "Why don't you tell me all about it?"

I sigh. "They should assign you to interrogate criminals with the

Boston police," I reply. I take the book out of his hands. "You could definitely wear down even the most hardened criminal." I flip to the section about Piccadilly Circus, London's classier approximation of Times Square.

"This is called the Shaftesbury Memorial Fountain," I say as I read, running my finger along the tiny text as I skim for the pertinent information. "It was built to commemorate a famous Victorian philanthropist named Lord Shaftesbury. When it was built, many Londoners were angry with the presence of the naked winged archer, Eros, at the top. They felt it was too erotic an image for such a respected and conservative man. And also that the statue was in a vulgar part of town. As a result, Eros is often called the Angel of Christian Charity. I guess because a *naked love god* is a bit too scandalous."

At the mention of the words "erotic," "vulgar," and "naked love god," I brace for Jason's inevitable dirty joke, but all I get is a distracted "uh-huh." He's typing away on his phone, not even looking up.

Jason continues with his nose in his phone, so I find another empty spot at the foot of the fountain and open my guidebook. I can be distracted, too. But as I flip the pages, I find I can't focus on any of the words or pictures. I feel strangely anxious. I haven't seen Mark at all today or heard from him, either. I did get a text from Chris, but it didn't give me the buzz of excitement it has in the past.

All my attention is on Mark, and my attempts to be rational about his sudden appearance in London are not working. Sure, we had a great day yesterday, and he walked me home and let me keep his sweatshirt (and I totally *didn't* sleep with it, I swear), but that's hardly a declaration of love. Still, I can't seem to shake the *blah* feeling that's overtaken me.

It doesn't help that Jason is acting stranger than normal. He's barely spoken to me, though he has managed to impersonate me falling into the pond three times today. The only things that seem to be distracting him right now are the living statues scattered around Piccadilly Circus, and that's only because he's taking great pleasure in taunting them. I feel bad for them (really, I know their pain all too well), but I'm also thankful he's teasing someone *other* than me. With the icky feeling resting on my shoulders, I mostly just want to be left alone.

But as the day wears on, Jason's cold shoulder makes me feel worse and worse. I can't help running through the last few days: the almost kiss on the London Eye, the full-on make-out session in Stratford-upon-Avon, the note in which he called it all a mistake.

And then yesterday's weirdness with Mark. Jason was so *hostile*. There was definitely something going on, some kind of history between them that even Mark didn't realize, because he acted cool and calm in the face of Jason's insanity. I tried bringing it up once or twice already, but Jason got all cagey and changed the subject. It's downright bizarre. I could ask Mark, but I don't particularly want to bring him into all the ridiculous drama that is my junior class trip. Maybe there *isn't* a good reason for it. Maybe Jason is just taking pleasure in being an ass, which really wouldn't shock me in the slightest.

I close my book hard, pressing the covers together between my palms. I close my eyes and try to clear my mind of all the craziness that seems to be hopping around like a million little Jasons playing pranks on my psyche.

"Uh, I hate to interrupt your meditation, but I'm headed into Lilly-whites." I open my eyes to see Jason towering over me again, his thumb pointed over his shoulder at the famous London sporting goods store. "I want to get a soccer jersey to take back with me."

"Football," I mutter wearily.

"Whatever," he says. "I'll be back in a bit. I'll find you here later?"

"Yeah," I sigh. "Sure." I rub my temples, but it doesn't soothe the dull ache in my skull. I put my head down in my lap and take a few deep, cleansing breaths like my swim coach has us do before a meet. The oxygen floods my lungs and brain, and I actually do feel a little better. When

I look up, the scenery isn't so painfully bright anymore, the tourists not so cacophonously loud.

I scan the square and spot Jason. He's stopped outside the entrance to Lillywhites. He's engrossed in that damn phone again, but he quickly snaps it shut. His eyes dart around like he's looking for someone, and then he turns and walks away.

He's ditching me.

I'm suddenly furious. He wouldn't let me ignore him—no, he wore me down by being nice . . . all so he could use me as a cover!

What a manipulative little . . .

His ball cap bobs across the square and disappears down the steps of the Piccadilly tube station. Without consciously deciding to follow him, I hop up from my spot on the step and hurry after him. I'm sick of being lied to. I'm tired of being used.

And I want to know where in the heck the little weasel is going.

When he gets to the bottom of the stairs, I jog after him. I find a particularly tall businessman with broad shoulders and duck behind his pinstripe suit. When the train arrives and the doors slide open, I hop on the opposite end of Jason's car. I can see his reflection in one of the windows, and I keep my eyes trained on it so I'll know when he gets off.

The train whooshes down the track, and I grab the pole to keep myself from toppling over into the tired-looking woman next to me with the screaming baby in her arms. I make a mental note to find the hand sanitizer in my bag when I get off the train. Each time the train stops, I have to strain to keep Jason in my sight while people rush onto and off the train. First Green Park, then Hyde Park Corner. As we approach Knightsbridge, I see him move toward the doors. This is it. I take a deep breath. The train stops; the doors slide open.

"Mind the gap," the automatic voice trumpets, and people begin rushing off, including Jason. My heart pounds hard as the electronic ding alerts us that the doors will soon close. And right when I think I might burst from waiting, I finally leap off the train as the doors are sliding closed.

Jason moves fast along the platform, weaving through commuters and tourists. He's hoofing it with such purpose and speed that I don't worry about him turning around to catch me following him. He jogs up the stairs to the street and down Brompton Road, and I follow him, leaving a half block between us.

We don't go very far before he reaches his destination. Harrods. Famous like Macy's but expensive like Bendel's. Looming over an entire city block, the ornate building just *screams* "money." If the Gossip Girls came to London, this is where they'd shop. In fact, I'd be willing to bet all the books in my bedroom that this is where Evie and Sarah have been spending their cultural hours.

Jason disappears through one of the brass-and-glass doors, and I scurry after him. I pause by the door, though, and give myself a quick once-over in one of the spotless store windows. I remember vividly the passage in my guidebook detailing the Harrods dress code. There are stories about the staff denying entrance to all manner of famous people for even attempting to enter in flip-flops, no matter how diamond-studded. I am not about to be thrown out of here looking "unkempt," as the vague language stipulates.

Unfortunately, one look at my reflection, and I realize that "unkempt" seems to be my personal style. I run my fingers through my tangle of curls in a failed attempt to tame the frizz, and press my hands along my shirt. My sweaty palms do have a sort of steamer/iron effect on the wrinkles, and I feel satisfied that I'm probably not going to get booted from the store.

Once inside, I'm assaulted by an oppressively spicy smell. I've entered right into the men's fragrance department, and sexy suited men are all around, offering squirts of the latest designer scent.

"Craving by David Beckham?" a thick, syrupy British voice asks.

"What?"

Apparently, that's the magic word, because a spritz of something ends up right in my face and up my nose and in my eyes and on my tongue. I hack and gag and nearly spit right on the floor of Harrods.

"So sorry, sir," the clerk says. *Sir?* I stop coughing long enough to give him the nastiest look I can muster, and he hops back in shock. "Oh, dear me. I'm so sorry, ma'am. I, uh, didn't realize."

"Whatever," I mumble, brushing past him. Great. Now I'm dressed like a homeless person and I smell like a gigolo. They're going to have bloodhounds on my trail to get me out of here, and thanks to this stupid cologne, I'm going to be way too easy to find.

I wander away, rubbing my eyes to rid myself of David Beckham's latest celebrity scent. I blink hard a few times to clear up my foggy vision, and I have a brief moment of burning panic when I think I've lost Jason. But I quickly spot his rusty mop bobbing up the escalator. I scurry through the dense crowd of shoppers and hop on, trailing him slowly, mechanically, to the next floor.

I keep my focus trained on Jason's back, noting that when he reaches the top, he makes a quick U-turn off the escalator. Seconds later I emerge into the most glorious displays of designer shoes I've ever seen. Phoebe would be in heaven.

I see a flash of red hair underneath a navy Sox cap; Jason has hopped another escalator. I tuck my shoulders and duck my head as I follow him onto the escalator, positioning myself directly behind a blue-haired old lady in an enormous honey-colored fur coat. She's got a fluffy little yip of a dog tucked under her arm, and the color of the pup's fur is so close to the color of the coat that I worry she's destined to become a matching hat.

Safely hidden behind Cruella de Vil, I am able to follow Jason up three floors, past towers of luggage fit for a jaunt on the *Titanic,* mountains of fluffy towels I'd never dream of washing my face with, something called the Bed Studio. I immediately imagine Jason using all the beds as a personal trampoline; then, as soon as I have *Jason* and *beds* in the same thought, visions of wet grass start to snake into my brain. I lift my right foot and stomp down hard on the left to rid myself of the image.

We finally arrive at the fourth floor, where Jason steps off the escalator and pauses to look around. I have to perform a complicated shimmy-hop off the top of the escalator to avoid crashing into his back, and I duck behind a Juicy Couture–clad mannequin.

I count to ten, then peek out from behind the swaths of candy-colored terry cloth. Jason is on the move again and once again I follow him, ducking low behind dresses and blouses until he hangs a sharp left. I pop up from behind a display of Burberry trenches. He's headed into the Pet Kingdom, an opening flanked by two large porcelain Dalmatians on pedestals. I wait a moment until he's safe inside, then hurry across the crowded hallway to follow him. I'm temporarily distracted by the glass cases filled with dog shoes.

That's when Jason turns around. Maybe he's lost for a moment, or maybe he senses he's being followed. Whatever the reason, he throws a quick glance over his shoulder. Fortunately, I have just enough time to dive behind the counter of the doggie bakery in the corner. I crouch behind the pink-and-white striped counter, trying to block out the smells of liver and bacon by nestling into my David Beckham–sprayed hoodie. When I'm satisfied that Jason hasn't seen me, I slowly peek my head up over the counter and peer through the display of biscuits shaped like signs of the zodiac. I see the back of his head disappear out the opposite end of the Pet Kingdom, and breathe a deep sign of relief.

"Miss? Excuse me?" A perfectly coifed middle-aged woman in a navy suit is looking down at me. "Is there some kind of a *problem?*"

"Oh no, I'm okay," I reply, sighing. "I just need a moment. You know, to rest."

"Well, I'm going to have to ask you to leave," she says with her clipped British accent. All of a sudden, she sounds exactly like that evil headmistress from *A Little Princess,* and I feel the same cold terror I felt when I was first introduced to the character when I was five. I look up to meet a gaze so icy I feel like she's shoved me into the Charles River in the middle of January. "We simply don't tolerate this kind of behavior at *Harrods*."

I mutter a quick apology and bolt for the exit before she can take my arm like some schoolmarm and march me out to the nearest Wal-Mart. I can escort *myself* out, thankyouverymuch.

21

✑

There's No Place Like Harrods

Be careful. I wouldn't want to see you get hurt —S

Great. I follow Jason halfway across London and then lose him in Doggie Heaven.

I start circling back toward the elevator that leads to the street. I wind my way through maternity, baby, children's, and juniors, an entire luxury life cycle unfolding before my eyes. It seems like I'm nearly back to where I started, and I have yet to find the escalator that brought me here.

By this point, it's a familiar feeling. Ever since that party and Jason and my little texting exploration, I've been trying to get back to the Julia Lichtenstein who boarded the flight in Boston. Heck, I'd give anything just to be Book Licker again. But as soon as I think I've found her again, she's gone, replaced by this crazy girl who leaves a field trip to follow Jason Lippincott.

Up ahead is something simply called the Diner, where I can see that the Brits have decided to approximate a real American diner experience. Red vinyl booths, gleaming white Formica countertops, and shiny chrome as far as the eye can see. Of course, the luxury version of a classic American diner gets one very important thing wrong: it's all too clean, too shiny, too perfect. My favorite diner back home, the Deluxe, features tarnished chrome, chipped counters, and duct-taped stools at the bar.

Still, for a moment, I feel a sharp stab of homesickness. Deluxe was Dad's place, and as soon as I was born, he made it *our* place. He used to take me there every Sunday morning for breakfast, even when I was an infant. He loved to tell me how he'd put my car seat right on the counter next to his bacon and eggs. It was Mom's morning, he said, for her to sleep. But it was also our morning.

As I grew older—old enough to sit on my own stool, my little legs swinging below the counter, old enough to order my own pancakes—it became less about Mom sleeping in and more about me and Dad.

I spot Jason, his Sox cap resting on a tabletop, his red hair running wild across his forehead. He's sitting across the table from a blond girl, though "blond" isn't enough to describe her shiny, luxurious, perfectly straightened locks. Her flawless skin looks like a team of angels has been standing around spritzing her all day. She's wearing a perfect swipe of ruby-red lipstick. This girl is so classy she can wear what my mother refers to as "hooker lips" at midday and not look a bit like she's charging. A pair of milk shakes sits between them, Jason's half gone and hers nearly untouched.

They lean over the table at each other, talking conspiratorially. She pushes a slip of paper across the table, and Jason gives it a quick read, then shoves it into his pocket. He pulls the straw out of his milk shake and tosses it onto the table, tips the glass back, and finishes it in one long gulp. She laughs and reaches out and touches his hand. For some reason, seeing that—the gentle way she brushes his skin with her finger-tips—makes my stomach dive all the way to my toes.

When they stand, I see she's nearly as tall as he is.

She leans in closer to him, and my heart stops. . . .

Are they going to kiss?

Just then a very large Hawaiian-print monstrosity slips in front of my view. A large man in pleat-front khaki shorts and a silk shirt in an abomination of colors points a fat finger toward the diner. "Honey, look! I bet I can get a cheeseburger just like at home!" Of course a guy like that travels thousands of miles to eat the same crap he'd eat at home . . . for twenty dollars more a plate. I lower my gaze, and it's what I suspected: he's wearing socks and sandals. I hop left, then right, finally getting a clear shot around Mr. Hawaii, but Jason is already giving the girl's hand a final squeeze and turning to go. Whatever happened, I missed it.

Then, abruptly, he turns in my direction. Now that Hawaii has moved on, I realize I'm standing right out in the open. There's nothing for me to hide behind, so I simply spin around and walk quickly in the opposite direction, my sneakers squeaking on the marble floor as I scurry. I spot a sign for the "Ladies' Lounge," which I assume must be a bathroom, and make my way straight for it.

Inside, I'm greeted by a gleaming entryway, a luxurious gilded sofa against one wall. I sink into it and take some deep breaths, willing myself to stay calm. My brain won't stop firing questions at me, though: *Who was she? Is that who Jason's been texting all day? Where did he meet her? Did they kiss? He kissed me. Now he uses me as his alibi so he can go kiss her?*

As quickly as the questions come, my brain provides the answers: *She's a supermodel. She met Jason at that house party. She was charmed by his American sense of humor and brash behavior. They've been carrying on an elaborate affair via text message. They met up to cement their newfound relationship. He wants her. Bad.*

"Ugh," I groan before bending over and placing my forehead on my knees.

"Can I get you anything, miss?" I look up to see a grandmotherly attendant in a Harrods uniform looking concerned.

"No thank you, I just need a moment," I reply. I try to arrange my mouth into some approximation of a smile. What appears must look more pathetic than anything else, because she pats me on the shoulder.

"I understand, dear," she says. "Take as long as you need."

I thank her, then drop my head back into my lap. I wish I could drop to the floor to do some push-ups, but somehow I do not think Harrods tolerates *that* kind of behavior, either. All my muscles are tight, and that spot between my shoulder blades starts to ache. I take a deep breath, rolling my head to loosen my neck. *Quiet, quiet,* I repeat to myself, and after a few more deep breaths, I finally feel ready to leave. I thank the attendant on the way out, dropping some coins into the silver bowl by the door, and head back for the escalator. This time, Jason really *is* nowhere to be found, thank God.

I ride the series of escalators back down to the street, and with each floor, I descend deeper into a foul mood. He was supposed to be helping me; that was our deal. But I don't have Chris, and he's done nothing but sabotage things with Mark. He's been playing me all along, and I have no idea why. He flirts with girls to get room keys and Internet access and also, apparently, just for sport! And he's good at it, which is what really kills me. He's managed to find out enough about me to manipulate me (like playing on my love for the Beatles) so that he can get exactly what he wants, from a kiss to a cover to a pile of reflection papers. He's not helping me; he's helping himself. And now he's helping himself to the most gorgeous girl in Britain. Jason has been carrying on some kind of secret romance? All this time I've been confiding in him, *kissing him,* and he hasn't even bothered to mention the supermodel he's got in his pocket? I mean, sure, I've been asking for his help with Chris . . . and it's not like Jason *owes* me anything. . . .

I feel like I've swallowed a bunch of live eels. It's true. Jason doesn't owe me anything.

But he made me think that he cared. . . .

My thoughts are ping-ponging so fast it makes me dizzy. I am completely mortified. Why settle for the girl who pretends to be a supermodel when he can have an *actual supermodel?* It's utterly humiliating, and I feel the shame in my stomach rolling around with my breakfast.

I can't shake the image of her ruby-red lips, and the next thing I know, I'm imagining them kissing. I try to tell myself I don't care if he did—if he does. *I* want to kiss someone else. Someone like Mark. I try to imagine what it would be like to have Mark's strong arms around me, pulling me close. I try to imagine his lips on mine, but the image keeps disappearing right before I get to the good stuff. Instead, all I can see is an alternating slide show of Jason kissing me, then Jason kissing that girl. And then it all makes sense. That's why kissing me was a mistake. He was probably thinking about her the whole time, and once he came to his senses and realized it was Book Licker in his arms, he bolted.

No wonder Sarah keeps telling me to back off. Thinking back to that awful look of pity she gave me at Buckingham Palace, I realize she wasn't trying to keep Jason for herself. She was trying to protect me from Jason and his lies. She was only warning me away from him! Maybe she's not the super villain I've always thought, but now my whole world seems upside down. Mark is flirting with me, Jason kissed me, and Sarah Finder is being *nice* to me? Up is down; down is up!

When I'm back on the street, I turn to head toward the tube and the rest of my class. Jason is probably headed there himself, and it won't take him long to realize I'm gone (or will it?). As I make my way down the street, I feel the anger building up inside me, and also the pain of the shock.

I don't know why I'm so surprised by the way Jason has been using me. But I am surprised. Surprised and hurt. For a while, it seemed like he was turning into something else. *Someone* else. Like maybe he was going to let me see some other side of him. But even that was all a lie. There *is* no other side. It wasn't a betrayal, really, since we never had anything to begin with. A *mistake* isn't a relationship.

If I can go back to ignoring him, just like before this trip began, then I can forget. Jason isn't important. Mark is my MTB! Mark never makes me feel so horrible and confused and conflicted. Mark makes me feel good. That's what an MTB is all about.

It doesn't matter. IT. DOESN'T. MATTER. I repeat the words in my head with each step, over and over, until I'm actually whispering them aloud as I march down the street.

22

✑✑✑

A Stroll Down Memory Lame

I thought I saw u today, outside of Harrods?
(not stalking u I promise!) ;) —C

———

J ason is standing in front of Lillywhites. He's got one foot hiked up on
the building and I notice his knee poking through a hole in his jeans.
(How did he not get kicked out of Harrods for that?) He leans against the
brick exterior like he's been there all day, and when I walk up, he lazily
looks up from his phone.

"Hey, Book Licker, where ya been?"

"Where have *I* been?" I say, the anger starting to bubble up, but I
quickly slam the lid down tight on that pot. *I don't care. I don't care.* I
repeat the mantra over and over until, instead of exploding, I return a
lazy shrug and pull my phone from my bag to click through it. "Oh, you
know, just exploring."

"You blowing up?" he asks, nodding at my phone while he flips his
own shut and returns it to his pocket. "Met lover boy yet? He get a hold
of you?"

"I'm actually hoping to hear from Mark," I say, not taking my eyes off the phone, a sly smile on my face. *Can he see that I don't care?* "I think we might try to get together tonight, maybe go for a swim or something." Jason jerks back a little bit, as though I've reached out and slapped him. "What happened to Chris?" Jason says. I keep moving, so he's forced to direct the question to my back.

"Well, I don't know Chris. I *know* Mark," I reply. I don't turn around.

"Do you?" he says, his voice edged with coldness.

At this, I whip around to face him.

"I know he's a totally sweet, totally nice, totally cute guy who doesn't act like a five-year-old or *push me into ponds,*" I say.

"Touché," Jason says, but he doesn't smile. His expression is completely blank. There's a moment of thick silence between us, and I refuse to speak first. I will not speak first. I. WILL. NOT—

"What have you been up to?" I ask. *Dammit.* My curiosity and desire to catch him in a lie trump whatever other game my head wants me to play.

"Oh, you know," he says. He lets out a long breath. "Exploring. Taking in the culture. Readying myself for the excitement yet to come."

"What kind of excitement are you expecting?" I ask. I want to trip him up; I want him to mention Harrods or that girl or the texts he's been getting all damn day. He's too smart, though. Or maybe too good a liar.

He doesn't get to answer. We're interrupted by a stream of our class-mates pouring out of Lillywhites, some loaded down with bags. They move en masse toward the fountain, our designated meeting point. Ryan runs between us, a shiny new lacrosse stick in his hand. He's waving it so wildly that I have to duck to keep my front teeth. When I stand back up, Jason is pushing off the wall with his foot.

"Never a dull moment with me, Book Licker," he says.

✻ ✻ ✻

I trudge through the doors of our hotel behind the rest of the class. Everyone is chatting excitedly about their new purchases. All I can think about is a swim. Or a nap. Maybe a swim and then a nap.

The class rushes for the elevators, so I head straight for the stairs. I want to fall right into my bed, and I don't want to run into anyone between here and there.

I climb the three narrow flights to my floor and throw my body into the heavy metal fire door. It flies open and I stumble through it.

Colliding directly with Mark.

"Hey!" Mark exclaims, reaching his arms out to steady me. My face lands right in his chest, my cheek nuzzling the softest butter-yellow sweater ever.

"Oh my gosh!" I say, breathless from the climb. I step back out of his arms and straighten my hoodie, red creeping into my cheeks. "So sorry!"

"Hey, no problem. Just my luck, actually. I've been looking for you all morning!" he says, that big almost-perfect grin I love so much spreading across his face. "I was hoping we could do some more exploring, maybe grab some lunch. I loved wandering with you the other day."

"Of course!" I burst out. I guess playing hard to get isn't my forte. I can feel the muscles in my neck and shoulders melt like butter the color of his sweater, which goes perfectly with his dark hair and spring tan. While I've been running around looking after Jason, Mark has been looking for me *all morning*? Finally, someone who's chasing *me*. Just like that, I'm not tired anymore. "But maybe we could avoid ponds or other bodies of water this time?"

"Of course," he says, grinning. He leans against the wall, his arms crossed over his chest. I swear, he looks like a cologne ad I saw last month in *Teen Vogue*. "You crack me up, Julia."

Oh my God. He thinks I'm funny. And not in a clumsy-funny or dorky-funny way. I'm filled with the warm, happy sensation of sipping hot chocolate in front of a fire on a snow day.

Mark nods toward the elevator in one of the effortless nonverbal communication moves that only truly cool people are ever able to pull off. I follow him.

"What did you have in mind?" I ask.

"I don't know, let's just walk. How does that sound?" His voice is relaxed, easy.

"Perfect," I reply. My chest feels full, and I let out a long breath. The fullness is still there, though. But this time I know it must be happiness. "Let me run to my room and grab my map."

"No way," he says. He presses the brass down button, and the elevator bursts open like it was waiting for us. He gestures into the elevator. "Let me be your guide." Then, in a tone of deliberate casualness: "You don't need to find Jason or anything, do you?"

"Why?" I try to keep the edge out of my voice, but I have no interest in talking to or about Jason right now.

"Isn't he your trip buddy or whatever?"

"He can take care of himself," I reply firmly, and that seems to satisfy Mark.

Mark leads the way through the streets toward the Thames. We pass Cue-2-Cue, the record shop Jason and I visited on one of our Chris hunts. They've changed the window display since the other day, and now it's filled with oversized cardboard replicas of the original Beatles albums—British releases, not American, of course. I do my best not to think about Jason and our song . . . which is *not* "our song."

"Oh man, I love the Beatles!" Mark says, leaning into the window until his forehead touches the glass. My heart throbs and I feel myself smiling with my entire body. *Thank GOD he likes the Beatles. . . . Of course, he is my MTB.*

"What's your favorite song?" I ask. I hope he says "I've Just Seen a Face." Or "Here, There and Everywhere." That would be so perfect.

Mark thinks for a second before replying. " 'Imagine,' " he says with a smile, his crooked tooth staring right at me. "Man, I love that song."

I bite my lip. I don't want to correct him, but I *have* to.

"Um, that's not a Beatles song," I say, working hard to keep my voice even so as not to sound like the know-it-all I am.

"What do you mean?" He looks completely puzzled.

"It's a John Lennon solo song," I say gently, hoping that will nudge him in the right direction, but from his face, I can tell this is entirely new information. "From after the breakup."

"Oh yeah. Huh," he says, though he doesn't seem particularly perplexed. "Oh well, whatever. It's all the same, right?"

I swallow back the urge to say that it's definitely *not* all the same. It's one thing to correct Jason, who already thinks I'm the biggest nerd to walk the face of the earth. Mark doesn't seem to have that impression, and to correct him would only plant the seed.

Besides, it's an easy mistake. He at least knew a Beatle sang it. Easy mistake. And *double* besides, "Imagine" is a really good song. A little cliché, but still a really good song.

I take a deep breath, and even though it kills me, I choke out the easiest, breeziest, most casual "yeah" I can muster.

When we get to the end of the block, we can see the Thames. I step off the curb and into the crooked British crosswalk. I breathe in a deep gulp of the foggy London air, the smile returning to my face.

"Julia!" Mark's voice, firm and urgent, jolts me out of my reverie. The loud, long honk of the cab that's barreling straight for me follows closely behind. Mark grabs my hand and pulls me up onto the curb.

"Close one," he says when we're safe on the other side of the street. "You okay? Didn't even see that coming."

"Yeah, fine," I reply, but my eyes are focused on his fingers, which are still interlaced with mine. He doesn't let go. When I look back up at him, I notice that he's staring down at our clasped hands as well. I have to clamp my mouth shut to keep from bursting into a "Yippee!" I have to say something—I know it's the cool thing to do—but my brain can't put three comprehensible words together.

I turn my gaze back to him. For the first time, I notice that his eyes have a little caramel color in them. It surrounds his pupil like a sunflower bloom in his iris. The attraction I feel is so intense, so chemical that I have to take a few deep breaths to keep from throwing him down in the middle of the sidewalk and making out with him until graduation. He smiles at me, and my brain reminds me that this isn't a fantasy. It's real life. *My* real life, and he's just caught me staring.

"First time in London?" He breaks the tension perfectly.

"Yeah," I reply dreamily.

"Pretty cool, huh?"

"That's an understatement," I say. "I've been hearing about London since I was old enough to listen. My parents came here on their honeymoon and loved it."

"That's cool," he says, and then he goes on, suddenly: "I remember your dad. He died, right?"

I feel a knot form in the pit of my stomach, but whereas it usually builds slowly when thoughts of my dad hit, this time it builds really fast. I feel like I've swallowed an entire potato.

"Um, yeah," I reply. "When I was seven."

"That's rough," he says, shaking his head. "I'm sorry."

"Yeah," I say. I accidentally scuff the toe of my shoe on the pavement and pitch forward. Mark grabs my elbow and pulls me back upright.

"Thanks," I say, feeling incredibly awkward, partly because I tripped, and partly because his strange line of questioning threw me literally and figuratively off balance.

"No problem," he says, then smiles at me. "I got your back."

We stroll along the Thames, watching boats skim along the surface in the spring chill. We wander; we don't talk at all. It's like Mark dropped an atom bomb on our conversation with his "dead dad" comment, and I think even he knows it. The silence between us is starting to feel oppressive.

Up ahead I can see Big Ben. "Did you know that even though the Germans bombed London like crazy during the Blitz and two sides of the clock got damaged," I say, reciting directly from my guidebook, "it still ran accurately and chimed on time?"

"The Blitz?"

"The London Blitz," I reply. A glance at his face tells me that he's still lost. "World War Two?"

"Oh, right. I remember," he says, and I relax a little. AP history *was* a whole year ago for him. "Wow, you're really smart, huh?"

"Um, I guess so," I reply, because really, what do you say to that?

"I had no idea there was all that trivia stored behind your pretty face," he says, smiling. The words halt me in my tracks. He only takes another step before realizing I've stopped, and he turns to face me. "Everything okay?"

"Yeah," I reply, distracted. I bend down and fuss with my shoelaces, though there's nothing wrong with them. Still, I untie and retie them. I want to focus on the fact that he called me pretty, but the other part of his comment keeps nagging at me. What did he mean by that? Did he really think I was *stupid*?

"Hey, remember that time when we were little, and Robbie Hart said that if someone stuck a bean up their nose, it would grow in their brain?" Mark asks. "And you said that wasn't true, so he stuck a bean up his nose to show you?"

I laugh. I definitely *do* remember that. Robbie's mom had to take him to the emergency room to get the bean removed because he'd shoved it so far up there.

"I was wrong," I say. "Turns out a bean actually could sprout into your brain. I read about it online."

We're quiet again, but I feel slightly less awkward. Sure, a bean up

Robbie Hart's nose isn't the sweetest of memories, but I appreciate his effort to alleviate the tension.

We wander some more, chatting. I keep the conversation light, and Mark doesn't seem to mind. We talk about favorite movies (mine: *A Streetcar Named Desire*; his: *Fight Club*), favorite bands (mine: um, duh; his: Phish), favorite TV shows (mine: anything on A&E; his: anything on Cartoon Network). So his taste isn't *exactly* what I always pictured it would be, but at least we're talking easily and I haven't turned into a stuttering mess. Phoebe would be proud of my conversation skills.

We stroll until we find ourselves in a little park in the middle of the city. A wrought iron fence and tall trees shield it from the bustle of London. A sign reads St. James's Square. I'm about to suggest we go read the historical marker to see how this pretty little park came to be, but Mark is already breezing past it. The path at the entrance splits into little estuaries that meander around the trees before meeting up again in the middle of the park. We walk through the gate and choose a path that leads straight toward a pond in the center of the park.

We stop and Mark bends down to pick up rocks to skim across the water. He gives a couple a sideways toss, like he's throwing a Frisbee, but they plop in and sink to the bottom.

On the other side of the pond is a wedding party, bridesmaids in soft blue and groomsmen in gray tails, white flowers pinned to coats and falling out of arms. They are gathered under a willow tree across the park. A flower girl at the front of the gathering keeps tossing her empty basket into the air. One of the bridesmaids looks to be wrestling with her dress, tugging it in various places and looking irritated. A groomsman is engrossed in his cell phone, while another keeps sipping from a flask in his pocket. A frenzied photographer darts around the scene.

The bride and groom stand off to one side. Her long white dress is pooled around her feet, and the wind is disrupting her artfully arranged updo, but she doesn't seem to care. She doesn't seem to *notice*. She's looking at her new husband; he has his arm wrapped around her waist, and one hand on the small of her back, and he's looking right back at her.

Mark chucks another stone into the pond, then ambles over to me. "Whatcha thinking about?"

I hesitate. But when I look at him, I can tell that he genuinely wants to know. He's not just making conversation.

"So this is probably totally ridiculous, and I can't believe I'm even bringing it up now," I say, then take a deep breath before the words tumble out quickly. "But do you remember that day when we were little and you and I pretended to get married in my backyard?"

"Of course I remember that!" Mark says. He leans back against a tree and laughs. In the stillness, the sound is loud and hollow. "My mom loves to tell that story. She even has a little snapshot of you and me in our pretend wedding clothes."

I remember the photo now. His photographer dad snapped it after we were done and had run inside to change clothes. If memory serves, we were hoping to run in the sprinklers on our honeymoon.

"I always remember little six-year-old Mark, so serious about that fake wedding," I say. I can feel the smile creeping across my face. "You said you wanted to find the kind of love you read about in books."

Now it's Mark's turn to pause. He snorts hard, then proceeds to laugh to himself in that silent, shoulder-shaking kind of way.

"What's so funny?" I search his face, but it betrays nothing.

"Oh, it's just what you said," he sighs, still laughing a little. "Or I guess, what *I* said. I was probably hoping for a kiss."

"What do you mean?"

"*The love you read about in books?* Are you kidding? There's no way I came up with that on my own. I probably picked it up from one of my mom's soap operas. I probably thought I'd get a little kindergarten action." He winks at me. "You were cute, even back then. Is that pervy of me to say?"

I look away from him. Heat is flooding my cheeks. "Well, there is some pretty fantastic love described in books," I say quietly, feeling the weight of *Pride and Prejudice* in my purse.

"Yeah, maybe," he says, shrugging. "I'm not really into reading. I don't have the time, ya know? I can barely get through the crap they assign us for class."

As he says it, I feel almost like I'm receding, or as though he's receding; everything is blowing away around me, and suddenly, even though he's still standing next to me, he seems impossibly far away. I look back across the park, where the wedding party is packing up, probably to head off to some beautiful reception somewhere with champagne and cake. I want to go with them. As they make their way across the park, flowers and taffeta trailing behind them, I feel something inside me vanishing, too—an image, an idea, that blinks out all at once.

Mark is now just chucking rocks into the pond with reckless abandon. He's not even trying to skim. The guy in front of me is *not* the guy who was in my head all these years. Sure, it's the same crooked smile and perfect hair, but he hates books? He was delivering me a line at *six years old*? His favorite movie is *Fight Club*? It's like when you see an interview with your favorite studly movie star only to find out he's really a mumbling, pompous asshole.

Right now, I want nothing more than to run to my hotel room and bury my head in the pillows while my world comes crashing down around me. I've spent the past ten years building this fairy tale about Mark that's all make-believe. And this is when I'm pricked with a moment of déjà vu. I've heard that line somewhere before . . . Jason. Back when I first told him about MTB and he made fun of me. Great, now I'm giving myself philosophical advice courtesy of Jason Lippincott.

But he was right.

I study Mark's face, trying to see the guy I imagined, but he's not there. There's only a big handsome smile and a guy whose favorite "Beatles" song is "Imagine."

"I forgot how much fun you are," Mark says. He pushes off the tree and steps closer to me, giving me what I think is meant to be a soulful look. It's like he watched one too many eighties teen movies before coming on this walk, but he picked up all the moves from the villain. There's no Jake Ryan outside the church in *Sixteen Candles,* no Lloyd Dobler holding a stereo over his head. He's that asshole preppy guy from *Pretty in Pink.*

I feel sick to my stomach.

He slips his arms around my waist and starts to lean in closely. This is it: the moment I've been dreaming about for years. But I know what's coming isn't what I pined for.

I don't think I can take another disappointment today, so as his eyes start to close and his lips aim straight for mine, I blurt, "I'm late . . . for, uh . . . an appointment. With homework. I have an appointment with homework. I need to get back to my room."

He doesn't let go. He leans in even closer and whispers in my ear, "Let me come with you. I'm a *really* good tutor."

I leap back. "No!" I reply, my voice high and squeaky.

"Hey, look. It's no airplane bathroom, but we can still have some fun," he says. I go completely stiff. I feel as though I've been plunged headfirst into ice water. Oh my God . . . he heard . . . he thinks I . . .

I flash back to one of the first things he said to me in London: *I heard you had some excitement on the flight over.*

I close my eyes and sway for a second. I'm worried I'm going to be sick.

"Ryan told me about your little adventure at thirty thousand feet," Mark continues, and then laughs and takes a step toward me again. "Don't look so upset, Jules. I like a girl with a wild side."

I don't even respond. I just whirl around on my heel and bolt.

23

❧

Various Types of Homesickness

Feeling so lost —J

By the time I'm out of the park, I've broken into a slow jog. I turn left at the gates, and when I hit the next block, I'm running. The houses whiz by me, but I don't look. I keep my eyes trained ahead, quickening my pace with each passing block. I don't want to stop for anything. The more I run, the more tired I get, and the more tired I get, the harder it is to think about what I'm running away from.

I hit another park, and I make a sharp turn into the entrance. I run down a winding path to the stone archway that leads out onto the street. My heart is pounding, I feel a stitch in my side, and my shins burn like they haven't since I ran track freshman year. I skid to a halt, doubled over and breathing hard, my hands resting on my knees. I put my hands on my sides and start walking in little circles, trying to work off the cramp and cool down. It's only now that I'm able to look around.

I'm outside the park in a mostly residential neighborhood. Three-story brick town houses line the streets in every direction. The only things that distinguish one from the next are the differently colored front doors. I look for a street sign or some indication of where "here" is, but I can't find anything. This is when my heart *really* starts to pound. I've run so fast and so far that I have absolutely no idea where I am. I have no map. Because Mark was supposed to be my guide. Great.

I walk to the corner and stand there for a moment, looking around, hoping something will seem familiar, but when it doesn't, I make a left and start walking. I set off down the road, which quickly becomes a trek up a small hill. When I reach the top, I realize I have a slightly better view of my surroundings, and that's when I see it: the church with the crooked-looking spire. The very one Jason pointed to that day on the London Eye. And if that's the spire, then I must be close to–

I look up to see a street sign pointing at the road ahead of me: Ebury Street. I walk ahead and watch the numbers pass by. Fifty-two. Forty-eight. Forty-four. And suddenly, there it is. Forty-two Ebury Street.

It's a modest brick two-story, exactly like every other house on the street. It has a blue front door with a wide bay window on the first floor. Two windows on the second story are flanked with shutters, painted blue to match the door. I try to imagine Jason inside with his mother and his father. I peer in the window, hoping to see the spot where the Christmas tree might have been, little Jason eating popcorn off the end of the garland.

I don't see a little Jason, though. I see a little girl, maybe five or six, sitting on an overstuffed couch with her mother. A book lies across their laps, and the little girl is running her chubby finger across the lines, her mouth moving slowly to form the words. Her mother smiles and nods, encouraging her to continue. A man enters carrying a newspaper, and he settles into a wingback chair.

No. Not a man–my father.

I blink a few times and the image fades. The man inside is not my father; the girl is not me. I realize I've been holding my breath, and I can feel tears pushing at the backs of my eyes, so I take a step back, breaking my gaze on the family inside. I look at my shoes, my laces still tied as tightly as they were when I put them on this morning, perfect double knots.

I don't know if it's the running or the sight I've just seen, but my legs feel like they're made of jelly. I grasp the edge of the low brick wall in front of the house and lower myself onto the stone steps that lead up the path to the front door. When I'm sitting, I lean over to rest my forehead on my knees, my breaths coming quick with the approaching tears. I blink through them and notice something stuck to my shoe. It's a little white slip of paper. I reach for it but realize it's attached to the sole of my sneaker, connecting me to the pavement with a big juicy wad of gum.

Grape gum.

I pluck the paper off, scraping the gum off my shoe onto the pavement. The edge where the paper was stuck to the gum tore off, but most of it is still there. The printing is slightly faded, but I can read it enough to see it's a receipt from the Only Running Footman. As I squint at the front, I notice there's red ink bleeding through, and I flip the scrap of paper over. I recognize the handwriting immediately, the crooked, haphazard chicken scratch. There's a phone number at the top, and underneath it, there's the line he recited at the bookstore, only this time it's right.

Love looks not with the eyes, but with the mind;
And therefore is winged Cupid painted blind

It's the line. The one from *A Midsummer Night's Dream*. The one he mangled back when we were dancing. The one that is my all-time favorite.

Jason was lying. He *did* come to visit his old home. He must have stood right here, his grubby sneakers on the pavement, his perpetually untied laces dragging through the pile of leaves on the sidewalk. Did he see the new family inside? Was he remembering his own family, just like I did? The times when it was good? Before everything fell apart?

The thought of him here, on the outside looking in, causes my heart to shatter. Now there's no way to stop the tears. They come in big, fat, rolling drops. My head falls into my lap, and I let myself cry. I cry for Jason, and I cry for myself. I don't know for how long, but I cry until there's nothing left.

And when I finally pick my head up, wiping the last of the tears from my cheeks with a sniffle, I realize what I should have known all along.

I have completely fallen for Jason.

All that time I spent hating his obnoxious jokes and his bizarre behavior, I was kidding myself. I've been falling for him since that first day in the skate park, when he sang to me. I've been denying it, chasing my fairy tale of Mark, a fairy tale I built for years that fell apart right in front of me in minutes. And then there's Chris, the fairy tale I've only had for a few days, but the one I've already ruined by lying. Maybe I could have had something with him, but I never got the chance to see because I ruined it right from the start. *Supermodel?* What was I thinking?

I suck in a deep breath, the kind that comes when I emerge from underwater after a long, hard swim. I feel like I'm taking in air for the first time in a week, and my lungs burn. My chest feels heavy and full. I'm finally surfacing, facing the truth.

But the truth makes me feel even sadder.

Because Jason said I was a mistake. He doesn't feel the same way. And then there's the blond at Harrods.

I came all the way across the ocean to discover my Mark fantasy is a total myth, to fall for my least favorite classmate, and to find myself once again pining for someone who doesn't want me back.

24

⤳

A Midsummer Night's Disaster

"so quick bright things come to confusion" —J

I pull myself up off the steps before the family inside notices a sobbing American girl parked in front of their house and calls the police. I start down the street. More than anything, I want to have a heart-to-heart with Phoebe, but I glance at my watch and see that I'm supposed to be at the Globe Theater in exactly twenty-six minutes, and I *can't* be late. We're seeing a production of *A Midsummer Night's Dream* and everyone will notice if I come in after it starts. After everything else on this trip, if I miss the play, I'll probably get expelled. Not to mention that Mrs. Tennison will know for sure that I went off by myself. I'll be totally screwed.

I take a quick scan of my surroundings, searching for the busiest-looking street, which seems to be at the end of the block. I know I'm at 42 Ebury Street, but I don't know where 42 Ebury Street *is,* and I have no idea how long it will take to get to the Globe.

I manage to hail a cab fairly quickly this time; I pray the ride won't cost me more than the twenty-five pounds I have in my wallet. The cab ride is the fastest, jerkiest, scariest twenty minutes of my life, but when we screech to a halt in front of the theater with five minutes to spare, I tip the driver generously.

The entrance to the Globe, nearly empty a week ago, is now packed with people. Cabs are trying to squeeze down the road, dropping people off for the evening show, and they keep having to honk to get pedestrians out of their way. It's loud and chaotic, and it looks like Mardi Gras, with tourists and theatergoers milling around, only everyone is sober. I tuck my chin and try to make a beeline for the entrance. The crowd is so thick that I find myself ducking under elbows and backpacks and babies perched on hips.

When I get to the entrance, I am greeted by a rather official-looking and angry ticket taker. My heart sinks further into my sneakers as I realize that Jason must have both of our tickets. Without him, there's no way I'm getting in.

I rise up on my tiptoes and even take a few vigorous jumps as I attempt to see over the crowd. A dense crowd of tourists is clustered around a life-size diorama of *A Midsummer Night's Dream,* complete with fairy mannequins and a donkey costume, entirely blocking my view. Damn short legs. I'm about to give up and go sit on the curb and cry when I spot a rusty mop of messy hair in the back of the crowd. Jason is standing with Ryan Lynch and they're talking animatedly. Ryan's got a dusty, ratty Hacky Sack out and the two of them are passing it back and forth between them, barely missing knocking over the people around them.

"Jason!" I call out, waving my arm over my head like a crazy person, but his back is to me and he doesn't notice. I wedge my way through the crowd of theatergoers and tourists, and as I get closer, I begin to hear snippets of his conversation. I hear him say "she," and realize he's talking about a girl. "Intense" comes through and "long time," but I can't catch it all. Intermittent honks from the cabs trying to get through keep interrupting my eavesdropping.

"And she's really cute, but–" HOOOOONK. "You know what I mean?" Jason says.

"Totally, dude," Ryan replies. He executes some weird hopping motion, passing the Hacky Sack behind his back, then over his head to Jason. "I really think you should just–" HOOOOONK.

Dammit. I can't hear a thing. They must be talking about that blonde from Harrods, but none of the good stuff is coming through. Stupid cabs.

Ryan gives the Hacky Sack a hard kick, and it comes at Jason so fast he has to flail for it. His toe barely gets a piece of it, but it's enough to send it flying over his head to land right at my feet.

Jason turns to grab it, and I realize instantly that he's going to spot me. I don't want him to think I was eavesdropping, so I duck quickly and sort of hop backward away from him. I spot a Globe employee wearing a sandwich board bearing the image of Queen Titania and race to get behind him. Only I don't look where I'm going and bump into a grizzled, potbellied man, who looks down at me and grunts angrily.

"Sorry!" I squeak, and try to dodge him. I collide face-first with the guy wearing the sandwich board. It's kind of hard to retain your balance when you're wearing a giant piece of cardboard, so he goes flying backward. I reach for him and manage to grab the edge of Titania's face, but he's too heavy. He tumbles backward and I tumble with him, landing right on top of the pile. I actually bump noses with the poor guy. He grins at me.

"Hello, lovely," he says. I realize I am now practically straddling him.

I quickly roll off him, thudding down on my butt.

"That was graceful, Book Licker."

Jason extends his hand to me. He's laughing so hard that he has a tough time pulling me off my butt. I scramble to my feet, feeling as though I've been stuck headfirst into the sun. My whole body is burning. I forget that I was actually *trying* to find Jason, and instead wish I were back in the cab, panicking over not having my ticket.

"Don't look so glum," he says in a faux-British accent, chucking me on the shoulder. "No one was looking."

Clearly, he's lying. A Globe employee is trying to haul the sandwich-board guy up off the ground, muttering to herself and casting me dirty looks. A couple of other groups are still chuckling, and a nearby mother with a toddler on her hip looks concerned that I'm injured. I feel so ridiculous and so out of control I'm worried I'll start crying again.

"Julia!"

I whip toward the sound of my name, but all I see is a giant furry donkey head bobbing next to me. I hear cackling coming from inside the donkey head as it starts performing some kind of weird, shuffly dance.

Now people are staring, but at least they're not staring at *me*. Ryan is laughing and squeezing his legs together, like he's trying not to pee his pants. Even I have to admit Jason looks pretty funny, and I manage to crack a smile, right before Mrs. Tennison lets out a horrified shriek and barges toward Jason.

Jason whips off the donkey head and gives me a wink. As Mrs. Tennison shakes her finger in Jason's face and launches into her Why-Can't-You-Have-Any-Respect spiel, which at this point I seem to have memorized, I feel a rush of gratitude for him. It's followed quickly by a wave of sadness. Things seem slightly back to normal, whatever normal is for things between us. Just two buddies, having a good time being buddy-buddy.

I try to forget my revelation today—that I've totally and completely and pathetically fallen for him and become sad crush girl—and instead concentrate on getting us both into the theater. I don't know whether to feel relieved that things seem normal, or sad that they're not different.

I follow the rest of the class into the theater. Or at least, I *try* to follow them. There's a bottleneck at the entrance, and the crowd is getting tight and a little testy.

"You always do this," a woman snipes behind me. "I tell you ten times, and you get annoyed that I have to tell you ten times, and then you still forget. If I didn't love you, I think I'd have to kill you."

"How about next time you only tell me once, and maybe we can avoid these stupid arguments?" a man replies. There's a bit of an edge to his voice, and it cuts through the hustle and bustle of the crowd.

"Or maybe I tell you twenty times, and you *finally* remember to bring the camera," she snaps.

We all make our way through the door onto the floor of the theater. It's standing room only, and the angry couple winds up right behind me. Great.

The lights go down and the play begins. I'm nearly taken in by the magic onstage, but I can't shake this overwhelming feeling of *ick*. It doesn't help that midway through the second act, I hear the woman whisper to her husband, "I *really* wish we had the camera," and he just sighs heavily in response.

The headache that's been building since the lights went down has become a dull ache at the base of my skull. It creeps around to my forehead and by intermission is throbbing heavily in my temples. As I suffer through act three, I can't believe I'm actually hoping for the play to end. This performance, which I've been looking forward to since I got the itinerary (my favorite Shakespeare play performed *at the Globe*? Um, awesome!), is turning into the nightmare of my life. I'm totally miserable, and miserable about *being* miserable.

The crowd is packed in tight all around us. I look up to see that the balconies all around us are packed, too. It feels oppressive, faces everywhere bearing down on me. I want to sit down, even if it's just on the ground, but there's not enough room. I can't focus on the stage. The actors dart around in a total blur. I feel like someone's shoved cotton balls soaking in Jell-O into my ears. I hear muffled laughter from the audience, which only makes my head pound harder.

Onstage, the actors are shouting at each other: one lovers' quarrel after another, layering over the audience like a big quilt of angry noise. I lower my head to try to block out some of the chaos, but as soon as I close my eyes, I get a flash behind my eyelids. Sounds: inside my head, inside my memory.

I hear the yelling, two distinct voices, muffled as if coming from behind a door. I close my eyes tighter, and then I can see it. I'm sitting on the floor of my room, lights out, my pink flowered nightgown pooled around my ankles. I've got my ear pressed against the door to hear the sounds coming from down the hall. I know I should be in bed, but I can't sleep. I can't stop hearing the shouting, and I want to know what it is.

I snap my eyes open. The memory makes me feel all off-kilter, and I don't know why. Everyone fights, right?

And like another zap to the brain, I know why I feel so off. *Because I've always thought my parents never fought.* Sure, everyone's parents fight, but not *mine.* Because they were perfect. Weren't they? As soon as the thought occurs to me, I realize how ridiculous it sounds.

I can't focus on the rest of the play. The actors finish their lines; the story wraps up; the audience applauds; the lights go up. Suddenly, the crowd is flowing toward the door. I follow Jason out of the theater. I keep my eyes focused on his back. He's wearing his North Face fleece, and I notice a short brown hair stuck to the back. It looks like a dog hair. Does Jason have a dog? I want to reach out and pluck it off, but I don't. I'm too busy forcing one foot in front of the other.

"I have to say, Book Licker," Jason says when we're in the lobby, "that was actually pretty awesome." His smile is so big it touches his eyes with sparkling color.

"Yeah, great," I say, and that's all I can muster. Talking produces a strange echo in my skull that I can actually *feel.* It only makes my head-ache worse.

"Hey, are you okay? You don't look so great," he says. He reaches out like he's going to rub my back or put an arm around my shoulders, but after a second, he thinks better of it and drops his arm.

"Gee, thanks," I reply, still staring at my shoes.

"That's not what I meant and you know it," Jason says. "Why do you always take everything I say the wrong way?"

Before I can respond, he turns and heads over to Ryan. I'm too tired and distracted to chase after him. I can't focus on anything at all; the only thing I can hear is the muffled yelling from behind a shut door echoing through my head. Over and over and over.

25

Picking Up the Pieces

@ the Spice of Life pub if ur free
Will wait all night if I have to —C

"Dude, she looks sort of pale. Is she gonna ralph?" Ryan's voice barely registers.

Jason ducks so his face is directly in front of mine.

"Julia? Yo, Julia!" he says. He snaps his fingers in front of my face, but his expression is concerned. "Seriously. Are you okay?"

I blink a few times and then shake my head. I didn't even notice that we'd emerged onto the sidewalk in front of the Globe and were waiting for cabs to take us back to the hotel. A whole line of them, shiny and black, are about to pull up, and we'll group up and distribute ourselves into them. In my pocket, my phone vibrates. I jump, then pull out my phone and flip it open.

"Of course *that's* what gets you to stop being a zombie, Julia," Jason mutters. "You have to be on the other end of a freakin' phone."

"It's Chris," I reply as I scan the text message. "He's at a pub and wants to know if I want to come by."

"Well, sounds like it's finally time, then," he says. I'm still feeling a little foggy, so I barely register the edge to his voice.

"Do you think I should go?" The words are swimming on the screen, forming and re-forming.

"Why not?" he says neutrally. "Time to man up, I guess."

"Alone?" I mumble, my mind racing.

"Why don't you take Mark with you? He's a real gentleman, from what I hear."

At the mention of Mark, I look up. Jason is giving me a dirty look.

"What are you talking about?" I ask. I feel a slight tremor starting in my fingers, and I have to grip the phone tight not to send it clattering onto the pavement.

"Forget it," he says.

Great. On top of everything else, it sounds like gossip about Mark and me has made the rounds. The potato that has been sitting in my stomach all afternoon becomes a five-hundred-pound anvil. I guess that settles that. Mark was a stupid childhood fantasy, and my absolutely insane feelings for Jason are clearly unrequited. I've spent this entire trip talking about, thinking about, and chasing romance, and I am *not* leaving this country without actually finding some. I *won't* spend another minute pining for someone who isn't available, not when there's a perfectly sweet guy who's been pursuing *me* all week. And I've been blowing him off. For what? For Mark? For Jason?

For nothing.

But Jason obviously isn't done with me yet.

"Last time we talked, it was Mark. Now we're back to Chris," he says. He throws his hands up in the air. "Jesus, Julia, you could get whiplash following your stupid love life."

"It's not even like that," I reply with a touch of venom in my voice. If he's going to dish it out, he'd better be able to take it. "I spent some time with Mark, and I realized that maybe he's not who I thought he was."

The cabs have begun to arrive. Our classmates swarm them, until only Jason and I are left standing on the curb. We have to take the last car by ourselves. Together. Jason jumps in first, shouting through the window. "Didn't I already say that?"

"No, what you said was that Mark was too good for me," I reply, sliding in after him.

"I *never* said that. You hear what you want to hear, don't you?" He turns toward the window so I can't see his face. The cab jerks into motion.

"Whatever, Jason," I sigh. I turn away to look out my own window. Our cab races across the Thames by way of a narrow stone bridge, then dips into a dark tunnel. There's nothing to look at to distract me from my anger at him.

"Exactly, whatever. Brush me off, just like you brush off everyone else."

"What are you even talking about?" I struggle to keep my voice from trembling.

"If you would pull your head out of your guidebooks for point two seconds, maybe you'd see that you're not the lonely victim you're always pretending to be. There are people who actually care about you."

"What, like you?"

I hear him draw a quick breath; then there's a long pause.

"Maybe," he says finally.

"Oh please," I sputter. "What a great friend you've been. You ignore me when it suits you, throw me in the pond, ditch me to buy 'soccer jerseys' and who knows what else, embarrass me twenty-four seven, and practically get me booted off the trip."

"If it wasn't for me, you would have spent the entire trip *alone,* too busy looking up facts and dates to have any *fun,* and spending all of your time daydreaming about your stupid MTB, *Mark.* You should really be *thanking* me."

"Thanking you? Thanking you?" I slam my hand down on the leather seat in frustration. The muffled thwack is hardly satisfying, and now my hand sort of stings. "You're delusional, do you know that? You're delusional, and . . . and immature, and—"

"And selfish, and a child, and an ass," he finishes for me, practically spitting. "I know, you've said it before. You've said it many times, in fact." He turns to face me. His eyes are half-narrowed, and he's staring at me with such intensity I draw backward. "You know what your problem is? Nobody's good enough for you. You live in a fantasy world. And if you don't wake up, you'll end up alone, with your books and four million number-two pencils."

My vision flashes red. I can't even believe what I'm hearing. I want to pinch myself to see if I can wake up from this nightmare.

"How *dare you* say that to me," I choke out.

"What, *dare* to tell you the truth?" Jason is laughing now, but it's an angry laugh, harsh and cutting. "See? You can dish it, but you can't take it. You act like you're the only one with feelings."

"The day *you* show feelings is the day I—" I mutter, but he cuts me off.

"What? Put down your guidebook? Use a pen? Break the rules?"

"I've been doing nothing *but* breaking rules since I got here," I shout, nearly lunging out of my seat at him.

"Yeah, and you seem to have had more fun than you've had in your whole life."

"No, I've been stressed and miserable! I've had more trouble than I've ever had in my entire life *combined* since I started breaking rules."

"Why are you saying that like it's my fault?"

"*Because it is!* From the moment we left Boston, you've been picking at me and pushing me. And I'm sick of it—sick of your jokes and your smirk and your dimples and your immaturity." I'm breathing hard and raggedly and I can feel my cheeks turning red. The driver flicks his eyes in the rearview mirror, unable to ignore me.

"Immaturity? Is that the best you can do?" He finally turns to face me. "C'mon, Julia. You can do better than that. Go crazy. Use a bad word." He narrows his eyes, and all I can notice are his eyebrows, which are as fiery red as his hair. Suddenly, I'm distracted by them; they're all I can look at. I focus on them instead of the pain and anger and frustration in his eyes. I ignore the fact that he appears on the verge of tears.

"You want me to do better?" Steely anger is bubbling inside me, hot and molten. "You're not immature. You know exactly what you're doing. You *choose* to be a jerk. And what's sick is you're so good at it. You've lied and manipulated my feelings all through this trip, and you enjoyed it, didn't you? You've probably been off with Ryan just cracking up over how much you screwed me up. Tease me, comfort me, mock me, kiss me, blow me off for some supermodel. Was that fun for you, to screw with my head? Did no one ever teach you it's not okay to treat people like that? Oh wait, probably not. Your mom ditched you before she could get to *that* lesson."

I regret the words as soon as they leave my mouth. His whole body tenses up, like he might pounce on me or break into a sprint and run away. If his eyes were laser beams, he would have bored two perfect holes straight through to the back of my skull.

For a quick moment I actually feel a little scared. I instinctively scoot back against the door of the cab. But his body loosens, really quick, like someone plucked the tension right out of him from above. He leans back against the seat and raises his hands in a slow, labored clap.

"Wow. Really great, Julia. A-plus for that rant. That's all you really want, isn't it? A good grade? That's real life to you—books and school and grades. Your dad would be so proud."

Our cab screeches to a halt in front of our hotel. I fling the door open and bound out, then turn and duck my head back into the cab.

"Fuck. You," I say, my voice even. "There's your bad word."

I can barely see as I march through the door of the hotel, shoulder-checking anyone in the lobby who gets in my way. I don't even apologize. My fight with Jason keeps replaying in my head like it's the only song on my iPod and the device is set to repeat.

When I get back to my room, I slam the door hard and the photos of London rattle in their frames. I go to the sink and splash some cold water on my face. The icy water breaks through my rage, and all that's left is confusion and pain. I start to shake. I don't know if it's from the cold water or what, but I wrap my arms around me to try to steady myself. I can't stop. My teeth chatter. I wait for the tears to come, but they don't. My eyes are dry and itchy, and I rub my face hard.

I want my mom.

I pull out my wallet and unzip the front pocket with such force that the zipper comes off in my hand. I yelp and fling the broken zipper at the floor. I take out the red calling card Mom gave me for emergencies. And this is *definitely* an emergency. I can't shake the repeating thought: *I want my mom.*

I punch the numbers in on the cordless phone in my hotel room, carefully following the instructions on the back of the card. I'm so anxious that I mistype and have to dial three times. Finally, though, the line starts ringing, the sound slightly crackly as my distress signal travels over the ocean.

"Hello?"

"Mom!" I cry, clutching the phone with both hands.

"Julia? Are you okay?" Her voice is thick with worry.

"Everything's fine," I say, trying to swallow back a lump. "I just missed you and . . . I really needed to talk to you."

"Oh good," my mom says, letting out a long sigh. "I was so nervous when I heard you on the line! I miss you, too, honey. How are things?"

"They're okay," I reply. Suddenly, I don't know what to say. How do I even begin?

"You don't *sound* okay," she replies gently. Mom can always read the tones in my voice. She's always telling me I should never play poker.

"I'm just a little homesick," I say, then inhale. "Nine days is a long time."

"You're telling me! I've been wandering around this house trying to figure out what to do. Things got so bad I was even thinking of taking up knitting."

The tension starts to break apart in my chest. "What about line dancing?" I say. "Or underwater basket weaving?"

My mom laughs, and the sound is warm and clear, even through the phone. I imagine her in our tiny kitchen at her usual place at the head of our rickety wooden table, twirling the cord of our ancient phone around her finger. I take a deep breath. Just the sound of her voice calms me.

"Well, actually . . . ," she says, and then pauses. "I was out with Dan last night. He took me to that new tapas place."

And just like that, the heaviness in my chest is back. "Wh-what?" I stammer. "Who's Dan?"

"Oh, you know, the one Kathleen from next door set me up with. The accountant in her office," Mom explains, her voice a little clipped.

My mind has gone completely blank. "So . . . he was second-date material?"

"Third, actually. Monday we went to a movie, that new alien one?"

A third date? I know that Mom's been on several *first* dates. Every time, she ends up coming home, plopping down on the couch with a big sigh, and flipping through the channels for whatever reality TV marathon is on that night. I never ask for details, partially because I don't want to know, and partially because six episodes of *Teen Mom* sort of paint the picture for me.

But a third date?

Stupidly, the only thing I can think of to say is "Well, how was it?"

"Well, you know. I hate 3-D movies. They make me feel a little motion sick," she says.

"Not the *movie,* Mom! The date."

"Oh! It was great. He's a sweet guy. Funny. And at the tapas place he ordered in Spanish, which was pretty impressive. I think we're going to the farmers' market on Saturday morning."

My *mom* went on a *third date,* and she has plans for a *fourth.* My mom has a more active romantic life than I do at this point.

"I—I'm just surprised," I say.

"Julia." My mom sighs. "You're acting like I've never been on a date before."

I'm clutching the phone so hard my knuckles hurt. "I know you used to date. . . ."

"I'm not talking about in high school, honey."

"I just mean . . . I didn't think you'd actually start, I don't know, *seeing someone.*" I have to sit down on the bed before I can hear the answer.

"It was bound to happen sometime," she says, her voice gentle. "It's been almost ten years. I loved your father very much. I still do. But that's not a reason to shut down."

"I guess. . . ." I pick invisible lint off the shiny down comforter and accidentally draw out long, thin feathers from the stuffing.

My mom sighs again. "Listen, Jules. You know how hard it was when your father died, but it's important to pick up the pieces and try again."

"Try again?" I run a feather back and forth across the comforter, then take it between my thumb and forefinger.

"Of course."

"But Dad was your one." I hear my voice as I say it. It sounds desperate, childlike, as though if I say it enough, I can make it true. I let the feather go and watch it float gently to the floor.

"He was, and then he died," she says softly. "I can't imagine that love only comes around once, and I know your dad would say the same thing. You can't simply turn off love. It's part of life, and it's everywhere. You have to reach out and try to take it."

"Wow," I sigh, taking in everything she's said. The image of Mom sitting in a tapas restaurant with some accountant keeps butting up against the idea that Dad was Mom's MTB. She *can't* be looking for someone else. Isn't her MTB supposed to find *her*?

But of course she's looking. *Of course*. I've only known this for about five minutes, and already I feel silly for having ever believed something else. It's the same ridiculous feeling I had when I finally remembered their fight.

It's like I've been believing in Santa Claus all this time.

"Julia, I didn't mean to bring all this up on the phone," Mom says. "It's a lot to take in."

"Don't worry, Mom," I reply. I kick my shoes off and flop down onto the bed. "It's actually exactly what I needed to hear."

"So I didn't make you feel worse?"

"Nope," I reply, hoping she can hear the smile on my face. "Quite the opposite. I feel much better."

The minutes are racking up, so we say our goodbyes and I tell her that I can't wait to get home. She encourages me to enjoy the last bit of my time in London, and I know that I will.

I've been holding my breath, swimming underwater for too long. Maybe there *is* no such thing as the perfect person. Or maybe Jason's right: there are perfect people, many of them, and it's up to you to grab one when you find each other in the random chaos of life and love. Jason. Maybe he could have been one of those people.

He was right—all along he's been right—and now I can't believe how hurtful I was. I can't see how he'll ever forgive me.

I want to call Phoebe next, to talk about everything: my mom, her date, my dad, and my musical chairs of guys here in London.

Unfortunately, I don't think there are enough calling cards in all of London to get that story out. Instead, I take my cell from the bedside table and text her the only truth I know right now.

P— I fell for Jason and screwed it up BIG-TIME.
Don't ask. Will need lots of ice cream waiting for me.
Love and miss —J

I wait on pins and needles, staring at the tiny phone in my hand, but it doesn't vibrate. Did Phoebe get my text? Is her phone off? It must be, or she definitely would have written me right back, probably to ask me if I've gone barking mad. Maybe she's skipped writing me back and is simply trying to find a British mental institution where she can have me committed.

I wait another minute or two, maybe to let the shock wear off her so she can respond, but nothing comes. The only new text on my phone is the one from Chris about the Spice of Life pub.

The whole fight started when I said I was going to go meet Chris. Nothing to lose now. Jason hates my guts and is probably off with that blond girl, anyway, so what does it matter? Best not to fight for nothing, I guess.

I take my bag off the bed, sling it over my shoulder, and march out the door.

26

e~o

The Mysterious Chris

It's on. —J

I pop out of the tube at Leicester Square. It's late. As my last act of re-bellion on this trip (and hopefully for the rest of my natural life), I've ditched my hotel, blown off dinner, and come looking for my mystery guy. Hey, go big or go home, right? And since I am going home tomor-row, I figure I might as well go HUGE.

The streetlamps are just coming on all around me, and the sun is beginning to set. As I stand on the sidewalk, trying to get my bearings, people push past me. I haven't been to this area before, so I'm forced to pull out my laminated map of London. I step back against the outside wall of the tube station so I don't get trampled, and run my fingers along the brightly colored streets until I find my way. It should only be a short couple of blocks' walk to get to the pub.

I pass colorful shop fronts painted like Easter eggs, their equally colorful wares displayed in the windows. One shop displays a window packed with mannequins clad in hand-knit sweaters in every color of the rainbow. A watch shop has a display case crammed with brightly colored bands, and the jewelry shop next door features costume pieces so large they look like they'd weigh me down. Rhinestones in red and purple and blue are piled on top of each other.

Only a few blocks later, I've reached the address I found online. The pub takes up an entire corner block and is lit up like a Christmas tree. The sight of the big brick facade overwhelms me for a moment, and I have to pause on the sidewalk and take some deep breaths. After all the disappointments I've faced this week, I want this to be good. Even though I probably don't deserve it, I need it to be good.

Please don't disappoint me.

I step through the doors and instantly realize that Spice of Life isn't just some typical English pub. Sure, there're a bar and booths and tables, but a stage dominates the first floor. There's a band, a bunch of guys playing instruments with a female singer at the mic. The music is loud but calm, and I breathe a sigh of relief that I haven't walked in on a Black Sabbath cover band. I don't think I could take that.

I scan the crowd, searching for a rumbled mop of dark hair, a pair of black glasses, a well-worn flannel shirt. I look for the pocket Shakespeare. But I don't see him anywhere. I shrink into my shoulders and pull my sleeves of my gray cardigan over my hands, as if this will somehow render me invisible. Damn. I was hoping he'd already be there so I could have a moment to see him before he sees me. I want a moment to breathe, to prepare, to organize my words and thoughts before I approach him. Resigned to wait, I make my way over to the bar and perch on one of the high wooden stools, my feet dangling below me. I give the bartender a wave and order a beer, my first *ever*. It flies out of my mouth before I can even think, and once it's out, I go with it. I don't even know *how* to order a beer; I just say, "I'll take a beer."

"What kind?" the bartender says through his thick red mustache.

"What?"

He gestures to the colorful row of taps along the bar.

"Whatever's cheapest," I say. I don't even know how much beer costs, and I definitely don't want to order one and then not have enough money in my wallet to pay for it.

I realize now how my classmates have gotten away with it all week. Ask with enough confidence and a cold pint glass will appear in front of you, no questions asked. I take a sip and try not to grimace at the bitter gulp. It doesn't burn like the drink Jason made me at the house party, but it certainly isn't pleasant. I swallow twice more, quickly, hoping my taste buds will catch up, but they don't.

I pull out my copy of *Pride and Prejudice* and flip it open. I'm nearly finished, though I hope I don't get to the end while I'm sitting here. There's nothing I hate worse than being stranded somewhere alone with nothing to read.

"That's my favorite book!"

I look up. A girl is sitting next to me, smiling broadly. Her teeth are dazzling white. Her long blond hair cascades in waves down her shoulders. It's the kind of hair that looks like it came from an animated movie, with perfect bounce and shape. She's seated, but I can tell she's tall. Her legs drape effortlessly down the barstool. She's wearing skinny jeans with up-to-her-knees black leather boots. An oversized blue button-up that on me would look like a cotton shower curtain draped across my body somehow makes her look tall and shapely and glamorous. A pair of gold-rimmed aviators is shoved on top of her head, holding back her fringed bangs. Her blond hair is streaked with pink, and she looks vaguely familiar.

Then I remember: she was at the party Jason and I crashed on our first night in London. I saw Jason chatting her up in the kitchen of the house party and then, hours later, her boyfriend, with his matching hairdo, tossing Jason out onto the street.

She obviously doesn't recognize me, though, so I don't say anything. I've always been really good with faces, which means I tend to get a lot of creeped-out reactions when I recognize someone who has absolutely no idea who I am.

"Yeah, me too," I reply. "I've probably read it ten times."

"Same. I'm always so jealous when I see people reading it for the very first time. Lucky bastards don't know how good they've got it."

"Totally," I say. I know that feeling. I feel it for Jane Austen, and for Shakespeare, too. I remember vividly the first time I read them: all the excitement and energy of taking in something new and amazing.

"I wish I'd thought to bring a book," she sighs into her pint glass. "I didn't think I'd be sitting here this long."

"Oh, I never go anywhere without a book," I reply. I pat my messenger bag, thinking with a twinge of anxiety that I should have packed a spare. But if I finish the book and Chris isn't here yet, I might take it as a sign that it's time to give up. "Sometimes I actually hope the person is late so I get more reading time!"

She laughs. "I hear you. Today I'm a little antsy, though. Not sure I could focus on a book."

"Are you waiting for someone, too?"

She nods. "Broke up with my boyfriend last week after I realized he was a daft meathead, so I'm kind of excited for this new guy. Though I'm starting to get a little worried he's not going to show," she says. But her voice sounds chipper. If she weren't so genuinely nice, her happiness would be irritating, like those people who go on and on about how much yoga changed their lives. "Shall we wait together, keep each other company?"

We chat about *Pride and Prejudice* for a few moments, and while I'm distracted, I'm able to gulp down a few more sips of beer without gagging. After a few minutes, my companion glances at her watch, then double-checks the time on the clock over the bar. "I think I've been stood up," she sighs.

"Me too," I reply. His text said he'd wait all night, but apparently he wasn't telling the truth (though to be fair, I've been pretty lax about telling the truth this whole time). It just feels like time to give up. "I'm pretty sure it's been way too long."

"Who's this boy who's stood you up?"

"How did you know it was a boy?" I ask.

"Oh, it's always a boy, isn't it?" She rolls her eyes and taps her purple-polished fingernails on the bar, one after the other in quick succession. I feel oddly at ease with her. Maybe it's because I haven't heard from Phoebe in a while, but it feels good to have someone to talk to. I don't mind opening up.

"This may sound weird, but I'm looking for a guy I met only once. We've been texting all week."

Her smile falters; her eyes narrow a bit. She looks slightly confused. "Me too," she says.

"What do you mean, 'me too'?" I ask.

"I'm waiting for a guy I only met one time. My mobile has been chirping away all week from his texts. I told him to meet me here."

"Wow. Strange coincidence," I say, but even as I say it, I can tell the word "coincidence" seems wrong. I hope my words aren't coming out as fuzzy as my brain feels. "I've been hunting this guy—Chris—all week long. He finally gives me a place to meet him and then doesn't show up."

She bursts out laughing. "My name is Chris! Well, Christina, but no one calls me that 'cept for my grandmum. Isn't that weird?"

"Weird," I repeat, accidentally mimicking her British accent. *Weeyad,* it sounds like. The throbbing from earlier is back, and I feel like my brain is wearing a big fuzzy sweater. It seems a little too hot in here, too, and I tug at the collar of my shirt to try to get some air circulating. *What is in this beer?* "Is it hot in here? Do you feel hot? I feel hot as hell."

"Well, you know what Churchill says. 'If you're going through hell, keep going,'" she says with a little chuckle into her drink.

The quote hits me like a fist to the face. Oh my God. It can't be. As I fumble around for something to say, the truth starts to take shape in the back of my brain. It slowly snakes its way to the front of my mind like a slow-motion bolt of lightning, and I feel the heat starting to roll down into my stomach.

"Who are *you* waiting to meet?" I ask, bracing for the answer.

"His name is Jason," she says. "I met him at a party last weekend. He's American."

Oh. My. God.

"I know Jason" is what finally comes out of my mouth after what I suspect is a full minute of opening and shutting it.

"You do?" She swivels on her stool until our knees are touching. Now she's starting to look confused.

"Yeah, he's one of my classmates. We're on this trip together. We were both at the house party last weekend. That's where you met him," I explain, as much to myself as to her.

"Do you think he's coming?" she asks hopefully.

"Uh, he's . . . well, he's . . . unavailable." I know it's a lie (or maybe not—there *is* the blond girl from Harrods), but even if he hates me, I can't bear the thought of Jason hooking up with someone else who isn't me, let alone this spunky, well-read, clearly very interesting and smart beautiful blond. Not to mention that her name is Chris.

I get my Chris before he gets his, dammit.

And just like that, realization breaks over me like a wave, dragging me into the undertow of reality.

I'm waiting for Chris. Her name is Chris. She's waiting for Jason. Our texts flash before my eyes. All addressed to and signed simply "J."

This *is* my Chris. Somehow, I've been texting *her*.

I feel sick, and I push my half-drunk beer back across the bar. I need a water. Now. I wave at the bartender, but he doesn't see me. My throat feels like someone poured the contents of a saltshaker into it, and I'm struggling to swallow without gagging.

"Oh my God. Listen—you haven't been waiting for Jason. You've been waiting for me." I can barely get out a whisper. "*I* sent you those texts."

"But you sounded like a guy on the phone!" she exclaims, and I instantly think back to that moment at the Tate when Jason wrestled the phone from my hand and answered it. Oh God. If only I had been quicker, held the phone tighter, this could have all been sorted out a week ago!

I can't even believe this is happening to me. How did this become my life? The beer is now sloshing around in my stomach like one of those water park wave pools.

I hear the door to the pub open, but I'm not ready to look at anything yet. I keep my face down and my eyes shut tight.

"Holy wow, he's cute," I hear Chris mutter, and my heart skips a beat. Even though I know Chris is . . . well, not my sexy dream guy, I still hold out hope that somehow, my bespectacled, Shakespeare-reading hottie is going to walk through the door. I open my eyes, and there's the shock of my life.

It's Mark.

He does look cute. He looks like he stole his outfit straight off a mannequin, in distressed jeans, a white oxford, and a gray cardigan. Only Mark could make a cardigan work. And though I know objectively that he's gorgeous, I don't feel the same stomach-dropping adoration I've felt every other time I've seen him over the last 242-plus days. I'm shocked to realize that I feel nothing.

"Julia!" he says. "I haven't seen you since you ran off. Did you get your homework done?"

"Uh, yeah," I say. The mumbly self-consciousness I felt every other time I've talked to him is gone. I've been dodging him since his indecent proposal. "What are you doing here?"

"Dad says this place is awesome. Thought I'd check it out," he says, and then his eyes catch Chris. "Nice scenery."

"Are you going to—" I start, but Mark cuts me off. His eyes are focused completely on the nearly six-foot-tall beauty sitting next to me.

"What's your name?" he says, practically bumping me off my stool as he wedges himself between Chris and me.

She giggles. "I'm Chris."

"Chris, huh? I like that name. It's sexy," he says, his voice like honey. I never noticed how smooth he sounds, and not in a good way. More like if this were the '70s, he'd be wearing a leisure suit. I grimace at the thought. "And *you* are definitely sexy."

Oh ick. Seriously?

"Okay, well, I'm going to—" I say, but again, Mark cuts me off.

He gestures to my stool, the one I'm *currently sitting on,* and says, "Do you mind?"

I can't believe he's asking me to vacate my seat so he can hit on some girl. Not two days ago, he was hitting on *me.* How did I not notice this guy is a total *dog?* I hear Jason's voice in my ear, calling Mark charming, only now I recognize the sarcasm. Everything he said about Mark suddenly makes so much more sense. He knew all along.

And he was trying to tell me.

I hop off the stool and look for a table. Behind me, Mark and Chris are chatting away. It's clear Chris no longer has any need for her mysterious "J," be it Jason or me. The jealousy monster has a tight grip on me. I suddenly feel the most alone I've felt on this entire trip. I need a friend. I need Phoebe.

I take out my phone and hold it in my hand, noticing no sign of any response from Phoebe, despite my earlier bomb-dropping text about falling for Jason. *Where is she?*

And this is when the last piece of the puzzle snaps into place. I drop my phone and it clatters to the floor.

If Chris was texting Jason, but I was responding, then I must have Jason's phone. *And he must have mine.*

I close my eyes—and now I see it. I'm tipping head over heels down the stone steps after that party last weekend, the contents of my purse scattered. My phone is at the top step; then it's gone. Next thing I know, Jason is dragging me off the pavement and telling me he has my phone. Only it's not my phone. It's his. Which means he still has mine.

Which means . . . The dots start connecting fast. All those texts from "C"? They were meant for Jason, not me. All those texts from Sarah? Same. And this explains why Phoebe stopped calling or texting me. . . .

Wait a minute. If Jason has had my phone this whole time, then . . . oh, NO. Phoebe has probably been texting Jason! No *wonder* he knew about Mark, and MTB, and . . . Oh God, what ELSE does he know?

I scoop the phone up off the ground and do the only thing I can think of to do. I text myself.

27

❧

All's Well That Ends with Hydrangeas

J— where the hell are you? —J

I'm about to press send when I feel a heavy hand on my shoulder. I spin around and come face to face with Jason.

His hair is still messy and covered with his ratty old Sox cap, but he's wearing the blue cashmere sweater from the night of the house party. Just as that night, the fabric pulls the blue out of his eyes, and I'm nearly blinded by the vivid color. His arms are full, a bouquet of hydrangeas wrapped in brown paper in one hand and a small green leather-bound book in the other.

I don't know what to say, where to start, so instead, I point to the book.

"What's that?" I ask.

"Oh, uh, I think it's a replacement," he says, clearing his throat, "for your Shakespeare book. The pocket one."

I take the book and clutch it to my chest like a security blanket. Nothing seems right-side up right now, but at least I have my Shakespeare.

"I read a few pages," he says, his eyes focused on the book. "It didn't suck."

With my arms now full of Shakespeare, he simply sets the flowers down on the bar. When I don't move or say anything, he gestures to the gifts. "This is—this is because I'm sorry. About our fight earlier."

A huge lump fills my throat. *I'm sorry, too,* I want to say, but what comes out is "I thought you would hate me."

His eyes are full of warm light. I want to dive into them and swim. "I could never hate you. I realized when you freaked at me about blowing you off that you must have seen me with my cousin Fiona. You're pretty sneaky for a rule follower," he says with a sheepish grin.

My cheeks start to glow red as I remember the blond girl, the supposed supermodel, sliding the paper across the table into Jason's hand.

"Your cousin?" I repeat, because I'm still too confused to produce full sentences or follow simple lines of thought.

"Yeah," he replies. He hoists himself up onto an empty stool, then pulls out the one next to him for me. I climb onto it, still clutching the book. "I haven't seen her since I was little, but I figured I ought to look her up. You know, after you encouraged me."

"I did?"

"Yeah. On the London Eye, when you suggested I go to the old house. Well, I did. And it sucked, but then it made me realize I could do something about it. So I called her up. She was actually pretty psyched to hear from me, and she showed me a bookstore where I could find your pocket Shakespeare."

"But what are the flowers for?"

He inhales deeply. "This is the hard part," he says, swiping a hand through his hair. "Your phone is . . . well, it's *my* phone. And, uh . . . ugh, well—"

"Jason, I know about the phone," I say. I release my—er, *his*—phone from my vise grip and set it on the bar in front of him, then give it a little spin with a flick of my finger. He looks at it whizzing around on the bar, then slowly raises his head until his eyes meet mine. I see a mix of terror and relief wash across his face.

"You do? For how long?"

"Um, about five minutes," I say, gesturing down the bar to Chris and Mark. "I believe you know Chris, from the party?" Jason leans over his stool and catches sight of the pink streaks in her hair, then quickly jumps back toward the bar and ducks behind me like I'm some kind of human shield.

"Don't worry," I say, rolling my eyes. "You're free and clear. Take another look."

Jason peeks out from behind me, and that's when he sees Mark. He sits up straight, and I notice his fist start to clench a little.

"That guy?" he says, and I can hear the disgust in his voice, loud and clear. "What is he doing here?"

"Oh, you know, bro, just pickin' up chicks," I reply in my most bro-tastic accent.

"I *hate* that guy," Jason says, but I see him start to relax a little. "He's always running his mouth about a different girl. Does the whole world have to hear about his conquests?"

"*Conquests?*" I sputter.

"Seriously, that guy is a walking high school cliché. He's also probably a walking petri dish. I can't imagine all the stuff he's picked up, if half of what he says is true." Jason glances down at the phone, then back at me, a few lines of worry forming across his forehead. "Wait, you're not still . . . are you? With him?"

"Oh God no," I say, and the force of the reply is enough to make Jason burst out laughing. "That guy is definitely *not* my MTB."

Jason stops laughing and looks right into my eyes. The pressure of his gaze nearly makes me lean back on my stool, but I want to be closer to him, so I push forward.

"Does that mean you know who is?" he asks. "Your MTB, I mean."

I bite my lip. Believing in an MTB has gotten me nowhere. Maybe it's time to start believing in something else. I look back up at Jason, smiling expectantly, and I feel a tug in my heart, and I know.

"I have no idea," I reply. I smile at him. "But I don't think I care."

Jason exhales. A slow grin spreads across his face. "So . . . you're not mad about the phones?"

"I haven't really had enough time with this information to be mad," I say, which is the truth. "*Should* I be mad?"

"I figured you would be," he says. "Hence the flowers. A preemptive apology. I hope you don't mind I texted Phoebe to find out which were your favorites."

"She knows me well," I say, taking in a deep breath of the sweet-smelling flowers. "How long have you known about the switch?"

"Since the Tate," he says, his eyes trained back on his knees. "I answered and heard the girl's voice, which made me wonder. Plus I was starting to get the texts that were meant for you. Like the ones from Phoebe."

Behind me I hear Chris's tinkling laugh, and when I turn, I see her head tilted back, her blond hair shimmering like she's starring in her very own shampoo commercial. Mark is grinning at her with that obnoxious crooked smile of his, and I can see why he wants her.

"But if you knew the Chris texts were from her," I say, shaking my head in Chris's direction, "why didn't you go after her yourself?"

"What do you mean?" he asks. I can see a little crease forming in his brow. Does he really not get it?

"She gorgeous! She's texting you! She wanted you!" As the words come tumbling out of my mouth, I cringe at the shaking, slightly shrieky voice that is apparently mine.

Jason laughs and shrugs his shoulders. "Girls like that go with guys like that," he says. "Do you think I'm a guy like that?"

"No," I say, shuddering at the memory of lecherous Mark and his hands all over me.

"Exactly," he says. "I was just hoping that you'd realize that guys like me go with girls like you."

"But why didn't you *say* something?" I ask. I try not to think about all the things Phoebe might have sent him, thinking they were coming to me. "Or switch the phones back?"

"I liked helping you with the search," he says sheepishly, stuffing his hands into his pockets. "And it seemed like you were having fun, too. It was like you needed me, or actually wanted me around. Before that, you acted like you wished I'd jump into the Thames."

"I did," I say, and he looks slightly wounded. I rush on: "But only because you were such a jerk all the time! If you had acted like a normal human being, then maybe I would have wanted to be around you, search or no search."

"Yeah, look." He rubs his forehead. "I'm sorry. I don't mean to be an ass. When I'm with you . . . well, I feel comfortable. I can talk to you. And you're smart and challenging, and you make me think about stuff. And you're also a complete pain in the ass."

"I'm not a—" I squeak, and then stop myself. I guess I can be a handful sometimes.

Jason's smiling at me. His eyes are so blue I can hardly stand to look at him.

"So you let me chase some made-up guy all over London like a fool?" I ask, burying my face in the hydrangeas.

"You weren't a fool," he says. He reaches out and brushes my arm with his hand. I stare at the spot on my arm that's now pulsing with electricity. He reaches back up and places his hand on my arm, firmly this time, then looks right into my eyes. "You were determined. I like that about you. You're so fearless."

I blush at the compliments, even if they aren't entirely true. If he knew all my fears and self-doubts, he really *would* jump into the Thames.

"Look, I thought once you knew, you'd be pissed," he says. "I thought you'd think it was another one of my stupid pranks, and then I wouldn't get to spend time with you helping you find your mystery guy. And with as much as you care about love and MTB or whatever, I didn't think you'd ever forgive me for messing with your idea of perfect romance. When all along . . . well, what I was hoping you'd realize was . . ."

"My mystery guy was you," I finish in a whisper.

"Well, yeah," he says. He reaches out and touches my chin—once, gently. "I really like you, Julia. A lot. I—I want to be with you."

A huge smile breaks across my face, so big my cheeks feel like they're going to detach from my jaw. I bite my lip. My whole body feels like it has been stuck inside an oven, and this time I let myself remember, *really* remember, our kiss in the field. "So the kiss . . . it was for real?"

"Yeah," he says, and this time it's his turn to blush. "Of course."

"But you told Sarah it was a mistake," I say, looking hard into his eyes. He jerks back a bit, looking shocked.

"How did you know about that?"

"I saw your note," I reply sheepishly. "You left it on the bus. I took it when I was getting off."

"The *kiss* wasn't a mistake . . . *lying* to you was the mistake. Kissing you made me realize how much I liked you, but also that now there was no way out of this without you finding out that I'm a liar. I thought I'd ruined it forever."

"Wow." I exhale heavily, feeling like a balloon letting out all the air. I can't tell if I want to happy dance through the streets or curl up under the bar and take a nap.

"So I guess I just have one question," he says.

"What's that?" I ask, and Jason grabs my hand and squeezes it tight.

"Do you care that I'm an obnoxious brat who thinks yellow Starbursts taste like lemon Pledge, doesn't believe in 'meant to be,' and doesn't fit any of the qualities you're looking for in your mythical Mr. Right? Even though I call it soccer and not football, no matter how many times you correct me? Even though I'll be a pen user until the day I die?"

"Well," I say, pulling him closer and rising up out of my seat, "someone once told me love isn't perfect—or predictable."

This time when we kiss, I'm ready. I want it, and I sink into him immediately. His arms wrap tightly around my waist, his hands on my back, pulling me close. He bends his head to meet my lips and I kiss him with all the urgency of a week of running around London looking for something that's been in front of me all along. It's not MTB.

It's better.

ACKNOWLEDGMENTS

First and foremost, thanks to Lauren Oliver and Lexa Hillyer, who took a chance on me and then whipped me into shape over many months of drafts. I was but a wee babe of an author before you two taught me that my characters should, you know, *do stuff,* and slapped that *-ing* construction out of me. Thanks to everyone at Paper Lantern Lit: Angela and Rhoda and Beth, for line edits, roller derby cheering sections, and always being sassy at parties. Thanks to Stephen Barbara, agent extraordinaire. Thanks to my editor, Wendy Loggia, and everyone else at Random House. I couldn't ask for a better home.

Thanks to Mom, who always has sensible advice (and supports me even when I don't take it!) and who never lets me get away with poor grammar (even on my blog). Thanks to Dad, who said from time to time, "What about writing? You were really good at that." He has always known better than anyone that I'd someday find my way back to it (even if I did ditch the journalism major). Thanks to my entire family, who have cheered me on since the moment I entered this world. I'm a very lucky girl to have you all in my life.

Thanks to Alana and Meg, who encouraged me when I wanted to ditch my career in education and become a writer. I couldn't have done it without those Facebook messages of support. Thanks to John Hayward Williams, the first non–publishing person to read any of

Meant to Be, who let me use his name in my book. Buy his music; it's pretty awesome (haywardwilliams.com). And thanks to all my friends who said, "I'm totally going to buy your book!" Um, now's the time, folks! And if you said it, and now you're reading this, I like you very, very much.

I was also lucky enough to have some really great teachers in my life: Professor Glenn Gass, who wouldn't remember me because I was one of a billion students in giant lectures, made quite the impression on me with his zest and passion for music. You can thank him and his Z401: Music of the Beatles class at Indiana University for all the references. Also, Mrs. Sarah Williams, who taught me my first lesson on "show, not tell" and got me excited about creative writing; Mr. Mark White and Mrs. Penny Piper, who showed me that history is really about the story; and Mrs. Cynthia Freeman, who inspires every student she teaches, and I'm so thankful to have been one of them. Every time I think about walking the halls at Maryville High, I'm reminded of Cher Horowitz: "Oh, well, this is a *really* good school."

Thanks to everyone on Twitter and Facebook and in the blogging world who's followed me and beamed out messages of love and support. The Internet is a pretty cool place if you're a YA author.

And finally, thanks to Adam, who let me quit my job to become a writer and asked in return only that I use some of my newfound free time to walk the dog and do some dishes.

Sorry about the dishes.

A NEW NOVEL FROM LAUREN MORRILL
ABOUT FOLLOWING YOUR DREAMS . . .
AND FINDING YOUR HEART.

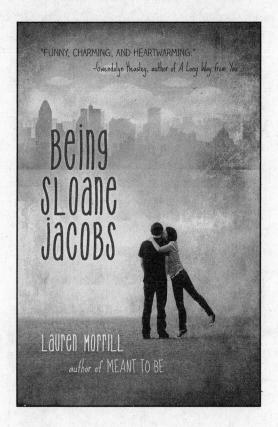

"FUNNY, CHARMING, AND HEARTWARMING."
—Gwendolyn Heasley, author of *A Long Way from You*

Being Sloane Jacobs

Lauren Morrill

author of MEANT TO BE